THE GILDED CROWN

MARIANNE GORDON

The Gilded Crown

A RAVEN'S TRADE NOVEL

HARPER Voyager

An Imprint of HarperCollins*Publishers*

For my mother, with all my love.

THE GILDED CROWN. Copyright © 2023 by Marianne Gordon. All rights reserved. Printed in the United States of America. No part of this book may be used or reproduced in any manner whatsoever without written permission except in the case of brief quotations embodied in critical articles and reviews. For information, address HarperCollins Publishers, 195 Broadway, New York, NY 10007.

HarperCollins books may be purchased for educational, business, or sales promotional use. For information, please email the Special Markets Department at SPsales@harpercollins.com.

Harper Voyager and design are trademarks of HarperCollins Publishers LLC.

Originally published in Great Britain in 2023 by Harper Voyager UK.

FIRST U.S. EDITION PUBLISHED JULY 2024.

Library of Congress Cataloging-in-Publication Data has been applied for.

ISBN 978-0-06-324877-9
ISBN 978-0-06-324876-2 (hardcover library edition)

24 25 26 27 28 LBC 5 4 3 2 1

CHAPTER ONE

The first time Hellevir visited Death, she was ten years old.

It happened in the depths of a long winter so brutal that some called it cursed. The cold stilled creatures in their sleep, made skeletons of the trees, and carved hollows from the cheeks of children.

The village where Hellevir lived with her parents and brother was on the edge of the forest which sprawled over most of the north-western lands of the Chron, tall and old and full of stories. Hellevir would sit at her father's feet as she helped him tan hides and carve bone. He told her about the No-Eyed Witch, who turned young boys into starlings for her aviary just to hear them sing, about the Silver-Beaked Hawk who tried to fly to the moon, and about the Antlered King whose armies had once scorched the lands, his smile grisly with the heart-blood of his enemies. The stories kept the cold at bay as it scratched at the door, but sometimes she felt like it was already inside the house, in the frost-glisten of worry in her father's eyes.

Hellevir was too young to hunt, but she was not too young to set the traps. Every morning she would walk through the woods to see what had been caught, and to reset the snares for the next night. Her older brother accompanied her with his bow and arrows to shoot down squirrels and rabbits.

One morning, when a new layer of snow was crisply fallen and the sky was a bright blue, Hellevir and her brother were out foraging when she found a bush coated in red berries. She took a handful.

"Not those," Farvor said. "They'll make you sick." Hellevir pocketed them anyway, not to eat, but to look at. They trudged on through snow as high as Hellevir's thighs, pausing to strip bark for kindling now and then. When they came to the frozen river, Farvor pointed to the left-hand bank. "I'll take the north side, you take the south. We'll meet back here before nightfall, yes?"

Hellevir followed her usual trail through the woodland, and found the first of the traps by a part of the stream where the wildlife came to drink. It was hidden under last night's snowfall. She brushed the snow away, but it stuck to her gloves and made huge mittens of her hands, so she pulled them off. The trap emerged, sharp and angry-looking. One of the teeth caught her and she winced, putting her finger in her mouth and tasting copper, sharp and sweet. She continued clearing snow, and her hand brushed fur, spiked and sharp, dull and brown. It was a fox, but its eyes were flat.

She took a few minutes to free it, stiff as it was, and with one finger still in her mouth, but eventually it came loose and she laid it across the snow. She had always tried to tame the foxes she saw in the woods with scraps of food, loving the wildness in their yellow eyes, but she had never been this close to one before.

She stroked the pretty fur, the dark tufts of its ears. The tail was thin and wet, not the bushy broom it should have been. She picked up the poor thing and wrapped it in her arms. Years later she couldn't have said why she did it. She'd just felt like she should, because it had seemed unbearably sad.

Never fall asleep in the cold, her father had always warned her. *You'll never wake up again. Get warm, first, any way you can. Then you can rest.*

She hadn't meant to fall asleep. She was tired from the trudge through the forest, from her parents' bickering through the night, and this was a pleasant place to sit, with snow creased around her legs like a blanket shaped just for her.

When she awoke she didn't at first see how the world had changed around her. She didn't feel the different cold against her skin, biting deeper into her bones than any winter, even this one. She didn't notice the smell, or rather, the absence of it. She didn't notice how the sounds had stopped. All she saw was the flick of a bushy, white-tipped tail vanishing between the trees.

"Wait!" she called, and was on her feet after it, wading through the high snow. "Come back!"

The fox didn't listen, but led her deeper into the forest, darting here and there between the boughs, and she rushed after it. She didn't stop long enough to realize that these trees were unfamiliar, or that they stood unnaturally still. The fox's bright pelt drew her on like a will-o'-the-wisp.

She rounded a heavy drift and found herself in a small clearing. The fox stood in the center, watching her, its eyes fire-orange and not flat at all.

"There you are," she panted. "Why did you run away?" The fox lowered its head, still watching, and its ear flicked. It glanced to the side, behind her.

She frowned and turned back, but there was nothing there, just endless trees. But . . . now at last she looked, really looked, and realized that these were not *her* woods. The boughs were too grey, like bone, and the knots in the wood were like eyes that watched her. The edge of her vision blurred and shuddered as if with a heat haze.

Slowly, she knelt down and held out her hand to the fox. It took a step forward and flicked its tail.

"Come here," she whispered, noticing for the first time how odd the air made her voice sound, as if it were muted and yet thundering, audible throughout the forest. "I'll take you back." She swallowed. "Please."

I must take you back, she thought, but she couldn't think why it felt so important.

The fox came a little closer and sniffed her bare fingers. Its ruff was speckled with snowflakes. Its tongue darted out to lick the melted snow from her fingertips, the drop of blood that had dried on her finger. Again, it glanced behind her. This time she didn't let herself turn back to see what it was looking at. She was too afraid.

"Why don't you come home with me?" she asked it. "I'm sure Ma and Pa won't mind. It's got to be better than being alone out here." She reached into her pocket, drawing out the berries she'd found earlier. "Are you hungry? Do you want these?" It twitched its nose at them, nuzzled them so they fell from her palm to the frosty ground. Its snuffling felt warm.

Again its amber eyes flicked over her shoulder.

This time she turned, too quickly to think twice about it, and the edge of her vision caught upon a black shape that made her heart tighten, but when her glance came to a halt there was nothing but trees and snow.

"Hellevir!"

She started, nearly frightening the fox into fleeing. It was her brother's voice. Distant and worried, as if he were trying to find her.

"I'm here," she whispered.

"Hellevir!"

She shuddered and held her hand out to the fox.

"Please," she said. "Come with me."

"Hellevir!" A hand seized her arm and hauled her around, and suddenly she was sitting upon the ground in a snowdrift, looking up into her brother's face. Twilit gloom sat heavy among the trees. A wave of cold passed over her, as if she were emerging from icy water.

"What are you . . ."

The fox wriggled against her chest, twisting out of her reach and making a dart for escape. Its tail brushed against her face, soft and full and smelling of earth and wild things. Her brother caught it by the scruff of the neck before it could get away, and it yelped and tried to bite him.

"Don't . . ." she started, but he'd already wrung its neck.

"That'll keep us for a few days," he said. "Ma can make you some new gloves that don't gather snow all the time. You were right about the stream, it's a good place for a trap."

Hellevir burst into tears. She couldn't help it. Her brother was at first bewildered—she'd seen him kill things before—and then annoyed when she refused to tell him why. He took her roughly by the hand and marched her home.

The second time Hellevir visited Death, she was twelve years old.

She sat with her father under the cherry tree by their house, fletching arrows. In spring, the blossoms would coat the grass, but for now there was only the snow, and the tree stood skeletal and bare. It was beautiful and still as they worked, their breath pluming, and everything—the lack of food, Ma's shadowed eyes as her hand

4

brushed worriedly over her swollen belly—seemed very far away. A magpie landed on the branch above Hellevir and fixed her with one ink-blot eye.

"Hello," she said to it with a smile. It cocked its head to one side, its eye darting to the shiny penknife on her lap that she was using to trim the feathers. "I'm afraid that's Pa's," Hellevir told it. The magpie chittered.

"I'll trade you some rowanberries for it," it offered.

"I can't eat rowanberries."

"How about I tell you where the hares burrow? They're lean but I'm sure there's meat on them."

"Wicked thing. You can't have the knife." The magpie let out a cackle and swooped down into the thicket, vanishing into the shadows of the forest. Hellevir shook her head and returned to her fletching, only pausing when she realized her pa was watching her. Her smile faded. She wasn't supposed to talk to things like that anymore.

"Please don't tell Ma," she asked him quietly. He brushed her hair away from her forehead with his big hand.

"I won't tell Ma," he promised.

"She doesn't understand."

"I know, my girl." He sounded sad. He returned to his binding, his expression thoughtful. She let him think, because he was a lot wiser than her. A pair of hawks circled slowly on the currents overhead.

"Is it very bad?" she asked quietly. "Should I stop?"

He put an arm around her and pulled her against his side, scooping her easily along the bench and sending the feathers fluttering to the icy ground. She could smell the heavy leather of his coat.

"Do you know where your ma is from?" he asked.

"The East," she said. "Gargoyle."

"The Galgoros," he corrected. "In the Galgoros they have a different way of doing things. You know the twelve-pointed star carved into the lintel above our door? Your ma carved that. It's from the Galgoros. It's a symbol of their god."

"Their god?"

"Onaistus, God of the Promise." Hellevir frowned. He caught her expression. "Her single god may seem odd to you and me, but many things seem odd just because we don't understand them.

It doesn't mean they're wrong. Our way is odd to her too. She doesn't understand that we do things differently, that we could believe in things that are not her single god. That one person could see something or talk to something that another person couldn't, and for it to be no harmful thing."

Hellevir thought about it, and suddenly felt quite distant from her ma, as if she'd always assumed they were looking through the same telescope—her pa had bought one from a passing trader to use for hunting, and Hellevir thought it was the prettiest thing in the cottage—but in fact her ma's was trained somewhere completely different, watching a landscape Hellevir couldn't hope to see. At least her pa understood.

"So you don't mind me talking to things?" she asked.

"As long as it feels right to do. Just don't let your ma see. I'm afraid it's just one of the many things I've not been able to make her budge on in all the years we've been married." He smiled. "My ma used to do the same, you know. Speak to things. She used to talk to the cherry tree. Said it liked to sing to her." He smiled briefly, and took a cord from around his neck, pulling up a pendant from under his shirt. Hellevir recognized the pendant, remembered playing with it when she was tiny and sitting on her father's lap. It was still warm from where it had lain next to his heart. She held it in her palm, rubbing the face of the snarling lion with her thumb.

"This was my mother's," he said. "She gave this to me when she died. She said she found it by the edge of the woods, when they were digging the foundations for our house." He squeezed her hands. "Before she died she said that we're a lion-hearted family, and I'd better make sure my children were as lion-hearted as she was." He smiled. "Tough woman, she was." He picked up the pendant and put it over Hellevir's head. "My lion-hearted girl," he said. "It's yours now. To remember there are always others like you."

Hellevir hugged him so tightly he laughed, and seemed about to say something else when an enormous clatter from inside the house made them jump to their feet. Pa had run inside before Hellevir had caught her breath, and a moment later he emerged, eyes wide, and told her to fetch the healer woman from the village. Her mother had fallen.

*

It was a long, long night. It was lost to Hellevir in a blur of running in and out of the cottage to fetch kindling from the store by the house, and then, when that dwindled, in and out of the forest, following the sharp orders of the healer woman. The sounds her mother made were cacophonous in her ears.

Hours later, when the first birdsong littered the air even though it was still dark, Hellevir stood in the doorway looking at her mother's body. Time had contorted that night; every moment had seemed weighted, pressured, long, a heavy tempo of blood in her head, and yet now she felt like she'd taken a breath and . . . and Ma had slipped away when Hellevir wasn't paying attention. There was a sheet over her, a sharp peak over her nose, gloaming dips for her eyes. To the side was a swaddled bundle, small, silent and unmoving. Hellevir couldn't look away from it. Exhaustion sat at the back of her mind, heavy as wet sand, and it numbed her to the shock.

Hellevir's pa sat beside the bed, bent over the body, his large shoulders hunched. The healer who had come to help with the birth, Milandre, stood behind him and put a hand on his back. In the gloom her face looked weathered, lined like an old map. She had her hair pinned back and the bare side of her head, missing its left ear, shone in the firelight.

"She was too early," the old herbalist muttered. "She shouldn't have had another when she was so weak." Her pa's shoulders tensed.

"It was her choice to keep the child," he snapped, looking up at her. "You would have had me force her to get rid of it?" He clenched his jaw and took control of his temper. A beat of silence, palpable, with a heartbeat of its own. He pressed his lips into Ma's palm. "You can bring her back," he said quietly against her skin. Hellevir saw Milandre stiffen.

"If I couldn't keep her alive what makes you think I could bring her back?" Her tone was curt.

"I know you can. I've heard . . ."

"You've heard nothing," Milandre said. Her expression softened a little as Pa closed his eyes. "I will stay with the body until morning," she added more softly. "Hellevir and I, we will prepare the rites." A bone-deep tremble went through Hellevir. She clenched her fists so they wouldn't see her start to shake.

"No," Pa murmured. "Piper is of Eastern faith. She wouldn't want to be among the cairns."

Milandre sighed but bit back the sharp words she might have spoken.

"Then your boy will fetch the Peer from the next village temple to do it. But nothing can be done now. Go and sleep."

He nodded again, as if he had only half-heard her. Hellevir took his hand and led him out of the room. Farvor had run away when they'd told him his mother was dead. He was out in the woods somewhere, and Hellevir envied him as she pressed a bowl of stew into her father's hands, wishing she was among the trees, a deer with nothing to do but run or an owl with nothing to do but fly. When food had passed her pa's lips, she helped him into bed like a child, pulling off his heavy boots. Only when she was sure he was unconscious did she steal back into the bedroom. The herbalist was asleep in the chair by the fire, breathing heavily by its glow.

Hellevir glanced at the bed. It seemed as if at any moment the shape under the sheet would move, would breathe, but it didn't. She knelt down before the hearth, stirred it with the poker.

"I want to try," she told it. The fire within the hearth roused itself and the crouching spirit made of burnt wood and coal watched her through heat-glow eyes. It had burned so strongly while Ma had been in labor. Pa wouldn't know to thank it, but Hellevir nudged some dry kindling closer to feed it.

"Then try," it replied.

"What if I can't do it?"

"The outcome will not be any worse."

"Will you come with me?"

"I cannot leave your homestead, you know that." Hellevir bit her lip, ashamed of her fear. The burnt creature rolled a hot coal towards her across the ash. A tongue of flame licked round it. "It'll be dark," it said. Hellevir picked up an empty lantern and used the iron to roll the coal inside.

"Thank you."

"Hurry, before morning wakes her."

Hellevir got to her feet and went over to the bed. She clambered up and lay alongside the still shape under the sheet, curling around the lantern at her stomach as she looked up at where the head rested. The coal flickered in the lantern, and its soft light lulled her eyelids closed.

The sound of the front door swinging open startled her awake.

There was silence. She was still in her mother's room, but . . . the body had gone. Milandre had gone. Even the baby had gone. The bed was rumpled, one edge of the covers raised as if someone had just flung them off to get up.

Hellevir slid off the bed. The kitchen was empty. The pot that had held the broth sat by the door to wash in the snow. The front door was wide open, still on its hinges, although it had always had the tendency to swing shut again if left ajar.

Outside there was no wind, only the head-aching silence. Her own breath seemed loud as a bellows, her footsteps echoing like rocks dropped down a well. Even her heartbeat, quick and heavy, seemed to announce her presence to the strange world and she felt—suddenly and completely—that it watched her.

The light was so odd—a permanent dusk, it seemed—that Hellevir looked up to see if the sun was out, and froze. There was no sun, no stars, no moon or clouds. When she looked up, another Hellevir looked back. The whole sky seemed to be a still surface upon which the world reflected, like the surface of a lake. Far, far above her was the snowy earth, the topmost branches of the cherry tree, the pointed roof of her own house, an angle of her home she'd never seen before, and her own reflection, staring down at her. She raised her arm experimentally, and the small figure did the same. It gave her an odd feeling of vertigo, as if she were about to fall upwards, and she quickly looked away.

She went into the woods. The trees were motionless, their grey bark soaking up the light.

"Ma!" she called, ignoring the odd timbre of her own voice. "Where are you?" She caught movement from the corner of her eye—the end of a shawl, the heel of a shoe?—vanishing between the trees, flitting in the same chase as the fox. "Ma!" She ran after her. "Wait!"

She came to the bank of the river; it was frozen a foot thick. Something moved on the other side of the water and she darted down the snowdrift towards it, slipping and sliding as her feet hit the ice. Her heart skipped a beat as she heard the heavy crack of the ice giving way, and she might have fallen through if a hand had not caught her by the arm and pulled her sharply back up onto the bank.

She whirled around, eyes darting among the trees, but there was no one there. She rubbed her arm, certain she had not imagined the hard grip. It had hurt too much for her to have imagined it.

"You're a little lively to be out here," a voice remarked. She jumped and turned.

Leaning against a tree was a man of black. His hair was black, his coat was black, his gloves were black. An absolute black, as if no light could reflect from it. It drew her gaze and held it, threatened to pull her in and drown her in its absence of light. His eyes were the blackest of all and watched her with amusement.

"Hello, child," he said. At least she thought he said it. His voice did not seem to come from one place, but all places, everywhere, from the very air beside her cheek.

"I'm not a child," she retorted, her voice high. "Who are you?"

"No, forgive me. I see I have a lady before me." His mouth curled into a smile. His lips seemed to shape oddly around his teeth, as if they were too long and too sharp, but then he spoke and she could see that they were normal. "Now, I must ask. What is a fine lady like you doing here? I don't think this is a place for you." He took a deep breath, as if he had smelled something sweet. "Oh no, you do not belong here," he said. "Not yet. Not for a long while yet." His voice was low and warm, the only warm thing about him.

"I . . . I'm looking for my mother," she said honestly. His smile broadened in a way that made her feel as if she were missing a joke, and he held out his hands in a gesture of peace. The smile and the gesture seemed at odds with each other. She couldn't tell where his edges were; he seemed to be made of the darkness between the trees.

"And why do you think she'd be here?" he asked.

"She . . . she's dead."

"So you do know where you are. I did wonder. But then again, it's not your first time here, is it?" As if from nowhere he held out the lantern, balanced by its ring on one gloved finger. "Your mother's right over there," he said, his eyes bright as if he were enjoying himself. "Your sister too."

He pointed out over the river, and Hellevir drew in her breath sharply.

Ma was sitting out on the ice, her legs crossed, holding the baby in her arms. She was rocking it gently, and singing to it. Something in Hellevir's chest ached. She couldn't remember Ma ever singing like that to her.

"Ma!" she called. Her mother didn't look up from smiling down at the baby's face, tracing its cheek with one finger as she sang. The ice cracked quietly around them. "Ma!" She didn't react, as if she couldn't hear her. Hellevir felt her fists tighten by her side, and she turned to the man, her jaw set.

"I brought that fox back," she said resolutely. "I want her to come back with me too." The man watched her but she tried not to waver. It felt like she was in the shadow of something tall about to topple upon her.

"And what will you give in return?" She didn't know what she had expected him to say—or how she knew what authority he held in this place—but it wasn't that. For a moment she was speechless, aghast.

"I . . . I don't have anything."

"What a pity."

"Why do I have to give you something?"

"You can't take anything from this place without paying the price. For natural deaths especially, there is a cost." His gaze slipped to the lantern by her foot. "But that will go some of the way to striking a balance." Hellevir followed his look.

"The coal? It's not mine. I can't give it to you. I . . ." She shook her head, trying not to cry. "I didn't know that's how it worked."

"You left the berries for your fox, and a drop of blood too. I thought you an adept." He knelt down beside her, watching her mother singing over her baby. Hellevir suddenly felt like they were two strangers looking in through the window of someone else's house. "Something from life that is full of life, and another blood gift," he went on. He reached out and took her hand, tiny in his own, and she shuddered. He was as cold as a dead thing. He began to press down her fingers to her palm, one by one. "For your mother to be safe with you again, alive, healthy, happy, and able to grow old . . ." He paused, when only her little finger was left, and all the rest were pressed down. "The coal and a small blood gift are all you'd need to give."

She looked at him, into his dark eyes. It felt like she was looking into the mouth of a deep, empty cave.

"Who are you?" she asked for a second time.

"If you come here again, you can ask me again."

Hellevir swallowed, looking down at her hand. Then she nodded. "All right."

That smile again, rapt and eager.

He stood, and with the motion her mother's attention finally seemed to be caught. She grinned and got to her feet, walking easily over the ice towards them as if she were simply crossing a spring meadow.

"Hellevir," Ma said with a sunlight in her voice that Hellevir hadn't heard in a long time. "What are you doing here?"

"I came to save you," Hellevir said. There seemed to be no air in her lungs, and it suddenly sounded a silly thing to say. Her mother didn't look like she needed saving. She looked happy. Hellevir turned without a word and held out the lantern to the man in black, and he took it with a courteous inclination of his head.

Hellevir held out her hand.

"Come on, Ma," she said. "I want to go home." Ma's smile broadened, and she moved towards Hellevir but the man in black stopped her. Hellevir stared up at him. "But you said . . ."

"We only bargained for one," he reminded her. She felt the words go through her, but she'd been afraid he would say them. She looked at the baby in her mother's arms, happily asleep and looking as healthy as a newborn lamb.

"But . . ."

"One or the other. Not both."

"Why not?"

"Because of a way of things older than I am."

"What if I come back? With more coal?"

"No. You must choose now."

"Hellevir, what are you waiting for?" her mother asked, as if she couldn't see or hear the man.

It should have been a difficult choice, but it wasn't. It was painfully easy.

"Mother, then," she whispered, looking into the green eyes that matched her own. "Ma." He reached out, the movement too quick for her to catch, and a moment later there was a bead of red on her finger. She stared down at it, watching as it slid and dripped onto the ground.

Her mother started, as if just noticing the tall man with the black coat standing beside them. She frowned, confused.

"I feel like I know you?" she asked. The man held out his arms.

"Here, let me take her," he said. Uncertain, Ma drew away a little, putting a hand protectively around the child's head.

"No, I . . ."

"I'll take care of her for you until you return. Go and be with your living daughter." Hellevir watched as her mother blinked, clearly struggling to think. The man's warm voice played on her, wrapped itself around her, belied the mocking smile.

"If you think it's best," she said, and reluctantly let him take the baby into his arms. Numbness gripped Hellevir from head to foot, as if she were finally feeling the chill of the snow. The man dressed in black looked down at her, her little sister cradled in his arms. For a second she thought tines were rising from his head, antlers as black as the snow was white.

"Time to go," the world around her rumbled.

"Time to go." Hellevir shuddered, her bones aching as if she'd been standing in a mountain river for an hour. She looked up blearily, and saw Milandre peering down at her.

"Time to go, pet," Milandre said again. "Come now. We have a lot to do." Hellevir shook herself awake and raised herself to look at the figure under the sheet, her heart hammering with hope and the almost painful certainty that she was hoping in vain and it had all been a horrible dream.

The figure coughed, a brief billow of the sheet, and began to shiver.

Milandre stared for a moment. Then she sharply drew Hellevir from the bed and pulled back the sheet. Ma sat upright, her hair wild about her and her face creased as she coughed and coughed. Milandre just stood there, her lips slightly parted in amazement.

"I don't understand, how . . ." She looked at Hellevir, but before she could say anything the door opened and Pa came in, Farvor at his heel.

"We heard . . ." He stopped, stunned. "Piper? Gods . . . Piper?"

"Water," Ma gasped. Milandre shook herself from her stupor and poured some from a jug by the bed. Hellevir didn't miss that she checked the bundle in case it also had signs of life, before letting it be. Ma gulped the water, letting it pour down her front. Pa looked like he wanted to swoop towards her and bear her up in his arms, but he was too shocked—too frightened—to get closer. Hellevir picked up a blanket and went to soak up some of the water, but as soon as she came near her mother roughly pushed her away, her hand hitting the center of her chest with a violence Hellevir would remember until the day she died. Only Farvor stopped her from falling.

"Curse you!" Ma screamed. "Curse you!" She threw the cup. It may have been aimed at Hellevir, but it hit the wall instead and cracked into a thousand pieces.

There was stunned silence as Ma began to sob uncontrollably. Then Milandre caught Hellevir by the shoulder, and gently guided her out of the room as Pa and Farvor stared after them.

"Come, child." She led Hellevir outside, where the sunlight was seeping through the wisp-layer of cloud, weak and watery. Milandre sat her down on the bench under the cherry tree and took her hands. The old woman frowned and glanced down at them, as if she'd felt something odd that she hadn't expected.

"Oh, child," she said, her voice heavy. She brushed the sensitive skin at Hellevir's knuckle where her little finger used to be on her left hand. It was scarred over as if the wound were many years old. The old woman's hand drifted up to her own head where her left ear used to be, bare as if she'd been missing it her whole life. "You did this, didn't you?" she murmured. "You brought your ma back."

Hellevir nodded, and held her breath to stop the tears, but it didn't work. Milandre gathered her up as she began to cry.

CHAPTER TWO

The third time Hellevir entered Death, she was twenty-two years old. This time she went prepared.

She was returning from the forest as the evening sun blazed warm and golden, her shadow long and thin ahead of her on the trail into the village. Sparrows were having dust baths along the road, and dandelion seeds twirled lazily in the humid air. Her basket was heavy with wild garlic—although she'd thought their season past—as well as elderflowers, some chicken-of-the-woods mushrooms she'd found clinging to an old oak, and blackberry leaves. She'd even found some wild strawberries.

She and Milandre lived as hedge-witches in the village. Hellevir had moved there shortly after raising her mother from the dead. Her ma had never been fond of the village by the woods, and after her miscarriage she had found nothing could induce her to stay. More than that, the sight of Hellevir seemed to burn her, and Hellevir would catch her watching, gaze lingering and dark. Although he had resisted his wife's pleas to move to the capital city before, Hellevir's pa had found himself unable to argue with her in the shadow of their grief. It came as no surprise—when her ma, pa and brother announced that they would be moving to Rochidain—that Milandre offered to take Hellevir under her care and teach her the arts of healing and herbalism.

As Hellevir walked she cheerfully swung the basket, and recited the morning's lessons she'd had with Milandre, whispering them to herself under her breath—*Rosin rose. Oil is a good balm for wounds, bruises, burns, and stings. Helpful for women past childbearing age. A treatment for sadness. Parts for use: the flower, seed and leaf. Not for use during pregnancy or breastfeeding. Flowers midsummer . . .*

She stopped. Something felt wrong. On a lovely evening like this, the streets should have been filled with children playing, and old men and women sitting at their doorsteps getting the sun on their faces, but instead there was only quiet. Her foreboding grew as she passed the stream where the parents took their children to paddle, and saw abandoned shoes and toys left on the banks.

The soldiers had stopped outside Milandre's house. Their horses were bay, a fiery color in the sunlight. They champed at their bits and tossed their heads in irritation at the flies attracted by the white sweat lathering their necks, the armor on their faces and necks clinking quietly. The standards they held hung limp in the still air, scarlet flags embroidered with a golden ship, the symbol of the Royal Court of Rochidain. One of the soldiers standing by the gate came forward as she approached.

"Be on your way," he said. "The old woman is busy. Come back when we've gone."

"The old woman is my mentor," Hellevir replied sharply. "And I live here. Let me past." He looked her up and down.

"Fine," he said. "I'll announce you." She nodded and let him lead her through the gate. In the workshop, the afternoon light cast all things in a monotone amber: the tools on the workbench, Milandre's hair and the long, uneven object wrapped in sheets lying on the center table. Hellevir knew the shape of a body beneath sheets. She could smell something bad.

"Are you refusing to help?" a voice demanded. Hellevir looked up into the sharp eyes of a woman in the same armor as the soldiers. She was stately, in her autumn years, her neatly coiled hair the color of steel. The cloak sweeping to her heels was dark and beautifully embroidered. She spared Hellevir a glance, before returning to Milandre.

"I'm not sure what you expect me to do, Your Grace," the healer replied, taking Hellevir's arm and drawing her aside. The lady seemed to grow impatient, as if she thought Milandre was wasting her time. She reached out and with a severe gesture drew back the sheet. Underneath was a young girl, not much older than Hellevir, although it was difficult to tell her age for certain. Her face was dark and bloated, days if not weeks dead. A band had been wound around her head and jaw to keep her mouth closed. The smell became so overpowering Hellevir had to cover her nose and mouth with her hand. Even Milandre blanched.

"I suppose it could have been hemlock," the herbalist said. "Or perhaps . . ."

"Wolfsbane. We have doctors in the city who can identify the toxin well enough, that's not why I'm here." The lady wouldn't look at the body; she only had eyes for Milandre. "I've heard about you. The strange ability you displayed during the war." Hellevir saw Milandre's hand tighten around the back of the chair. She seemed to choose her words carefully.

"Sometimes, Your Grace, the works of a clever healer can appear miraculous to simpletons. Stories fall from mouth to mouth and take on life they never should have had."

"Are you calling me a simpleton?"

"No! Of course not, my lady . . ."

"So you didn't resurrect a boy?"

Milandre said nothing. The silence in the hut became so thick Hellevir could taste it.

"Yes, Your Grace," she said with an edge to her tone. "I raised a boy, once. My nephew. He died at the Battle of the Prye, helping you to win your crown." Hellevir blinked, looking with fresh eyes on the fine armor the lady wore, the tall standards she could see swaying through the window. If Milandre had hoped the woman would look chastened, she was disappointed. "It was not an easy resurrection. The cost was high." Her hand drifted up to the smooth side of her head. "I have tried to raise others, fruitlessly. It's impossible for me now."

"You will tell me why."

Milandre raised her arms, palms up, a helpless gesture, but her eyes were reserved, cold. "Look at me. When I was young I could lift a goat on my shoulders; now my apprentice must help me with a pail of milk. Would you command me to lift three times my weight, or perhaps flap my arms and fly? Besides, the body then was freshly dead, and his death was by unnatural causes. It makes things . . . easier." She pointed to the body. "She has been dead for days."

"She was poisoned," the lady interrupted. "Someone did this to her. A most *unnatural* death." She said it in a mocking way, as if it were some absurd belief Milandre adhered to which she could not fathom.

Milandre put her hands together and pressed her fingertips to her lips.

"Your Grace, I am sorry. I cannot do what you ask of me. It's not that I will not, it's that I cannot. I am not strong enough." She hesitated, as if debating whether to continue, and then added, "I've never been able to repeat what I did during the War over the Waves. Not for lack of trying. I am sorry."

The lady looked as if she would argue further, or perhaps even strike the old woman. Hellevir tensed, but the lady just cast her sharp eyes back to the body—briefly, as if it scalded her to look—and covered the face again. She jerked her head, and the two watching soldiers came forward to take the stretcher the body was lying on. The lady went out first and held the door open for them as they passed through with their burden.

Hellevir watched them go up the path. Milandre stood beside her with her arms folded.

"We're leaving," the lady called to the group outside the gate, her voice clipped. "Back to Rochidain."

The words pushed up out of Hellevir's chest and rolled past her teeth before she could think to hold them back, and she heard herself say quietly, "I can do it." The entourage paused as the lady looked back, the hem of her cloak sliding across the cobblestones.

"What did you say?" she demanded. Hellevir found herself trapped under the lady's gaze, like a butterfly pinned to a board.

"I can do it," she said again, more loudly. The lady stepped around the stretcher and came towards her, hand resting lightly on the sword at her hip. Milandre caught Hellevir by the arm, pulling her back with a violence that nearly tugged her off balance.

"Forgive her, Your Grace," she said sharply. "She doesn't know what she's saying." Her fingers dug a warning of silence into Hellevir's skin.

"She says she can do it," the lady said. She returned her regard to Hellevir. "Is this true?"

"I can try," she said, raising her chin. Milandre's grip tightened unpleasantly.

"You can do it, or you can try?" the lady asked her.

"I can do it. I know I can."

18

The lady watched her for a moment, lips pressed thin. Then she gestured for the men to bring the body back inside.

"At least you're willing to try," she said as she passed them in the doorway, directing her words to Milandre. The old woman towed Hellevir back.

"What do you think you're doing?" she demanded, her eyes blazing. Hellevir had never seen her so angry in all the years Milandre had been her mentor, but she braced herself against it.

"I can do it," she said again. "I've done it before."

"That means nothing," Milandre snapped. "Just because you did it once doesn't mean you can do it again. Do you think I was lying, that I haven't tried a hundred times and failed a hundred times? It doesn't always work. And say it does, look what it took from you when you raised your ma." She raised Hellevir's four-fingered hand, and her tone became desperate. "Do you think there won't be another price to pay?

"Think, child, think what it'll mean if you do succeed. If you do it once do you think they'll let you fade back into the countryside? They'll take you away, order you to raise every sickly relative they have, every fallen soldier. They have the power to make you. Don't do this, for your own sake!"

Hellevir knew what she was saying was true. She knew she should listen.

"The girl is my age," she said. "I wouldn't want to be dead yet." She placed her other hand over Milandre's. "I'm going to try. You can't dissuade me."

"You don't even know the girl. Why are you doing this?"

"Because I can." *Because I want to know if I can.* "Because I should." *Because I have to try.* "Because I can save her life."

It felt like a locked door that was just waiting for her to turn the key and pull it open. Her heart beat with an odd trepidation, as if she were about to start a race which she knew she could win, if she only pushed herself hard enough. Every day since she'd raised her mother she'd felt the pull of it, had waited with breath held for the opportunity to see if she could do it again. But she didn't say this to Milandre, because she wasn't certain how to explain it herself. She just knew this was something she had to do, like when she'd held the fox to her heart as a child.

She loosened Milandre's grip and went back into the house.

19

"I said I'll try," she told the lady. "But you have to promise me something." The lady narrowed her eyes and tapped a heavy ring on her finger against the pommel of the sword. "If I succeed, you have to promise you won't make me do it again. You or anyone else from your court. You let me stay here."

The lady inclined her head.

"Fine," she said. "Done. Now give the skeleton of your boasts the meat of your actions."

Hellevir swallowed. The lady's presence filled the little workshop like iron poured into a mold, her watchfulness scalding. "What was her name?" she asked.

"Sullivain," the lady said through tight lips. Hellevir knew the name. She doubted there was anyone in the Chron who did not.

Hellevir glanced at Milandre.

"I need to go to sleep," she said to her. The old woman nodded, and reluctantly went about creating a sedative. While she began to fill the burner with a mixture of herbs, Hellevir stepped outside.

She stood in the road, watching the dandelion seeds drifting by, as calm and slow as if there wasn't a dead body rotting not ten feet away. One floated past, and she reached out and caged it gently in her fingers. She caught two more, making sure they still had their seeds attached, and carried them inside, careful not to let them be crushed. She put them underneath a bell jar and sat beside the body. She tried to look calm, like she knew what she was doing, but her heart was beating quickly and heavily as if it wanted to be free of her chest. A part of her screamed at herself, as if watching her from far away, *why are you doing this? Why are you going back to that place?*

I just have to, was the only answer she had. *I have to see if this is something I can do. I have to save her if I can.*

"Please wait outside with your men," she asked the lady.

"Why?" she demanded as the old woman tried to usher her outdoors.

"I'd find it hard to go to sleep with you in the room too," Milandre snapped, then added, "Your Grace." Reluctantly, they filed out. Milandre took out her tinder box and lit a candle.

"Are you sure you want to do this?" She said it through gritted teeth, but her tone was pleading.

Hellevir nodded, although suddenly she wasn't sure at all. Milandre lit the herbs in the bowl and put a wax cloth over the top, handing Hellevir a tube to breathe the smoke through. Hellevir put it over her nose and mouth, and took a deep breath. Her eyelids grew heavy far more quickly than she thought they would, and her head sank slowly onto the table. She wrapped her arm around the jar and let herself be pulled under. The last thing she was aware of was Milandre putting a cushion under her head.

Hellevir now knew what to expect, although it had been so long since she had been here. She'd recalled it to herself in the years since, wandering the still woods that were not her woods in her mind, remembering the conversation she'd held with the darkness that lurked there. The odd half-light, the roaring silence, the stillness of the air. The things left on the workbenches and tables as if whoever had been using them had stood and fled midway through. The sudden cold. At least the smell of death was gone. The irony was not lost on her.

She stood, picking up the bell jar under one arm. The scrape of the chair leg against the floor was cacophonous, and it made the hairs all up her back and her neck stand on end. She went outside, and—taking a moment to gather her courage—made herself look up.

Even though she knew what she would see, it still jarred her. Her own distant reflection staring up-down at her, Milandre's house and garden from the viewpoint of a bird. A wave of dizziness flowed over her, and she fought the urge to sit down, to anchor herself more firmly to the ground.

She walked down the cobblestone path, her footsteps echoing, and pushed open the gate. Dandelion seeds hung suspended in the air, still as a moment caught in the blink of an eye. Hellevir tapped one with the tip of her finger, but it drifted only a little distance before halting as absolutely as before. She walked through them, brushing them aside as she went, leaving a tunnel behind her in the seeds.

"Sullivain!" she called. "Sullivain!"

Nothing. Just the sound of her own staccato heartbeat. The absence of people was tangible in the very air.

She came to the river and climbed up onto the bridge. The water below had no current, but stood still and silent like a lake. It looked far darker than before.

"Sullivain!" she shouted. It occurred to her that on the two occasions she'd entered Death, the ones she'd been looking for had died very close to where she had begun searching. She had no idea where Sullivain had died, but she assumed it was the capital. Did that mean she wouldn't be able to find her?

It suddenly felt hopeless. She stopped, looking down at the bell jar under one arm. The seeds swirled around inside as easily as in life, and were a brighter color than everything around them.

"What am I doing?" she asked herself quietly. "Am I a fool?"

"People who ask themselves that usually aren't fools," the man in black said. She jumped, almost dropping the jar.

He was standing at the head of the bridge, leaning against the wall. The light bowed around him, stooped before him; it made her eyes hurt to look his way. He still wore the heavy winter coat which bled into the darkness, the dark gloves. He was exactly as she remembered him.

"Do you know why I'm here?" she asked. Her voice was high. He laughed—a short, sharp exhalation of breath which made her flinch—and looked out over the grey fields. She felt her cheeks heat. "Do you?" she demanded. She didn't like to be laughed at.

"Yes," he replied slowly. "I do."

"Will you give her to me?" He walked over at an easy pace, his hands in his pockets, black eyes unreadable as they lingered on the bell jar in her arms. She tensed, and realized she was shaking, whether out of fear or trepidation, she wasn't sure. She hated it, though, hated it because she knew he could see it.

She had been watching him so intently, the darkness that surrounded him swallowing her attention as completely as it swallowed the light, that she didn't at first notice that the world had changed around her. It wasn't until he stopped moving towards her that she realized the river and the village had gone. The cobbles under her feet no longer belonged to the bridge, but to a small courtyard, surrounded on all sides by trees that went up and up, as far as her eyes could see, vanishing into gloom.

In the center was a stone fountain, its waters frozen as they fell into the circular pond around it. Moss caked the stone, and for the first time a scent caught Hellevir, an earthy dampness that made her think of waterfalls. It wasn't an unpleasant smell. Lanterns hung from the branches at random intervals, their light a steady beam, unwavering and blue, unlike any flame she had seen. He watched her, assessed her.

"Where are we?" she asked.

"A little further into Death," he replied, kneeling by the pond to run his hand through the water. It left a valley as if he were running his fingers through sand. He looked up at her. "Does that frighten you?"

"I . . ." She shook her head, but it did frighten her. He frightened her. "I'm here for Sullivain," she said. "Please can I take her back?" He stood up as if he had not heard her and brushed the droplets from his hand. They hung suspended in the air where he discarded them like beads of glass. Hellevir made herself go up to him and hold out the jar.

"Are these enough?" she asked. He seemed nonchalant at first, but his eyes kept coming back to the seeds, drawn to them. He did want them, she realized.

"Yes," he said slowly. "Her death was far from natural, so I suppose it is fair."

"So she *was* poisoned?"

"Yes."

"Who did it?"

He didn't answer the question, but instead met her gaze so suddenly that she wasn't prepared for it. She resisted the instinct to back away.

"You come here with an alarming ease," he said with that smile she remembered from when she was twelve years old, the one that had crouched in the corners of her dreams and gleamed at her in the depths of the night as she tried to fall asleep. "Are you going to be making a regular habit of asking me for the dead?"

"I . . . hope not."

"Now, that doesn't sound like the full truth." She thought of the soldiers watching her as she prepared to go to sleep, of Milandre's warning. Word would spread. It was impossible that it wouldn't. It was so hard to think of these things, to think straight at all, when she could feel him watching her like that.

"Then I won't lie," she said. "I might have to."

"Well, if that's the case, I think I'll make a more sensible merchant of myself."

"What do you mean?" she asked.

"If you're going to be flitting between the living and the dead, we may as well make use of it," he said. "Make a deal of it." Hellevir's hands were sweaty against the glass jar, leaving palm-prints of condensation. His lip twitched. He liked watching her reactions, she could tell. She wondered if she was the only soul he could talk to, or whether others paid him visits. Did he hold conversations with the dead?

"What sort of deal?"

He *hmm*ed, and the world rumbled low with the sound. She felt it against her skin, like the vibrations of a violin string.

"There are things from life that are precious in a place like this. Treasures. Bring them to me whenever you seek the dead, and I'll make you a fair trade, and only demand a few drops of blood at a time."

"A few drops of blood?" Hellevir repeated, unconvinced. "Like this?" She held up her hand, the gap where her little finger used to be. Except there was no gap. She blinked, turning her hand over.

"We are all whole in death," he said.

"Will it . . ."

"Be gone when you wake up? Yes." He lowered himself to sit on the low wall encircling the pond. "But no, I don't mean more than a few drops if you bring what I ask. A pricking of your finger."

"Why so little? What if I come again asking for someone who died naturally?"

"If you bring me what I tell you, it won't matter. The treasures have their own source of bloodshed, of weight, that will tip the balance. A treasure, in exchange for your self. Or would you rather keep bringing me bits of coal and seeds and run through all your fingers, all your toes?" That smile, as if he liked the sound of it.

Hellevir swallowed, looking around her at the trees. The fear crept up her spine and sat like a live thing upon her shoulder.

"I don't think I understand the rules," she said.

"It's not a game. There are no rules, not in a place like this. Only laws."

"What sort of things do you want me to bring you?"

"Nothing monstrous. Particular things that someone like you will be able to find."

"Someone like me?"

"Someone who can see things the way that you seem to be able to see them."

"I . . ." She suddenly felt dizzy again, and put a hand to her head. Making a deal with Death—because what else could he be?—it was absurd. But she knew exactly what he meant by *someone like her*. Someone who talked to fires and magpies, who listened to the arguments of sparrows as she lay in her bed every morning. Who she was had turned her mother's gaze dark and glowering, even before Hellevir had raised her. She'd noticed the way the villagers whispered to each other, glancing and not-glancing in her direction.

I could simply never return, she thought, but in her heart and bones she knew she would. She was . . . pulled here, as if she were on a cord. She'd felt it in the intervening years, since she had brought back her mother. A curiosity, the half-acknowledged need to slip away and come back here. Like the urge to stand at the edge of a cliff with one's back to the drop, and look up.

She found herself nodding. Slowly, she sank onto the wall beside him, setting the jar down on the stone between them.

"What do you want me to bring you?" she asked. To her surprise, he reached into his pocket and drew out a charcoal pencil and a slip of paper. He gestured for her to turn around, and numbly she complied. She felt the press of the paper on her back, the scratching of the pencil as he wrote. Perhaps it was because she half-expected his hand to pass right through her that the tangibility of it felt so bizarre. He drew away and held out the paper between two fingers.

It was a riddle. It was written with a fine hand.

"I thought you said this wasn't a game," she said. She was surprised to find she was angry.

"I am . . . restricted. I cannot tell you directly where to look. The signs will make themselves known to you, as time goes by, and make sense to you when you see them. They will call to you when you are near."

"What if they don't?"

"Then you'd better not come asking for more bodies." There was a warning in his tone and she felt, suddenly and completely, the danger of him.

"Why?" she dared to ask. "Why do you need these things?" He didn't reply, but she felt the danger deepen. It was there in the way the air tautened in her throat, pressed with livid stillness against her skin. This was not her world. It was not her place to question its laws.

She put the paper into her dress pocket.

"But what about this time?" she asked instead. "For Sullivain. Is what I brought enough?"

He picked up the jar, turning it over and letting his eyes rest on the vibrancy of the seeds. "She has been dead a long time," he said. "And the poison has wreaked havoc on her body. I will need more than a few drops of blood, just this one time, to restore her to health. The law of this place dictates it. Hereafter the things you bring me will be enough." She braced herself, and held out her hand. He gave that bark of laughter again, which died on the still air as soon as it had left his lips.

"So willing to lose parts of yourself," he commented. "And for a girl you do not know."

"If I can save her, I should. I knew what I would be giving up when I came."

"I doubt it. Even so . . ." He took her hand, turning it over in his. His skin was cold to the touch, sapping her warmth as if he were made of marble. He bent her ring finger gently. She could see it, as clear as if it were already missing, and repressed a shudder. "This, and a lock of hair, will be enough."

"Why a lock of hair?"

"So many questions. Call it your signature for our contract. I will keep it here, in my pocket." She let out a breath, pulling her hair into a tail and draping it over one shoulder. Her curls caught on the chain of the pendant about her neck, and it fell haphazardly from her shirt.

The man in black's reaction was immediate. His gaze locked on to the lion pendant that her father had once hung over her head as they sat under the cherry tree.

"Where did you get that?" he asked. His voice, for the first time, had none of the scorn or disdain, none of the mockery, that

Hellevir had assumed was inherent to it. It was the first time he had sounded like a real person, and not an actor on a stage of his own. She put a hand to the lion's head.

"This? My pa gave it to me." She frowned. "Is this what I should give you?" she asked. "Instead of the seeds? Is it worth more?"

He half-reached out for it, and then seemed to check himself, letting his hand fall back. "Keep your trinket," he murmured.

"Isn't it good enough?"

"It is not a fair trade," he replied. "It is too seeped in blood. This thing would earn you legions, a hundred lives, if I were willing to give them. Which I am not." She looked down at the pendant with new eyes, her curiosity burning, but before she could ask another question he had reached out and taken a lock of her hair between thumb and finger. She flinched at his proximity. Obligingly, she pulled from her pocket the small trimming shears that she used for taking plant cuttings, and snipped it free. He knotted it neatly so it wouldn't escape, and tucked it into his breast pocket. Hellevir felt like she could see it burning through the fabric of his coat, a lock as black as everything else he wore.

"Will you give me Sullivain?" she asked.

"She is behind you," the man replied.

There was a girl with wheat-colored hair standing in front of the trees, looking up at the boughs with her hands on her hips. She seemed confused, searching for something. Without the touch of poison, the days' worth of death, Hellevir was struck by how lovely she was. In this place, surrounded by grey and shadow, she shone as if she were made of gold.

"You," Sullivain said, turning and seeing Hellevir. "Have you seen my grandmother?" Her voice was low like a bell. Hellevir collected herself.

"Yes," she said. "I think it was your grandmother who sent me. I'll take you to her."

"Oh, good. We were supposed to be having lessons."

The man in black was beside her in the time it took her to draw breath. He moved too quickly, like a figure from a bad dream.

"Who are you?" Hellevir asked him again. That smile, as if he'd caught her.

"If you come here again, you can ask me again."

27

"Does that mean you'll never tell me?"

"It means I'll never promise an answer. It depends how long we carry on our trade."

He held out his hand, and for a moment Hellevir just looked at it. Thinking that nothing would be able to unnerve her for the rest of her life, she pressed her palm to his. A handshake to seal it, as normal merchants would do.

"A deal," she said, and heard the trepidation in her own voice. He smiled as if he heard it too. He bowed his head over her hand, as if they were about to dance, and she shivered.

"A deal," he replied, and the words grew and deepened and engulfed her, until she was drowning in their blackness.

She awoke with a start. Her head swam, still under the influence of the incense. Cold flooded her bones and left her gasping.

"Hellevir!" She heard Milandre draw close and felt a hand on her shoulder. She shook her head to clear it, blinking to bring her vision into focus.

"Is she . . ."

The figure on the tabletop shot upright, clawing the sheet and the band from her face, and vomited onto her own lap. Hellevir and Milandre recoiled automatically, tripping over Hellevir's chair. The girl gasped and heaved in breath, putting a hand to her forehead.

"Onaistus," she muttered. She looked up blearily and took in the two of them staring at her. "Who are . . . ?"

Milandre handed her a towel to wipe her face, just as the door burst open and the lady rushed in, hand once again on her sword as if she meant to do battle. She stopped dead when she saw the girl on the table.

"Sulli?" she murmured. The girl turned around shakily, still breathing heavily.

"Grandmama?" she said. "What's happening?" The lady didn't answer, but came forward and held the girl's face between her hands, for a moment speechless. Then she wrapped her arms around her and held her close, resting her cheek on her granddaughter's head and closing her eyes tight.

Night had fallen by the time the entourage was ready to leave. The soldiers attached lanterns to their standards, and in the gloom they looked like a ritual procession. The girl, Sullivain, sat on her grandmother's horse at the front of the saddle, her shoulders wrapped in a heavy blanket despite the sultry night. She couldn't seem to stop shivering.

Sullivain's grandmother stood with Milandre and Hellevir outside the house. Hellevir was leaning heavily against Milandre, trying to hide her own trembling knees. She was exhausted.

"I don't have the words to express my gratitude," the lady said. From the stilted way in which she said it Hellevir wondered if she had to thank people often. "You can't know what you've done."

"I hope you will remember what you promised, Your Grace," Milandre reminded her. "Such things cannot become a commodity."

"You have my word. None from my court will trouble you for such services again." She turned to Hellevir. "The court is in your debt, however," she said. "The De Neïd House . . . no, *I* am in your debt. If you ever need our help, send a messenger."

"Thank you," Hellevir said, attempting another bow.

The lady inclined her silver head, and made to turn back to her cohort. She hesitated a moment.

"What is there?" she asked. "On the other side?" The question was a slip, Hellevir thought, that she had asked despite herself. The lady was getting old, and the fear of what was to come was growing slowly around her like vines climbing the oak. Even royalty could not escape the fear.

"It's empty," Hellevir replied. "But I think I've only seen the surface, a place that is a stepping-stone to death. I don't know what comes after any more than you."

The lady nodded, thoughtful, and returned to her soldiers. She swung herself up behind her granddaughter and took the reins around her. The Princess watched Hellevir, holding the blanket tightly under her chin, her face grey with fatigue. Hellevir inclined her head. She nodded slowly back, as if she knew Hellevir had just done something important for her, but couldn't quite understand what. Hellevir wished that she could explain it to her, that she didn't have to go quite yet, but the lady had already kicked their horse onward.

As they watched the entourage vanish down the road towards Rochidain, disappearing into the night, Hellevir suddenly felt very,

very tired. She put her head on Milandre's shoulder, and the old woman absently stroked her hair, her touch firm as if she were stroking a cat.

"Was that really the Queen?" Hellevir asked quietly.

"Yes," Milandre replied. "You have been graced by the sight of royalty, Hellevir. Consider yourself blessed beyond all measure. The girl you just brought back was her granddaughter, her only living successor, and I've no doubt in saving her you helped this country to avoid civil war."

Hellevir swallowed, feeling a sense of vertigo.

"Is that why someone poisoned her?" she asked.

"No doubt."

"What if they try again?"

"Who knows? Maybe they'll be more reluctant when they see the dead walking."

Hellevir felt suddenly as if she'd just exerted a lot of effort for not much gain, as if she'd run the fastest in a race only to realize she'd run in the wrong direction.

"Come, child," the old woman said. "Help me open some windows to get rid of that stench. Royalty of course would not deign to mop up its own mess."

Hellevir nodded as the herbalist went back inside. Her gaze lingered on the lanterns of the retinue as they faded, glimmering, into the night. She brought out the slip of paper she'd been worrying in her pocket, and holding it in the two remaining fingers and the thumb of her left hand she read it by the light spilling from the workshop.

Where a stern bow will impress a Queen,
The gift of a song
Will console her when she weeps.

Hellevir slept all through the night and the next day. Her sleep was dreamless and complete. Her fatigue was so absolute that she later wondered what she'd given in a single finger. Something was gone, just as there had been something missing the first two times, something deeper. When she finally surfaced, it was night again.

She wandered blearily from the bedroom through to the workshop, where Milandre sat in front of the fireplace darning an apron. She cleared her sewing things from the other chair so Hellevir could sit. Milandre poured them both a glass of the nettle beer that they'd brewed the previous year, and they sat in silence, listening to the crackle of the fire.

"Did you know Death has pockets?" Hellevir asked quietly. Milandre raised her eyebrows, tilting herself slightly, as she always did, so that her good ear could catch what the missing ear couldn't.

"Death has pockets?" she repeated.

"Yes. He has pockets. Why would Death need pockets?"

"Are you a little feverish, child?"

They lapsed into silence, watching the flickering firelight and the slow-gleaming seams of the wood. Hellevir felt Milandre watching her.

"You're wondering why this man in black talks to you," the old woman remarked. "When he has never shown himself to me, in all the times I've gone to that place."

Hellevir nodded. "I wonder if it is because he sees me as an opportunity," she said. "An idiot he can trick into doing his work in the living world."

Milandre gave it thought. "Perhaps," she replied slowly. "But I don't think you're an idiot, or that you shouldn't have accepted. You made a sensible deal, because you're very right, you will have to do this again. Take me as a cautionary tale; things come back to bite, and there will be others who will want you to bring back their dead, and just like today you won't be able to refuse, not easily. It's best that you don't spend your life giving away parts of yourself for strangers' deaths, or soon you won't have anything left." The old woman glanced across at Hellevir. "Death picked you, but it's not because you're an idiot." Her expression suddenly became sad as she looked at Hellevir's face. "You talk to things, to creatures and spirits, in a way few others can, even me. You enter the afterlife as easily as entering dreams. Perhaps that's why. You have an affinity for souls."

Hellevir could think of nothing to say. She just drank her beer, and wondered what it would be like not to have to think about Death so much. If her only worries were the harvest and the herbs in season, her hair and the weather, or even the politics of a court.

It would be a tame life, she thought, taking a sip, and realized that was probably a great deal worse.

31

CHAPTER THREE

Every year, Midsummer Eve began with celebration, and this year was no different; the best food in the village, far too much drinking, and dancing until dawn. The next morning they would all take offerings to the cairns on the hill and leave them for the spirits of the dead, singing their dirges, before they went to pour beer along the edges of the fields for the Harvest Court. But, for now, the villagers flung themselves into the festivities with gusto and delight, seeking only to please themselves before they took thought for their gods.

The market brimmed with fruits and vegetables, all the larger and riper for the harshness of the frosts, and with cured meats and pies and cheese and beers and wines. An ensemble of musicians was set up in the marketplace where a large space had been cleared for dancing, and they played so many jigs, one after the other, it was a wonder they could remember them all.

Hellevir and Milandre had a little stall by the corner and sold their nettle beer and elderflower wine. It was a balmy night, and Hellevir enjoyed the excuse to smile. She even enjoyed the dancing, spinning and swirling in formation as if she were part of a flock of birds.

The village baker, Sofiah, lingered by their stall. She was the only one who wasn't smiling. Her eyes had a distant expression, clouded with unhappiness. Hellevir poured her a glass of elderflower wine and held it out to her.

"The finest we've made," Hellevir said cheerfully. "I hope you like it."

Sofiah looked at the wine for a moment, and then at Hellevir. Hellevir hesitated.

"Are you enjoying the celebrations?" she asked, just for something to say. She felt Milandre's hand brush her arm, a light caution. Sofiah narrowed her eyes.

"It's hard to enjoy yourself when the man who should have been dancing with you is buried at the cairns, under two foot of stone, while the girl who could have saved him dances without a care in the world." The words were sudden, sharp as ice, shot so violently at Hellevir that when she parted her lips to speak, she couldn't think of a word to say. "Not worth your time, was he, my Anir?" she spat. "A simple farmer, not worth the trouble of bringing back, not like a granddaughter to the Crown." She lashed out, knocking the cup of wine from Hellevir's hand. She swept away, leaving Hellevir standing there with the wine sinking into the cobblestones. Hellevir swallowed, mortified, and came around the stall to pick up the cup, trying her best to ignore the eyes darting in her direction.

It was the first symptom of a disease that had taken the village. Where she had once felt welcome, if not entirely one of them, now she started to feel people watching her. They would look away when she glanced across, or worse, meet her gaze with open resentment. People who had once smiled as she entered their shop—who had asked after her pa, after the healer woman—were now curt and cold, as if she were a stranger. She no longer enjoyed the long walk from Milandre's house to the woods; all along the way she could hear whisperings and though she could not make out the words she knew from their tone that they were unkind. Everyone had been touched in some way by death, and she, who could protect them against it and yet had not, slowly became a symbol of their pain, a thing to hate.

"What if they're right, Milandre?" she asked, looking out between the curtains of their cottage. "I should have done something, shouldn't I? To help Anir, and the others who died in the frosts?" She felt ashamed that she hadn't even tried. That she hadn't even thought to try.

"It's not your job to wipe out death," the old woman remarked as she set the table for supper. "If they thought about it, they'd realize that."

"Perhaps it should be my job," Hellevir murmured as she watched the street. "If I can do something, surely I should? No one would need to die at all."

"Death is an eventuality, not a probability. You can put it off, yes, but you can't halt it completely. You should spend your time making sure you grant full lives where they are cut off too soon, bring back those who were lost before their time."

"Anir was lost before his time."

Milandre stopped what she was doing and put her hands on her hips, and Hellevir could tell from the way she huffed that she was growing impatient.

"My dear, there is no right answer. You cannot save them all, because you are a finite thing yourself; if you give too much away then there will be nothing left to save others."

"So I have to choose?"

"Yes, and choose wisely."

Hellevir shook her head, a little savagely.

"I don't like it. I should save anyone who needs it, bring back anyone it's in my power to bring back. Who decided death had to be an eventuality?" Her heart was beating harshly at the bull-headedness she could hear in her own voice.

"Then you are more foolish than I thought," Milandre remarked.

Hellevir scowled at her, but the old woman had gone out of the back door to fetch kindling, finished with their conversation.

The heat broke with a storm that night. The rain sounded like snakes hissing in the thatched roof, and dripped in streams onto the garden path. Hellevir was halfway through drawing a sweet-pea flower in her journal, but her ink sat forgotten at her elbow as she turned the quill pen slowly in her hand, listening to the crack of thunder overhead.

"The rain had better not last," Milandre muttered from where she sat sewing herb pouches. "It'll drown all the spring onions we just planted."

Hellevir nodded, only half-listening. She was thinking about running through the storm, standing in the middle of the fields with her arms wide open as the lightning crashed overhead. A peal of thunder rolled over the village; she could feel it in her bones, an energy that made something in her want to roar or tear down walls. It called her outside, invited her to play as surely as if someone had called her name.

She got to her feet, closing the notebook with a snap that set the candle flames flickering, and put the stopper back in the inkwell.

"I'm going out," she said.

Milandre raised an eyebrow at her. "Feeling the need for a breath of fresh air?" she remarked as a thunderclap rocked the house.

"Feeling something," Hellevir replied, already pulling on her coat and boots, although she had half a mind just to run outside barefoot. Milandre stood and pulled aside the curtain, for a moment illuminated by the lightning.

"I won't be long," Hellevir said. "I just want to . . ." She stopped, seeing that Milandre was watching something outside, her brow furrowed as she tried to make out whatever it was through the pouring rain. "What is it?" Hellevir asked.

"There's someone at the gate."

"At the gate? At this hour?"

"Yes, three people, I think, they . . ." She put a hand to her mouth, standing back so abruptly that she upset the chair Hellevir had been sitting in. "They've got . . ." She seized Hellevir by her sleeve and pulled her back. "Get away from the door!" she snapped.

A heavy knock came on the wood, shaking it in its frame. Hellevir stared at it with wide eyes, her hands gripping the old woman's.

"Who's out there, Milandre?" she asked.

"No friends of ours, not anymore."

Hellevir dared a glance through the curtains, and could just make out three figures dressed in black coats, their hoods drawn low. They were leaving, the gate swinging behind them as they ran back into the rain.

"They've gone," she said.

Milandre went up to the door and began to unbolt it, her lips set in a thin line. The wind flew around her skirt as she opened it wide, spitting rain onto her shoes. The old woman bent and picked up something black and sodden that had been left on the doorstep, closing the door against the wind and rain. Hellevir watched as she brought it over to the table and laid it out flat. It was a raven. Its neck had been wrung and adorned with hemlock, the white flowers dripping rainwater onto the tabletop. Mud clung to its beak, to its staring eye.

"Why have they done this?" Hellevir asked quietly.

Milandre's jaw clenched.

"Because they're frightened idiots," the old woman said through her teeth.

"This is a message?" Milandre touched the stem around the raven's throat.

"The hemlock. A symbol of death. The raven . . ."

Hellevir stared down at it, eyes wide.

"The raven is me?" Milandre went to put a hand on the girl's arm, but she shook it off. "No," she said. "No."

"Hellevir . . ."

"No. Why should they be allowed to do this? No."

Before Milandre could stop her she took up the bird and the hemlock in her arms, and strode towards the door, flinging it open to let in the crackling air. She stood on the doorstep, letting the rain spray her cheeks and the wind catch her hair.

Without thinking how she would do it, without knowing how she did do it, Hellevir closed her eyes and entered Death.

The cold hit her like the wave of rain, but the air felt charged in a way it never had before. This time, awake as she entered, she felt fully what it was like to step across into Death. It felt like a tearing, a ripping of something vital deep within her, and she gasped at the sudden pain of it, a pain that was not physical but still resonated from her hair to her bones. When she opened her eyes it was to a world caught mid-storm, the rain in glistening shards around her, the lightning forked and blinding white like a crack in the world, yet there was no thunder, only the earsplitting silence of Death. She looked up, and saw that the mirrored sky was pooled and dripping with the rain, that the lightning was causing fractures across its surface that shifted and made her eyes hurt, as if she were witnessing something that should not be seen.

She gathered herself together, put her fingers to her lips, and whistled. A pure note in the cloying silence, shooting from her like an arrowhead, until it seemed the whole world put its hands to its ears and screamed from the sound. With that whistle came the caw of a raven, and the black bird emerged from the trees, sliding through the static raindrops and leaving a hollow space in his wake. Hellevir put out her arm and it landed heavily, claws biting into her sleeve. She held out her other hand, palm flat.

"Draw blood," she ordered, and the air rumbled with her command. The raven fluttered nervously, and with a quick flash of its beak, obeyed, slashing open the skin. Hellevir clutched the hemlock in her fist, coating it in her blood, and flung it to the ground.

She emerged again just as the lightning hit the ground, and the thunder rattled the windowpanes in their frames. The raven tried to take flight in its confusion, crowing and beating its wings, but she held it close and hushed it, telling it that everything would be all right. She patted its feathers dry with her apron and it quietened with shock, feathers spiked and bead eyes bright.

Milandre watched all this with a hand to her chest.

"Hellevir?" she asked. She spoke quietly, as if afraid of what the girl would do. Hellevir glanced over.

"He's hungry," she said. Numbly, Milandre brought out the sack of seeds they kept for the garden sparrows and poured a few on the table for him. Hesitantly, he hopped among them, pecking them up, shaking his feathers to discard the raindrops. In silence, they watched him eat. Outside, the rain continued to pour. For a moment it felt as if there was nothing in the world outside but rain, and they were all that was left.

"How did you do that?" Milandre asked. "Cross without sleeping? I've never seen that before."

"I don't know," Hellevir replied, honestly.

"It . . ." Milandre shook her head. "You must not do that again, Hellevir," she said. Hellevir glanced up at her with a fire in her eyes.

"And what, just let them get away with it?" she said sharply. "They killed him. It was an unnatural death."

"Because it was an unnatural death with a message," Milandre replied. "They are already angry with you. Do you want to make them frightened too?"

"Is that not better?" Hellevir remarked haughtily. Milandre blinked, and then took her by her hands.

"This is not you, child," she insisted. "I know you are wiser than this. It's just fear making you speak this way." Hellevir held her gaze for a moment, and then looked away.

"They killed him," she said again, more quietly. "I was just supposed to let him die?"

"My dear, I understand, I do. But crossing like that, it was a . . . a callous way of doing what we do. A sacred thing done in anger rather than with devotion, with understanding of its importance. You walk a thin line with Death . . ."

"What do you know of Death?" Hellevir snapped. "You've never seen him."

Milandre pressed her lips together, making a visible effort not to let her temper rise to meet Hellevir's.

"I know, but . . ."

"I know more about Death than you ever will. Why should I not enter and leave and do as I see fit?"

"Will you not listen to me?" Milandre exclaimed. "You're not a god! This isn't a game!" Hellevir shrugged her hands away, causing the raven to jump skittishly.

"No, it's not," she retorted. "And there are no rules."

She left Milandre standing by the worktop strewn with muddy feathers and claw prints, and slammed the bedroom door behind her.

That night she dreamed, as the thunder rumbled ever more distantly and the rain was all that was left of the storm, but they were not good dreams.

The world shuddered as if in a heat haze. She put her hands to her head, her mind thick and her limbs heavy.

She was in an elsewhere she did not recognize. It felt like the world of Death, for all its roaring silence. But surely in Death the walls did not crack and draw themselves apart, the wood not behaving like wood at all but fibrous like old flesh torn slowly asunder. Surely in Death there was a roof, and if not a roof then the mirrored sky, and not the endless black that shuddered and trembled like a living thing afraid of being whipped. An endless black that swallowed whole her house and enclosed it on all sides and above and below.

She crouched upon her bed, seized with a dreamer's terror. She tried to move but her limbs stuck sluggishly to her, as if she were a being made entirely of mud. Her eyes were drawn to where the walls had been, and she saw a figure made of black, featureless and radiating malice, his regard fixed upon her so entirely that she felt as if she cowered before a thousand eyes. He advanced with a dreadful slowness, and it was only when his face was inches from hers that she could make out his eyes; black eyes that bled with fury and the shuddering madness of the void around them. *Void* was the only word she could think of to describe the absence of this place; the absence of light, sanity, hope.

"How dare you," the world rumbled around her. She tried to turn away, but he caught her jaw in his hand. She tried to scream, but as in all dreams it came out soft, as if it had no air behind it. His grip was hot and ached, biting into her bone.

"Death is not your plaything, little girl," the world around her snarled. "It is not your garden to idly pluck what grows there. Do you understand?" The girl who in waking was Hellevir tried to nod, she really did, but it was as if the weight of a mountain sat on her neck.

"We have a deal, and you will honor every word of it." The hand tightened on her jaw until she thought it might crack. Her teeth began to split. "If you ever again snatch from my realm as you did," came the thunder, "I will bite the hand from your arm and the arm from your shoulder. Do you understand?"

"I do," she breathed, the words a flicker against the maelstrom of the world's fury. "I do. Please. Please."

The hand tightened, as the being contemplated her with its thousand stares. Then it withdrew, dropping her with a suddenness so sharp her stomach roiled and she retched. She curled in on herself as the nausea swept over her and her head swam, and when at last it passed, she looked blearily around her and saw the walls were where they should be, the roof was overhead, and outside the rain was pattering quietly against the windows. Dawn had tainted the sky a vicious red, an infected color.

She lay there, curled in a ball with her eyes squeezed shut, until at last her head began to pound a little less, and the nausea began to subside.

Milandre was already awake and kneading the dough ready for the day. As Hellevir entered the room the raven, sitting atop the workbench, turned his ink-blot eyes to her, and leaned into her arm as she scratched his head. She tried not to remember how his eyes had looked when they were sightless.

"Thank you," was all he said. She just hugged him, breathed in his smell of wind and feathers.

"What's your name?" she asked him.

"Elsevir."

"I'm Hellevir."

"Thank you, Hellevir."

Milandre stopped kneading and put her hands on her hips, the flour creating white handprints on her apron.

"Up early?" she said sharply, clearly still angered by the night before. Hellevir said nothing, just came over and wrapped her arms around her middle, hugging her tightly. Taken aback, Milandre stroked her head without thinking, leaving flour in the girl's hair.

"What's this?" she asked, her anger melting under concern. "Are you all right? You're shaking."

"I'm sorry," Hellevir said quietly, and buried her head in the old woman's shoulder.

CHAPTER FOUR

Two letters arrived a week later, when Hellevir was in their back garden, pulling weeds from the vegetable plots. The raven sat on the fence post watching her work and keeping an eye out for worms. Elsevir refused to leave her side, even taking to sleeping in a bundle of scarves as a makeshift nest by her bed.

Milandre called for her at the door, the letters held to her stomach. Hellevir shucked her gloves and pushed up her straw hat as Milandre held out the letters tied in twine. The sweat painted her hair to her forehead, and she wiped it away with the back of her hand, leaving a dirty streak.

The top letter was in her father's blocky handwriting, and Hellevir's heart leaped. He rarely wrote these days—Ma never wrote at all—too busy in the capital city to spare much thought for letters.

Hellevir turned to the next, and felt her whole body go still.

"What's wrong?" Milandre asked. Hellevir wordlessly showed her the wax seal that held the envelope closed, imprinted with a sailing ship, the royal coat of arms. Milandre paled, and gestured impatiently for her to open it. Hellevir swallowed nervously and broke the seal.

Milandre waited as Hellevir read it twice, tapping her nail on her arm.

"Well?" she asked. Hellevir folded it slowly, lips pressed thin.

"It's the Princess," she said. "Sullivain. She demands my presence in Rochidain."

Milandre's eyebrow rose.

"Demands, does she? Let me see." Hellevir handed it over numbly.

"She doesn't say why," she said as the old woman skimmed it. "Just that I must attend on her. She says she's sending a carriage in two days."

Milandre scratched the side of her head where her ear used to be. "It's not too hard to guess why she wants to talk to you. People become morbidly curious about death the closer they come to it. She probably wants to find out more about where she was."

"But I . . . I *don't* know much more, not really. The place we go is just an in-between, a bridge, I don't know what comes after."

"You'd better be prepared to say something. But . . ."

"But what?"

"I think it also likely she will want to know if you can save her again, if she needed you to."

The thought sank like something solid and cold into Hellevir's stomach. She rubbed her chest with her fist, recalling the last time she had seen Death. Her mind flinched from the shuddering void, the grip of his hand on her jaw.

"But the Queen promised me that no one from her court . . ."

"The Princess did not promise anything. She is not yet a part of her grandmother's court." There was a beat of silence. Hellevir suddenly wanted to tear up the letter, pretend she'd never received it, but the old woman added, "Perhaps this is fortuitous."

"Fortuitous?"

"I think it's time you left the village. Saw a bit of the world outside."

Hellevir's face fell. "Is it because of Elsevir?" she asked. "That's why you want me to leave? The villagers don't know what it means when I bring someone back, what it takes from me, maybe if I explained . . ."

Milandre put a hand on Hellevir's cheek. "*I* don't want you to leave," she said. "I just think it'd be wise. One day the villagers may forget their anger. Their moods are like the seasons, you know, nothing lasts. Besides," she said, more cheerfully, patting Hellevir's hand, "you promised your pa you'd visit, didn't you? Long overdue, I think."

Hellevir hesitated, looking down at the letter.

"Will you come with me?" she asked, without much hope. Milandre's expression softened. She brushed a wayward lock from Hellevir's face.

"I can't, my dear. I must tend to the house and gardens," she said. "The village needs a healer, even if a lot of them don't deserve one. Rochidain was never the place for me. Too many people, too many spies, too much intrigue. And now too much of the Galgoros." She glanced outside at where Elsevir was pecking at the beans he knew he wasn't supposed to touch. "Take the raven with you. He'll be good company."

Hellevir nodded, suddenly feeling a bit at sea. Milandre tucked her hand under her chin.

"Cheer up," she said. "It will do you good to fly the nest."

Hellevir made herself smile and nod, and tried to tell herself it was for the best, but what Milandre had said disturbed her.

"Could I refuse?" she asked quietly. Milandre kissed her gently on the top of her head.

"No, my dear," the old woman said into her hair. "I wish you could, but you can't refuse a summons from the Crown."

Hellevir sat that night in the little home by the woods where she used to live with her parents. It had fallen to wrack and ruin in the years since they'd all left, her father, mother and brother to Rochidain, and she to Milandre's cottage. The cherry blossom had grown wild and unruly, and ivy clambered up the walls both inside and out. Hellevir sat with the raven on her knee, stoking up the fire in her parents' old room and patiently feeding it twigs she'd collected, until a charcoal figure turned over lazily and opened one sleep-drooping eye.

"Hello," Hellevir said with a smile. The fire yawned, mouth bright and hazy with embers, and rolled up into a crouch.

"If it were not for you I don't think I'd ever need to wake up again," it said.

"I like to make sure you're still here."

"I'll always be here." The night was black and thick as honey. She sat in a cocoon of the hearth's light, her knees drawn up to her chest and her arms wrapped around them, the raven nestled in the crook of her lap, as she told it of the news she'd had from Rochidain, reading the Princess's letter aloud to it.

"If I go, who will come to wake you?" she asked the hearth quietly.

"You do not need to keep coming to wake me," it said.

"Don't you want me to?"

"I do and I always will. But you do not need to. Even if I am sleeping, it is no bad thing. I do not mind it."

"I know, but . . . I feel I should. After what you gave me to bring back Ma . . ." She offered the fire a few more twigs. It took them from her and wrapped its arms around them. "The coal was yours, a part of you. I had no right to give it away, no matter what it was for. For that, it's the least I can do to wake you now and then, to keep you here."

The firelight sighed, and breaths of ash went brushing along the hearthstone.

"I knew what would be demanded when I gave it to you," it said. "These bargains have a price. And I would give it again for anyone who lives under these eaves. More besides. It is my duty as the hearth."

"An unfair duty."

"It is what I am. I don't know if it is unfair, but it is my privilege and belongs to no other." Its flames began to dim and flutter. Hellevir reached for the basket, but all the pieces of wood were gone.

"I'll come back again," she promised. "One day."

"As you wish," it murmured sleepily, and turned over under its bed of ash.

"I don't want to go," she told the fire, but it had already faded to low-burning embers. Hellevir sat there for a while, worrying the already dog-eared letter by the dim light. The wax sailing ship insignia was losing its ridges under the warmth of her thumb as she rubbed it. Something stirred in her mind, and she drew out the riddle again. She always kept it in her breast pocket, just as she imagined Death did with the lock of hair he had taken. She stroked Elsevir's head thoughtfully.

"The Queen's symbol is a sailing ship, isn't it?" she thought aloud. "A galleon?"

"Yes," the raven said, and ruffled his feathers. "Although why you'd wish to cross water I have no idea."

"The war was fought over the sea trade to and from Rochidain,"

Hellevir mused. "It's why they called it the War over the Waves. When the Queen won, she changed her emblem from a lion to a type of ship used both for trade and warfare."

The charcoal writing of the riddle was still clear and unsmeared, but felt just a little colder than it should have done. She read it through again, wondering if the phrasing of the first line meant anything, *Where a stern bow will impress a Queen* . . . it couldn't mean the bow of a ship, could it, rather than something a courtier would do? The Queen's ships? There was a shanty that had gone around the inns not long ago about a seafarer, and each verse had started "Mine all mine, from stern to bow, and brig to star."

She shook her head, pocketing both the letter and the riddle. It was a ridiculous reach, far too abstract to mean what she was thinking. And what was she thinking, that the first instruction was sending her to Rochidain? Death's clues would have to be clearer than that.

As promised, the carriage arrived two mornings after the letter. It was the smartest thing Hellevir had ever seen; the horses were sleek and healthy, and the doors had a polished shine. The man who drove it was dressed in livery, and the two guards who accompanied him on horseback wore fine armor, the galleon insignia on their chests glinting in the sunlight. Hellevir wondered why she needed guards.

As they stood by the carriage, Milandre took her hands.

"Look after yourself," the herbalist said. "No one else will."

Hellevir gave a wry smile. "Thank you for that. Will you be all right here on your own?"

"I've lived alone far longer than I've lived with you," came the retort. Elsevir was perched on the carriage window, and she stroked his glossy neck. "Look after her, handsome thing."

"As long as I have feathers," he replied.

"We'll look after each other," Hellevir said. She squeezed Milandre's hands in hers, suddenly not wanting to let go. "I'll miss you," she said. Milandre surprised Hellevir by placing her hands on either side of her face.

"Do not do anything you don't want to," she said, her tone firm. "Rochidain, it manipulates. I should . . ." She sighed. "I should have hidden you. Kept you from their eyes better. I never expected them to arrive on my very doorstep." Hellevir realized Milandre was frightened. She tried not to feel it too.

"I'll be all right," she said, with more courage than she felt. "Perhaps she just wants to thank me." The hope in her voice fell flat. It was the tone her father had used when he said everything would be all right in the long winters of her childhood, even when he couldn't possibly have known.

"There's always a home for you here," Milandre said. "Look," she continued, leaning down and picking up a small basket she'd brought from inside, "I got these for you." Inside were a pestle and mortar, a collection of jars and bottles, some linen and a few other oddments from her workshop. Even a few boxes already filled with dried leaves, roots and berries. Everything a herbalist could need.

"I expect you to make your way in Rochidain," the old woman said gruffly. "I've taught you a trade, and you should use it."

It sank in suddenly that this was really it, and Hellevir wasn't coming back for a long time. She flung her arms around the old woman, wishing keenly and painfully that she didn't have to go. She tried to commit to memory the herbalist's smell of thyme and lavender, the sight of their little cottage in the sunshine and the way the sun glinted on the charms at the windows. Milandre stroked the back of her head.

"Be safe, child," she said. "And trust sparingly. Now, off you go." Hellevir peeled herself away and climbed into the carriage, her jaw tight to keep from crying. Milandre called up to the driver, and he flicked the reins. The carriage jolted forward, and the guards' horses whickered as they were urged on. Hellevir watched the old herbalist standing by the roadside, her hands clasped together, until the carriage rounded the bend and the cottage was lost from sight.

CHAPTER FIVE

Hellevir spent most of the journey fretting about what would meet her in Rochidain. Every time she thought about what the Princess could want, what their meeting might entail, her stomach tightened. But between her fears she found her mind drifting to darker thoughts, the memory of the sickly dread, the trembling haze of the void and the thousand-eyed stare pinning her down. What if she never found the "treasure" he wanted, and he inflicted that wrath on her again? The riddle burned a hole in her pocket and she worried it between her thumb and finger, running over the verses in her head.

> *Where a stern bow will impress a Queen,*
> *The gift of a song*
> *Will console her when she weeps.*

Anxiety knotted in her stomach. If the stern bow was taking her to Rochidain, then what was the gift of a song? A shanty, or was it another play on words? What if she was completely wrong about what the stern bow meant and she was no further forward? With only her own anxious thoughts for company, the days dragged, long and tedious. She heard the guards chatting together jovially as they rode alongside the carriage, and tried to alleviate her boredom by talking to them. They closed up whenever she spoke, resorting to monosyllables, and she soon gave up.

On the tenth day, the city began to grow from the landscape like a forest, beginning with a scattering of hamlets that became thicker and thicker until the city gates loomed before them, ten men tall and five men wide. The gates were swung open and traffic was filtering through. The carriage stopped a moment in front of the guardhouse—she caught a glimpse of gold-rimmed armor, the emblazoned golden ship—before being ushered through as the driver showed his seal. The guards didn't accompany the carriage further, but exchanged a few words with the driver before splitting off in another direction.

The sight of the city momentarily scattered her fears. The road broadened into a bridge as it crossed a wide lagoon, dotted with white sailing boats that meandered lazily over the waves in the bright sunlight like seagulls. The bridge itself was ample enough to host market stalls and street vendors. Hellevir, despite herself, leaned out of the window, caught by the smells of food on the market stalls, the flash of trinkets, the throng and push and noise of so many *people*. Traders pressed against the carriage and tried to hawk wares to her as she passed, holding up multicolored scarves in loops and necklaces made of beads, before the carriage reached the other side and drove into the town proper.

Canals split the houses apart where there would have been roads; boats slid up and down them where there would have been carriages. They nipped to and from the wharves, bringing wares and produce to riverfront shops, mooring at ladders by the small footpaths that lined the waters. Hellevir continued to hang out of the carriage window, drinking it all in. Her father had described it, but his letters had never prepared her for how beautiful it was; Rochidain was a city of water, but it was also a city of light, the sun glinting from the waterways and the windowpanes, the red roof tiles and the sparkling fountains. The thin houses were pressed together like books on a shelf, each one painted brightly in reds, yellows, oranges and blues, and their windows hung with luscious assortments of flowers. She found herself spellbound, all thoughts of Death and darkness and gifts of songs dissipating like mist in the dawn.

At last the carriage stopped and the driver climbed down, opening the door for her.

"I thought we were going to the palace?" Hellevir asked, settling Elsevir on her shoulder.

"I'm to take you to your family's home first," the driver said.

"A carriage will pick you up to see the Princess the day after tomorrow, when you've settled." Hellevir nodded her understanding, that word—Princess—bringing her back down to earth. She would at least have a couple of days to catch her breath, but part of her disliked the extra time she'd have to fret.

The driver clicked his fingers at a young boy leaning on the rails overlooking the canal, and threw him a coin. "Hold the horses' heads until I get back," he ordered, and the boy nodded eagerly, taking up his post with a business-like manner. The driver picked up Hellevir's bags and guided her off the street along the canal, leaving the bustle of the road and entering a hushed maze of water, hanging baskets and cats that watched drowsily from shadows. At any other time, as she stopped to pet a ginger tom, Hellevir might have said she was enjoying herself, but she found it hard to think of anything besides what was waiting for her at her family's home. She hadn't spoken to any of them face-to-face in years. What would she find to say? For the first time she worried about what she was wearing, simple travelling clothes all dusty from the road. Would they think she was too rough for their new city life?

"How did the Princess know my family was here?" she asked.

"There aren't many people from your village living in Rochidain," came the reply over his shoulder. "The Palace finds out these things."

The driver stopped them by a heavy green gate, and pulled on a metal cord that rang a bell somewhere in the house. Hellevir rubbed her sweating palms on her shirt. There was the sound of footsteps, and then a woman in a simple grey dress opened the door. Hellevir didn't know her, and wondered if the driver had the wrong house. She had a pendant around her neck, a twelve-pointed star, and Hellevir recognized it as the one which had adorned the doorway of their little house by the forest.

"Yes?" the woman asked, but before the driver could answer there was the thud of footsteps and Farvor—older and taller and with longer hair—erupted onto the street, catching Hellevir in a bear hug which sent Elsevir into the air in a flurry of feathers. Hellevir was so surprised she just hugged him back and tried to concentrate on breathing through her crushed lungs.

"You're here!" Farvor exclaimed, and released her, holding her at arm's length. "Took you long enough! Here give me the bags, come inside!" He seized her bags from the driver in one hand and dived back through the gate, dragging her after him. She found herself in an elegant courtyard with a fountain bubbling in the center, fig trees lining the high walls and a pomegranate tree hanging over the fountain's pool, the red petals of its newly budding flowers crinkled and dew-wet. Hellevir had never seen such plants before, only knew their names from Milandre's books showing flora of the Archipelagos. She wondered how they were cultivated to withstand the colder climate of the Chron.

Then her pa came through one of the doors, and she forgot everything else as he wrapped her up in his arms, smelling of the same leather and wood as he always had, despite his fine clothes and the shine to his shoes. For an absurd moment she had to fight back the urge to cry. When he released her his smile was all warmth.

"Come inside, my girl," he said.

The family was flourishing in Rochidain. A year before, Pa had been promoted at the butcher's and made a partner. He had his own set of butchering knives that he sat sharpening with a whetstone as they talked, a gift from his business partner imported all the way from Gal Earith. Her mother, he said, admiring their shine by the lamplight, took a small stipend from the Temple for her work, and they'd been sent a servant from the Temple too. Hellevir watched the woman in the grey uniform fussing about the kitchen, helping the cook—a large lady with flour in her hair—to prepare dinner, and from the looks of things generally getting in the way.

"Where is Ma?" she asked as she helped the cook to shuck peas. The kitchen was downstairs; below the water level, Hellevir realized. The only natural light came from thin slits of glass high above their heads, still above the surface. Pa had sent Farvor to bring them some fruit from the market, because Hellevir had never eaten an orange and that just wouldn't do.

"She's at the temple, as always," he replied, pouring her a mug of tea.

"She spends a lot of time there?"

"As much as Onaistus demands." She couldn't help but hear some salt in his tone. When they had shown her around the house, Hellevir had seen evidence of two warring beliefs; her pa's old bear-claw charm hung on the lintel to ward off evil from the household, but there were also unfamiliar symbols, curling and complicated, painted tidily and discreetly on the wood of the windows, or inlaid in copper over the hearth where the cook had her pots. Hellevir knew they were called Dometiks, but didn't know what they meant. Pa saw her eye lingering on a pile of books at the other end of the table, written in the Galgarian script, and he sighed, putting the teapot down. "Listen to me. I complain when I shouldn't. She's happy to be somewhere that feels more like home. Here she's free to practice her faith, follow her Promise."

Hellevir nodded, feeling unsure. On the one hand, she felt like she knew next to nothing about Onaistian, and was upset her mother hadn't tried to share it with her or Farvor. On the other, what Hellevir knew about the afterlife conflicted completely with what the Onaistian faith preached. Eternal life in the embrace of the God of Light did not fit well with what she knew about the grey half-light and the brooding man with the eyes like pits, the void shuddering behind them. Hellevir shook the memory from her.

"What Pillars has she chosen to follow?" she asked instead.

"Honor and Grace, I believe," he said. "She's put the Dometiks for all the Pillars around the house." He gestured to the symbols carved above the hearth. "Can't pretend to know what those ones mean. Compassion or some such. She'd have them painted on the floors too if she had her way."

There was a beat of silence where Hellevir wondered how much of her mother's silence about her faith during her childhood had been because of her pa, and realized how much her mother must have resented that. No wonder she'd been miserable by the woods. It surprised her how darkly he was scowling at the Dometiks, but she didn't have the heart to challenge him right then. She was just glad to see him.

"You never described the city to me in your letters," Hellevir remarked, changing the subject. "From the way you said you wished to come home, I was imagining something drab and grey."

"Well, it was, until you came." He brushed her cheek, and she took his hand, suddenly wishing she'd come sooner. His smile faded as he took her hand, turning it over and looking at the spaces where her fingers had been. "Milandre wrote and told me what the village has been like for you recently," he said quietly. Hellevir shifted, uncomfortable, and resisted the urge to draw her hand away.

"That's what convinced me to come," she replied. "She thought it would be a good idea for the villagers not to see me for a while."

"Well, I'm sorry for their stupidity. I would have thought them more sensible folk." He looked like he was about to say more, and she had the sudden sense that he wanted to ask her about Death. Instead he just patted her hand.

They were interrupted by the clatter of Farvor's footsteps as he came down the stairs. He had a bag in his arms and dropped it on the table in front of them, toppling what Hellevir assumed were oranges from inside across the tabletop. The kitchen filled with a heady citrus smell.

"Feast your eyes!" he exclaimed. "All the way from Land's Groves." He picked one up and peeled it with a knife from his belt, holding out a segment to Hellevir. "Give it a try."

She popped it in her mouth. It exploded with flavor, sweet and fresh and foreign, refreshing as a cool breeze on a hot day. They both chuckled as she held out her hand for the rest of the fruit.

That evening they took her for a walk through the city. The sun had set and the waters were the lavender dusk of the sky. Hellevir had told Elsevir to go free for the night, to roam where ravens are wont to roam.

They meandered aimlessly, showing her this statue or that fountain, this pleasure boat that belonged to so-and-so, the broad and decorated doors of that rich merchant. Hellevir let it all wash over her, surprised by how nice it was just to be taken places she'd never been before. Her village by the woods suddenly seemed very small and a whole world away. Hellevir walked with her arm looped through her father's, enjoying the scents of the summer night and the bright lanterns along the pathways, and felt the knot inside her—the knot made of her fears of what the Princess could want, what she would find when she knocked on her family's door, and not least where she might begin hunting for the riddle and gifts of song, the knot that had tightened and tightened the closer she'd come to Rochidain—start to loosen.

In fact, the riddle was pleasantly distant from her mind, until she caught sight of an arched gateway with a heavy brass knocker on its painted blue doors. It stopped her, and she stood in the middle of the pathway, looking at it across the canal. Her pa and brother walked on towards the thoroughfare, not realizing she had paused. Above the arch she could see the swaying tips of trees, but that wasn't what had stopped her. There was an emblem above the gate, a round disc engraved with a bird mid-flight, beak parted. As she watched, a low song began on the other side, first one voice, then two in chorus, sweet and slow. More joined in until there was a flock of harmonies.

The gift of a song, she thought. Her pa noticed they had left her behind and came back to join her. The three of them stood and listened, until the many faded to two, then one, whose voice rose and fell in solitude, and ended on a single high note.

To anyone else it might have meant nothing, but to her it was obvious, as if the emblem had been placed there for her: the evening song had been sung for her ears alone, to catch her as she passed. She realized what Death had meant when he'd said the signs would show themselves and make sense when she saw them.

"What's in there?" Hellevir asked her father.

"It's the Order of the Nightingale. Their priestesses sing well, don't they? Every evening they sing."

"I've not heard of them before."

"There are pockets of them here and there in Rochidain. They keep to themselves, follow the older traditions in a quiet sort of way. Offer food and shelter to those who seek it, listen to the waters, talk to the winds, that sort of thing. I do wonder how long they'll be able to practice," he added sadly.

"Why is that?"

"The Onaistian Temple," he replied. "Their Promise is putting down roots, and old foundations are crumbling because of it. They're everywhere in the city now. Look." He stopped them and tapped his shoe on the ground, where there was a copper circle embedded among the cobbles. There was a snake . . . no, an eel etched into it, curling into an intricate geometric knot. "They've put these all down this street, marking out the route of one of their annual processions. It starts outside the city and ends at their central temple." Hellevir looked down at the disc, delicately shimmering in the lamplight of the road.

"What does the eel mean?"

"I'm not sure," he replied honestly. "The Onaistians are big believers in symbols. You saw your ma's symbols at home. They have a Dometik for everything, all of them knotted like this." He tapped the emblem again. "Perhaps that's why they chose it, the eel. It knots itself."

Pa made to walk on. Hellevir looked at the gate of the Order, its brass knocker shining in the lantern-light, and reluctantly drew herself away. She'd visit the next day, she told herself, without her pa and brother in tow. She didn't know how she knew, but it was something she needed to do alone.

They wandered homewards as full night came on, although the streets were as busy as during the daylight. Hellevir wanted to stay out longer, but exhaustion dogged her steps from the day's journey. She was glad then that Princess Sullivain had given her a couple of days to breathe before she had to attend on her.

When they returned home, Hellevir didn't see her ma sitting by the fountain until she stood up. A tall, slim man in a grey uniform had been sitting beside her, and he also rose.

"Hellevir," her ma said, giving her a kiss on the cheek. "Welcome to Rochidain." Hellevir braced herself against the chill in her tone, unsurprised by it. She remembered how it had been after she had brought her back to life—the cold glares, the icy silences—but even so it made her sad that her voice still had a rimed edge after all these years apart.

Despite that, her ma looked well. Her black hair was braided and had a healthy shine and the gauntness was gone from her cheeks. She held her head high. Too high, Hellevir thought, as if she were trying to look over a wall. She'd never walked so tall at home.

"Thank you, Ma," Hellevir said. "Pa and Farvor have been showing me around." She glanced over at the man dressed in grey. He wore the twelve-pointed star upon his chest, a copper color.

"This is Peer Laius," Ma said. "The Peer Leader of our temple. Laius, this is my eldest daughter." Hellevir sensed her father stiffen behind her.

Hellevir bowed, well-practiced since the Queen had visited.

"It's nice to meet you," she said politely. The Peer inclined his head. He was clean-shaven, the lines on his face pronounced as if he had been drawn in ink.

"It must be good to be home," he said. His voice was clipped with the delicate accent of the city proper.

"The village is my home," she found herself retorting, before realizing it sounded rude. "But I am glad to see my family, sir," she amended.

"I do not doubt it. Well, I won't keep you from each other." He took her ma's hand and bowed over it, before inclining his head to her father and turning towards the gate. Ma accompanied him.

"I will come to the temple the day after tomorrow," she said. "There will be a delivery to sign for."

"I trust all to your capable hands." He added something in Galgarian, and she replied formally. It shook Hellevir a little, hearing her mother speak in another tongue. She had never uttered a word of her native language in the house by the woods.

The Peer paused as he was pulling on the gloves the servant brought him, looking at Hellevir. "You should come with your mother and help us at the temple, Hellevir," he said. "We can show you around the place."

"Hellevir won't want to see that," Ma said sharply.

"Come, Piper," he said, with a reproach in his voice that Hellevir knew her pa would never dare use with her ma. "Let her come and see the temple, see what you do there. She must be curious. Besides, we may convert her yet." He fastened his cloak at the shoulder—although it was a simple thing, Hellevir could tell it was well-made by its weight, the gloss to the fabric—and tapped his forehead in what she supposed was a gesture of farewell. Perhaps it was a city thing.

As the servant locked the gate behind him, Hellevir exchanged a look with her father. Her mother must have caught it. She swept past them with a sniff.

"Come inside, then," she ordered. Pa followed her. Farvor caught Hellevir's arm as she made to go in.

"So," he asked. "What do you think?"

"Of Rochidain?"

"Well, that too," he said. "But I meant the Peer. Pa and I have been wanting to know what you'd make of him. Or I have, at least." Hellevir glanced through the window into the sitting room, where her mother was lighting candles around a small altar laden with fruit.

"I'm not sure I could make anything of him after two minutes," she remarked.

"First impressions, then."

"I thought all Peers were from the Galgoros, like Ma, but he looks Chronish."

"He *is* Chronish, through and through. He learned his trade over in the Galgoros, I believe, then came back and named himself Laius after another priest in his temple. No idea what his real name is, Ma probably knows." He nudged her with his elbow. "Go on, first impressions. I won't tell Ma."

"I . . . He reminds me of . . ."

"Go on. Say it."

"An eel. He makes me think of an eel. Like the ones from the street."

Farvor laughed at that. Hellevir had to wonder when his laugh had become so easy, so full. She wondered if it really was just the city.

"I have missed you," he said. "Let's go inside."

They put Hellevir in one of the top rooms of the house.

A room each? she found herself thinking. The bedsheets were fine linen, simply but expensively embroidered. The curtains were thick and heavy, the iron lattice on the windows elegantly wrought. Her family moved through these riches easily, happily, almost blindly. Hellevir wondered how she would feel returning home to her simple cot, the shutters and thatch of Milandre's cottage, the herb garden. The thought of it brought a pang of homesickness.

She sat in a chair at her open window and rested her chin on her arms as she looked out over the rooftops and the canals, stroking Elsevir's feathers while he preened her hair. The air smelled wonderful, with hints of the fruit trees she'd seen growing in the neighbors' gardens and the drifting scent of honeysuckle, all laced through with a saltiness she guessed must be from the ocean, although she couldn't see it. Seagulls drifted overhead, pale in the night sky, calling noisily to each other. The sounds of city life rose and fell on the breeze, laughter from the inns, music coming from one of the wine-houses. She liked it here. It felt alive in a way the village hadn't.

She should have fallen into a deep slumber after the business of the day, the exhaustion of the road. But she just couldn't. She tossed and turned, her legs tangling in the fine sheets, the thick weave unfamiliar and cloying against her skin.

Her mind wouldn't let her sleep. The riddle kept reverberating around her mind like coins, until the sound began to hurt her head.

The gift of a song
Will console her when she weeps.

Her thoughts kept being tugged back to that nightingale above the gateway, its wings wide and its beak open as if mid-song. At last, when dawn was beginning to edge under the curtains, she flung off the covers and swung her legs out of bed, putting her head in her hands.

She had to know what was behind the gates. She *had* to.

"Where are you going?" Elsevir asked her, clicking his beak as she got to her feet and pulled on a simple coat and trousers, her only spare clothes besides those she'd travelled in.

"To find the first precious thing," she replied, swinging her coat around her shoulders. "Will you come?" In answer, Elsevir flew up to alight heavily on her shoulder and nestled into her neck.

Hellevir stole quietly through the sleeping house, pausing only when she heard the sound of movement in the kitchen. She peered down the stairs to see the cook getting the dough ready for the morning's bread. Hellevir unhooked the key from by the door, and quietly let herself into the courtyard.

It was blissfully cool outside. Cobwebs hung between the branches of the fig tree in the courtyard garden, beaded with dew. Birds were singing as if it were the last day in this world they would sing. Hellevir cracked open the gate and slid through. She could hear the sounds of activity from the thoroughfare as traders set up their market stalls for the day, a low bustle accompanied by the drip and thunk of boats slipping up and down the canals with their wares, pushed along by poles.

The dark night sky was fading to lavender, and as she made her way across the bridges and along the canals it continued to lighten and the city continued to awaken. By the time she reached the Order of the Nightingale, streaks of cloud were illuminated in reds and golds. She put her ear to the wood of the door. Inside, she could hear stirrings, footsteps and voices. Not really knowing what she would do when someone answered, she raised her hand and took hold of the knocker, dropping it once, twice. She stood back and waited, glad of Elsevir's reassuring weight on her shoulder.

There was a shuffling on the other side, and the heavy thunk of bolts being drawn back. A small door in the left side of the gate opened up, and a face peered out. She wore a blue scarf over her hair.

"Are you all right?" she asked with genuine concern.

"I . . ." Hellevir had hoped she'd know what to say when the time came, but words failed her. "May I come in?"

The woman blinked. "Of course, my dear," she said, and stepped aside to let her through.

Inside the gate a small path ran between two high walls dotted with arching windows, hung with fuchsia. Even in the low morning light Hellevir could see the bright pink flowers and recognized them from Milandre's books.

"Have you come looking for help?" the woman asked her. She was dressed in loose blue robes like a uniform, and Hellevir remembered her pa saying that priestesses ran the Order. "We have food and a bed if you need."

Hellevir found herself oddly touched by her offer.

"No I . . . I don't need shelter." She shook her head, feeling foolish. "Is there . . . is there a weeping woman here?"

"A weeping woman?"

"Yes."

"Are you looking for someone in particular? We had a couple of people come in last night, but . . ."

"No, I don't mean them. At least I don't think I do."

"In that case, I don't . . ." She paused, as if a thought had occurred to her. "You don't mean the willow, do you?" she asked. "The weeping willow?" Hellevir's heart fluttered. She nodded. The lady assessed her for a moment, not unkindly. After a moment she gestured with her hand.

"Come with me," she said.

She led her up the small path between the walls of fuchsia. Amid the foliage, Hellevir could see eyes watching her: eyes made of leaves, the flowers with yawning pink mouths like cats' tongues. Hellevir let her hand brush past the delicately hanging blooms to say hello, felt from their softness a dozing smile, and wished she had brought her notebook so she could sketch them. The path opened up a little, winding between the curve of buildings with arched doorways. Another priestess was coming out of one of them, a pile of books under one arm.

"A little early to have opened the gates," she remarked as they approached.

"She knocked and asked to see the willow," Hellevir's guide told her. The other priestess glanced at Hellevir, and then at the raven on her collarbone.

"All right," she said slowly, and waved them past.

"Why is the willow important?" Hellevir dared to ask. Her guide raised an eyebrow.

"You don't know?"

"I . . . I was just told to look for a weeping woman," she replied honestly.

"The willow is the center of the city. Its heart. The city was built around it. The Order protect it."

They came to an iron gate surrounded by curling leaves, and the priestess brought a hoop of keys from her pocket, unlocking it with a clink. She swung it open and led Hellevir down another small stone corridor.

On the other side was the lushest garden Hellevir had ever seen. Trees were dotted here and there on carefully cut lawns, and flower-beds—neatly tended and bright with flowers even Hellevir couldn't name—sloped down towards the small river that ran between them, from grass to water with no real bank to speak of. Through the trees she glimpsed great vines that sagged under the weight of fruit as they hung from the high wall encircling the garden. Birdsong filled the little air that wasn't pressed tight by the canopy.

The priestess walked onwards across the grass and Hellevir followed, wanting to take off her shoes and feel the earth under her feet. They passed herb gardens heavily scented with thyme, rosemary and sage of all varieties. The scent conveyed her instantly back home, and Hellevir had to resist the urge to stop and rub the leaves between her fingers, or take cuttings to send to Milandre. Old ceramic likenesses of the harvest gods—chipped and moss-encrusted, smiling wickedly through boar tusks, antlers adorned with vines—danced across one of the walls.

"My father seems afraid of the Onaistian hold on the city," Hellevir commented. "Says they threaten ways like yours."

"New faiths come and go," the priestess replied over her shoulder. "The old ways remain, and always will." She spoke with a confidence Hellevir wished she shared. "Whenever our order, our gardens, come under threat, either from people wanting to build on the land or do away with us for whatever reason, the Houses who believe in our work have helped us stand our ground and weather the storm. We are the heart of the city, its firmest foundation, and in the end I don't believe a new faith can threaten that." Hellevir hoped she was right.

They followed a bend in the river. Through the trees there appeared a willow standing upon the riverside, ancient and high, trailing its leaves into the water. A bed of tulips surrounded it, stopping where the leaf canopy brushed the ground. There was a stillness to the air, something hushed, which the sounds of the thoroughfare couldn't breach.

They walked underneath the boughs, parting the hanging leaves like a curtain. Hellevir looked up at the brightening sky between the branches. She felt, suddenly and completely, that she was in the right place.

A bell rang, and the priestess glanced back the way they had come.

"I have to go," she said. "I don't normally leave visitors with the tree, but . . ." She glanced at the raven. "I don't think you'll do any harm."

"I'll wait here for you," Hellevir replied, surprised by her trust. This place was sacred, she could tell by the priestess's hushed tone, the way she looked up almost tenderly into the high boughs.

"I won't be long."

The priestess left her there, ducking back through the leaves. Hellevir pushed back her hood, and Elsevir stretched his wings and flew up among the branches.

"What now?" the raven asked. Hellevir lowered herself to sit with her back against the big old trunk and rested her arms on her knees. She looked up into the canopy.

"I'm not sure," she admitted. Her blood was buzzing in her veins as if a storm were brewing, the anticipation that *something* was going to happen alive within her. The tree was silent, slumbering as the birds bickered and darted among its leaves.

Hellevir rolled the riddle along her tongue again.

Where a stern bow will impress a Queen,
The gift of a song
Will console her when she weeps.

Perhaps there was another layer to it, she thought. Perhaps the riddle wasn't just telling her where to find the first treasure, but how to draw it forth.

Not really certain what else she could do, she began to sing. She'd never liked her own singing voice, as she never could hit the notes, but as she kept going she gained confidence and let her voice trickle up into the boughs. She sang the old sea ballad she'd heard in her home village.

Mine, all mine, from stern to bow, and brig to star.

I forgot to bow, she thought, and clambered to her feet, still carrying the tune softly. She dipped her head and bowed low at the waist.

When she raised her head again, there was a figure woven out of bending branches where she had been sitting moments before. It leaned against the trunk in much the same way Hellevir had done. Its branches were braided together like the baskets for holding fish at the market, and its head turned towards her slowly with a low creak of boughs. Hellevir's breath caught in her chest.

"I feel like I was asleep a long time," it said, voice drowsy. The sound was of breaking branches, the shift of earth by roots. It glanced up into the sky, and pointed with a long, trailing finger up at Elsevir sitting among the branches. "You have hemlock about your throat," it murmured.

Hellevir slowly lowered herself to sit cross-legged in front of the figure. Its head came back down to look at her, sapling branches forming the ridge of a nose, the hint of brows, the slightest dips above high cheekbones. Hellevir felt her heart skip a beat.

"And you," it remarked, the voice murmuring from somewhere deep inside the twisting boughs. "You are missing parts. Where have they gone?"

"I traded them," Hellevir said softly. "For souls. I brought them back from Death."

"Ahh." The figure sighed and leaned back its head. "I know death. As a seed I was watered by blood. My roots still feed on

61

the memories." Hellevir had the sudden half-imagining of a night-ingale, skewered on the tines of a stag. She blinked it away.

"I'm sorry to wake you from your sleep," she said honestly.

"I'll return to it soon enough."

"Do you know why I woke you?"

"I suppose you don't want to be missing any more of those parts. You might start to feel cold." The figure looked down to observe the holes in its own chest between the woven branches which were slowly beginning to sprout buds.

"I . . . Yes. That's right."

The figure was by the waterside. Hellevir had blinked and missed its movement. She got to her feet, and went to stand beside it as it looked down into the running waters dimpled with the tips of leaves. It was slender, and taller than her by at least a head. Long leaves cascaded down its back and drifted in the breeze. Small creatures, ladybirds and spiders, hid in the nooks of its shoulders.

"I suppose it is providence," the figure said. "The priestesses sing to me, but always the same things. You sang me something new. For that I'll give you what you need."

"Thank you."

A trailing hand reached up and brought down one of the willow's branches. On it were seeds, curling like caterpillars.

"Take them," it said. "They're yours." Hellevir reached out a hand and gently pulled them loose. They left pollen on her fingers.

"Am I doing the right thing?" Hellevir asked. "Gathering these for Death?" But when she looked up the figure was gone.

She emerged from the canopy, feeling a little light-headed as she folded the seeds in the riddle to keep them whole. She found the priestess already waiting for her.

"Have you been there long?" she asked.

"No," the priestess replied. "But I . . . sensed I should not disturb you."

"You could see . . ." She didn't know how to phrase it.

"We talk and we sing," she replied. "Some of us to things most people would say aren't there. But we always pretend it's in prayer, so they don't call us mad. The Peers of Onaistus would not tolerate us otherwise."

"I've talked to spirits in the hearth, the wind, the ivy," Hellevir murmured. "Magpies, ravens, but never anything like that." She glanced back at the willow. "You should sing it something new."

"Something new?"

"Yes. It would like to hear something new." She slipped the seeds into her pocket. "Thank you. I won't take up more of your time."

"Did you find what you needed?" the priestess asked as she took her back towards the garden gate.

"I think so." She paused. "My pa said you were built on the founding stone."

"That's right. It was at the end of the war fought against the Antlered King. You've heard of it, the Nightingale War?" Hellevir nodded. Every child had. The Antlered King was the bogeyman used to keep children well-behaved, or he'd come and eat their hearts. Her father had told her the stories in the village by the woods. "Once the Antlered King was finally defeated, the Nightingale Queen, leader of the surviving peoples, came here to bury her brother, who'd been killed in the war, on the banks of the river. It's where she put aside war, and it's where the willow grew."

She pointed back to the tree, its branches low over the water.

"The Queen turned this land into a prosperous place where her people could grow. It's why the symbol of our order is a nightingale, in her honor, in the memory of peace."

When Hellevir returned to her family's house, she went upstairs and sat down heavily on her bed, running her hands through her knotted hair in an attempt to calm it. She gave up quickly and just sat there, letting her mind catch up with her body. Her eyes felt gritty from too little sleep, and she wished she could just curl up in a ball under the covers. Elsevir sat on the back of her chair and watched her with an ink-blot eye.

"You found it," he commented. Hellevir took the paper out and spread it flat on the bedside table, the seeds curling in its center. She put a hand over them; they felt . . . warm. Something giddy bubbled within her, something elated. She couldn't quite believe it had been so easy.

"Yes," she said. "Somehow." She pressed her lips together. "Now I just have to sit and wait for the time when I need to use them."

CHAPTER SIX

Her brother let her nap for most of the morning before he barged into the room and loudly complained that cities don't tour themselves. Groggily, Hellevir descended into the main room after him, straightening her shirt and tucking a flyaway lock behind her ear, which Elsevir quickly untucked. Her ma was sitting by the window, making use of the daylight with some embroidery on her lap. When she saw Hellevir, her lips pressed together.

"Have you nothing better to wear?" she asked. Hellevir looked down at her shirt and trousers. They were simple but they were clean.

"My travelling clothes need a wash," she said. Her ma stood up, laying aside the embroidery.

"You look like a farmer," she remarked. "We need to get you some better clothes."

"I can take her shopping," Farvor offered, helping himself to an apple from the side table. "I'd like to show her the Merchant Quarter. We can stop by the Cuckoo's Corner this evening." He caught his mother's narrowing eyes. "Just for one drink," he quickly added. Ma sighed.

"Fine. I also have a dress for you. I was going to keep it until you met with the Princess, but you can't be running around the town like that." She glanced pointedly at the timepiece on the wall. It was a fine-looking thing, all intricate coils and springs like a folded flower. There'd never been anything like it in the village by the woods. Hellevir couldn't pretend she could read it. "You've slept most of the morning, I'm going to be late for temple." Hellevir didn't miss the reproach in her tone. "Hurry. Upstairs."

Hellevir followed her up to her room, and waited patiently as her ma opened the wardrobe and hunted through it. It was the first time she'd been into her parents' room, and her eyes were arrested by the small table in the corner, laden with candles and the twelve-pointed star leaning against the wall. There were various other icons she didn't recognize, discs inscribed with Dometik patterns. She wanted to take a closer look, but her mother was already pulling a sheaf of fabric from the wardrobe and laying it out on the bed in front of her.

Hellevir looked over it as she straightened out the sleeves. It was a dark color, at least, and she was glad of that. She was surprised she liked it.

"How can we afford this?" Hellevir asked, rubbing the fabric between thumb and finger. It looked expensive, much more sophisticated than anything she'd worn before.

"The Temple has been good to us," Ma replied defensively. "So has your father's shop. Put it on."

Hellevir did as she was told, quickly undressing and sliding it over her head while her mother pooled out the skirts around her hips. She caught sight of the two of them in the wardrobe mirror, she with the neck of the dress loose about her shoulders, her mother fussing about the hem with a frown, and suddenly wanted to capture this moment—being with her ma, doing mother and daughter things—in her memory forever.

Hellevir's mother seemed to have forgotten what she had seen in Death. If the memory had lurked in the moments after her awakening, there was no trace of it in the long years after she'd brought her back. All she seemed to know, all she seemed to remember, was that Hellevir had saved her by unnatural means, and had not saved her newborn daughter. It had led to a coldness that Hellevir felt every time her mother looked at her, spoke to her; Hellevir had long since resigned herself to it, but now something ached in her, wishing things could always be like they were today. Her mother had never helped her into a new dress before.

Her ma pulled on the sleeves, and then laced up the back of the bodice.

"That's too tight," Hellevir said, putting a hand to her stomach.

"You're not supposed to be comfortable at court," her ma remarked, tying the cords. "You're supposed to have good posture."

"But I'm not going to court today."

"You will tomorrow."

"I'm just seeing the Princess."

"Who will one day be Queen. It may as well be court." Hellevir saw her shake her head in the mirror, as if mystified. "I must admit, it's not something I'd ever thought I'd see," she murmured. "My daughter calling upon royalty." Hellevir thought it might be the closest to pride she'd ever heard in her mother's voice. She undid Hellevir's hair and set about combing it into respectable waves, pinning it up again in a manner Hellevir couldn't have achieved with hours in front of the mirror. Hellevir let herself enjoy the feeling of her mother's cool touch. "Don't let that bird on your shoulder," she said. "It'll pull the threads."

"He."

Her ma gave her a look in the mirror, and the illusion was broken. Just like that.

Hellevir had hoped her ma would come with them to explore Rochidain, but she made her excuses and vanished with the servant in grey, Weira, to the nearby temple. Farvor swept her up and away before she could feel any disappointment, and flagged down one of the little boats that always seemed to be nipping up and down the canals. She was unsure at first, disliking how wobbly it felt under her feet, but once they were seated the ride was surprisingly smooth. They chatted happily with the boatman, who pushed the vessel along with a long pole. The waterways were often too narrow for oars, he explained, enjoying that she found the ride a novelty. It took real skill to keep the boats from being scuffed by the stone walls, and new boatmen often lost a pole when the end was sucked down in the canal silt and they couldn't pull it free.

The canal opened up and soon there were dozens of little craft like theirs sliding past, laden with well-dressed Rochidainians reclining on plush cushions, laughing and enjoying the sunshine of the day. Some had emblems painted prettily on the side.

"Those boats belong to the Houses," Farvor explained. "You can see their shields on the hulls."

"The Houses?"

"The ruling families of Rochidain. I work for one, House Redeion." He squinted, holding a hand up to shield his eyes.

"Harrow," he said, pointing to one boat with a shield bearing a rose. "Dunfeld." He pointed to others. "Greerson, Haliwell, Mordig."

The boat pulled up to a small quay and Farvor helped her alight, throwing the boatman an ade—the Queen's face glinted on the coin as it was tossed—before leading her up the stone steps towards the bustling thoroughfare.

"Welcome to the Merchant Quarter," he exclaimed, gesturing grandly and clearly very much enjoying showing it all off. Before them was a sea of tents, as multicolored as a fleet of ships bearing the world's sails. Before she could take a breath, Farvor had seized her hand and dived in. The sky vanished above striped fabric as her brother wove through the crowd, past stalls selling food and wine and books and birds in gilt cages, the smells of roasting meat, fruit and beer assailing her. Hellevir was overwhelmed by the sheer number of people, cacophonous, everywhere, and all she could do was grip her brother's hand as Elsevir huddled close to her neck. A gap opened up where a fountain trickled water, and a bare-chested man juggled knives to the whoops of the onlookers around him, his teeth glinting with gold.

"Where are we going?" Hellevir shouted at her brother, breathless.

"The tailor," Farvor flung over his shoulder. "You need clothes for next week."

"What's happening next week?"

He grinned back at her. "Next week we dine at House Redeion," he announced over the clamor around them. "My knight heard you were visiting town and asked me to invite you for dinner."

Hellevir felt herself go still like a rabbit sighted by a hound. It was only Farvor's pull on her hand that kept her moving.

"Me?" she asked. "Why does he care about me?"

"He wants to meet my notorious sister!"

"Notorious?" she repeated, anxious.

"Well, the story of the herbalist who healed the Queen's grand-daughter wouldn't stay quiet for long. Did you think it wouldn't spread?" She relaxed a little, exchanging a glance with Elsevir as he struggled to cling to her shoulder. If the running story was that she'd healed Sullivain using her knowledge of herbs, saving her *before* she died, it would make things easier.

"No," she muttered under her breath. "I suppose I shouldn't have let myself hope."

Farvor stopped them at a double stall, one-half laden with fabrics and the other crowded with wooden mannequins hung with clothing. Her brother greeted the tailor like an old friend, letting him show him the latest cloths from Inthira and the Galgoros. Soon Hellevir was standing on a stool, being measured this way and that, the shopkeeper draping her with fine green cloth embroidered with fish.

"Can we afford this?" she asked Farvor quietly. He just rolled his eyes with a smile.

"Have fun, won't you?" he replied, and made her pick out a waistcoat. She chose one in a dark violet with delicate silver embroidery on the lapels, and a matching coat.

Soon they had a small pile of clothing wrapped up to deliver to their parents' home, and more which would be made for her in the next couple of days. Farvor bought her a sweet pastry—more buttery than anything baked in the village back home—and as she followed him through the throng she found she was enjoying the bustle, the constant movement around her like the rush of a river.

They lingered at the market for the rest of the day, Farvor pressing drinks and sweetmeats she simply had to try into her hands until she felt full to bursting. They wandered until the stalls were beginning to close up for the evening, and Farvor led her back out and down the side streets. In the setting sun the canals looked like molten gold. He stopped by a tavern where warm lamplight, music and the babble of voices were spilling from inside. A sign hung above the door showing a heavy-looking bird in a nest far too small for it. *The Cuckoo's Corner* was scrawled underneath.

"This is one of my favorite haunts," Farvor explained, pushing open the door and letting the smell of beer pour out. "I promised Ma only one drink, but you can't come to Rochidain and not try a pint of Overdawn." Inside, the air was thick with pipe smoke, curling like vines above Hellevir's head. A trio of string players sat in the corner of the room, playing a lively old jig. The tavern was busy but not thronged, the sound of voices like the hum of bees around her, split now and then by a trill of laughter.

"Overdawn?" Hellevir repeated as they approached the bar and took a seat. Elsevir hopped onto the bar-top and pecked at some loose crumbs.

"Cider from Ennea," Farvor explained. He waved to the barkeep, holding up two fingers, and tossed down a half-ade. The barkeep must have known him by sight; a moment later two golden pints appeared in front of them. Farvor raised his.

"To you, little sister," he said to Hellevir with a wink, "finally making it to Rochidain." Hellevir smiled a little sheepishly and clinked her glass to his. She took a sip; the cider slid down her throat, cool and fresh, sharp and clean.

"Milandre makes better," she lied with a shrug. Farvor put a hand to his chest, wounded.

"With all the respect in the world for the woman," he replied, "but the village has never seen a pint this good."

"It's all right, I suppose."

"You're just goading me. This is the best cider in the Chron."

"I'd need a second one to really tell. So I get the full flavor you know."

"Oh, sure, sure. And a third to dispel any lingering doubts."

"If you're buying." She looked around the bustling tavern with a smile. "I'm glad I'm here. I can't believe I put off coming to Rochidain for so long. It's so . . . alive here."

"And it only took a summons from the Crown."

Hellevir shrugged, taking another gulp of her cider to quell the flutter of nerves the reminder sparked within her.

"The Princess wants a good herbalist," she said with an attempt at nonchalance. "I saved her once, so I suppose she trusts what I do."

Farvor tapped the side of his drink with a nail, suddenly pensive. "But what I don't get," he mused, "is why would the Queen take the Princess all the way out to the woods to find a herbalist? There are very good ones in Rochidain. Why come to you and Milandre in the first place?"

"She'd heard of Milandre's work during the War over the Waves," Hellevir replied. "I suppose she knew she was good."

"Right." She felt him watching her. She didn't look up from her drink. "You know," he went on, "Lord Redeion and some of his friends were dining with the royal family that night. A few noble families were." A loud laugh beside her made her jump, but Farvor didn't react.

"Calgir—Lord Redeion, that is—said it was a pretty horrific evening," he went on. "Everyone was wondering if anyone else had been poisoned at the same table. But no, just her. He heard first-hand from a servant, later on, that it had been a quick affair, mere hours before she died." Hellevir blinked, staring at him with wide eyes. She glanced around them, but no one was listening.

"She didn't die . . ."

"I'm not an idiot, you know," he added quietly. "I remember what happened with Ma."

She stared at him.

"You knew about Ma? Everything?"

"Yes, everything."

Hellevir realized she was holding her breath. She let it go slowly. It didn't shock her that he knew, and part of her was even relieved. She wouldn't have to pretend with him, now.

"I thought Milandre had told you . . . well, not the truth."

"Milandre tried to make up a story—she'd been mistaken, Ma had just been asleep—but I'd seen the body. I went in when you were all asleep."

Hellevir's jaw tightened and she looked down at the knots in the wood of the bar-top. Her memories of that day were crystalline, etched into her as if they'd happened yesterday, although she had only been a child. The shape of her mother under the sheet, the stillness of the bundle by her bed, the glint of that man's smile as he took the lantern from her. There was a beat of silence as they both tried to disentangle themselves from the memories of that day.

"I don't think she'll ever forgive me," Hellevir murmured. "For bringing her back and not the baby." Farvor took her hand in his, his thumb tracing the smooth scars where her little finger and her ring finger used to be, and raised his eyebrow in a question. She nodded.

"I gave them up," she said. "The first for Ma, the second for the Princess." He hummed thoughtfully, and let her draw her hand away.

"Ma is . . . a stubborn woman. But Pa and I, we know what you did. We'll always be glad you did it."

Hellevir gave him a small smile. "Thank you, Farvor," she said. He sat back, drawing circles in the spilled cider on the bar-top with the tip of his finger.

"So," he said. "You brought back the Princess. I'm guessing she knows she was dead?"

Hellevir finished her drink.

"I don't know. I assume so. I . . . I don't know what she wants from me tomorrow. Maybe she wants to ask about Death, about what's on the other side? Milandre thinks she wants me to protect her from Death indefinitely."

Farvor pulled a face. "It's Rochidain," he remarked. "And it's the De Neïds. I wouldn't put it past them to aim for immortality."

Hellevir laughed. She couldn't help it. It was a high-pitched sound, nervous, and her eyes immediately flickered around her to see if anyone had noticed. Farvor glanced down at the anxious way she was playing with a loose thread on the hem of her sleeve. The music picked up pace, and patrons began to take to the dance floor like flocking birds, linking arms and whirling around in time with a trilling jig. Farvor finished his drink and seized Hellevir by the hand.

"Enough morbidity," he announced. "More dancing."

"I don't know the steps," she protested, pulling back.

"Nonsense. I'll teach you. Off your backside, herbalist." He yanked her forward, laughing, and they joined the throng on the dance floor, the music giddy around them and their heads light with Overdawn cider.

The next morning Hellevir woke up with a blistering headache. Ma was knocking on the door. She opened it blearily, rubbing her face.

"Your carriage will be here soon," Ma said. "You should get ready." She didn't offer to help her into the dress or put up her hair again. Hellevir got ready and went downstairs to the kitchen, anxiety chewing at her stomach. She tried not to think about what might lie in store for her at the palace.

She forced herself to eat some bread and cheese in the kitchen, to soak up the remnants of Overdawn in her stomach as much as to ground herself. A light trill rang from the bell at the gates, and her heartbeat picked up.

This is it, she thought.

A moment later Weira let in a carriage driver, in finer livery than the last one. The golden ship was stitched on his upper arm, and he had a yellow feather in his hat.

The driver led her through streets back to the main thoroughfare, where the carriage was waiting for them. It was open to the air, and as he handed her into it, she thought nervously that the whole world would be able to see her as they passed through the city. She'd left Elsevir behind, arguing with the doves over seeds, and now wished she had someone to keep her company.

As they neared the richer areas of the city the houses grew taller, the canals broader. The boats on the rivers grew larger too, and wandered more slowly, taking their time. Many of them had glass roofs and decks where Hellevir could see men and women walking arm-in-arm in their bright clothes, or sitting and drinking from tall flute glasses, as if they were in their own gardens and not on a river. The carriage crossed a huge square with a fountain the height of five men in the center, adorned with statues of figures and fish. Hellevir craned her neck to look at it, wanting to go closer, but the houses slid across her view. She saw it all through a haze, unable to enjoy the sights as she had yesterday, too mindful of where the carriage was taking her.

At last, they passed through another set of gates like the ones leading into the city, and across a broad moat. On the other side there was an open space surrounded by carefully squared lawns and shaped trees, and the carriage circled around to stop in front of the heavy doors of the palace.

The red walls loomed over her, their green ivy alive with small birds that chirruped and fluttered above the courtyard. Flags hung heavy in the summer air, sporting the shield of the De Neïds and the older, gracefully aged heraldry of the former royal Houses. Hellevir recognized among them the gull of the Bergerads, the royal House which had fallen to the De Neïds during the War over the Waves, and was surprised the Queen allowed enemy colors to remain flying. Iron-crossed windows glinted in the sunlight, and stone faces, austere and expressionless, stared down at her from beneath the window-ledges. Hellevir saw other carriages coming and going, and nobles wandering in and out of the building as if it were their home.

A servant in red met her as the driver handed her down.

"Miss Hellevir Andottir?" he asked. "Please come this way." He didn't lead her through the front doors but down the side of the palace. "The Princess is in the courtyard practicing," he explained, as if that would mean something to her. They crossed a small bridge into another part of the castle, and Hellevir heard the clash of metal against metal and the scuffing of boots. They entered another courtyard, where men and women wearing loose army gear were engaged in various forms of training. In the middle was the future sovereign, halfway through a bout of fencing. Her face was covered by a protective mesh, but Hellevir could tell it was her from the flaxen color of her braid, so bright against the typically Chronish chestnut hair of the soldiers around her. Her chest tightened, wondering what the Princess would think of her, whether all these people would be witness to her awkward bowing.

The Princess moved elegantly, even Hellevir could tell, and she found herself absorbed in the effortless way she leaned forward and back, the careful placement of her steps, like a cat on a fence. She lunged forward, her point evading her opponent's defense and hitting the center of his padded chest, eliciting whoops and claps from the watching soldiers. The Princess pulled off her visor and tucked it under one arm, sweat plastering the hair to her forehead, grinning broadly. One of the trainers put an arm around her shoulder, pleased with her, and as the soldiers passed they patted her on the back and congratulated her. Her opponent pulled off his visor and grimaced, looking surly, but she held out her hand to him before he could say anything.

"Best fight I've had in a while," she said. "You nearly got me with that first feint. I learned something new with that footwork, too." His expression lightened a little, and he shook her hand, mollified, before he let his friend untie the back of his fencing jacket. The Princess said something to the two of them in a foreign tongue, eliciting a laugh.

Princess Sullivain caught sight of Hellevir. "Herbalist," she said, pointing at her with the foil. Hellevir blinked, feeling pinned by the sudden attention. "Good. You're here." She handed her sword and visor to an attendant before pulling her arms out of her padded jacket and dropping it to the ground. She took a proffered cup and drank its contents in gulps as she came over to where Hellevir was standing.

"Walk with me," she said, striding past like a whirlwind, and Hellevir followed. The back of the Princess's blouse was stuck to her with sweat, clinging to the curve of her spine. Hellevir noticed and looked away.

They entered a room finely decorated with upholstered chairs and marble-topped tables. The place was lined with books, on everything from poetry to history, fairy tales to politics. There was a balcony door letting in a warm breeze which played with the lace curtains.

"I stole this room from one of the captains," Princess Sullivain said as she went over to a washbasin in the corner and splashed water on her face. "He didn't mind really, he's never around. I always preferred the view here, although Grandmama doesn't like me being so far from the main house. She thinks it gives ample opportunity for another attempt on my life. But the first time I was in the main hall surrounded by guests, so it hardly seems to matter, does it?"

"I suppose not, Your Grace," Hellevir said noncommittally, unsure how she was supposed to respond. The Princess's way of speaking was so quick, to the point. Hellevir felt a little like she was constantly in her wake, a slow horse in the dust of a fast one.

"Your Grace is my grandmother," the Princess said. *Princess* seemed the wrong word, too flowery. "Call me Sullivain. After all," she added, turning to face her with the towel around the back of her neck, "you did bring me back from the dead. It should make things a little less prim, don't you think?" She winked.

"You remember, then?" Hellevir asked.

"Not much," Sullivain admitted. "Bits and pieces. Mostly just some awful smell. Grandmama wouldn't tell me anything at first, but I pestered it out of her in the end."

"So what do you want from me, Your Gr . . . Sullivain?"

"Please sit. Water?"

"Yes, thank you." Sullivain poured her a cup and handed it over. The water was crystalline, clearer than anything Hellevir had drunk before, and tasted vaguely of lemons.

"Honestly, I wanted the full story. I want to know how you did it."

"How I brought you back?"

"Yes. Every detail." Hellevir took another sip to buy herself some time to think. The idea of telling her what happened in Death felt like a breach of some secret, of Death's confidence.

"I . . . can't," she said. "Not everything."

"Why not?"

"It's complicated."

"Hmm. I see. Actually, I don't." Sullivain frowned thoughtfully, going over to a small cabinet. Without a care in the world she pulled off her sweaty shirt and undershirt, and drew out clean ones. She didn't seem to care if Hellevir watched, so she didn't let herself avert her gaze again, refusing in part to be intimidated by her.

Sullivain glanced back and saw Hellevir studying her. She smiled wryly.

"I used to have scars, you know," she said. "All up and down my back, from training. You have to move from wood to steel at some point, and with a proper blade too, not just a foil. All gone now, since you brought me back. It made me quite angry to begin with. I'd earned those scars."

She pulled on her shirt, tucking it into her trousers, and dragged her braid from the collar. "Let me be straight with you," she said, turning around with a point-blank look. "As you might expect, I've never died before, and I have absolutely no memory of it. Quite simply, that terrifies me, that something that *important* can happen to me, and I don't remember a thing." She looked so earnest. She was watching Hellevir with those copper eyes as if there was nothing else in the world that concerned her. Hellevir felt her resolve waver. "It would help me a great deal to get on with my life if you could fill in the blanks," she pressed.

Hellevir sighed.

"All right," she said quietly. She wondered if everyone had this much trouble refusing the Princess. Sullivain dropped onto a long couch and gestured for Hellevir to sit opposite, pushing a bowl filled with fruit across the table towards her.

"So," she said. "Tell me how you did it. Please."

"I entered Death for you," Hellevir said. "I found you, and I made an exchange for you, and I brought you back."

"What sort of exchange?"

Hellevir raised her hand, her empty knuckles.

"A finger. And a lock of my hair." Sullivain's eyebrows rose as she popped a grape into her mouth. She took Hellevir's hand before she could stop her, turning it over. Her hands were wet with the condensation from the grapes. Hellevir was surprised by how calloused they felt, like a blacksmith's.

"This looks years old," the Princess was saying. "Amazing. The stuff of stories."

"The exchange requires something else, something from our side that is . . . full of life," Hellevir went on. It was odd to describe it in such terms, and she realized it was the first time she had laid out the rules, even to herself. "A seed freshly released, or a burning coal. For you, it was three dandelion seeds."

"But is that all?" Sullivain asked. "A finger and some hair? Are souls usually so cheap?"

A finger, a lock, and a slice of my soul, Hellevir thought, but didn't say it. Sullivain caught her silence.

"Forgive me, *cheap* is the wrong word," she remarked. "It just seems little for a whole life. So, how does it work?"

"The degree of what is taken from me depends on how the person died. How much the body has been damaged. How long they have been dead. How natural the death was."

Sullivain released her hand. She was frowning, fascinated.

"So, what, I was an unnatural death, and easy to save?"

Hellevir nodded, although *easy* was not the word she would have used.

"Unnatural deaths demand the least," she said. She shrugged in an attempt at nonchalance. "But you'd been dead a long time, and your body was decomposing, so it cost me more. Honestly, I'm still learning the rules. The laws."

The Princess nodded, thinking. She leaned her elbows on her knees, regarding Hellevir intently.

"I see. Well, it goes without saying that I am in your debt." Hellevir wondered if all De Neïds had trouble with the words *thank you*.

"I couldn't *not* bring you back," Hellevir said truthfully. She remembered the feeling, seeing the body on the table. The urge, to find out if she could, and the crowning certainty in her own heart that if she could, she should. An imperative that almost had nothing to do with her. Sullivain regarded her a moment, thinking, and then she sighed.

"I owe you a great debt," she said again, "which is what makes what I'm about to say next very difficult for me, I hope you understand."

Hellevir felt her stomach sink.

"Oh?"

"You probably already know that I wouldn't ask you all the way here if I just wanted a story. You must know what I need. The first time was a poisoning and we still don't know who it was. The next time might be something else. I want you here to make sure I won't be left for dead."

She spoke as if she had rehearsed the lines. Tension slid over Hellevir's limbs, but she couldn't say that she was surprised. Milandre had predicted this, after all.

"You want me on hand in case you die again?" she said slowly, just making sure she understood.

"Exactly."

"And if I refuse?"

Sullivain smiled. Oddly, it didn't look like her own smile; it was too cold. On her lovely face, it seemed foreign, as if someone else had drawn it on her. She stood, coming to sit on the arm of Hellevir's chair. Hellevir stiffened at her proximity. She still smelled of the sweat and dust of the training grounds.

"Your family is doing well in Rochidain," she said. "Very well. Your brother is Calgir Redeion's squire, your father has work at the butcher's. Your mother has found favor at the temple. But Rochidain belongs to the De Neïds, and we can change all of that good fortune in a day." Hellevir stared at her, and then stood abruptly, cutting off the threat, not letting the Princess lean over her in such a manner.

"Your grandmother made me a promise," she retorted. "That no one from the court would ask me to raise the dead again."

"The promise covers my grandmother's court," the Princess replied. "I have my own, or I will, in the not-too-distant future. For the time being, I am not part of it."

"That's splitting hairs and you know it. It's not true to the spirit of the Queen's promise."

Sullivain stood. She was tall, and Hellevir had to look up. The copper color of her eyes was molten, but did not flicker. Again, Hellevir was acutely aware of how close she stood.

"Promises and good faith did not build this city," Sullivain replied. "Money and politics did. And consider this: Grandmama has no other blood heir, and she's not a young woman. If I were to die and she were forced to name one, it would have to be from among the Houses, and she's hardly going to allow the crown to pass to one of them. And if Grandmama dies without a successor, civil war will be inescapable, with all the Houses falling over each other for the crown." She smiled as if it were a trite concern. "And I'm sure you don't want that. So if you won't do it for me, do it for the Chron." She said it a little mockingly, calling upon a subverted sense of patriotism. She saw the dark way Hellevir was staring at the ground. "Chin up. I may not die again after all. And I will pay you well." She said it brightly.

"If bringing you back will prevent war," Hellevir remarked hotly, "I would have continued to do so without threats. You didn't need to bring my family into this."

"Is that so? How interesting. The countryside must breed more honorable stock than Rochidain. I don't imagine many of the noblemen's sons or daughters would bring me back if it meant losing their fingers." She laughed. "They wouldn't if it meant losing even a lock of hair."

"Then no wonder there would be a civil war, if none of them would sacrifice to keep the peace."

"Peace is not something of which the noble-born are particularly fond. Peace is not good for the business of seeking power."

"You're not going to let me go home, are you? Back to the country."

"It will take you far too long to get here if I'm attacked again. The longer I'm dead, the longer people would have to know it, to use it. Besides, I heard your village had become quite unpleasant for you recently, after we left."

Hellevir stared at her.

"How do you know that?"

Sullivain smiled, and tapped her nose.

"Nothing stays a secret in Rochidain," she said. "No, you may stay with your family, but go no further." Hellevir felt the arguments burn hot and turn to ash in her chest, as she opened and closed her mouth like a fool. "And before I forget," the Princess added. "You should probably carry this." She held out a golden brooch, fashioned into a galleon. "It will let you access the palace when you need to. I don't want you being detained when my life might depend on you coming here quickly." Hellevir reached for it, but the Princess held it back. "You should make a habit of coming by regularly, as the royal herbalist would. Let the servants and the nobles see you, become a familiar sight to them."

"And what am I to do here?" She could hear the sourness to her own tone.

The Princess shrugged. She reached forward to put the pin on Hellevir's lapel. Hellevir hoped she couldn't feel the ponderous beating of her heart as she pressed the pin to her chest.

"Be my herbalist. We'll say I called you here since you did such a good job last time, no one will ask questions. I have trouble sleeping; bring me something for that. Next week, Markday." She patted the brooch, and then reached out past her—too close for comfort, but Hellevir resisted the urge to step away—to tug a bellpull by the door. Sullivain paused a moment to look down at her as she reached over, and tilted her head to the side, as if she found something curious in the way Hellevir was glaring at her.

There was a knock on the door before Hellevir could speak, and a servant appeared. "Miss Andottir is leaving now," Sullivain told him. "Please escort her to a carriage." The servant bowed and held the door open. Hellevir had much more to say, most of it indignant, but her anger clogged the words within her. She forced a bow before turning to leave, aware of the Princess's thoughtful gaze following her out.

The servant led her to where a line of carriages was waiting, ready to take the palace's visitors back to the main town whenever they needed. Hellevir gave the driver the address, only half-paying attention, and sank back into the carriage seat. The city slipped by, but she saw none of it.

She had never felt so powerless. Her heart was beating too fast, thrumming in her chest as if she'd just been physically attacked. The arrogance, the brashness. She'd never come across anyone like the Princess, anyone who'd left her feeling so infuriated after such a brief conversation. A bitter twist of indignation curled in her belly.

She felt like she was caught on two fronts. On the one hand she'd made a deal with Death. On the other, the Princess now demanded—although she couldn't know it—that Hellevir keep the precious things she found on hand in case there was another attempt on her life. If there was anyone else whom Hellevir needed to save . . . it would come out of her own body. And there was nothing she could do about it, besides try to find the riddles as quickly as she could. But if saving the Princess stopped civil war, it was worth it, surely?

She brooded all the way home, toying with the brooch, remembering how vehemently Milandre had warned her to keep silent when the Queen first brought her granddaughter to be saved. If this was what her life was going to be now, at the beck and call of the queen-to-be, perhaps she should have left the Princess as she'd found her, civil war be damned. But when she remembered her bloated corpse, the pallor of her skin, so very different to the golden-haired woman of today, so graceful as she fought and so full of life that it shone from her, Hellevir could only feel glad she hadn't.

CHAPTER SEVEN

The temple was only a short walk away from her parents' house. Amid the brightly painted houses and the glistening waters, it looked a pale thing, all dove-grey stone and white doorways, as if the color had been washed away. Hellevir had tried to excuse herself from the visit, still angry after her meeting with the Princess, but her ma had brooked no argument.

"Peer Laius was gracious enough to offer to show you around," she had said sharply. "You'll do him the courtesy of showing up."

Ma took her through a side entrance, into a courtyard where two priests were sitting talking over their books. One of them rose, and Hellevir recognized Peer Laius. He smiled and took her mother's hands.

"Piper, good to see you. Hellevir, how are you enjoying the city?"

"It's beautiful," she said honestly. She bit back a comment about the royal family. Ma glanced over the Peer's shoulder towards the back gates, where they could see a boat was pulling up to the temple mooring.

"The delivery is coming at the back. I should . . ."

"Go. I'll keep Hellevir company. Peer Endus will help you." His companion with the book inclined his head and went with her mother to greet the boat.

Peer Laius smiled at Hellevir—it was a placid smile, with no force behind it at all—and gestured with his arm towards a door in the side of the temple.

"Come, I'll show you around."

Inside the temple there was a circular hall with a high domed ceiling plated in gold leaf, the pillars prettily etched with geometric patterns. Stone seating descended in semicircles towards a central podium, where a table stood arranged with fruit and ornaments. Before it was a pit in the floor filled with white sand. There was a single arched window, the pane criss-crossed with lead to create a pattern on the sand below.

"What's that?" Hellevir asked, pointing towards the sandpit and the table. She'd never been inside a temple before, and her ma had never described it to her.

"That's where worshippers pray and place their offerings," he explained. "Come, we'll have a look." She followed him down the stone steps—marvelling at how straight he could keep his back; perhaps that was where her ma had learned it—and stopped before the table. It smelled rich, but none of it had been allowed to rot, not like the offerings sometimes left at the cairns where Hellevir had grown up. Those had been left for months, humming with swarms of flies attracted by the sweet-sickly smell of rot. But here there was only the distant hum of the thoroughfare, and the air smelled of stone, clean and cold.

Among the fruit there were flowers and handmade trinkets too, small statues and portraits studded with jewels and ornaments in the shape of eels and flames. Some of them were like the discs Hellevir had seen at her mother's home altar, engraved with complicated patterns; she went to pick one up, but the Peer stopped her.

"We do not tamper with the offerings," he said. "Not until we collect them all at night for Onaistus's treasury."

"I'm afraid I don't know much about Galgarian religion," she admitted, withdrawing her hand.

"There's no harm in not knowing something if one has not come across it before," he said, perhaps trying to be kind, but she found his tone condescending. He stood beyond the light coming through the window, and in the dimness his steel-grey hair and featureless uniform suited the simple style of the temple. "You should come to the next service," he added. "I have a book or two about the faith that may interest you, too."

Hellevir nodded, despite herself. She was curious to know more, if only to understand her mother.

"Thank you."

"Let's find you something, then."

He led her through another door in the side of the hall, and down a narrow stone corridor that was cold despite the warmth outside. As other priests passed they nodded to Peer Laius.

He came to a door and unlocked it with a key from his pocket, leading her into what must have been his private study. The walls were lined with bookshelves, and nooks containing scrolls, but otherwise the room was as sparse and clean as the rest of the place.

"Ma seems to like it here," Hellevir said as the Peer gestured her to a chair.

"I think she missed being able to practice the faith," he commented, his back to her as he looked over the shelves. "In her hometown she said the temple was right next door, and she would help her own mother gather oranges for the altar." Hellevir looked down at her hands on her lap. She didn't have a clue what her mother's hometown was like, even what it was called. Only that it was over the sea.

"Here," the Peer said, pulling down a book. "This roughly sketches the faith. There is no cohesive text of our practices. It was only recently that they started to be written down; before that it was considered a sin."

"A sin? To write about your own faith?"

"It was passed more from mouth to mouth. It was believed that while it was an oral tradition it had greater power. The theory was that if it were trapped in a standardized text, our Peers would rely on it too heavily and the faith would lose its organic nature, and they would stop memorizing and building on the texts. Part of the beauty of the faith, I've always found, is that it is fluid and open to interpretation. It grows with stories and adds things it finds useful. This is why our temples are such simple places; our practice is rich enough as it is."

"Why is it a good thing? For it to be open to interpretation?"

"Because then people can find in it what they need to help them on their way. They can find their own reason in it that will encourage them to follow the faith and embrace the Pillars of its tradition." He put the book in her hand. She noticed for the first time how thin his fingers were, and the nails, bitten halfway to the cuticle. For some reason she had assumed his hands would have been immaculately kept like the rest of the temple, and was again reminded of eels, although she couldn't have said why. Perhaps that was why he always stood with his hands behind his back.

She opened the book's first pages. To her surprise, she saw that the frontispiece was adorned with the golden ship of the royal family. He saw her looking at it. "The royal family likes its staff to know the religion well," he commented. "This was a surplus copy."

"Are all of the court Onaistian?"

"Most of them. The Queen I know is devout, and encourages the Houses to adopt the Promise too. After her granddaughter's near-death at the hands of the poisoner, I believe her faith has only strengthened. She and the Princess's donations to the Temple have doubled in these last few months." He sighed regretfully. "I would like to think it is in thanks for her granddaughter's life being spared, but I worry it is out of fear lest another attempt occur. Once the assassin has been found, I imagine she will feel considerably more at ease. As will we all." He frowned. "Miss Andottir?"

Hellevir realized she was frowning, her eyes fixed on the middle distance. A thought had just occurred to her. She gave herself a mental shake and patted the book.

"Thank you for this."

"Consider it a favor to your mother." He opened the door again, and she quickly got to her feet.

"Why do you think the Queen adopted Onaistian?" she asked.

"I could not presume to know," he replied. "But many turn to the Promise as a form of structure in their lives." He glanced down at her. "Perhaps it could offer you a structure too?" he commented. "I heard you have had troubles in your home village."

Hellevir stiffened a little, but made herself smile. His description of the faith had not been what she had expected. From what her pa had said, she had thought to find charlatans, an obsessive cult, and not what seemed to be a largely sensible practice. But—and she could not have said why; perhaps it was her father's blood in her—she felt a sense of being at a tangent to their ways, as out of place as a raven among doves.

"Perhaps," she said politely, and didn't mean it at all. Hers were the old ways of spirits and blood.

*

That evening she sat with her mother in the living room, by the fire. Ma was doing her needlework, and Hellevir sat with the book Peer Laius had given her open on her lap, her cheek on her hand as she leafed through it. Her mother seemed pleased—surprised, too, but she hid it well—that Hellevir was taking an interest, and left her to it.

It began simply enough with what the Peer had told her, tracing the history of the faith rather than detailing its practice, its spread from the Galgoros across the sea to the western continent. She unfurled a handy map pressed into the pages. There was nothing particularly ground-breaking, and as she read she found she was actually growing bored. It was just a list of ways to follow the Path of the Promise, to ensure an eternity of bliss in Onaistus's company. It jarred with what she knew of What Came Next; the half-life of Death was only a stepping-stone, but she couldn't imagine that what lay beyond it could be something as . . . simple as what the Onaistians envisaged.

With a yawn she flicked further into the book. A page caught her eye, and she opened it with surprise. Here was something new.

It was a wood engraving, showing creatures circling a man with his eyes closed. They looked horrific, all teeth and horns. They were depictions, the book said, of dark things made of lies, intent upon pulling men and women from goodness, from the Promise.

Hellevir didn't know what to make of that. It didn't explain what the evils were, whether they were just metaphors for temptation. She glanced over at her ma, quietly stitching away, her black hair loose from its braid about her shoulders. Perhaps this was why Ma had always hated her talking to the fire as a child, to the trees. She'd thought her daughter was talking to evil things, dark things. Things that would condemn her to the Nothing that awaited those who weren't worthy of Onaistus's eternal company, things that would pull her away from the Pillars of the Faith, away from the Path.

Hellevir had the abrupt urge to throw the book into the hearth, angered by it and its claim to know what was real. But her ma was sitting there so calmly, pleased with her daughter for listening to the good Peer and reading his book.

She took it up to her room with her when Ma turned in, and sat in a chair by the window, listening to the noise of the city, but she didn't read any further. She found herself staring out at the canal again, pondering what the Peer had said to her about the Crown adopting the Promise. The whole conversation had left her feeling a little uncomfortable, but it had given her an idea. Perhaps a foolish idea, but after the morning with Sullivain, the sensation that the walls of the city were closing in around her, she was open to considering anything. The gifts to the Temple, the threats; the Princess was simply afraid, and for good reason. She wanted Hellevir close because she was predicting another attempt on her life, but what would happen when—if—the assassin was found? She hoped it would mean the Crown would let her go home, return to the village and her cottage with Milandre. She wondered how far along the investigation was, whether they had any suspects yet, and felt a sudden and painful sense of urgency.

I wonder if there's anything I could do, she thought as she looked over the gleaming canals. *There must be a way I can help, some way I can use my deal with Death*. As soon as she thought it, she shook her head, wondering at herself. It was a daydream. How could she hope to find the assassin when the entire court had tried and failed? Nonetheless, the idea bit at the bars of her fear, the crack of its teeth overwhelming her as she tried to come to grips with the madness her life had become in only a few days. Princesses, courts, assassins, Peers, riddles and dark things; how on earth had her small world in a small cottage spilled her into such chaos?

CHAPTER EIGHT

She must have dozed.

Her head jerked as she awoke and she nearly fell off her chair. The city had quietened, and she was relieved to realize that even Rochidain must sleep eventually. Her oil lamp had gone out in a wayward breeze, but she didn't relight it. With a yawn she closed one of the windows, leaving the other ajar for Elsevir, and turned towards her bed, dismissively dropping the book on her bedside.

She hesitated, her hand upon the bedsheet. She waited, thinking, feeling. Letting her senses drift. Trying to figure out what was wrong. Then she looked up.

He sat in the corner of the room, watching her. She stood straight abruptly, almost knocking her lamp from her bedside, the oil sloshing around within it.

The moonlight didn't reach his body, only his boots. He had one leg crossed over the other. She could see the white of his hands, folded on his lap, of his face, indistinct and chalky. His eyes were hooded darknesses in his head.

Hellevir swallowed, and made herself stand tall, head held high as her mother did. Her heart was beating sickeningly.

"What are you doing here?" she demanded. At first she didn't think he would answer her, that he'd just continue to sit there and watch. If she were to close her eyes, she knew it would feel like being back in that nightmare, a thousand-soul stare bearing down upon her.

"You know," he murmured, his voice a hint of that roar it had been. "I did wonder if you'd notice I was here."

"How could I not?" she asked him sharply. His presence filled the room like fog.

"I often sit in the corners of dreams," he said. "Some dreamers can tell there's something there. Most can't."

"And am I dreaming?"

"Only half."

They watched each other in silence.

"Won't you come into the light?" she asked. For a while she thought he wouldn't, but then he slowly uncrossed his legs, and leaned forward with his elbows on his knees so his face was in the moonlight.

"Is that better?" he asked, a little derisively. "Now that you can see?"

It wasn't. Here, in the real world, he seemed shockingly out of place, as if he obeyed different laws. Everything about him was too intense, the black of his hair so thick it made her feel almost blind to look at it, the white of his skin like bone.

"Much," she lied. She sat on the edge of her bed, resolving not to let him see how shaken she was, although she was almost certain he could see right through her like the moonlight. "What are you doing here?" she asked again. He put his palms together, looked away, as if deciding how to phrase himself.

"I fear I was too . . . brutal. When last we met."

Hellevir thought briefly—only briefly, like putting her hand near a flame—of that nightmare place where the world shuddered around her. She watched him, seeing how at odds his expression was with his words.

"You were too brutal," she agreed simply. His black eyes grew impossibly darker, as if the thin light was being drawn into them. Then he inclined his head stiffly.

"I have always had a . . . temper."

Hellevir made a conscious effort to stop herself from playing nervously with the bedsheet in her hand. She'd been nothing in that place. Her jaw ached with a phantom pain from the memory of where he'd gripped her. And all that had just been his temper.

She gathered herself and opened the drawer of her bedside table, taking out the slip of paper with the two seeds resting upon it.

"Were you worried I'd abandon our deal out of fear?" she asked sharply. She felt his regard slide from her to the seeds as she put them by the lamp.

"You found them," he remarked, surprise arching his dark brows. "That was . . . quick." He tore his eyes away. They were not his to take, not yet, as much as he might want them. Not until she came looking for a soul.

"Did you think I wouldn't?"

"I thought you'd find the place. I did wonder whether you'd know how to *get* them, however."

She took a savage sort of pleasure from his underestimation of her. She tapped the slip of paper under the seeds, creased and torn from so much handling, but his sharp scrawl was still clear. "Couldn't you have written plainer instructions?" she asked. "If it's so important to you that I find them?"

"I knew it would be plain, once you saw the signs. I knew they would reach out for you, and I was right. You found them; you have them." Hellevir shuddered, remembering how they'd walked past the archway, and the singing had seemed to start right then, just for her. She wondered if there were such a thing as coincidence, in a world where Death could walk through dreams and willow seeds could bring the dead back to life.

They watched each other. She wouldn't let herself look away.

"Your Princess," he remarked, "she called you here to keep her alive." Hellevir blinked, uneasy with the sudden change of conversation, but nodded. "And I assume you have agreed?"

"I didn't have much choice," Hellevir retorted. "She's threatened my family if I don't."

"There's always a choice. What will you do if someone else needs to be raised?" He seemed to like the idea of her being faced with such a trial, curious to know what she would do.

"I . . . don't know," she replied honestly. "I will just have to make sure I find your treasures quickly." She said it bravely, but it was a very real fear, weighing her down. To lose more of herself . . . The thought of it made her flinch, chilled the bare knuckles on her left hand. She swallowed, afraid of what she was about to ask, whether it would anger him. "If I can hand over the assassin to her, she may not need me here. She might let me go."

There was silence, marked out by the beat of her heart.

"Are you asking me who killed her?" he remarked slowly.

"I suppose I am. Will you tell me?"

He smiled, incredulous at how much she dared, and shook his head.

"I am not a service for you to make use of," he replied slowly. "And I don't divulge the secrets of the dead. If you want to find your Princess's killer, you'll have to do it by yourself. But I admire your optimism in thinking it would make any difference. The city is a carcass crawling with creatures that want nothing more than to consume her, and plucking out one will not stop the decay."

She blinked, and the corner of the room was empty. There had been no hint of his withdrawal, no breath of air. Just the sudden absence of his regard. She released a breath and realized she wasn't sitting on her bed, but in the chair by the window where she'd dozed off. She hadn't moved at all.

Perhaps it all had been a dream. But the seeds were still out of their drawer and on the bedside table, white in the moonlight.

"All right. Stop fussing. *All right.*"

"No, just . . . Not like that."

"Like what, then?"

"Higher, stitch it higher."

"Pa taught you to sew. Why am I darning your clothes for you?"

"Because you're my sweet sister who knows how to do everything?"

"I'm a pushover is what I am. There." Hellevir straightened, holding the pins between her lips. Farvor lifted his arm and looked at the seam on his side. "Now take it off and I'll sew it up."

He waited in his shirt while she darned the waistcoat, pulling out the pins holding the fabric together as she went. It was a lovely piece, pale blue to bring out Farvor's dark hair, with the shield of his knight stitched on to the lapel. By an odd coincidence, the House symbol was a nightingale, in almost the same configuration—wings mid-flight, beak open as if mid-song—as the symbol of the Order of the Nightingale.

"So," he said while she worked. "Did you find out what the Princess wanted?"

Hellevir kept her head bent over her work. She didn't want to think about it, but after a moment she sighed. It would be good to tell someone, and so she did, including the threat that life could be made difficult for the family if she didn't comply. When she was finished, Farvor whistled.

"Well, it is the De Neïds," he remarked. "Threats and blackmail, it's how they stay in power."

She glanced at him, wishing he'd warned her.

"If she dies the Queen has no heir," she went on with a sigh, "and if the Queen dies with no heir there will be civil war."

"Most likely. What are you going to do?" he asked.

"Nothing. There's nothing I can do." She gave a half-laugh, slightly bitter, and made herself return to her sewing. "Short of finding the assassin myself, all I can do is hope the person who did try to have her killed has been put off."

"Is there anything I can do?"

She hesitated.

"You could . . . no, never mind." It was stupid. What was she thinking?

"No, go on."

"What if . . . Could you help me to keep an ear out?" she said, half-heartedly. "You're in the service of a noble; could you listen for anything that might help to find who did this?"

"Wait, you meant what you just said? Finding the assassin?" She shrugged a little helplessly. He blew out a sharp breath. "Are you sure you want to get mixed up, Hellevir? This sounds dangerous."

"I'm already mixed up. The Princess says I can't leave Rochidain, can't go home. Maybe if I find who did it, she'll let me go. She'll revoke her threats."

Doubt hung between them in the air, thick as smoke.

"This is your home too," Farvor said quietly, then added, "I can try, but the nobles are as slippery as eels. They never say what they mean." He *hmm*ed. "You might hear something at the small dinner this evening. The poisoning has been just about the only topic of gossip since it happened, so it shouldn't be too hard to pick up something."

"Thank you, Farvor."

"What are brothers for, if not to help their resurrectionist sisters find assassins."

She laughed again, more genuinely this time.

"If you really want to help," she said, "you can make sure Ma doesn't drag me to that temple of hers again."

He grinned.

"Just wait until a Markday sermon. They can last *eons*."

"You can also stop clicking your knuckles. It sounds like your bones are breaking."

"My hands hurt if I don't!"

"And for the love of goodness please stop smoking whatever it is you're smoking out of your window, you're not fooling anyone."

"You're the herbalist, you can't tell what it is?"

"We can *all* smell it on you."

"You've been here *one week*, Hellevir."

"And your shoes! Do you not know what shoe polish is? I thought you were a proper city boy now."

"Oh, shush, you," he laughed. "I'm still the hunter's son. I can still shoot a buck at two hundred paces."

Hellevir rolled her eyes, but she couldn't keep herself from smiling. "I'm glad you're still you at heart, at least. Here, try this on." She held out the waistcoat and helped him into it. He flexed his shoulder and rolled his arm. The seam held, and it fitted well.

"Looks good." He took it off for her to press. "I do hope you like him," he said, resting his chin on his hand.

"Like who?" she asked over her shoulder.

"Lord Redeion. My knight."

"I'm sure I will."

The "small dinner" Farvor had promised turned out to be a gathering of about a hundred people. There may have been more; Hellevir lost count of the number of carriages pulling up in front of the estate doors. Most of them were knights of some kind, or held rank in the Queen's army. Some were wealthy merchants from overseas, dressed in clothes she didn't recognize, their accents sharp. Whether they wore foreign garb, the colors of their House shield, or the reds and golds of the military uniform, Hellevir wasn't sure she'd ever seen such wealth all in one space.

She looked down at her dress as they climbed down from the carriage.

"Is this drab?" she wondered for the first time. Farvor glanced over at her, looking fine in his squire's blues. He plucked a red rose from one of the garden pots lining the path to the house, pinching off the stem and the thorns, and threaded it into her braid.

"Better?" she asked.

"Better. Ready?"

"No."

They were led into a high-ceilinged dining room bright with candles, a chandelier glinting overhead. Hellevir wondered what Milandre would think of all this finery, and with a smile imagined the old lady would turn up her nose at it, eat as much food as she could, and get out of there as fast as her legs would take her. That didn't sound like a bad idea.

Farvor, as the lord's squire, was seated on the right-hand side, at the lower end of the table, with Hellevir next to him; there was a reason to all the seating but Hellevir couldn't fathom it. Farvor said they were lucky to be seated at the table at all, considering their station. She'd hoped to be able to talk to Lord Redeion herself, just to see whether he lived up to Farvor's stories, but he was seated at the head of the table, far away from them, talking with an eagle-faced man Farvor said was his uncle, Auland Redeion, one of the wealthiest men in the city. It was hard to judge Lord Redeion the younger from such a distance, but she could hear his laugh even from her end of the table.

Farvor was chatting as easily as if he'd been born into this sort of life. He threw himself into conversations loudly and with a confidence Hellevir wished she shared, but she was happy enough letting it all wash over her.

Farvor ended up being right that the attempt on the Princess's life was on everyone's tongues. Hellevir didn't have to wait long to overhear hushed conversations with that word, the word that had been poised in her brain, a shining hook to catch slippery eels. Assassination.

She turned her attention as inconspicuously as possible to a pair of young squires she'd been introduced to earlier in the evening. The one in yellow Farvor had said was from House Senodin; her name was Cayne. The one in purple and silver was from House Hannotir, called Yvoir.

"No," the House Senodin squire muttered, "I've not heard much else about it. It's frustrating, really, no one knows what's going on."

"Is there an investigation?" Yvoir asked.

"Obviously. Wasn't your Family questioned? All the Houses who were at the dinner are being spoken to." She blanched. "Lord and Lady Senodin threw the investigator out on his ear."

Yvoir tossed a chestnut curl over her shoulder.

"I'm sure Lady Hannotir would just love that." She ducked her chin to give the impression of a heavy neck, and affected a jowly tone. "You dare question me? In my own house, like a common servant who has stolen the cheese? How dare you, sir?" She spluttered as if with indignation and the Senodin squire laughed loudly.

"Yvie," she remarked with a smile. "You shouldn't mock your lady like that. The walls have ears."

Yvoir shrugged, halfway through her glass of wine already. "She can't be bothering with spies," she retorted, downing the rest.

There was another group to Hellevir's right, whose names she hadn't caught. Two squires in dark green, a wolf on their lapel, and another in violet with the symbol of a chalice.

"Do they have any suspects?" a wolf squire was asking.

"I heard the palace cook is still locked up," the chalice commented. "They think he did the deed, but don't know who put him up to it." The wolf grimaced.

"Makes sense. Someone poisoned her and had to know what to use, like a cook."

Another conversation, opposite. Two squires both in black, an oak on their chests.

"Thing is," one of them mused, popping a grape in her mouth as if they were discussing the best breed of hunting dog rather than the death of the country's future sovereign, "someone's behind it all, someone hired the cook to do it. He didn't do it on his own."

"He's been with the royals since she was a child," her companion added. "It must have been one hell of a bribe to convince him." He flinched. "Or a threat."

"The list of suspects is positively endless," Hellevir heard someone crow, voice loud and bawdy, from further up the table, a woman in white with a rose stitched to her shoulder. "I can't think of anyone in all of the Chron whose death would benefit more people than that of the Princess." She was shushed immediately by those sitting around her.

Hellevir recalled Sullivain's rather morbid words about the civil war her death would undoubtedly cause among the noble Houses: *Peace is not good for the business of seeking power.*

"It was probably a noble," she heard Cayne say from her left, an echo of Hellevir's train of thought.

"If it was a noble, why did only the Princess fall ill?" Yvoir asked. "Why did they try to do away with her alone when they could have got rid of the lot of them at once?"

Cayne seemed to ponder.

"It would only make sense if the person behind it all were at the dinner themselves, surely?"

"Exactly. Think about it. Wouldn't it have been easier just to poison everything instead of one bowl? The nobles are always out to eat each other, it'd just be a wasted opportunity. Unless they didn't want to poison themselves too."

"Yvoir!" Cayne chided. "Lady Hannotir might not bother with spies, but the Queen certainly does. Don't forget you work for one of the nobles who was there."

"Please, tell me I'm wrong. Your Lord Senodin would sting my Lady Hannotir in a heartbeat if it bought him an extra ship."

"Yvie!" Cayne hissed. "You're drunk."

"I'm not drunk, you're drunk." Yvoir saw she'd upset her friend, and put her glass down more soberly. "Sorry. I'm on edge. My father's still fuming after last week and he's making the house unbearable."

"Has he found somewhere else to work?"

"No, but he found out they're bringing in a whole new staff, and it's irked him. The Queen even brought in a *herbalist* from the countryside."

Cayne sniffed. "A country bumpkin? What joy."

"I think it'll be funny, if their remedies don't kill her faster than whatever poison she took. They'll have the Princess taking peasant potions, a regimen of rat toes and snail slime."

"An owl plucked and stewed in a copper cauldron."

"The guts of a cat, grease of a hedgehog, bubble bubble pip pip."

"Oh, stop, you'll put me off my food!" They chuckled, before being distracted by another conversation. Hellevir stared down at her food.

*

The meal ended, but Hellevir didn't have much time to ponder what she'd overheard. Most of the guests milled around talking for a while after the meal, and Hellevir noticed a few saying good night to Auland Redeion, but then it seemed as if a secret signal was passed through the gathering and suddenly the music became loud and fast and blaring and there were bodies everywhere laughing and spilling wine and couples whirling on the dance floor, insignias and glinting fabrics, a menagerie of bees and swans and nightingales and boars and peacocks and dragonflies, flashing by in a whirl of color and noise. Farvor had vanished and it all became a bit too much. She was used to the village dances, but never had she been surrounded by so many *people*. A drunken squire tried to drag her into a dance, staggering into her as he pulled her around, ignoring her protests until she wrenched herself away and ran.

Hellevir shrank out of one of the doors and into the garden, welcoming the cold night air on her flushed cheeks. She stumbled forward without knowing where she was, following a string of lanterns until she found a small fountain with a bench, and sat down with a sigh of relief. Someone had spilled brandy on her new skirt, and she doubted it would come out. She wanted to go home, not to her parents' house but to Milandre's cottage, where she could just picture the old herbalist sitting by the fire, darning something or making herb pouches. But no, she was to stay in Rochidain, by order of the Princess, surrounded by drunk squires and assassination attempts and people who hated herbalists. She fought the sudden urge to cry.

"Are you all right?" asked a voice, and she jumped to her feet. It was Lord Redeion the younger. He was dressed in a smart blue waistcoat, embroidered with golden birds. She gave an awkward bow.

"Yes, my lord," she said. "I was just . . . getting some air." The knight gave a half-laugh and glanced back over his shoulder towards the hall, to the sounds of laughter and music.

"It doesn't usually get that mad," he said. He paused. "I saw you run out and thought I'd better check on you. You're my squire's sister, aren't you? Hellevir?" She blinked and nodded. He made an annoyed sound, but it wasn't directed at her. "You know this was supposed to be a small affair for me to meet you?" he said. "It started off with ten people. Then those ten asked another ten and soon I was catering for a hundred." Hellevir glanced towards the light of the ballroom.

"This was all to meet me?"

"Yes, Farvor's told me a lot about you. He's . . . well, he's grown very important to the household, and I want to get to know his family." He gestured towards the bench. "May I?"

A little on the back foot, Hellevir stepped aside to make room for him, and sank down onto the seat. She wondered briefly what the Rochidain etiquette was for a young woman like her being alone with a lord, but felt so frayed at the edges that she couldn't bring herself to care.

"How are you finding Rochidain?" he asked politely. He had a gentle way about him.

"I like it," she said. "I like the waters everywhere. Our parents seem happy here." She hesitated. "Shouldn't you be in there?" she asked, inclining her head towards the lights of the ballroom.

"Honestly, it was getting too loud for me as well. When I saw you fleeing the scene I told Farvor to meet us out here when he'd made my excuses."

"He likes working for you."

"I should hope so!" he laughed. He had an easy laugh and an easy manner. She felt herself relaxing a little. "You know," the knight added thoughtfully, "I think he scared the other pages when he was first employed."

"How so?" Hellevir asked.

"Well, there was a rat in among the pheasants—the groundsman keeps them—and all of the pages were running around fluttering and being generally pretty useless. Farvor takes out a slingshot—a *slingshot*—and hits the thing right on the head, not touching a feather on any of the birds. Picks it up by the tail and without thinking twice throws it into the canal."

Hellevir chuckled.

"That sounds like him. He kept our home clear of rats when we were children. But he was better with a bow." Hellevir heard footsteps, and glanced up to see her brother coming down the path.

"Oh, I've heard plenty of boasts!" the knight chuckled. "I hope he'll come with me on our next hunt and give substance to them."

"I wouldn't want to show up your usual entourage," Farvor said. He was carrying three full wine glasses balanced by their stems, and held out two. "Are you telling Hellevir stories?"

"Only the good ones," Lord Redeion said, accepting a glass.

"There *are* only good ones." Farvor sat down on another of the benches opposite. Lord Redeion wanted to know more about their home by the woods, and Hellevir was happy to tell him, with Farvor chipping in his opinion. The topic turned to court life and they fell into an easy cadence, talking about who had been seen stealing silver, why this person was no longer allowed into that lord's house, which serving boy Lady Such-and-such had been caught with in the stables, all the gossip of a busy city with a vibrant elite.

"I must confess," Hellevir said quietly. "I know next to nothing about Rochidain, about the Houses. I feel like I'm staring at a knot that I have to unpick."

Lord Redeion laughed. "You're not the first one to liken Rochidain politics to an incomprehensible knot," he remarked. "I admit, I'm glad my uncle handles most of our House business himself at court."

"It's that complicated?"

"It's complicated, but also a lot of responsibility. Uncle Auland revels in it. Loves being at the heart of the action. Some of the decisions he has to make I don't think I could."

"What sort of decisions?"

"Well, for instance, our trade relies on ships. We've been dealing with one ship-building family for generations, and Uncle Auland has just decided to switch to another who are offering cheaper rates, leaving the original family . . . well, out in the cold is putting it mildly." Lord Redeion grimaced. "I'm not sure I could have done that."

Farvor snorted.

"That's because you're a human being. Auland revels in it because he has a heart of ice and a soul of flint, like some elemental being from a fairy tale about ghouls and lost maidens. He's made for the court."

Hellevir glanced at him, surprised at his candor in front of Lord Auland's nephew, but Lord Redeion just chuckled and shrugged.

"You forgot *skin thick as steel*. I don't have that either."

"Good, it'd make you no fun to tease."

Their casual chatter, their ease with each other, made her anxieties fade bit by bit. By the time they returned to the ballroom many of the guests had left—it was long past midnight—and those who remained were in small groups talking quietly among themselves. Lord Redeion called a carriage for them.

Hellevir sat on the steps looking out over the front gardens, watching the swans drifting like dropped petals along the nearby canal. The moonlight glinted off the thin collars about their long necks, and she wondered absently why they wore them. She felt tired but pleased that the evening had at least ended well. She glanced back to ask Farvor a question, and saw him standing by the door, close to Lord Redeion. The knight's hand was resting on the back of her brother's head, and they were smiling as they pressed their foreheads together, dark hair to light. Farvor said something, and they both laughed quietly.

Hellevir stood up as the carriage came around, brushing off her skirts, and heard them come down the steps behind her. Lord Redeion handed her into the carriage, and saw them from the door with a wave.

"So," Farvor asked, moving from his seat opposite to come and sit beside her. "What did you think?"

"Of the party? Awful."

He laughed. "That bad? I suppose I did rather leave you to fend for yourself."

"Yes, thank you for that."

"But Lord Redeion looked after you, no? What did you think of him?"

"I like him," she said, honestly. "I like anyone who'll try to make someone feel less uncomfortable." She paused. "He's very fond of you," she commented. Farvor glanced at her, reading her tone, and she gave him a wry smile. He laughed.

"How did you guess?" he asked.

"Please, I saw you. So there's no rule about knights fraternizing with their squires?"

"There's no strict rule about it, no," he said, stretching his arms over his head until his shoulders popped. Hellevir thought she heard the seam of his waistcoat tear again.

"You've smiled more in the week I've been here than in the

whole time we lived by the woods," Hellevir commented. "So something must be right."

His expression softened as he watched the canals slip by.

"I've never felt more right," he replied quietly. Hellevir took his hand and squeezed it.

The carriage left them on the thoroughfare and they walked back along the streets to their gate. Farvor suggested a nightcap before bed, and left her sitting by the fountain in the courtyard as he fetched them some brandy, the rose he'd braided through her hair dangling lightly between her fingers. The pomegranate tree was in bloom, its flowers frilled and so red that they almost glowed in the dim light. She spied eyes shaped like seeds watching her from the foliage, and smiled as the tree reached out with pollen-dripping fingers to play with her hair.

Farvor appeared with a bottle and set it beside them on the edge of the fountain, oblivious to the spirit in the tree as it plaited a neat braid in one of his locks.

"That looks expensive," Hellevir remarked as he poured the brandy into two glasses.

"Oh, it is," Farvor remarked carelessly. "It was a gift from the Temple. Ma brings it out whenever the Peer is here."

"Farvor," she chided.

"As if she'd notice a few thimblefuls missing. Besides, who knows, perhaps one sip of the Temple's finest is all I need to be converted to the Path of the Promise and a life in praise of the God of Light. Cheers." They clinked their glasses together and took a sip.

"Salvation tastes dusty," Hellevir remarked. Farvor grimaced.

"Oh well, what did I really expect. Stingy coots, the lot of them." He leaned back, pushing his hair out of his eyes. "So," he began. "Did you overhear anything interesting? If you really were serious about trying to do your own investigation."

Hellevir sighed. The problems that had seemed quite distant while she'd talked with Lord Redeion flooded back as if to reclaim the space they were owed.

"I don't know. I'm not sure what I can do that the Queen's spies can't. The squires seemed to think one of the nobles did it."

"I mean, that would be my first guess. Did you hear anything else useful?"

"Well, they were quite drunk. One of them suggested that the House responsible was at the dinner where Sullivain was poisoned."

"Sullivain, huh?"

"I mean the Princess."

"It would be an easy way to ensure the poison had done the trick, I suppose. It narrows your list down to six Houses; not a bad start."

"You know who was there?"

Farvor leaned forward, and started counting off on his fingers. "The Hannotirs," he said. "The Dunfelds. The Greersons, Scelligs, and Senodins. And of course, the Redeions." He caught her look. "Go on, ask me the question."

"There's no way that Lord Redeion . . ."

"Not a chance in this life or the next. I've seen the mental preparation it takes him to shoot a pheasant. He couldn't kill anybody."

"Or his uncle?"

"Auland Redeion may be a pompous stick-in-the-mud, but he fought for the De Neïds during the war. He's as loyal as they come." He thought about it. "They all did, except for the Dunfelds." She stared down at the ground as she tried to piece things together. He nudged her gently. "Hellevir, you should get some sleep. You're not going to solve this in your first week here."

She sighed, rubbing her face.

"I know, I just . . . I want this to be over. I want to be able to go home. I feel like I'm just waiting for the next attack, for the next time I have to raise her."

He put an arm around her shoulders and squeezed. "It may not come to that."

"Maybe. I just feel at sea. The Houses, the politics, the intrigue, it's easy to drown in it all."

"Well, maybe it's time you learned a bit about it. I can ask Calgir to give you pointers, if you like. He helped me get to grips with it all."

"I don't want to impose on him."

"Rubbish. I'll ask him." He stretched, joints popping. "Well, I'm turning in, and you should too. Besides, you're not going to solve anything after drinking this rubbish," he remarked. "I can feel my own brain dissolving." She chuckled, relieved that at least she had him to confide in. It would have felt awfully lonely otherwise.

They both fell up the stairs, saying sleepy good-nights as they stumbled into their rooms. Hellevir couldn't reach properly to untie the knots of her bodice and ended up pulling them tighter—"Stupid thing," she muttered to herself—so in the end she just pulled the whole garment over her head and left it draped, smelling of brandy, over her chair. With her last vestiges of energy she took out the journal she had used at Milandre's to record the properties of plants. She opened it to the back and wrote down what she could remember of the conversations she'd heard at dinner, and the names of the Houses. It was a half-discernible scribble, but Milandre had always told her to write down things while they were fresh in her mind, unspoiled by sleep. Then she collapsed in her bed, still in her slip, without bothering to un-braid her hair.

It felt like she'd only been asleep for five minutes when she heard the front-gate bell being pulled. She rolled over groggily and saw that it was still dark outside. She listened, still half asleep, as there came the sound of the door and then the gate being opened, and voices, one of them shrill. There was a moment of silence, and then footsteps coming up the stairs.

It came as a surprise that it was her door they knocked on. Elsevir, nesting in a scarf on her chair, irritably fluffed his feathers.

Hellevir sleepily pulled herself up, drawing the blanket around her bare shoulders, and went to open the door. Weira, the Temple servant, was standing outside, still dressed for bed, holding a lamp.

"I'm sorry to wake you, miss," she said. "There's a lady downstairs wanting to see you."

Hellevir rubbed her face. "Who?" she asked.

"She says she's from the Order of the Nightingale."

Hellevir started. "What does she want?"

"She won't say. Shall I tell her to go away?"

"No, I . . . I'll come down."

They both glanced back as her parents' door opened. Her pa put his head out, his hair dishevelled from sleep.

"What's the fuss?" he grumbled.

"Nothing," Hellevir said. "Go back to bed." She nodded to

Weira, and the servant led her back downstairs. She heard her father's heavy steps following behind her.

The priestess was in the courtyard, pacing in front of the fountain. It was the same woman who had shown her around the Order the previous week, or at least Hellevir thought it was; it was hard to tell in the dimness, even by lamplight, and it didn't help that all the priestesses wore their hair covered. When she saw Hellevir step through the threshold she came forward.

"Please, you must come with me back to the Order," she said without preamble.

"Why?" Hellevir asked. "What's happened? Is it the willow?" But the priestess was shaking her head.

"Not the willow. It's . . ." She glanced at Weira and Hellevir's father standing at the door, both listening with open curiosity.

"Weira, will you get us some tea?" Hellevir asked the servant. She looked about to argue, but instead she just nodded and went back inside. "You can talk freely in front of Pa," Hellevir said to the priestess, who hesitated, but went on.

"There is a boy—a man—at the Order. He's been badly hurt, a duel gone wrong. I've come to you for help."

"A herbalist's help?" Hellevir asked, although she knew she was wrong. The priestess shook her head.

"Not a herbalist's help," she said. "No."

There was a beat of silence.

"All right," Hellevir said quietly. "Give me a moment to fetch my things." The priestess nodded, rubbing the web of skin between her thumb and forefinger, and Hellevir ducked back inside. She rushed upstairs without looking at her father, but he caught her by the arm.

"Do you want me to come?" he asked.

"No, it's better if I go alone," she said, putting her hand on his. "But thank you."

In her room she changed quickly without bothering to light the lamp, annoyed with herself for not stopping to un-braid her hair before going to sleep as she forced the strands apart. It was so wild that she gave up trying to comb it, and simply lanced it up with a silver hairpin her pa had bought for her to keep it out of her face.

The seeds were still in the drawer. For a moment she looked down at them, taking in a deep breath, releasing it slowly. Then she picked them up with care, folded them in the paper, and slipped them into her pocket. As she turned back to the door the moonlight shone oddly on the glass of her window, and for a moment she thought she saw the reflection of a figure behind her, a dark figure with tines growing from its head. She gasped in fright and looked back, but there was nothing there.

Her heart pounding, she tapped her shoulder. Elsevir flew over and nestled against her neck, flapping his large wings for balance.

The priestess was waiting downstairs, agitated. Ma was also there, her black hair in a cloud about her shoulders. She had her arms folded in a shawl, and Hellevir's heart sank as she saw the fire in her eyes.

"Where are you going at this time of night?" she demanded.

"The Order have a wounded man. I'm going to help."

"Rot!" Ma exclaimed. "They have their own healers. Why would they need you?"

"I'm . . ." But her mother cut her off with a sharp wave of her hand.

"This is . . . you're going to do it again, aren't you?" she exclaimed. She shook her head. "No. I won't let you go."

"You go," Pa said grimly. "I'll handle your mother." Ma whirled on him.

"*Handle* me, will you?"

"Ma," Hellevir said, trying to be gentle. "I have to go. Please." Hellevir pulled on her cloak, and gestured the priestess towards the gate. Her ma tried to step in the way, but her father took her arm and held her back.

"No! It's wrong!" Ma shouted.

"Why?" Hellevir had to ask, her voice sharp, stopping with her hand on the gate's handle. "Why is it so wrong?"

"Because it ruins lives! It ruined ours. It's an unnatural thing, flying in the face of what's proper."

"Ruins lives?" Hellevir gestured to the rich garden, the large house. "How is your life ruined?" She shook her head, trying not to let her anger get the better of her. "I'll be back soon," she said, and left before Ma could throw anything else at her.

The priestess led the way, over the silent bridges lit by lamplight flickering between the wings of moths, through archways echoing

104

with their footsteps. Hellevir felt like she was trailing her thoughts behind her, scattered by lack of sleep and the sheer number of things that had happened in the few days she'd been in Rochidain. She focused on the blue of the priestess's cape in front of her, the weight of Elsevir on her shoulder.

"How did you know to come for me?" Hellevir asked. The priestess glanced at her over her shoulder.

"I'd heard a few stories," she said. "About the Princess coming back from the dead. About the new herbalist in her employ from the woods, the one who'd saved her. You had the right accent. It was easy enough finding your address." She paused. "But mostly I just had this sense. As if you weren't quite here. And then there was the willow . . ." She petered off, as if it were too peculiar a thing to voice.

"I've left a bit of a trail," Hellevir remarked, more to herself than the priestess.

"Our Order recognizes the truth more easily than most, but we will not be the last to find out what you are." She hesitated. "You should be careful who knows, especially in Rochidain. The city is beautiful but . . . it is not safe."

They came to the archway, and the priestess tapped lightly on the door. It opened immediately, as if someone had been waiting for them on the other side, and they were ushered through. The priestess led her down the narrow path, the fuchsia whispering as they went, and then turned to enter one of the buildings, heading through corridors and up winding stairs. At last they came to a small room which looked like an infirmary; jars containing different herbs sat on shelves, bottles and ointments were set in neat rows on the countertop, drawers labelled in a neat hand lined the walls. All clean and tidy, an orderly workspace, but the center of the room was chaos. Hellevir put a hand to her mouth.

The body had bled profusely. It was all over the floor. The boy lay on the table, his shirt open and his chest bare. His eyes were looking off somewhere into the corner of the room, his hair spiked with drying blood.

There was another priestess present, her eyes dark and her hair coming loose from its scarf. Her hands were covered in blood, and Hellevir guessed she was a healer. She sat on a stool by the body, leaning forward with her forehead resting on her wrists, and looked up as they came in. Her expression was hollow.

"I hope you're not about to disgrace the dead by trusting a charlatan, Edrin," she said curtly to the other priestess.

Edrin shook her head.

"What harm can come from trying?" she asked. She glanced at Hellevir. "Can you do this?"

The herbalist in her recognized the smell of vinegar and honey for cleansing, soaked into the bandages that had been used to put pressure on the wound. There was a gauze dressing sitting on the table, ready to be applied, which had a dry paste rubbed into it; she guessed it was a mixture containing myrrh, perhaps egg-whites and maybe chalk or flour to prevent infection. There was a jar of copper salts open on the table beside the body.

"What happened to him?" she asked.

"He was in a duel, the stupid boy," the seated priestess said. "He drank too much and challenged someone he shouldn't have challenged. And that someone lacked the humanity to refuse, despite his state."

"So he's a drunk with a quick temper?"

The priestess raised her head and regarded Hellevir coldly.

"You want me to justify why you should try to help him?" she asked. "Yes, he was a young idiot, but he came here to use our library. He liked to read, he liked to learn, and we liked to teach him. He wouldn't have been a young idiot for much longer. Does that satisfy you?"

Hellevir didn't answer at once. She just stared at the body, unable to make herself move.

She wanted to raise him. His face was young, handsome, beneath the grey pallor of bloodlessness. The urge to take his hand, slip into Death, to put an end to this ugliness, to lift the horrific pressure in the room that only a death could bring, was palpable. The thought of turning her back, leaving him here, put a crooked edge of shame against her throat, and she knew she'd bear the scars from it if she left. But she was paralyzed by the *what if.*

What if the Princess was killed again? What if she died, and Hellevir had nothing to give besides her self? She'd have no choice but to raise her, but she'd have no treasure to trade.

I am finite, she told herself, *I can't give parts of myself away without considering the consequence.* Her muscles braced to turn away, towards the door. She teetered on a tortured edge of indecision.

She realized her fists were clenched. The thought of leaving the body, leaving death where she could bring back life simply because she was afraid of what the future might bring, felt unclean.

No. She forced her fists to unfurl. If she were going to use her gift to raise the dead, she'd use it her way. Princesses be damned, she'd just have to find the next riddle quickly.

As soon as she made the decision, decided not to turn away, that feeling of grime slid away from her, and she knew she'd made the right choice. There was a body in front of her, and she could do something about it. That was all that mattered right then.

"All right. What is his name?" she asked.

"Ionas. Ionas Greerson."

Hellevir started, recognizing the name. "He's a noble?" she asked. "One of the Houses?"

"Yes. He's Lord Greerson's son." The priestess's eyes became hard again. "Does that change your decision?"

"It . . . it makes it easier." Still hazy with the wine from the evening, Hellevir strained to think back to earlier. Greerson. They were one of the Houses who'd been at the dinner where Sullivain was poisoned.

Hellevir looked at the body with fresh eyes. Perhaps this was an opportunity. This boy might be able to tell her something. He might even be the one who'd hired the cook.

The priestess's eyes drifted over to the body, then glanced away as if it hurt to look at him.

"Do you need us to go?" she asked.

"No. Not if you don't want to. I need to sit, though." The priestess stood up—slowly, achingly, as if her legs were tired from standing—and shifted the stool towards Hellevir with her foot. Hellevir moved it over to the boy's side, and sat down.

"Keep watch," she told the raven, setting him down on the table. Elsevir clicked his beak.

She took the boy's hand, and in her pocket tightened her fingers around the seeds.

She knew she didn't have to be asleep, ever since she'd brought back Elsevir. She just had to close her eyes and reach for Death—

the cold of her own shadow, the breath against her neck—and there it was. It was still painful, though, as if she were ripping herself from life.

The stillness, the silence, felt like a weight against her skin. It felt as if it would be too thick to breathe, but the air rushed cold into her lungs, and she shivered. She stood, her hand resting on the table where the body used to be.

Perhaps it was providence, but she knew where she was supposed to go.

The corridors slipped around her like a maze. Up and down grey stairways, in and out of arched doors, until she had the surreal feeling that she was ascending when the stairs led down, and moving through doorways with arched floors, her feet upon the ceiling and her hands trailing the undersides of banisters. Doors creaked shut as she opened them, and windows looked out onto the corridors where she had just been. Patiently, she walked them all.

When at last she found a door that led outside, there was no mirrored sky, just blackness. Absolute. Complete. She walked the winding path and came to the iron gate, the long corridor. Beyond, there were no trees, as in the living garden, no flowerbeds. Just the grass, grey in this world, which descended bankless to the still waters of the river. She followed it, and there, motionless like a statue of itself, stood the willow. It grew in complete solitude upon the edge of the water, surrounded by darkness as if it were the last thing left in the world. Its bark had an odd smoothness, and she knew it wasn't the actual willow, but only a semblance of it. Everything was dusted with the grey shadowlight of Death.

As she paused before the canopy of leaves, a hand reached past her shoulder and pulled the long branches aside. She jumped, turning around, and saw the man with the black eyes standing beside her.

"Welcome back," he said, or the world said around him. He wore his black coat that sank with him into the darkness as if he were a part of it. He held the canopy wider, and she ducked her head to go inside.

The willow seemed to have grown. The branches seemed far higher above her head than before, the drooping leaves domed like a temple ceiling.

The man with the black eyes sat down on the ground and leaned his back against the trunk, looking up into the boughs as the willow figure had done in life. He glanced back at her, as if surprised to find her still standing.

"Sit," he said, inclining his head. She stayed where she was.

"I'm here for Ionas," she said. "I've brought your precious thing, the willow seeds."

His eyebrow rose and his lip curled. "Very kind of you," he commented. "Please sit."

Numbly, she went over and lowered herself to the ground beside him. The trunk felt wrong against her back: too smooth, too cold. Too empty. There was no spirit of wicker and bough here, only the semblance of its home.

"Why does this place look the way it does?" she asked.

"Why is your sun in the sky?" he countered.

"I thought you controlled this world."

"In part," he said. He seemed to be in a mood to talk, not eager for her to hand over the seeds and her blood. She wondered how much she could get him to tell her about this place.

"So you like to watch me walk labyrinths?" she asked. He leaned his head back against the trunk and smiled, his teeth white as sun-bleached bone.

"I sometimes think I have control," he amended. "And then I wake and realize it was a dreamer's trick. I controlled nothing."

"You sleep?"

"Vast swathes of time seem to pass, laden with the souls of the dead. And then I am trapped in the same moment for an eternity. This place is me, and I am it, and I exert the same control over it as you do over the beating of your own heart."

Hellevir looked down at her legs stretched out in front of her with a frown.

"That makes no sense," she said.

"This is Death. It does not obey your rules of sense."

"And what about that nightmare place? That void you sent me to after I raised Elsevir?" She resisted the urge to brush her jaw where he had gripped her.

His smile faded, and for a moment she thought she had asked too much. The darkness pushing against the boundaries of the canopy seemed to press harder, a building pressure.

"This place is me, and I am it," he said again, his voice low. "Anger one, and both will act upon it." His tone was even, controlled.

She didn't know what to make of that. She wasn't sure she understood his answer, or why her question had caused him to withdraw. She swallowed, daring a glance across at him, but he wasn't paying attention to her. His expression was unreadable and closed, his gaze resting on the motionless waters.

"Who are you?" she asked. The darkness eased, and that smile returned.

"If you come here again, you can ask me again," was all he said.

"You know I will. Will you ever tell me?" He did not reply, his gaze distant as if he was only half-listening. "Anyway," she allowed herself to ask, risking his anger again, "if we are to be partners in trading souls, it seems we should know each other's names."

He turned to her then, pulling himself back from the middle distance, his expression sardonic.

"Bold girl," he said quietly, his voice a rumble through the worlds. "But then I suppose you would have to be, to keep coming into my home."

Hellevir didn't answer. Instead she took out the seeds wrapped in their riddle, but as she did so the rose that Farvor had threaded into her hair for the party—now slightly crumpled—fell from her pocket onto the grass between them, and for a moment they both looked down at it. In the gloom it shone like glass. Before she could reach for it, the man with black eyes had picked it up, turning it over. The starved light in his eyes devoured it. For a moment she felt as if she weren't there, and all that existed in this world was the dark man and his red rose. She might have been frightened by the hunger she could see in him, a desperate hunger that seemed inclined to push all else aside to seize the feast before it, but he seemed suddenly so unhappy. She thought she recognized the feeling; she'd watched Milandre's house vanish into the dust of the road with that same longing. A desire to be home. He pressed the flower to his nose and breathed deeply, before handing it back with a sad sigh.

"Alas, it has no scent here," he said with a quirk of his lip, as if that were funny.

"You can keep it," she replied. "There are other roses in life."

The smile broadened.

"Is that pity?" he remarked. "You pity me that I have no roses?"

"Yes, I do," she said honestly.

He laughed, and the sound was muted, unearthly. She shuddered.

"Pity can only be thrown downwards. Like scraps. I have no need of scraps." He took her hand and shoved the rose into it, harshly, and her fingers curled around it. "Besides, it would not be a fair trade. One day, for the right price, but not today."

She couldn't think of a reply to that. She didn't quite have the courage to tell him that she pitied him not because she thought him pitiable, but because she thought she knew how he felt. Instead she simply unwrapped the willow seeds from the riddle, and offered them to him.

She watched his eyes flicker to the seeds, grow bright with them. He seemed to look away, back to her, with a deliberate effort, as if denying himself the pleasure.

"Will you give me Ionas?" she asked.

"Oh, I suppose," he said with a sigh. "He's over there, admiring himself in the waters."

Hellevir followed his pointing finger, and saw a youth with reddish hair reclining by the water's edge, his head resting on his hand. He was trailing his hands in the water. Hellevir got to her feet and went over to him, acutely aware of the watcher at her back.

"Ionas?"

He glanced up, smiling lazily. He'd disturbed the stillness of the water, and the ripples were frozen around his hand.

"Oh, no, thank you," he said. "I'm tired today."

"I've come to take you home."

"You're sweet, but I'm already seeing another boy."

She thought she heard a laugh behind her. Her patience frayed. She sat down beside him.

"I need to ask you something," she said. To her surprise, he winced.

"No," he said. "No duels for me. I've had too much to drink."

"Do you know anything about who poisoned the Princess?" she asked.

"I said no, you won't goad me, Haralt."

"Please," Hellevir insisted. "Were you at the dinner? Is there anything you can tell me?"

He turned to look at her, face creased in an expression so hostile that for a moment it took her aback.

"How dare you!" he growled. "You don't know my mother!"

"It's all right," Hellevir said quickly. "It's all right. I'm sure your mother's lovely." His expression softened, as if he'd actually heard her.

"She was," he muttered.

"So you can't tell me anything about who tried to kill the Princess?"

"I said no, you won't goad me, Haralt."

Hellevir sighed. "Come on," she said. "This is getting us nowhere. Up you get. The priestesses want you back." He grumbled as she pulled his arm, but got to his feet.

"I'll give the book back when I visit next," he said. "I'm not done reading it."

She held him by the wrist, looking back at Death. He was gazing down upon the seeds, and his hand hovered above them as if enjoying their warmth. She must have blinked, for when she looked again the seeds were gone.

"You'd better be worth this," she muttered to the boy. He grumbled something incoherently, casting his gaze about as if he'd lost something.

The man with the black eyes was on his feet and in front of her, and she started at his sudden movement. She wasn't sure she would ever grow used to the twitching speed with which he moved.

"You're forgetting something," he said, his tone a rebuke. Hellevir raised her head high.

"I haven't forgotten," she retorted. She let go of the boy and lifted her hand to her hair, drawing out the pin. She pressed the tip of her hairpin to her finger to draw blood. She winced; it was too blunt to pierce the skin. He watched her.

"Here, allow me," he muttered after a while. He took her hand before she could protest and pressed his nail into the pad of her thumb. She blinked as blood dripped freely. She hadn't felt a thing.

They watched as the blood pooled and flowed down the side of her thumb, and dripped three times onto the ground.

"What about the next riddle?" she asked. That smile, that pleasure in knowing what she did not.

"It's already in your pocket," he replied.

And she awoke.

*

She had moved between life and Death often enough now to know to brace herself against the flood of cold. It was still horribly unpleasant, and she opened her eyes feeling like she'd spent the night in a snowdrift.

The priestesses started, surprised.

"That was fast," the healer remarked. "Is that it?"

Hellevir put a hand to her head, feeling nauseous. "I was gone for hours," she muttered, thinking of the serpentine route through the corridors and stairs.

"No," the healer said. "Minutes." She pointed up at the time-piece on the wall.

Hellevir was saved from having to explain—and admit that she still couldn't read the time—by a heavy groan from the table. The priestesses jumped.

Hellevir got wearily to her feet and backed away as the boy sat up, resting his elbows on his knees and kneading his forehead with the palms of his hands.

"Onaistus, what a night," he muttered. He looked up blearily. "Sathir?" he muttered as he saw the healer beside him. "What am I doing *here*?"

The healer brushed his hair back, checked his pulse. She pushed back his shirt, revealing an unblemished torso. She stared at it for a moment, and then put her hand to his cheek.

"Ionas?" she said, voice high. "You're. . . ?" She seemed to stop herself from saying the word *alive*.

"I'm fine," he grumbled. "Just drank something unpleasant." He glanced down at his open shirt, noticing the dried blood encrusting his skin. When he looked up there was worry in his eyes. "Did something happen?" he asked. He caught sight of Hellevir. "I . . . do I know you?"

"No," Hellevir said. She tapped her shoulder, and Elsevir fluttered up beside her cheek. She glanced at the priestesses who were watching her, waiting for a plausible explanation. "You were in a duel," she told the boy. "You were too drunk to fight. You slipped and hit your head. The priestesses have been looking after you."

"I . . ." He shook his head, rubbing his eyes. "That doesn't sound . . ."

Sathir cuffed him around the back of his head, and he made a noise of complaint.

"And that's for the trouble of it," she snapped. She was angry, but Hellevir thought she might have been closer to tears than she looked. Hellevir considered briefly asking Ionas again about the poisoning while he was lucid, but she felt suddenly exhausted.

"I should go," she said to Edrin. "Could you lead the way? I'm worried I'll get lost in the dark."

CHAPTER NINE

Hellevir arrived back home feeling like she'd run a hundred miles. Her hand was clasped around the new riddle in her pocket, already malleable from her touch, and she began to recognize a new urgency, nauseating and clammy, that came with an unsolved riddle. She could feel time ticking past; at any moment someone else could need her, or worse, the Princess might be attacked again, and she would have no treasure to show for it. She had to find it quickly.

Salt in the wound
Will bring tears to the eye
By causing irritation.

It was infuriatingly vague. She didn't have the first idea where to look. *Salt in the wound?* How on earth could that lead her to anything useful?

It was still dark by the time she reached their canal, but the birds were starting to sing again and the swallows were darting over the water. The gate had been left unlocked for her, and as she went in she saw lamplight inside the house.

She could hear her mother and father talking, but their conversation stopped as she opened the front door. Her pa appeared and took her cloak.

"Was it . . ." He stopped, not knowing what to say. There was no real etiquette for asking whether she'd managed to raise the dead.

"Fine," she muttered tiredly. "He's fine. He doesn't remember anything." She rubbed her eyes. "I'm going to bed," she said, but her mother appeared at the doorway. She was still in her nightclothes.

"We need to talk," she said. Her tone was sharp. Hellevir's head began to hurt.

"Can we talk tomorrow?" she asked. "Please, I am so tired."

"No. We're talking about this now."

"Piper, the girl's dead on her feet . . ." her father started, seemingly oblivious to his poor choice of words, but Ma cut him off with a look. Hellevir put a hand on his arm. She stroked Elsevir, and patted her father's shoulder. Feathers flat under the tension in the room, the raven obediently hopped over to him.

"It's all right," she said to her pa. "Let us talk." He made an annoyed sound in his throat, but left them there, going down into the kitchen with the raven.

Hellevir joined her mother in the sitting room. Neither of them sat down. She could see into the courtyard through the window, and it seemed to her incrementally brighter. On nights like this, when she was awake to witness the slow grey of dawn as it began to wick away the darkness, it seemed so gradual a change that it took a moment for her to convince herself it wasn't her eyes playing tricks.

"What do you want to . . ." Hellevir started.

"You can't keep doing this," her ma snapped. "It's not natural." The blood in Hellevir's temples pulsed.

"I'm not sure it's unnatural," she said. "Death doesn't seem to mind." Her ma winced, as if she hated to hear names given to the formless evil that her daughter was communing with.

"It's against the natural order," she said, and Hellevir couldn't argue with that. "You're playing with things mortals aren't meant to play with. What you're doing . . ." She hesitated, pressing her lips together, then let it out. "It flies in the face of Onaistus. You're stopping people from being given his Promise when he sees fit to bring them to it. You're putting their eternal souls in jeopardy."

Hellevir sat down heavily in one of the armchairs.

"Ma, I don't believe in your ways," she said.

"Fine," her ma snapped. "Whether you believe in them or not, you're playing with things that you don't understand, little girl."

Perhaps it was because she was so tired, or because she was exasperated by her mother's constant coldness and the sneer in her voice when she called her *little girl*, as if she had no experience of the world, or perhaps just because it was so *unfair*. Hellevir got to her feet, fists clenched by her sides, and the words bubbled out of her, scalding on her tongue.

"I brought *you* back," she said through her teeth, taking vicious pleasure as her mother took a step away. "I reached into Death and gave away a part of myself to keep you alive. You'd be dead now if it weren't for me." She held out her hand, the knuckle white and bare. "Do you think this is just a finger? Do you think it's just drops of blood I give? It's parts of *me* that are taken, parts of my *soul*. I can feel it in me, the gaps. I gave up a part of my soul for *you*."

Her mother was shaking her head, tears glistening in her eyes. "You ruined our lives . . ."

"You keep saying that!" Hellevir cried. "Look around you! You're alive, you're in a good home, you've found your religion. I saved you from an early grave. What more do you want?"

"You didn't save me at all!" her mother spat, and the little girl in Hellevir—for there was still a little girl within her, no matter how much she protested—wanted to hide from the anger in her eyes. "You just made your own life easier! Lives are always easier when your mother's there, your wife, to take care of you all. You didn't care that I'd left a good thing behind for you, you didn't think to take it on yourselves to care for her. You threw her away so you wouldn't have to handle a harder life. *She* was part of *my* soul, and you threw her away!"

Silence filled the room. They stared at each other. Hellevir blinked and it released tears down her cheeks. She wiped them away impatiently.

"I was twelve years old," she said quietly. "I had the option to save you. So I did. I didn't think beyond the simple fact that I wanted you back."

"I'd made the choice already," her ma replied. "It was not yours to make."

Hellevir swallowed, her throat hurting from trying not to cry. Her jaw worked. They stood looking away from each other. The time-piece on the mantel ticked, and the birdsong outside trilled mutely.

"I'm not sorry I brought you back," Hellevir muttered. "I'll never apologize for that. But I am sorry I couldn't bring her back too. I did try. Death wouldn't let me. I had to choose, and I chose you."

Her mother stayed turned away, her arms crossed over her stomach. Her long dark hair formed a curtain between them.

"Then Death is an evil thing," she said. "Are you certain you want to be dealing with such an evil thing?"

"No," Hellevir replied honestly. "But I don't think Death is evil. He . . . it, they have their laws. Like winter must have its frosts." She took her mother's elbow, gently pulling her around. "I'm trying," she said. "I'm not just running in blindly. I'm trying to be careful, to pick the ones who have died too soon, who haven't had their lives."

Her heart cracked a little—she could almost hear it—as her ma shrugged her off.

"Ones like your sister?" was all she said. She left Hellevir standing there, her hand still half raised to touch her arm. She sat down where she was on the rug and put her head in her hands. Her hair fell around her, and she realized—absently, abstractly, absurdly—that she'd left her hairpin in Death.

Hellevir slept poorly. She had nightmares for the first time since she was a little girl. Nightmares about a lifeless bundle, stiller than a stone. She awoke at noon. Her hair was in witchy locks around her head, and she spent a long time disentangling them, letting her mind catch up with her body. She was exhausted, the fatigue sitting at the back of her skull like unkneaded dough. She went downstairs to find something to eat, but when she heard her mother's voice coming up from the kitchen, she turned around and went back up to her room.

It was Markday, the day she was due to visit Sullivain at the palace. She chose to walk, enjoying the fresh sea air, the sound of the seagulls overhead. Elsevir accompanied her, flying away only briefly to fetch her a dropped earring he'd spotted between the cobblestones, blue and slightly muddy but no less pretty. He sometimes brought her such things when he could tell she was unhappy.

"Thank you, sweet bird," she said, scratching the ruff of his feathers.

As Sullivain had promised, the galleon brooch allowed her instant admission to the palace. A guard agreed to take her in, and led her through the double doors. She was so absorbed in her thoughts, miserably turning over the conversation with her mother in her mind, that she barely noticed that the guard was talking to her, chatting cheerfully as they made their way through the high-ceilinged corridors.

"Our mistress likes to write her letters looking out over the canals," the guard was saying as she took Hellevir out into a courtyard and under an archęd tunnel. It took Hellevir a moment to realize she meant Sullivain, not the Queen. "She travelled as a child to other courts, and made a good many friends. She likes to stay in contact with them."

Hellevir glanced up at her, surprised by her familiar tone. The guard caught it and smiled.

"She likes to sit in the barracks with us, on occasion," she explained. "Her lady grandmother doesn't approve, but we let her have a drink of rum and tell her about the places we've been stationed. I think she'll be a great traveller when she's sovereign. It's the stories she comes to us for, not the rum."

Hellevir didn't know what to say to that. She hadn't expected to hear such fondness for the Princess. She stroked Elsevir as they walked through the gardens. The trees and shrubs were in full bloom, the grass carefully tended and shaped.

Sullivain was sitting in a small parapet of the wall overlooking the waters of the lagoon. A slim table had been set out for her, and she sat writing away on reams of papers, wetting a quill pen now and then, her forehead tense as she frowned down at the missives. She brushed her flyaway hair from her face. Several books held the loose papers down in the breeze.

"Your Grace," the guard said, halting behind her. "Miss Andottir, to see you."

"Thank you, Kélé," the Princess said, glancing back with a smile. The guard bowed and left Hellevir standing there as Sullivain finalized a letter. Hellevir's gaze drifted over the blue waters. The smell of the salt sea was sharp as smoke, and she breathed it in, glad of a moment to gather her thoughts.

"Not a bad place to sit and write, eh?" the Princess asked. Hellevir lowered herself onto a stone bench by the wall.

"It's lovely," she agreed. "But isn't it . . . exposed?" She was no expert on these things, but if anyone was going to harm Sullivain, pulling up a boat and shooting an arrow into the gardens wouldn't be difficult at all.

"No boats are allowed within a certain range of the walls," Sullivain said, rolling an ink blotter along her signature on the page. "No divers can fish here without permission. No one can access the gardens without an escort. You do sound like my grandmama." She folded the letter and dripped wax onto it from a crucible, its flame fluttering in the breeze, and pressed her signet ring into it. "Besides," she added, winking at Hellevir, "if anyone does get in and catches me off guard, I have you to bring me right back."

Hellevir said nothing, feeling uncomfortable. She glanced around, but none of the guards were within earshot.

"I am a finite thing, Sullivain," she murmured. "I'd rather you kept dying to a minimum."

"Finite, eh? Then why'd you raise that Greerson boy? Shouldn't you be saving yourself for me?" Sullivain tossed the questions over her shoulder like crumpled paper. Hellevir went still. How had she found out so quickly? She'd heard about the Crown's network of spies but that was *fast*. Sullivain glanced back when Hellevir said nothing, and gave a wry smile.

"Oh yes, I heard about that," she remarked. She pressed her seal into another stamp. "So, how much did they offer you?"

Hellevir blinked.

"You think I was paid to bring him back?"

Sullivain got to her feet, shuffling papers to stack them on the other side of the desk. Hellevir felt her shadow fall across her.

"Why not? I'm sure a lot of Houses would pay you a fortune to be their personal key to immortality."

There was a pause. Sullivain was watching her closely, copper eyes bright and curious. The thought had never even occurred to Hellevir, and she folded her arms, indignant. A skiff drifted past, its sails white as seagull wings and leaving blue impressions on Hellevir's eyelids.

"I didn't come to Rochidain to make a commodity of myself," she said quietly, trying not to snap at the Princess. "I came because you summoned me. Ionas Greerson had died and I could do something about it, it was as simple as that. I don't do it lightly, Sullivain." She glanced at the ground, remembering her words to her own mother. "When I give up parts of myself, it's not just my body. It's a part of my soul, or whatever makes me what I am. What I do will never be for sale."

"A part of your soul, how romantic," Sullivain remarked with a laugh in her voice. "I suppose I should be jealous, then, that other people have parts of your soul as well as me?"

"And are you jealous?" Hellevir countered. Sullivain stood over her, a smile on her lips. Hellevir jumped as the Princess reached over, but it was just to tuck a wayward lock behind her ear, her hand lingering a moment on the skin behind it.

"Perhaps," she said with a light in her eyes.

Hellevir fought for something to say, and found nothing. She didn't like how much the Princess seemed to enjoy intimidating her.

"Again, however, I must ask you," Sullivain remarked, "if you are so finite, why should I let you waste yourself on some boy?" She didn't withdraw her hand. Hellevir felt a flush across her neck as the hairs stood on end.

"I . . ." Hellevir hesitated. She swallowed. "I'd also hoped that by raising Ionas I could learn something. I've heard . . . rumors, I suppose. Rumors that the killer might be a noble."

"Is that so?" the Princess asked, eyebrows high. She flicked a strand of her hair over her shoulder as she returned to her seat, and Hellevir felt there was air enough to breathe again. The Princess rested her arm on the back of her chair, the thin fabric of her shirt straining at well-toned muscle.

"Yes," Hellevir pressed on. "And likely one who attended the dinner where you were poisoned."

"I see. How did you work that one out?"

"Everyone seems to think only a noble would stand to gain from your death. And if it was a noble, wouldn't they kill all who were at the table, unless they were there themselves? Don't all the Houses hate each other?"

Sullivain brushed the feather of her quill pen against her cheek as she pretended to think. Hellevir had the distinct feeling she was being mocked.

"Actually, they don't all hate each other," Sullivain remarked. "Well, they do. But most Houses have agreements with each other, informal alliances. What if allies were at the dinner whom the killer did not want to harm? That would explain why no one else was poisoned too, and the killer wouldn't have had to be there at all."

That's a point, Hellevir thought, a little helplessly. Sullivain smiled at her, a generous smile which made Hellevir feel like a child who had failed a task. "Besides, commoners do stand to gain," the Princess added with a wink. "They'd get a public holiday for my funeral."

"I appreciate your trying to unearth the killer," she went on. "I really do. But these theories, they're as thin as gossamer. You are not from the city, and I don't expect you to understand how it works. Further, I'm worried you'll only stir up waters that Grandmama needs quiet for her own investigations. If she found out you were trying to play the detective, she wouldn't be pleased."

"You . . . you don't want me to help?"

"I would like you to do your job," Sullivain said gently. "Which is keeping me alive."

The vague hope Hellevir had nurtured that she might be able to help find the killer quickly, and that it might be her key to going home, fizzled and died. It left her feeling oddly bereft, but not surprised; she realized that a part of her had known there was nothing to her theories. Thin as gossamer, indeed.

"Fine," she said, trying to hide her frustration. "In that case, I have your tea." At Sullivain's blank expression she continued, "You said you had trouble sleeping. I am your herbalist, am I not?" She untied a pouch from her belt and held it out. Sullivain looked at it, then her, in surprise.

"I didn't think you'd really bring me something," she admitted. "It was just an excuse to get you here and get you seen around the palace."

"So you don't need it?"

"I didn't say that." She took the pouch and undid the drawstring, sniffing the contents. "Well, it smells better than what the physicians give me."

"What do they give you?"

"Mouse fat and something." Hellevir had heard of mouse fat being used before, but Milandre had said it was about as effective as the old-fashioned use of dog's earwax, and only a little less disgusting.

"This is valerian root," she said. "Lemon balm and dried hops. Ask a servant to make tea out of a spoon of it an hour before you go to sleep. I saw some lavender in the garden; you should make an oil out of it for your pillow. A glass of milk and honey wouldn't hurt before bed as well."

"Milk and honey. Noted." Sullivain looked amused by that, as if the suggestion were quaint. Hellevir wondered how severe her insomnia was.

"Let me know if it makes the insomnia worse, or causes nausea. Valerian can be fickle."

"Noted again. My tea is fickle."

"I'll be on my way, then." She stood to go, but Sullivain caught her sleeve.

"So soon? I'm your patient, remember? At least play your part."

"Forgive me," she said. "I would rather go. I had a late evening. An unpleasant morning."

Sullivain eyed her shrewdly.

"What happened that could be more unpleasant than raising the dead?"

"I . . . nothing. It was nothing."

"Come now, we can't have my herbalist with such a dour face. What has upset you?"

It was an invitation to talk. To have a conversation less as threatener and threatened, more as young women sitting side by side. Hellevir had to stop herself. Her eyes were watching the skiffs, their slow movement hypnotic, and she almost tricked herself into believing she could speak freely, talk about her mother and their horrific argument. Sullivain had a way of looking at a person, as if the rest of the world were put on temporary hold, making it too easy to trust her. Perhaps that was why the soldiers were so fond of her; she listened. But this was the same woman who had threatened her, threatened her family. Who had done so with a smile.

"If that'll be all, Princess?" she said. Sullivain raised an eyebrow. She glanced at Elsevir on Hellevir's shoulder, as if he would give her the answers she wanted. She almost looked disappointed, before she turned her face away and pulled out a new sheaf of paper, dipping her quill in the inkwell at her elbow.

"Have it your way," she remarked. Hellevir felt a pang, realizing that the Princess had withdrawn from her. "See you in a week. If this fickle tea of yours doesn't work, you'll hear of it."

CHAPTER TEN

At her parents' house, a letter was waiting for her from Milandre. Hellevir opened it with relief, cheered by anything that reminded her of home and trying not to feel guilty that she hadn't yet written to let Milandre know she'd arrived safely. Sure enough, the letter started with *Where's my letter you little heathen?*

Life is dull here and I need entertainment. The chickens are as much company as the weathervane. You are in Rochidain, girl. Where are the stories and gossip?

Nothing has happened here at all. A summer storm flooded one of the lower fields. The wind was enough to shake the house down; I'm afraid one of its victims was the old cherry tree at your house by the woods, I saw it when I was out foraging. Almost the whole tree was uprooted, and the topmost bough fell and caved in one of the walls. I'm sorry, my dear. But at least the tree is not dead; the roots are deep enough in the ground to keep it growing, and the bark is fresh. It's still strong.

One thing I do envy is how close you are to the sea. The things I could make with some seaweed! I've enclosed some recipes here for kelp, which may be useful, just don't forget to wash and dry it first or the salt will make you ill. It makes a good wound dressing, too, at a pinch. I wish I could get my hands on some of the yellow iris as well; you can find it in the swamps around Rochidain. If you get out there send me some of the seeds, I'm sure I could grow it here. The roots are good as an emetic but the garden could also use some color to it. The seeds make a good drink too, but you have to roast them for too long for it to be really worth it.

That's the excitement of the village for you. Send me a letter or I'll complain to your father.

Hellevir read it aloud to Elsevir, sitting on her windowsill as they watched the world go by. When she had finished she folded it up with a smile, feeling a pang of heartache. She missed Milandre, she missed their cottage. She missed the garden, and wished she was there to help Milandre harvest the carrots. Her smile faded, as she wondered if she would ever get to return, but she didn't let herself wallow. She quickly penned her own letter back before she forgot.

"Anything you want to add?" she asked the raven.

"That I'm a better conversationalist than chickens."

"Oh, of course."

She folded it up and sealed it, standing up to take it downstairs to Pa. She paused as she looked down at the canal below, seeing her mother walking with Peer Laius back from the temple. They stopped in front of the gate, talking in voices too low for Hellevir to catch. She saw her mother shake her head and put her hand over her eyes, and the Peer gently rested his hand on her arm, his manner consolatory. He gave her a smile that Hellevir would have thought should be reserved for small children who had tripped and skinned their knees. Something in her balked at that smile on her mother's behalf, so condescending, but her mother just nodded and seemed to stand taller, as if taking strength from what he was saying. He patted her arm, as if to say *There, there, it's not so bad now, is it?* and opened the gate for her to enter the courtyard.

Hellevir sat back down slowly, not wanting to go downstairs with the letter after all if Peer Laius was in the house. Every time she met him she felt analyzed, assessed for her promise as her mother's daughter and a member of the Temple; every time she felt it she had to resist the urge to shout at him that she wanted none of his religion, nothing that would reduce her as it seemed to reduce her mother.

I raise the dead and talk to trees and birds, she wanted to shout. *Do you still want me in your white temple, before the altar of your god? Would you still want me if I told you I talk to dark things that pull me from the goodness of his Promise?*

A little heathen, just like Milandre said. Just like her mother said.

She felt suddenly angry. The anger was fueled by fear, by her conversation with the Princess, by everything that had happened, spilling into an outlet where she could hate without fear of repercussion.

The book Peer Laius had given her still sat by her bedside, gathering dust after days of her having lacked the stomach to read more, and she put it into the drawer out of sight. She couldn't shake the feeling, the unnerving suspicion, that Peer Laius and her mother had been standing at the gate and talking about her.

She paced the room, her arms folded, trying not to let her temper get the better of her, telling herself she was getting worked up over nothing. Telling herself that her anger had nothing to do with the coil of guilt that sat looped in the base of her stomach because she had never asked Ma about her country where she grew oranges for the altars. Guilt that she had never thought how lonely she must have been, out in the middle of nowhere, miles from her home in a foreign land. Guilt for letting her daughter die.

Salt in the wound
Will bring tears to the eye
By causing irritation.

Hellevir sat in her parents' courtyard reading over the second riddle and absently pinching off dead leaves from the pomegranate tree.

Just like the last one, the riddle seemed meaningless. It was difficult, but she didn't let herself despair; the last riddle had made itself clear to her, and this one would too, in time. She already had a small inkling of where to start looking, she hoped. Unease drifted around her like a thin smoke, coiling around her worries. She felt an odd regret about the last conversation she'd had with the Princess, wishing she'd stayed longer and explained her reticence. Her thoughts lingered on the Princess's touch on the delicate skin behind her ear, and she found herself reaching up half-consciously to brush her neck.

She heard her brother's footsteps tumbling down the stairs, and quickly folded up the riddle. Farvor put his head out of the door just in time to see her slip it into her pocket.

"Love letter?" he asked teasingly. She gave him a look.

"No," she said. "I'm not the one receiving gifts from suitors." She patted a small spray of white roses on the bench beside her. Farvor's smile could have lit a temple.

"When did these arrive?" he asked, picking them up and putting his nose in them.

"A little earlier. The note just says they're for you. Would you like a buttonhole?"

"Please."

Hellevir put the withered pomegranate leaves aside, nipping one of the smaller rose heads and slipping it into the lapel of her brother's waistcoat.

"He doesn't seem to care much who knows," she commented. Farvor shrugged, happily admiring his flowers.

"It's not so unusual for knights and squires to form relationships," he said. "It's generally accepted that it makes them a stronger team."

"And if there's a war, he'll take you with him?"

"Yes, as his arms-bearer. But he's not a Knight of the Court, not yet, just a People's Knight, so he doesn't lead one of the five armies. Without a war all I have to do is keep his books and make sure there's enough food at the banquets. It's very boring really." He glanced up at the sky, where the sun was appearing between the pointed roofs of the surrounding houses. "Speaking of knights, my lord is expecting us," he said. "Shall we go?"

"Let me put those in a vase for you first."

She went inside with the flowers in her arms and descended to the kitchen. Her pa looked up from a ledger he was writing in.

"Who are those for?" he asked, nodding to the flowers.

"Farvor, of course."

Her father laughed. "No need to sound so bitter. Your time will come." Hellevir frowned at him, indignant that he would assume she envied her brother, but he continued oblivious, "From his knight?"

"Who else?" she said. "He sends gifts every other day."

Calgir Redeion had invited her to the Redeion boat on the lagoon ostensibly to give her some tutoring on Rochidain and its politics, but Hellevir suspected her brother had suggested it as a way of cheering her up after her argument with Ma. The atmosphere in the house had been as sharp as needle points since they'd fought.

The beautiful pleasure boat had the name *Tranquillity*, written in curling gold letters along the hull. Lord Redeion the younger— or Calgir, as he insisted she call him—led them on board from their private mooring, offering his hand to Hellevir as she alighted. Farvor went straight to the table laid with food that Calgir had brought for them to enjoy.

"You got Ennean honeyed ham?" Farvor said with delight. "What a treat."

"You did say you liked it," Calgir replied. "I asked Uncle Auland to have some brought in." He looped his arm with easy comfort around Farvor's waist. Black hair and gold, they looked well together.

As they sat down to eat Calgir brought out a deck of thick cards, unlike any Hellevir had seen before. There were twenty of them, well-thumbed, each decorated with a different emblem. Some were animals, some objects. He laid them out in a grid, emblem facing up. She recognized the galleon of the De Neïds, but the symbol looked like it had been stuck over the top of something older. Their original symbol of the roaring lion, Hellevir guessed.

"My mother designed this game," Calgir said, "as a way for me to learn the Houses. Make sure I didn't embarrass the family by getting names wrong at important events. Each card represents a House, and on the back is the House name and family members, and any important facts worth remembering." He reached out and tapped a purple card decorated with a swan, closing his eyes as he recited. "House Hannotir, currently ruled by Lady Ava Hannotir and husband Lord Gavon Hannotir, adopted heirs include Saviron, Ella and Juyne. Notable industries, marble, iron and coal, with mines in Savoi, the Eastern Archipelago and the Chron." He flipped the card over, unfolding it to show a small family tree and key information in various inks.

"These are fun," Hellevir said with a smile, wondering if she could do something similar with her herbs to help her remember their properties. She felt rather than saw Farvor roll his eyes.

"I knew you'd like them," he remarked wearily. "Bookish types and their memory aids." Hellevir and Calgir just smiled at each other.

It was a pleasant couple of hours, learning under the gentle Rochidain sun, eating delicious food from all over the Redeions' trading routes, and listening to the sounds of the lagoon. It was surprisingly easy to quieten the worries that had been constant companions over the last few days and weeks. Her thumb absently worried the dog-eared riddle in her pocket.

As the sun began to set Calgir declared her an expert and gathered the cards away, pouring them each a glass of pale wine.

"You know," he said, "I was rather worried my party had frightened you away. It must have been overwhelming for you, new to Rochidain as you were."

"Not as overwhelming as the palace," Hellevir remarked. "At least I had you and Farvor to keep me company. Mostly." She cast her eye at her brother, who pretended not to notice.

"Ah yes, you're attending our Princess on a regular basis? She must trust you very much to keep you so close after the attack."

"I think the experience shook her," Hellevir admitted. "Although she would deny it. I think it'll help her a great deal to have the assassin found."

Calgir popped a slice of orange in his mouth. He didn't look at her but studied the fruit.

"It's such a sordid affair. I'd half-hoped Rochidain was past the time of assassinations and threats of war, but that was naïve of me, I suppose. Of course, everyone is convinced a noble did it." His tone was flippant. Hellevir exchanged a rather startled look with Farvor.

"You believe that?" she asked.

"Princess Sullivain . . . well, she's rather beloved by the people. The De Neïds are an old House; they claim they can trace roots back to the Nightingale War and the Antlered King, but even so she would be the first De Neïd to be born with the crown. It would signal the beginning of a dynasty, and not all the Houses are comfortable with that."

Hellevir shook her head, watching the sparkling lights on the marina which seemed so at odds with this talk of death.

"Are they so desperate for the crown themselves? Do none of them want a peaceful city?"

Calgir shrugged, as if it were a common point of conversation, but there was a tension in the way he looked out across the lagoon.

"It's complicated. It's not so much about winning the crown as gaining from the chaos a war would cause. In war, some Houses benefit, some lose out. It leads to a reshuffling of hierarchies, a mix-up of assets. Loyalties are rewarded with trade routes and ships by whomever wears the crown, allies get a chance to move up the pecking order. But each House has its own fingers in various pies, which the Crown can't always touch. Overseas connections and networks and such, which also bring benefits to the victor."

Hellevir shook her head, bewildered.

"It's all about money?" she exclaimed.

Farvor snorted, his wine stem resting on his stomach. "Poor, sweet, baby sister," he commented. "It's always about money."

"It's about trade," Calgir amended. "The old royals, the Bergerads, House of the Gull, demanded too big a slice, and that's one of the reasons why civil war broke out, spearheaded by the De Neïds. Although to be honest the De Neïds aren't much better." He regarded his wine. "I probably just committed treason by saying that," he remarked.

Farvor clinked his glass to Calgir's.

"You anarchist, you," he teased.

Hellevir leaned forward, interested.

"Out in the sticks no one could really tell me about the politics," she said. "Or they weren't willing to remember anything about the war."

"I don't wonder why. Villagers were in the thick of it, not part of the politics but suffering for them."

Hellevir scowled down at the olive she was pushing around her plate.

"It never occurred to me that anyone would want war."

"If no one wanted war, war wouldn't happen," Calgir pointed out gently. "But it's not everyone," he said with a smile, perhaps seeing how troubled she looked. "I for one enjoy peacetime Rochidain."

"Says the man who fences every morning at dawn," her brother commented.

"Fencing is a peacetime sport," Calgir objected, sitting forward in his chair. "During wartime it seems to me bad taste to pretend at swordplay. Fencing is an artform, a combination of chess and dance, of . . ."

"'Strategy and grace,'" Farvor continued for him. "'Mind and body in tandem.'"

Calgir laughed, a healthy sound that rolled over the waters.

"Says the country lout who would rather use a sling. Mock me all you like, it's the gentleman's sport."

"So you want me to treat you like a gentleman, do you?" Farvor had a glint in his eye, and Calgir blushed a deep scarlet to the roots of his hair. Hellevir chuckled and choked on her wine, her eyes streaming as Calgir thumped her on the back.

That night she and Farvor arrived home tipsy and giddy. Farvor was singing at the top of his lungs, and although Hellevir kept shushing him she found herself laughing too much to really mean it. They fell through the gate and Hellevir collapsed beside the fountain, trying to ignore the rolling of her stomach and her spinning head. The lamp of her parents' room was lit and she hushed Farvor as he yawned loudly.

"You look like you need some water," Farvor commented. She didn't know how he wasn't on the floor; he'd drunk twice as much as her or Calgir.

"Mint," Hellevir muttered. "Fennel. Honey. Tomato juice."

"Not one for hair of the dog?"

"Fennel. Honey. Peppermint tincture. Willow bark. Boil one spoon of dried bark in water for a decoction."

"I can do fennel and honey and peppermint, but I might leave the tinctures and decoctions to you. Why tomato juice? Never mind, one minute."

She watched him vanish inside, feeling suddenly very fond of him. She saw the kitchen lamp brighten through the low window set into the foot of the wall. The light reflected in a pair of eyes and she jumped, but it was only one of the canal cats. He came over and leaped onto the bench beside her. He let her stroke his glossy black fur.

"You're out late," she told him. The cat gave her a haughty glance and deigned to speak.

"Night is our time," he said. "We prefer the quiet to your bustle." She scratched him behind the ears, and he purred. Hellevir was distantly aware of the clatter of her brother in the kitchen through the front door.

"We seem to make just as much bustle at night, in Rochidain," Hellevir commented.

"Yes, you can be loud," the cat remarked, rolling onto his back to accept stomach rubs. He put his teeth around her finger when she stroked him incorrectly, but didn't break the skin.

"If it's any consolation," Hellevir said with a sigh, scratching his chin instead, "I don't always like it either." Her stomach churned a little and she closed her eyes, wondering where her tea was. "Here it's all a little fast. The dancing here is like a whirlwind, but I used to enjoy the dances at home."

"We like dancing too."

"Cats like dancing?"

"Oh yes."

Hellevir was about to ask what a cat dance looked like, when a voice cut across the night.

"What are you doing?"

Hellevir glanced up to see her mother standing at the door in her nightdress, pulling her shawl around her shoulders. Hellevir gestured to the cat.

"Just playing," she said. "Farvor is fetching me tea."

"You were talking to it, weren't you?"

Hellevir sighed.

"Yes," she admitted.

"Why?" It seemed the only question that came to her mind, a single baffled syllable.

"What do you want me to say?" she asked her mother. "I talk to things. You know I do." Her ma glared at the cat, and his green eyes stared back, tail twitching. Her ma put her fingers to the bridge of her nose.

"I can't do this anymore," she muttered. Hellevir wasn't sure if it was to herself or not.

"He's just a cat," Hellevir pointed out. The cat's ear twitched at being referred to as *just* a cat.

"'He's just a cat,'" Ma repeated. "Hellevir, I can't do this. 'He's just a cat.'"

Hellevir shook her head, as much to clear it as out of bewilderment.

"What are you talking about?" she asked.

"You speak to things no one else speaks to. And you . . ." She seemed to have trouble saying it. "You bring back people. Nothing about you is natural."

Hellevir bristled, feeling too tired for this discussion. Sensing he wasn't going to get any more attention the cat jumped down from the bench and slipped under the gate into the night.

"I can't be someone I'm not," Hellevir remarked curtly, wishing Farvor would hurry up with that tea.

"No," her mother conceded, and somehow Hellevir disliked the resignation in her voice more than she would have any anger. "No, I see that now. You're too far gone." Hellevir saw her swallow and turn away. "Tomorrow I want you to leave," she said. "Go and stay at the Order. I don't want you here. The Peer was right about you."

She turned and left before Hellevir could gather her wits enough to realize what had just happened. Farvor came up the stairs and said a cheery good-night to his mother as she passed, and put a hot cup of peppermint-smelling tea on the bench beside Hellevir. He seemed to notice her expression for the first time, and he frowned, worried.

"What's wrong?" he asked. "Do you feel unwell?" She said nothing. She just turned her head towards him, her mouth slightly open as if she was trying to gather the words but they kept evaporating from her tongue.

"Hellevir? What's happened?" He took her hand. He seemed surprised when she just started crying, his eyes growing wide with worry. He let her put her head on his shoulder until she gathered herself enough to tell him what Ma had said.

Her mother had meant it. The next day she woke Hellevir early, and told her she'd sent a message to the Order of the Nightingale to expect her.

Hellevir numbly packed her bags as the sound of her parents' arguing came up the stairs, her father's voice louder than she'd ever heard it. Farvor helped her, his face stony. When they were done he looked at the bag with his jaw clenched. Hellevir put her hand on his arm.

"It's for the best," she found herself saying, knowing on some level that it was true. "I was upsetting her sense of order."

He shook his head, disagreeing not with her but with the whole situation.

"But why now?" he asked. "After you talked to a *cat*?"
Hellevir shrugged tiredly.

"I suppose it was the final straw," she said. "Just one more thing about me she couldn't bear."

They descended in silence, Farvor carrying her bag. The arguing downstairs stopped as soon as their feet could be heard on the staircase, and when they reached the bottom Pa was waiting. His expression was black. Her mother stood behind him with her arms folded and her head held high, as high as Peer Laius had taught her.

Pa took Hellevir's hand, his eyes hooded.

"You don't have to go," he said darkly. "This is my house. You can stay if you wish it."

"Pa, I . . ."

"No, I mean it. You can stay."

Hellevir put her arms around his neck, breathing in the leather smell that he always seemed to have even when he wasn't wearing his coat.

"It's all right," she said into his shoulder. "I understand why. I think it's best."

He heard her mechanical words, knew them for the rehearsed lines they were, and held her tight.

"Some people don't know the gifts they have," he muttered.

"I'll be all right."

"I know you will. That's not the point." He drew back, shaking his head. "You're not far, at least," he said gruffly. "It's not like I'll never see you." She quelled the part of her heart that asked why he wasn't doing more to make her stay, why she was being cast out instead of her mother, and realized that it was because he knew she could handle it. Her mother might not have been able to. That was enough for her.

"No," she agreed.

He stroked her cheek, his eye lingering sadly on the lion pendant on her chest.

"Lion-hearted girl," he said without smiling.

They left through the courtyard gate, Farvor with her bag. Hellevir heard her ma start to speak to her father, but he silenced her.

"Not a word, woman," he snapped. "I have no patience for you."

CHAPTER ELEVEN

Autumn was beginning to threaten Rochidain already. Hellevir could feel a cold edge on the air.

She sat on the banks of the river by the willow tree, watching the moonlight play upon the water. Sleep had evaded her, and the cool night had seemed a thousand times more welcoming than the cloying, clammy sheets, the darkness of her chamber. Her cloak was wrapped tightly around her shoulders, and Elsevir rested against her neck, his feathers cool against her cheek.

She'd been at the Order for four days. Her brother had sent word that he'd left their father's house as well to live with Calgir, and she worried about her pa all alone. She felt tired, unable to muster the energy to visit him, or to solve riddles, or to do anything that she knew was important.

She understood. She really did. She understood why her mother didn't want her in the house, that she was just afraid of something she didn't understand. Afraid of the damage it would do the rest of her family, to their standing among the Peers, to their immortal souls. And she understood why her father hadn't tried harder to keep her there. He knew as well as she did that the best place for her was somewhere she could do what she had to do in relative peace.

She understood it all. Perfectly. So why did it feel like there was a hole in her chest, as bloody and raw as if a real blade had been plunged into her? She knew the truth, the facts, but her heart just wasn't listening, because it felt like she'd been cast aside. It was startling, the level of pain. She'd been in and out of Death, she'd been threatened and intimidated, she'd even been left behind once before when her family had come to Rochidain, and it had never hurt as much as this.

Childish, she told herself. *It's for the best, you know that. It was time you left at any rate, you're a grown woman.*

But the pain didn't care what she thought she knew. She took in a deep breath, letting it out slowly as if she could release some of her unhappiness up into the quiet night sky. The river at her feet rustled past, talking to itself, and she listened with half an ear. As she watched, the river raised its head, hair long with weed, fish eggs tangled in its tresses, and rested its cheek on its arm as it regarded Hellevir with stone eyes washed bright by the water.

"Hello," Hellevir said quietly. The river spirit grinned at her with sharp teeth, before sliding back under the waters. Hellevir watched where it had vanished, feeling a little better. Here, at least, she wouldn't have to hide what she was.

The boat came from the palace to collect her the next morning. Hellevir shouldn't have been surprised that the Princess knew she was no longer with her parents. The servant in red who usually met her, Bion, she believed he was called, a tall man with a well-manicured beard, led her to the captain's rooms that Sullivain had commandeered for herself. The Princess was sketching, her fingers black with charcoal, and didn't seem to hear the door open. Hellevir had been worried that Sullivain would be annoyed with her after the sour note of their last meeting, but any strain melted in the soft sound of the scratching on the paper. Sullivain hummed to herself as she worked. Hellevir waited patiently, enjoying the chance to let her eyes wander over the books, the chess set, the numerous bits and pieces cluttering the shelves from their owner's various travels. She liked this room.

"What do you think?" Sullivain asked, standing up to lift the picture, and blowing the loose charcoal away. "A good likeness?"

Hellevir blinked. The Princess had drawn Elsevir. He had a gleam in his eye that she knew well, as if he'd just seen something shiny. It was good. She exchanged a glance with the bird on her shoulder and he began to preen, clearly pleased that someone thought him so handsome.

"A very good likeness," Hellevir said. "I didn't know you liked to draw anything but swords."

"I'm expanding my repertoire." She put the drawing to one side. "Here, coat, please." Before Hellevir could protest, the Princess was unbuttoning her jacket.

"What are you . . .?" Hellevir began, alarmed.

"It's your turn." She must have seen something in Hellevir's expression to amuse her, and winked. "Just the coat, don't worry." She slid it from Hellevir's arms, draping it over the couch, and then took Hellevir's shoulders and guided her backwards until the couch pressed into the back of her knees and she had no choice but to sit. All the while, Hellevir's heart was lodged firmly in her throat, acutely aware of every motion Sullivain made.

"You want to draw me?" Hellevir made herself ask. Sullivain went back to her easel and drew out a fresh sheet of paper.

"I need practice with Galgoric features." It was the first time anyone had ever referred to her as Galgoric. She wasn't sure how she felt about it.

"I'm only half Galgorian."

"Your mother, I understand? She's in your high cheekbones, your eyes. Sit, please. Face to the window." Hellevir tried not to feel self-conscious as Sullivain studied her by the light streaming through the big bay windows, sketching broad strokes across the paper. Hellevir felt suddenly like she'd forgotten what the natural resting state of her face felt like. "Goodness, herbalist, relax. You'd have thought I was using you as target practice at the archery range. Sit back a bit."

Hellevir watched her as she sketched. It was easy enough, as the Princess never met her eyes, instead studying her hair, the line of her jaw. When she concentrated, a thin line formed between her eyebrows. Hellevir remembered the first time she had laid eyes on her, not the body on the table but in Death, her hair golden against the grey half-light. She remembered thinking how striking the Princess was. The sunlight caught the finer filaments of her hair, made them almost glow.

"I understand you aren't living at home anymore," Sullivain remarked, rubbing at the page with the side of her hand.

"It . . . wasn't working."

"Can I ask why?"

Hellevir hesitated. It felt too raw to talk about, the edges still painful to the touch. Sullivain caught her reticence, and glanced at her over the paper. Hellevir found herself speaking before she could rethink the wisdom of it.

"My mother is Onaistian," she said quietly. "She sees what I do as a breach of her faith. We had an argument last week and . . . well, one thing led to another."

Sullivain nodded, as if she'd suspected as much. "This argument, it was what was upsetting you," she said. "Last week."

"I . . ." Hellevir was surprised she had remembered. "Yes, yes it was."

"Grandmama had similar worries, once," the Princess remarked. "After you brought me back. If we fall from the Path of Light, from the Pillars that Onaistus has set us, we don't get eternity in his embrace when we die." She spoke as if she were intoning a lesson. "We become nothing. Forgotten, like we never were." She glanced up with a shrug, as if it were a normal thing to believe. "Grandmama was worried that she'd damned me to nothing by having you raise me. She got over it quickly, though." She snorted, a half-smile playing on her lips. "Silly fear, really. It's not like I'm on the way to the Promise anyway. The nothing already awaits me." It was a heavy thing to say, with a twist of bitterness, but before Hellevir could ask her about it she went on. "You know," she suggested without looking up, "you could come and stay at the palace. We have rooms enough."

Hellevir opened her mouth, then shut it again. The invitation sparked a dual response in her. The notion of staying here, surrounded by the wealth of the palace, the courtiers, the servants, filled her with unease. But a meandering thought wondered what it would be like to be so near to Sullivain, seeing her every day. It wouldn't be awful. A glimmer, sparking somewhere beneath her sternum, played across her chest and along her skin. Hellevir did want to stay, and she didn't know what to think of this realization.

"I . . . I would rather stay at the Order," Hellevir made herself say. "But thank you."

Sullivain seemed surprised by this. "Whyever so?"

"Because they understand me there. They know what I am and don't pass judgement. Besides, I can be of help as a herbalist, use the trade I've been taught." *Because I don't think I trust myself around you*, she found herself thinking. *I find it too easy to talk to you, and I must be more careful.* Already she wished she'd kept the argument with her mother to herself. It was not something the Crown should know.

Sullivain stopped sketching, her blackened fingers pausing mid-air. She looked at Hellevir, and Hellevir suddenly had the feeling that she'd said something to offend her, but the Princess renewed her drawing, and said, "Tell me about your home village. I don't remember much of it. Only your mentor's workshop." She wrinkled her nose. "And that smell."

"That was you," Hellevir reminded her.

"Yes, well, it took a long time to get out of my hair. I had to throw those clothes straight into the furnaces."

"No wonder." Hellevir shifted, then stopped moving when Sullivain shot her a look. "I do miss the village," she admitted. "I miss the hedgerows, my mentor's gardens. But not as much as I did when I first got here."

"Herbalist, can it be Rochidain is growing on you?"

"It has its appeal." Their eyes met for a moment, a brief graze that sent a flush through Hellevir, an absurd sensation almost like freefalling, as if she'd missed the last step on the staircase, barely catching herself in time. Sullivain returned to her sketch with the edge of her lip twitched upwards. They didn't speak for a while; the only sounds to be heard were the scrape of charcoal on paper, the distant bustle of the palace, and the birdsong outside. The silence between them felt fluid, not completely tranquil, but shifting like the gentle back and forth of waves. Hellevir didn't hate it.

"Not my finest," the Princess said after a while. "But it'll do."

Hellevir shifted, a little stiff from sitting for so long.

"May I see?"

"If you insist." Sullivain stood and came over to sit beside Hellevir on the couch. Hellevir became very aware of the press of Sullivain's thigh against hers, as she turned the parchment around.

Hellevir found her own face looking back at her in smudged charcoal. The likeness was not perfect—the Princess had been careless with the shape of her hair, the set of her shoulders, done in quick blurred lines—but what troubled Hellevir was the look in her own eyes. The figure Sullivain had drawn looked deeply sad, her expression withdrawn, glancing at the portraitist as if afraid of what they could see and wondering—ineffectually—how best to hide it.

"Oh dear," she muttered, before she could think not to. Sullivain raised an eyebrow.

"You don't like it?" the Princess said. "No matter, I can do another." She made as if to rip it in half. Hellevir stopped her quickly, a hand over hers. The Princess's hand was cool, dusty with charcoal.

"No, don't," Hellevir said. "I don't . . . I've never seen myself this way. I don't know what to make of it. Is this how I look to you?" She'd had no idea she wore her heart in her features so much. This was not the face she prepared in front of the mirror every morning.

"One of the reasons I like your face so much is because you're easy to read," Sullivain said with a smile. "Not like the others of the court, who've been trained since birth to keep their features set in stone, to the point where I wonder sometimes how deep the ruse goes, whether they are stone to their cores." She studied her own drawing. "I think I've understood you rather well."

"Yes," was all Hellevir said. She realized her hand was still over Sullivain's, their touch growing warm, and quickly withdrew it.

Sullivain gave her a sideways smile, as if she'd just won an argument.

CHAPTER TWELVE

The sea was choppy that day. The boat hugged the shoreline, its
sail pulled taut, rising and diving with the swell. The sky was as
clear as a bell, for the time being, the sunlight striking glass shards
from the waves. The horizon was a fine thread from one edge of
the world to the other.

A wayward surge rolled over the deck and sprayed Hellevir with
salt water where she stood at starboard, her hand wrapped around
the briny mainstay to keep herself steady. She didn't care that she
was getting wet. She loved every second of it. Part of her wanted
to fall in among the waves, be carried away, consumed. She wanted
the sea to wash away the last week, the memory of the way her
ma had looked at her, as if she were an unknowable creature.
Another part of her kept thinking about the portrait Sullivain had
made of her, the candid way she'd caught the worry that Hellevir
felt was integral to her now. She was still trying to decide if she
liked how Sullivain saw her.

Pa came up beside her and took the back of her belt in a firm
hold. She gave him a look.

"It'd be just like you to fall overboard," he remarked. She had
to laugh.

"It's so *big*," she exclaimed, looking out over the waves. He
frowned at her.

"Is this the first time you've seen the ocean?" he asked, as
though it had just struck him. Hellevir nodded, enjoying the
feel of the wind buffeting her hair, blowing away her worries.
He shook his head. "Well, what kind of father am I, that I

haven't shown my daughter the ocean, and you here near a month?"

"I don't mind," she called over the wind. "I'm seeing it now." She leaned over the rail to look down at the waters cleft by the bow, and he tightened his grip on her belt.

"Just don't go seeing it up close," he told her. "If I jumped in to save you someone would have to jump in to save me."

Hellevir ignored him and raised her arms high, looking up at Elsevir flying overhead, a black speck. Pa glanced up at the bridge, but the captain was too busy controlling the wheel to pay much heed to the mad girl pretending she was a bird.

The boat plunged down into the trough of the wave, hitting the upward swell and sending a great spray crashing over them. Hellevir just laughed, shaking her hair like a wet dog. Her lion-headed pendant fell loose from her collar, glistening with salt water.

"Wild girl," she heard her father murmur.

They arrived at the town of Dunriddich mid-afternoon, salty and wind-beaten. Dunriddich was a smaller coastal town that had a little of Rochidain's grandeur in its high buildings and cobbled squares, but had been painted a few shades greyer by the relentless ocean wind. There were stories that the town—perched on the end of the headland—was where the winds liked to sit and swap stories about their different corners of the world.

Hellevir and her pa were visiting for two days so Pa could talk to some of the suppliers of the shop. She had agreed to come for a change of scene. But there was another reason why she'd wanted to come.

The first line of the second riddle was a constant in her mind, clicking around her head like the hands of a clock. *Salt in the wound.* It could mean anything.

So she did what she'd done for the first riddle; she guessed wildly, and took the riddle quite literally. Salt. Where in Rochidain could you find salt? Only by the sea, unless there was a salt mine she didn't know about. The signs would present themselves, the man in black had said, and when her father told her he was taking a ship up the coast, and asked her to go with him, she took it as one.

They will call to you when you are near. That was what the man with black eyes had said. But even if she was wrong, it was good to escape the city for a little while, to escape the Crown and its conniving.

Despite the whistling wind, the livestock pastured nearby was known for its excellent flavor, and for rarely yielding lean meat. Hellevir watched as some of the cattle were herded into huts by the harbor, ready to be taken by ship to Rochidain. They had great curved horns and shaggy coats she wanted to run her hands through. They were gentle, and let her stroke their noses.

"Are they slaughtered in your shop?" she asked her pa.

"No, at the Rochidain docks by their own farmers," he said. "Then they're brought to us."

"The farmers go all the way to Rochidain with them?"

"Yes, it's a tradition. They prefer to kill the beasts themselves. They sing to them before they do it."

Hellevir glanced up.

"They sing to them?"

"Yes. It soothes them." He looked up as the farmer came over, dipping his hat, and they drew away to discuss the business. Hellevir wandered over to the seafront, letting her eyes carry her over the waves. Elsevir pulled at her hair with his beak.

"It's too salty," he complained. Hellevir chuckled.

They turned back as her pa called her. He came over, his great coat flapping like wings about his legs.

"This might take a while," he said. "The farmer has said his son Griffud can show you around, if you like?"

Griffud turned out to be a ten-year-old who liked to walk along the harbor walls with his arms outstretched for balance. Hellevir joined him, putting one foot before the other on the uneven stones as the waves lapped a few yards below.

"So what is there in Dunriddich?" she asked. "Besides cows."

"There's the well," Griffud said over his shoulder. "You can make wishes into it."

"Do they come true?"

"I once asked for a pet and we found a baby rabbit at the end of the garden. I made Papa promise not to kill him. He's called Bim."

"A magic well, then. I could do with making some wishes."

"And there's the milk lake too."

"The milk lake?"

"Well, I call it the milk lake. It's white. Ma says something in the clay around here turns the water white."

"How interesting. Do you think the cows steal back their milk and keep it in there?"

He glanced at her with a look that suggested she was very stupid, and then seemed to realize she was joking.

"Well, it tastes funny. Not like milk."

"You probably shouldn't be drinking it."

"There are other places too. The Loom Lighthouse, and Alir's bakery. He does the best pastries. And there's Scar Bay," he added as an afterthought. "But Ma says not to go there, it's always too windy. A boy drowned out there last year. There're the old cairn lands, beyond the new ones. There are badgers over there."

Hellevir realized she'd stopped in the middle of the wall, and wobbled after him more quickly.

"Scar Bay?" she repeated.

He nodded, not looking back at her.

"I think it's because it looks like someone took a big sword and chopped the cliffs," he said, making a great slicing motion as if he were wielding a greatsword. "Ayre broke his arm trying to get down to the beach there fetching back that boy's body. Ma told me not to look but it was all fat and white."

Salt in the wound, Hellevir thought. She frowned down at the boy, wondering if it could be that easy.

"Were you put here for me?" she asked. The boy scowled.

"Well, yes," he said. "My pa told me to take you wherever you wanted to go."

"Can you take me to the bay?"

He seemed to think about it, but his mother's words clearly didn't have much clout.

"Yes, but can I pet your raven?" he asked.

Hellevir glanced at Elsevir on her shoulder, who looked like he'd rather dive into the sea. He endured a stroke on the head. Having taken his payment, the boy jumped from the wall and set off at a trot down the promenade.

Scar Bay was aptly named. As Griffud had said, it was as if part of the cliff had been gouged out, the red of the rock unnervingly like exposed flesh, and it reminded her of a man from her home village who'd split his lip in a bar fight, and forever had a cleft. She and the boy stood at the top looking down, the seagulls drifting lazily below them. The wind whipped at her coat. The tide was out, and had left a beach strewn with sea debris and rocks blinking with pools.

"Is there a way down?" she asked. Griffud pointed, and she could just make out an almost vertical path slipping this way and that down the rocks. He didn't seem to question why she would want to go down. She felt a little dizzy just looking at it.

"I might need all my concentration for this," she told Elsevir. "Can you stay with the boy?"

"What if you get hurt?" the raven asked, clamping his wings tight to keep from being buffeted off her shoulder.

"I won't. Besides, from up here you'll see if I fall." Reluctantly— and to Griffud's delight—Elsevir let himself be transferred to his shoulder. Hellevir took off her coat too and gave it to the boy to hold.

"If I fall, get help?" she asked. He nodded. She took a breath, and made herself start the descent. It was slippery, and her boots weren't made for it, but there were plants with roots embedded in the rock that gave a sturdy enough hold. She hoped. She reached the last couple of yards and skidded down them on her backside, resigning herself to filthy clothing.

The wind down here was less wild, but not by much. The tide crashed in the distance with all the menace of a building storm, and she cast about her. With nowhere else really obvious, she walked deeper into the cleft, balancing precariously on flat rocks that were slippery with weed. She wrinkled her nose at the salty stench. The further between the faces of rock she wandered, the quieter the wind became, and the more distant the world began to feel.

If she had been uncertain whether she was in the right place until now, the waterfall cast her doubts aside. The cleft was a natural formation, worn away by wind and the steady flow of water, a small stream which tumbled over the rocks. When a wayward breeze caught it, the spray was picked up and flung, gritty with the silt of the fields above, straight into Hellevir's face. Her eyes instantly watered and she blinked furiously, blinded. When her vision finally cleared, she saw at the foot of the waterfall a yawning blackness, the stream splitting over it like long white teeth. A sea cave.

"I suppose that's it," she said to herself, and picked her way over, still wiping the tears from her eyes.

The walls inside echoed dully with the splash of her boots in the rockpools.

"Hello?" she called. There was no answer besides her own voice. She went in further, trying not to shiver in the cold. The sunlight shone at her back, illuminating the floor, but beyond that she couldn't see deeper into the cave.

"Hello?" she asked again. Something cracked and she jumped, nearly hitting her head on the low ceiling. She saw movement in the gloom.

"I know you're there," she said, trying to ignore how high her voice had become. The cracking came again, and kept cracking and grinding until it sounded as if her own back teeth were beginning to fracture. In the dimness something jerked and flinched, sending a small tumble of pebbles and shells into the daylight around where she stood. Hellevir swallowed as something shifted in the gloom, turning over in the darkness.

"Won't you come into the light?" she asked. When no answer came she found herself growing agitated, the tide brushing against the back of her mind. She picked up a pebble and tossed it into the darkness. The vague shape flinched.

"Stop bothering us," it hissed like the ocean seethe. "Let us sleep." Hellevir heard something metallic, the scraping of an iron chain against stone, as the shadow rolled and creaked like breaking wood. The sounds, the groaning of metal and timber, made her think of the ship that had brought her and Pa to Dunriddich.

"I'm sorry to wake you," she said to what she could not see. "But you have something I need. A treasure."

The creaking and cracking stopped, sending another slide of pebbles and debris towards her. With them came the top half of a chain, long-rusted and green from the salt. It was pulled back into the shadows with an irritated huff that blew over her, smelling of seaweed.

"A treasure, it asks," the voice creaked. "A treasure to plug the gaps where the water gets in. It has many gaps, surely it must sink." She felt the owner of the voice peering at her, looking into her.

"Yes," Hellevir said. "Without it I will sink."

"And with it too." She heard a grinding, perhaps a salted laugh. "Sink like stone, like we did, like we did."

"What do you mean?" she asked.

"We bit and tore," it clicked. "Bit and tore and were bitten and torn, and dashed upon the rocks until there were gaps in our sides like yours. The ones we carried too were dashed, and the others from those we mauled."

"The ones you mauled?"

"Dashed and sunk and dashed, all the ones since then. The winds, the waters, they like to feed us. They like to dash too, they do. They bring us bones, they do, and blood, still dripping, when they crawl upon the beaches, thinking they are no longer at risk of sinking. Thinking that they are safe."

"Sailors," Hellevir murmured. "From shipwrecks." The darkness clinked as if with iron bracers.

"Wrecks, wrecked, wretched things," the figure said as if in agreement, jerking the indistinct shape of its head. "But none so many since we were made wretched too. All were sunk and all were dashed that day, but one."

"One?"

"He had our reins, he set us to our mauling, before we were wretches. He crawled and crawled across the stones, his bones run through his legs like needles." Hellevir tried not to flinch as it cackled, swaying with the sound of scraping salt. "Like all the ones that followed, crawling and wrecked things." It stopped moving, and she felt it fix her with its regard.

"But stories—no, not stories, not stories of wrecked blood and needles. It comes for treasures." Hellevir just nodded. "We have them here, come closer."

She obeyed, unable to make herself advance more quickly than a timid shuffle. The cracking sound, like trees being bent under heavy wind until they began to splinter, was making her head hurt. Her eyes could just make out the rocks and ancient ship-chains piled against the stony wall, but the figure in among them loomed indistinguishable and misshapen. She stopped, unwilling to go beyond the reach of the sunlight. It felt dangerous to do so. Her boot crunched on something, and when she looked down she saw she'd stepped on a bone. She couldn't tell if it was animal or human.

She looked up sharply as the figure came to meet her at the boundary of the shadows, straining and stretching with that awful cracking sound as if it were stuck to something at the back of the cave. The chains scraped against the floor.

"We have treasures, we do," the figure breathed over her. "A thousand of them. But the one we think it wants will not fix the cracks."

"Perhaps not," Hellevir said. "But they might stop me from getting more."

"No more cracks," the darkness lamented. "We tire of seeing broken things, though they feed us. It does not do to sink, we miss the time when we did not."

The figure moved with the splitting of wood, reaching into the darkness at its hip. Hellevir thought she saw it prying something from the cave wall, and wished she could see more clearly, but knew if she wanted to she'd have to step into the dark. The figure cracked its way up again, and into the daylight came a hand made of rotten timber. Upon its palm was an oyster shell.

"It's treasure," it hissed. The oyster shell looked unobtrusive, grey and unremarkable.

She gingerly took it in both hands. It was closed. The rotten hand withdrew, bits of stone and detritus dropping from its fingertips. Hellevir had the sudden sense she'd outstayed her welcome.

"Thank you," she said.

"It should let us be," the figure warned. "We're about to feed. It should not get caught with the other wretched things."

Hellevir glanced back, and to her shock saw that the water was visible through the mouth of the cave. It had snuck up behind her like a ghost.

She nodded to the darkness as it cackled and groaned with stone and old wood and chain, and hurried through the opening of the cave, the oyster clutched to her chest in one hand.

The sea was slithering across the rocks, filling pools here, crevices there, as it crept up towards her. The path that had led her down was still clear—just—but she'd have to hurry. She slid and skidded over the rocks, bruising her knees when she slipped. The mouth of the cave yawned behind her as if it meant to suck her back and swallow her whole.

It seemed an age before she reached the path. When at last she did, her boots splashing through the rockpools that seemed to be swelling even as she looked at them, it took another age for her to climb it. The oyster thumped against her leg in her pocket as she pulled herself up, searching for handholds and places that wouldn't let her boots slip. She paused for breath halfway up, and saw that the whole floor of rock had vanished beneath the sea. She shuddered as she saw the mouth of the cave gulp it greedily, the waves lapping about its maw, and continued her climb, her stomach churning.

When she was at the top a heavy hand gripped her by the shoulder and heaved her up. She gasped, surprised to be looking into the angry eyes of her pa.

"What do you think you're doing?" he demanded. He still had her by the arm and gave her a firm shake. "Are you trying to get yourself killed?" She glanced behind him and saw Griffud watching with wide eyes, Elsevir on his shoulder.

"I'm sorry I . . ." Hellevir began, but he just shook his head and pointed down at the bay.

"What fool would go down there with the tide coming in, eh?" he snapped. He was not the sort of man to shout, and she felt small before his anger. "You'd have drowned and your body would have been lodged down there for days!"

"I'm sorry, Pa," she said. "I had to. Please, just . . . I had to." He glared at her. He made an annoyed sound, perhaps seeing something in her that made him know she spoke the truth.

"We're going back to the inn," he muttered. He pulled her arm to take her back, but a shooting pain went up her leg and she hissed through her teeth. He glanced down and saw that there was blood on her trouser, and before she could stop him he'd pulled up the fabric to reveal a long cut down her shin. She must have got it from falling on the rocks, but she'd been so frightened of being caught by the tide that she hadn't felt a thing.

"We'll get that looked at," he said, getting to his feet. "What a state. And your ball soon, too." He lent her his arm as she finally felt the full pain of it, and led her hobbling back towards the town.

That night, lying in bed with her shin bandaged, Hellevir couldn't sleep. She swung her legs out of bed and hobbled to the chair by the window, where the lantern hanging outside the inn's front door cast a warm pool of light. Pa was sleeping in another bed by the further wall and didn't stir as she opened the shutters to let in the night air. The sky was starless and overcast; the hush of the sea, the gentle pulse of the waves, was soothing, and it lulled her.

She dozed, her head on her arms as she listened to the soft sounds. A half-dream disturbed her, a dream of roiling waves, and she saw a ship tossed upon them. Its figurehead was a carved boy, seashells all along his arms, an oyster shell in his raised hand. He grinned viciously into the spray, and as the ship dove down it hit the trough with a resounding crash, so loud that she awoke with a start.

She shook herself and sat up straighter, stroking Elsevir's soft chest. He leaned into her hand and closed his eyes, enjoying the scratches.

"I think it pitied me," she murmured, quiet so as not to wake her father. Elsevir looked at her with one ink-blot eye.

"The cave creature?"

"Yes. I think it saw a sinking thing and a part of it wanted to save me."

The raven cocked his head to the side. "And are you a sinking thing?"

"I hope not."

The raven nestled against her arm.

"What did it give you?" he asked.

Hellevir stirred herself, finding that her eyelids were suddenly heavy.

"I suppose we'd better look."

She reached into the pocket of her trousers, flung over the back of the chair, and pulled out the oyster.

"I've never opened one of these before," she said. "Do you know how to do it?"

"Should I use my beak?"

"If it won't hurt you." She held it up, and Elsevir lodged his beak into the gap between the two halves, prying and twisting. Eventually, it came open, and Hellevir pulled it apart. Inside was the oyster meat, and before Hellevir could stop him Elsevir had snapped it up in his beak and gobbled it down.

"Elsevir!" she exclaimed in a whisper. "Why would you do that!"

"I doubt your precious thing was the meat," Elsevir remarked. "Look again."

Hellevir resisted the urge to swat at the bird, and instead brought the shells up to the light. On each side of the shell was a pearl. Elsevir plucked each one out and dropped them into Hellevir's palm; they shone like teardrops as she rolled them around. They seemed a few shades redder than the pearls she'd seen on jewelry, but it was hard to tell by the lamplight.

"One less thing to worry about," she murmured, and closed her hand over them. She heard her father roll over, stirring from sleep. She heard him sniff.

"Hellevir," he muttered, his tone pained. "Why do I smell fish at this hour?"

"Sorry, Pa," she said sheepishly. He rolled out of his bed and knelt by the hearth, using a poker to stir up the embers of the slumbering fire.

"Why are there oyster shells on your bed?" he asked tiredly, rubbing his face. He'd clearly given up on sleep, instead encouraging a tongue of flame from the ashes.

"The caves, there was a creature. It gave me the oyster. The pearls will help me raise someone if I need to again."

Her pa glanced at her, the shadows heavy under his eyes, but there was a half-smile tugging at his lips.

"I can't pretend I understand what you just said," he remarked. "But I assume it's important."

She came over and sat beside him in front of the hearth, dragging over her blanket to wrap around them both. She put her head on his shoulder, watching the flames flutter in the draft from under the door. She thought she saw eyes peering at them from among the logs, but if there was a spirit, it was shy and didn't come out.

"Thank you," Hellevir said after a while. She felt her father shift.

"What for?"

"Just . . . for not asking. For letting me be who I am. Not being afraid of me. What I can do."

He humphed good-naturedly.

"The day I'm afraid of my own daughter is the day I've lost all sense of right and wrong." She looped her arm through his and hugged it to her like she used to do when she was a little girl, and he would tell her fairy tales by the firelight. "You're thinking about your mother," he guessed.

She nodded. She'd been trying not to think about it, letting the sea and the rush of finding the next precious thing carry her away, distract her. It had been a pleasant distraction. Her pa sighed.

"Your ma . . ."

"I understand it," she interrupted. "I really do."

"That's because you've got the most understanding soul of anyone I've ever met," he remarked. "It made me worry, you know, when you first came to Rochidain. That people would take advantage of it, abuse it." He shifted. "Your ma did try our ways, for years, when we lived by the woods. I have to give her credit for that. But part of her missed her own faith, and now that she's got it back . . . she clings to it more than ever. She's just afraid for you, afraid what your gift means for your soul."

Hellevir pulled away a little, looking up into his grizzled face.

"Gift?" she repeated. He raised his eyebrows, surprised.

"Isn't it a gift?" he asked. "Your ma is with us when she would not have been."

She smiled, feeling a flood of love for the old man, and hugged him.

"I like to hope so, sometimes," she said. "It's just nice that someone else thinks so too."

CHAPTER THIRTEEN

In return for her bed and board, Hellevir helped Sathir as a herbalist in the infirmary. Sathir was a strict mentor and seemed wary of her when she first arrived, but it turned out they had a lot to learn from each other. The priestess began to untense a little as time went on and Hellevir showed no sign of raising any more dead sons of noblemen.

The priestesses let her have free rein over the herb gardens, and the allotments became her little haven. The raised brick beds were overgrown with sage, thyme, mint and lemon balm, including some varieties she'd never seen before. There were perks to living in a trading city. The garden made her feel almost normal, like she was back in the village again and she and Milandre were in the kitchen brewing tinctures.

She was snipping some calendula to make an ointment for the wound on her leg she'd gained scrambling over the stones, and pointing out aphids for Elsevir to peck at, when she saw one of the priestesses approaching.

"Hellevir," she said. "There's a boat here for you."

Hellevir frowned.

"A boat? From who?"

"It has the royal insignia on the side."

Hellevir's heart seemed to rise and sink at the same time. It wasn't Markday, the day she usually visited the palace.

Oh no, she thought. She untied her apron and put it aside before following the priestess out of the front gates to the waterfront. A long boat was moored up in front of them, open-topped with three neat rows of plush red seats. The boatman tapped his cap to her, a flippant gesture at odds with the surge of anxiety his appearance had caused. He held out a letter with the royal seal. Numbly, she took it and cracked it open.

"Bad news?" the priestess asked, reading her sour expression as she skimmed it through.

"I don't know," she said. It gave no reason for the summons. A bad omen. She swallowed thickly, mindful of the two pearls in her pocket. "Can you let Sathir know I've had to leave?" she asked the priestess, who nodded, looking at the letter with open curiosity. Hellevir let the boatman help her down into the craft. Elsevir tucked himself into Hellevir's elbow.

The boatman brought them in to the edge of the marina at the royal palace, sliding the vessel in among the others like a dagger into its scabbard. He helped her to alight onto the jetty, where she was expecting Sullivain's servant in red, but instead a guard was waiting, hand resting on the pommel of his sword. Hellevir had to quell her disquiet.

"What's going on?" she asked, but he ignored her question and just gestured for her to follow.

The corridors they went down were clearly not used by the Crown, but by servants. They descended a winding staircase, the air growing damp, until they came to a room hewn from rough stone, the walls echoing as they walked. Bars crisscrossed in front of her, dimly lit cages with low beds and pails inside. This was the palace prison.

Are they arresting me? Hellevir thought with a stab of panic, although she had no idea why they would. Elsevir huddled close to her neck, as uncertain as she was.

The cells were empty except for one at the far back. Sullivain was there, pacing back and forth, her footsteps ringing, and Hellevir allowed herself a breath of relief that she was not dead.

Beside her, standing with the posture of a statue, was the Queen. Hellevir had not seen her since the night she'd raised Sullivain, despite the time she'd spent in the palace, and it struck her as absurd that it was here, amid these dark cages, that she laid eyes on her again. The Queen was talking in a low voice with a tall man dressed in the uniform of the City Guard. He had a pinched face and small eyes.

"Stop pacing, Sulli," the Queen said sharply to Sullivain. "It makes you look nervous." The three of them paused as Hellevir was led before them. The soldier bowed and departed quickly.

"This is her?" the City Guard officer remarked, looking Hellevir up and down as the Queen got to her feet.

"It is. Miss Andottir, come."

Hellevir did as she was told. Gods, she was anxious. Her whole body felt like it was made of lightning. She made herself bow, acutely aware of them all watching her. Even in the gloom of the prison cells, Sullivain seemed to glow, eclipsed only by the Queen herself. It was the first time Hellevir had felt her attention waver from the Princess, commanded elsewhere.

"How can I help, Your Grace?" she asked quietly. The Queen took her elbow and guided her past the officer and into the cell. Not knowing how to resist, Hellevir let her.

Inside there was a body. It lay at an angle, contorted from its final throes. Its skin was still slick with sweat.

"This man was the cook who prepared my granddaughter's meal the night she was poisoned," the Queen said. "He was discovered like this not long ago. Strangled, by the looks of it. Silenced before he could give us the name of his employer." She sniffed. "I will have to review the palace guards. We have another traitor among us, it seems."

Hellevir made herself look up from the man's twisted body.

"What am I here for?" she asked, afraid she already knew the answer.

"We want you to bring him back. We hadn't finished questioning him." Hellevir glanced at the City Guard officer, but he didn't seem to react.

"You told *him*?" she demanded, surprised at the anger in her own voice. "Are my secrets to be common knowledge?"

For a moment the Queen seemed taken aback by her tone. "This is the lead investigator into the attack. He needs to know such things. But that hardly matters. What matters is that you raise Loris." She said it as if it were a given that Hellevir would do as she was told.

Hellevir noticed marks on the body. Some older than others. Burns, cuts, bruises. His arm appeared to be broken. Marks of torture. She felt a little nauseous.

155

"No," she said quietly. She was surprised how easy the decision was to make, and by her immediate relief. Her hand had slid into her pocket, over the pearls, and she unclenched her fist, letting her arm hang loose by her side. The Queen made an astonished sound, placing her hands on her hips.

"No? He's the only one who knows who did this," she said coldly. "Someone paid him to put poison in my granddaughter's food. You're going to help me find out who."

"Grandmama," Sullivain said chidingly. "You're scaring my herbalist."

The Queen took a visible hold on her anger, and pointed a finger at Hellevir. Hellevir stood her ground, her own irritation spiking as the finger jabbed at her.

"You will go wherever it is you go and you will bring him back. I don't care what it costs you."

Hellevir could feel the Queen's ire, a thin sheen of oil across the depths of her fear. Fear that Sullivain would be attacked again, and that there was nothing she could do about it. Queen of so much, and yet she couldn't protect her own grandchild. But suddenly, Hellevir didn't care. She felt incensed. Everything she had endured over the past few weeks boiled within her, indignation at the constant anxiety, and she had to fight to keep her voice steady.

"No. I brought your granddaughter back from the dead, giving up parts of myself to do so on your sworn promise that you would never ask me to do it again." Elsevir ruffled his feathers in a show of anxiety, but to the Queen it must have looked aggressive, as she took a step back. "The dust had barely settled in your wake before Sullivain demanded that I come to Rochidain as her personal resurrectionist, threatening my family and forbidding me from going home. I have done nothing but comply with demands and threats, even trying to help in the investigation, and now you're saying you don't care at all what sacrifices I have made to protect Sullivain for no gain to myself. So no, I won't bring back your cook. I won't bring him back for you to torture and kill again when he's outlived his usefulness. I will not waste my self this way."

There was a beat of shocked silence. Out of the corner of her eye, Hellevir could see that Sullivain was smiling, hiding it behind a hand. Hellevir wondered how often people were brave enough to stand up to the Queen. Or stupid enough.

The Queen glared down at her.

"I feel I should make something crystal clear," she said, tone hard. "The threats Sullivain made to you when you first came to this city were not idly made, nor were they empty. It would be very easy for me to find reason for your brother to be dismissed from the Redeion household, your mother to be excommunicated, your father out of business, and for you to be thrown in one of these cold cells for disobedience to the Crown. It is a courtesy that we've let you remain outside the palace, comfortable. I would think very hard before shirking the duties we ask of you."

Hellevir swallowed, her mouth suddenly very dry.

"You told Sullivain to make those threats?"

"Indeed." She stepped forward, intimidatingly close. "With the knowledge that every threat made comes with the full weight of the Crown's displeasure, *my* displeasure, do you still refuse to raise the man who killed my granddaughter?"

Hellevir felt herself waver. It did change things, knowing that the threats came from the Queen; it made them seem more real, more enforceable. With Sullivain, there had always been the slim chance that if Hellevir refused to remain in Rochidain, the Princess would let her go, but there would be no such allowances from the Queen.

"I can't bring back everyone," Hellevir insisted more quietly. "There's not enough of me. If I save him, there's less to save your granddaughter if she's attacked again." A bending of the truth. The Queen folded her arms, jaw tight. An idea struck Hellevir. "But I don't necessarily have to raise him. I just need to talk to him. Will you let me do that instead?"

"What do you mean?" the Queen demanded tersely.

"I go into Death and talk to him—was Loris his name? I'll find out what he knows. He probably won't even realize he's dead."

"And I'm supposed to trust you to do this?"

"Yes. I brought your granddaughter back to life when no one else could. Even before your threats. What reason have I given you not to trust me?"

The Queen's eyes bore down on her. Hellevir made herself stand tall, raise her head as high, as her mother did.

"All right," the Queen muttered. "Be quick."

Hellevir released a breath. She sat down cross-legged on the ground by the body before the Queen could change her mind. She put her hand over the cook's, and slipped into Death.

The cold stung. She breathed it in, welcomed it, was relieved by its sharpness. The Queen, Sullivain, the officer, the dampness of the prison, vanished as if they had never been. She stood, looking around her at the empty cell. For a moment she was disoriented, casting around for the door of the prison that would take her above ground, but the more she looked the more she realized that there was no door, and no walls, just endless bars, endless locks, like a tangled hedge maze made of iron. It was so thick that she couldn't see farther than a few yards in every direction in the gloom.

She began to move through it, winding her way this way and that, unable to tell if she was wandering in circles. The rusting bars were uncomfortably oppressive in their closeness, their stillness, and the echo of her footsteps grew monotonous. Her confrontation with the Queen kept pace with her, a voice asking her what exactly she hoped to do if she did talk to the cook. She hadn't been able to make sense of Ionas Greerson, so why did she think this time would be any different? She dismissed the thought. She could only try.

"It'll be fine," she told herself, the words still as bone in the air before her, more solid than the iron bars. "It'll be fine."

The air brooded. The ceiling felt low, giving the impression of mounds upon mounds of stone and earth pressing down upon her. He watched her, she could feel his eyes tracing her through the iron bars.

It took her a while to realize that she couldn't go farther forward. There was nothing before her but iron, nothing but heavy air, but when she turned to retrace her steps, she found the way back was barred as well, that the bars had constricted behind her without her noticing. She was trapped.

Uncertainty gripped her, but she took a breath and leaned on the bars, looking through them. Death would appear. She waited in her cage, tried not to think of it as a cage.

It was the scent that told her to turn around. An earthy smell of moss and water, and when she looked back the fountain stood before her, frozen and cool. Still beyond her reach; the bars in front of her were thick, unbreakable.

"You are back so soon," the world murmured. "Back so soon. I wonder whether you can have had time to find another precious thing."

She sensed a thickening of the darkness and saw that he was before her, as if he had been all along. He watched her through the bars, leaning his elbows on them as he regarded her with those black eyes. He stood closer than she found comfortable, but there wasn't enough space for her to step back. It was hard to tell where the iron bars ended and the darkness of his cloak began, giving the odd impression that he was somehow pinned within the bars, part of them.

"I'm here to . . ." she started.

"I know why you're here. You want to talk to your Princess's cook. You are here, I believe, for a *visit*." His tone suggested he was insulted that she would ask such a thing, looking at her, as if she'd spat on the ground in front of him. He was angry, and she could understand why. This wasn't in keeping with the nature of their agreement. She was using Death, not to save lives, but because of politics. Even she felt unclean. She tried not to let him frighten her, but her memories of the void were stark. She didn't dare look at them directly.

"If you've been watching then you must know I don't have a choice," she said quietly.

"We have a bargain, you and I," the world said in her ear. "You bring me treasures, and I grant you souls. Death is not here for your convenience, and you should not be allowing yourself to become distracted by the politics of a city so rotten I can hear the flies hum from here."

"I don't want this either. But Sullivain . . . the Crown won't let me leave Rochidain."

"Yes, you are quite trapped. But it is neither here nor there to me whether your Princess's killer is found. Why would I let you disturb the dead with the insignificant quarrels of the living, if you do not intend to raise them?" The world shook with the violence of his tone. She stood taller.

"Because you lose nothing by letting me do it."

"I have nothing to gain, either. You're asking me to let you talk to one of the dead out of the goodness of my heart?"

"If you have one," she retorted before she could clamp her teeth around the words.

"Careful, girl," he warned, the world's voice low beside her. "I give you great allowances in letting you walk here."

"If I find her killer, they may let me leave Rochidain," she said quietly. She wished these bars would vanish. She felt so trapped. "Then I am free to find any treasures that aren't in the city."

He paused in thought, and the darkness hung still around him. She waited, her heartbeat growing heavier by the minute.

"Are you going to let me out?" she asked. "Or do you plan to keep me here forever?"

"He's by the fountain," he said, sounding displeased. The bars to her left were gone. She walked forward eagerly, glad to be free of the cage. As she passed the man with black eyes she felt a chill run along her skin, felt suddenly that he was about to reach out and touch her, but he didn't move.

Loris was sitting on the ground, his back to the low rim of the fountain. The heavy man had his head in his hands, as if protecting himself from something. As she drew closer she realized he was muttering, his voice high.

"Onaistus, Bringer of Light, keep me safe. Onaistus, Bringer of Light . . ." He was praying. Hellevir slowly knelt down beside him, wondering where he thought he was. Back in the palace prisons, or somewhere else?

"Loris?" she asked. He didn't seem to hear. "Loris?" She reached out a hand to his shoulder.

He reacted explosively, shaking her off and backing away.

"Please don't!" he cried. "I won't go back! You can't make me go back, please!" He began to sob. Hellevir raised her hands in a gesture of peace, watching him with wide eyes.

"It's all right," she said. "I won't hurt you."

"Don't take me back! Please, they'll brand me a traitor, hang me." He uncoiled suddenly and grabbed her hands before she could back away. "Tell them you found me dead," he begged. "It'll be better that way! Tell them I died fighting, or from some malady, just . . . not like this! Please!"

"Who do you think I am?" Hellevir murmured. She didn't expect an answer, and so was surprised when he gave her one, after a fashion.

"I know who you are, my lady," he said, still bowed over her hands. "I recognize your banners. My brother fights for you, for the new queen. My lady, I beg you. The fear took me. They conscripted us, we had no choice but to fight, but I'm not a fighter. Please understand, I'll do anything, just don't make me go back."

He ran away, Hellevir realized. *He's a deserter. Was it during the War over the Waves? Who does he think I am? Certainly not the Queen. A noblewoman?*

Whoever it was, they must have been lenient, or he wouldn't have lived long enough to become the palace cook.

"It's all right," she said. "I won't give you up."

He let out a sob, gripping her hands even tighter in his sweaty paws. "Oh, my lady, Onaistus be with you. Thank you."

Perhaps this is the way to speak to dead souls? she wondered, looking down at the crown of his head. *Play into the memories they're stuck in, guide them to give me the answers I need.* She had no idea if it would work. It was worth a try.

But as she watched him, crouched before her, she felt only a great swell of pity. He was terrified, reliving some cornerstone moment of his life. She felt guilty for using him this way, and wished she could make things easier, wished she could send him back wherever he had been, before Death had brought him before her.

He put poison in the Princess's food, she reminded herself. *Don't feel guilty about him.*

"It's all right," she said again.

"I'll repay you, my lady. Just say it, and it's yours." She thought quickly, wondering what the mysterious lady had said next. She wanted to keep the memory going.

"What do you have to give?" Perhaps if she kept her replies vague, capturing the spirit of what had been said rather than the exact phrasing, he would carry on.

"I can cook. Food to die for, my mother always said."

"All right," she hedged. "You will come to Rochidain and be my chef."

As soon as she said the word Rochidain, his demeanor changed. He stood up swiftly. He was a great deal taller than her, and it gave her a fright. In a moment, the harrowed, hunted look was gone from his eyes. He was smiling at her, leading her by the hand instead of cowering over it.

"Of course, the best in Rochidain!" he was saying. "From your own flock, of course." Hellevir followed, bewildered, wondering what memory she had triggered. "Try the sauce, my lady, all produce from your own plots. And the roast swan. Can I tempt you with a taste before the meal?"

"Er. Thank you."

"I chose the largest of the flock, the whitest, I could barely lift him! Such beautiful birds, a shame almost to eat them, but I've done him justice."

I'm so confused, Hellevir thought helplessly. *We're in Rochidain, and I'm eating a swan. This doesn't help me.*

Something niggled at her. Where had she seen a swan before?

"Loris, what House do you think we're in?" Again, that confused expression, as if he were finally seeing her for the first time. She desperately took him by the shoulders, scared of losing him again. "Loris, please, stay with me." He shuddered and withdrew, sinking down beside the fountain. A moment later and he was lost to her again, mumbling his prayers.

"Onaistus, Bringer of Light, keep me safe. Onaistus, Bringer of Light . . ."

"Loris . . ."

"I think that's enough of that." A moment later, the bars had curled up from the floor, thick as roots, thick as tree trunks, swallowing Loris and hiding him away from her. Protecting him from her. She looked back, coming eye to dark eye with the man in black. She started, but before she could back away his hand was on her arm. He didn't hold her tightly, but any touch as cold as his was harsh enough to feel like iron. She found herself apologizing, although she wasn't sure quite why. The tight grip reminded her of his hold upon her jaw, the darkness of the void shuddering at his back.

"You have disturbed the dead enough," the world rumbled. "I think it's time you left."

"I'm sorry, I didn't mean to hurt him."

The eyes, the darkness, the air, regarded her.

"You can't understand how ironic that is." She stared at him, not knowing his meaning. "Of course you can't. You say you don't wish to hurt him, and yet here you are, in service to someone who took such delight in his pain."

"I know." She flinched. "I know the Queen . . . she tortured him."

"No," he said. "I do not mean the Queen."

She blinked.

"The Princess? She did that to him?" The broken bones, the burns, the bruises . . . Sullivain did that?"

"Neither of them are innocents. Do you really think they will let you go?" he asked. "That you'll find her killer, present him to the Crown, and they'll release you?"

Hellevir stared at him. His tone was mocking, disbelieving that she could be so naïve. It felt as if she were being eclipsed, blotted from view. She drew her arm away, and he let her go.

"I have to try," she said, shakily, although she didn't really believe it at all, not anymore. "And you don't know Sullivain." He stepped closer, except she didn't see him move, he was just suddenly there.

"I do," the world growled. "I know her far too well. You have a bond, born from your traded souls. But your Princess, she may seem a woman made of fire, all the brighter to you because of what you have sacrificed for her, but you shouldn't let it blind you; hers is the shine of fool's gold."

"Why are you saying all this to me?"

"It is as you said. She's preventing you from finding my treasures," he murmured. "You cannot stay in Rochidain forever. Find a way out from under the Crown's control. For your own good."

Hellevir shook her head.

"Why not just tell me who the killer is? You must know." She knew he wouldn't, knew that it was somehow against the laws of this place to divulge the knowledge of the dead. She was already testing the limits by talking with the cook. It was infuriating. He didn't reply, and they watched each other in the gloom.

"I should leave," she whispered.

"Then leave."

She awoke. The cold felt like she'd just burst free from a block of ice. She looked up groggily into the Princess's face. For a moment she seemed worried, before she withdrew and folded her arms over her chest. The Queen stood behind her, eyes hard.

"That was swift," she remarked. "Did you get a name?"

"I . . ." Hellevir put a hand to her head. "No, not exactly." She stood, shakily, and Sullivain took her arm, steadying her. Her touch was warm, and for a moment Hellevir was distracted by it, surprised by the strength of her grip. To their credit, the royals were patient while she gathered her thoughts.

"He fled the front during the War over the Waves, and a noble found him but didn't turn him over as a deserter," she reported hesitantly. "Someone he called 'my lady.' I believe in return he offered to work for her as a cook in Rochidain, and felt he owed her still."

She didn't like relaying the information. It felt like a betrayal of Loris.

He was a killer, she reminded herself. *Why do I feel pity for him?*

"Is that all?" It wasn't enough; Hellevir could hear the archness in the Queen's tone.

"He was preparing a meal," she added. "A swan. They were in Rochidain I think."

The Queen did not react. Or rather, she went still, as if trying to hide her reaction. She said nothing, frowning down at the ground with her lips pressed thin.

"A swan?" Sullivain repeated behind her. "Are you sure?"

"Yes, he said as much."

Then it hit her. A swan, of course. She should have remembered the insignia from the cards Calgir had used to teach her the Houses. It was one of the names who had been at the dinner when Sullivain had been poisoned. The Hannotirs.

"Grandmama . . ." Sullivain began.

"Hush, let me think."

"But a swan, Grandmama."

"Perhaps the swan was a gift . . ." Hellevir suggested. But no, he'd said *From your own flock*.

"Only House Hannotir rear swans," the Queen interrupted sharply. "And traditionally only they are allowed to slaughter them." Her tone was grim. She wasn't pleased with this news.

"But that means Loris worked for the Hannotirs," Sullivain exclaimed. "Before he came here."

"We should find out for certain," the Queen said stiffly. She glanced over at the City Guard officer, who still stood by the cell door.

"I will renew my investigations into them," he said. "But you must understand, this doesn't count as evidence. Any number of people could have caught a swan from the canals without the permission of the Hannotirs."

"Miss Andottir said there was a noblewoman granting leniency. There are not many Houses with a matriarch."

"Your Grace, the girl saw a roast swan. To assume it leads to the Hannotirs is speculation at best." He glanced at Hellevir with a sneer. "And misplaced trust in the word of a heathen who claims to speak to the dead at worst."

Hellevir narrowed her eyes, but before she could reply the Queen cut him off with a sharp gesture of her hand.

"This 'heathen' has done more for House De Neïd than you could hope to achieve in a lifetime," she said. "She's done her part. Now you do yours. You have a place to start. Find evidence."

"Yes, Your Grace."

"But quietly. They shouldn't know they are under suspicion, or they may flee Rochidain. I won't have them vanish before we can find the truth."

He left. Hellevir realized Sullivain was still taking a lot of her weight, and for a moment hesitated, recalling the rumbling words the man with black eyes had said to her. What had he meant, that Sullivain was fool's gold? They were bound, she knew it, felt it, but his speaking it aloud gave it a solidity, a permanence, she hadn't let herself acknowledge. And what he had said about her being fire, brightness, as if Sullivain were some obsession of Hellevir's . . . The thought angered her, made her want to march right back into Death to demand to know what he meant. Abruptly she stood straighter, standing on her own two feet. Sullivain's hand brushed her arm as it dropped away, and Hellevir tried to ignore the trailing warmth it left on her skin. She was standing so close behind her, Hellevir could almost feel her heat.

"I'm disappointed you couldn't get a name," the Queen said, her tone like the iron bars that had held her. "But this is more than my network have been able to unearth. Loris has been working for us since Sullivain was a child, and before that I thought he worked somewhere in the country, so even if it was not Lady Hannotir you saw, this warrants investigation. Regardless, you've helped. We'll see if the Guard can find anything, although . . . I must admit, I wouldn't have expected this from her. Least of all her."

The Queen shook her head.

"We should put the body on the walls," Sullivain said with a casualness that completely belied what she had just said. Hellevir found herself staring at her, shocked. "Send a message to the city that this is what's in store for traitors."

Her grandmother scowled.

"I haven't used the battlement pikes since the War over the Waves," she mused. "But you're right, we must act strongly. We can't appear to show clemency for such a crime."

They both seemed to realize Hellevir was still standing there. She mastered her expression quickly, looking down at the stone floor. She felt them exchange a glance.

"Ava Hannotir will be at the ball, Grandmama," Sullivain remarked.

How can she talk of the ball with a body two paces from her, Hellevir thought, *and in the same breath suggest putting it on a pike?*

"Yes. You will have to put on a convincing act, my dear. She can't know we suspect her."

Sullivain grimaced. "I've had to pretend to like her for twenty-three years; I'm sure I can do it for another evening," she remarked. Her gaze slid to Hellevir. "You will still come, won't you?" she asked. "I heard Calgir Redeion invited you."

"I . . . yes."

"Good, I will need an ally. You'll be my first dance, and we can gossip about how poorly Ava is dressed together."

Her nonchalance was almost impressive. Hellevir glanced at the Queen, and saw the royal studying her, eyes narrowed slightly.

"You may go, Miss Andottir," she said.

CHAPTER FOURTEEN

The ball was to be on the pleasure boats along the royal canal surrounding the palace. Hellevir was dreading it. She'd rather have spent the time in Death than dressed up and feeling like a troll compared to all the noblemen and women of the court, pretending there weren't threats in every dark corner and a pair of pearls in her pocket just waiting for a body. But Sullivain had expressly told her to be there; and what the Princess wanted, the Princess got. The one saving grace was that Farvor, as Lord Redeion's squire, was also required to attend.

Hellevir chose an outfit with a dark green bodice, beautifully embroidered in gold, which flowed in strips over dark trousers. She pulled at the sleeves of her jacket, wishing the material on her wrists was less scratchy. The lion pendant her father had given her sat under her collar, hidden and warm against her heart, a counter to Sullivain's golden brooch, pinned cold and glinting to her lapel. She turned to look at herself in the mirror of her room, and wished again that she didn't have to go.

Loris's body had appeared on the battlements that evening, speared through the chest on a pike. She'd never seen anything like it, had never expected to in a city she associated only with clean waters and bright houses, but she had heard enough stories of the War over the Waves from Pa to know one body on a pike was nothing in the grand scheme of what the De Neïds had done to win the crown. When she'd talked to Pa about it, he'd just shrugged.

"Honestly, I'm surprised they didn't hang him publicly the

moment he was arrested," he remarked. "The Queen is getting soft in her old age." His nonchalance took her aback, and she began to realize just how sheltered her life had been in their little village by the woods. She told herself she was just too used to the ways of her village, to a time of peace, but even so it left a sour taste in her mouth. Perhaps it was because she'd talked with Loris, had known him.

As they made their way to the palace by boat, Farvor put a hand on her arm to stop her from tugging at her sleeve fabric, and left his hand on hers to reassure her.

"Are you nervous?" Calgir asked from the seat opposite her as they travelled to the ball by canal boat.

"I don't know what to expect," she replied. In honesty, she'd been nervous since she'd left the palace the day before.

"I'm afraid it will be rather like the dinner at my house," Calgir said with an apologetic wince. "But Farvor will look after you, I'm sure."

Hellevir doubtfully raised an eyebrow and Farvor elbowed her.

At first it was surprisingly easy. They embarked onto the broad pleasure barges as a group, she and Farvor trailing at a respectful distance behind the knight and his friends, and were greeted with a glass of pale wine and the rich smell of good food. The music was pleasant, and tables were laid for each party.

"This way," Farvor said quietly, pulling them away towards the stern of the boat where it was a little quieter. Hellevir saw other squires, resplendent in their knights' colors, and various servants-in-waiting, permitted to enjoy the ball with the rich and bright and beautiful elite out of the goodness of their masters'—and the Princess's—beneficent hearts. In the bow of the boat were the broad tables of the court, and she saw Sullivain seated in the center, resplendent in a golden waistcoat and trousers, her head high and glinting with a jeweled crown. Anxiety slid through Hellevir as she saw how open the boat was, thinking how easy it would be for someone to slip poison into Sullivain's drink or a dagger into her side. Why did she insist on taking such risks?

It was hard not to stare at her; all around her the nobles listened with interest as she spoke, captivated, and Hellevir could hardly blame them. The Queen was absent, and it only made the Princess shine brighter, her presence resonating through the hall and turning heads in her direction. She said something and those listening laughed, a genuine sound, and Hellevir wished she'd heard what Sullivain had said that was so funny. She made herself look away, those dark words—*fool's gold*—ringing in her ears again, irritating her anew every time she remembered them.

Hellevir found herself seated next to Yvoir, of all people, once again. Lady Hannotir's squire. There must have been a set priority to the seating that was followed at every dinner.

"You're that herbalist," the squire said. "The one from the Redeion ball. I'm afraid we called you names before we knew you were the herbalist to the Crown. Hellevir, right?" Hellevir smiled, and said she was. She offered to fill Yvoir's glass, which was sufficient for the squire to open up. It was surprisingly easy to get her to talk about her knight; Yvoir seemed both to love and to loathe her. Lady Hannotir was a Knight of the Court; the smaller group of warriors who were knights not just in title but in deed, who had been hand-picked to lead the Queen's five main armies should war arise again.

"That's quite an honor," Hellevir remarked.

"Oh yes, Lady Hannotir outdid herself in the war. Loyal as loyal can be to the Crown, that one." Hellevir recalled how surprised the Queen had been to learn that the Hannotirs could be suspected.

"You seem to like her?"

"Lady Hannotir? She's amazing. Walks into a room and the whole place goes silent to listen." Yvoir sighed and popped an olive into her mouth, and Hellevir followed her gaze up to the head table. She was looking at a stately woman in her late autumn years, a monocle resting over one eye. A cane leaned against the table by her leg, and she was silently surveying the Princess's conversation with the air of a well-meaning grandparent who has given up trying to understand the language of the youth. Hellevir's heart tightened. Lady Hannotir looked far too respectable to be behind a murder attempt, but Hellevir was learning that the court was a cast of actors, and what better persona for a murderer to hide behind than that of a gentlewoman? "One day I hope to have that kind of gravitas, you know?" Yvoir was saying, although Hellevir had missed the first part of what she'd said. "To make people listen."

"Got to have something to say first, though," Farvor interjected with a wink. Yvoir tossed the olive stone at him. He grimaced, wiping at his waistcoat where it had hit and inspecting the silk for a stain.

"Maybe I have got things to say, farm boy!" she exclaimed. "I won't be a squire forever." She took a sip of wine and glanced at Hellevir. "If you're the Princess's herbalist, you must know what's going on with the investigation. Any news?"

Hellevir kept her expression neutral. "They don't tell me anything," she said.

The dancing was held on one of the other boats, connected to the palace gardens by a broad walkway. The deck was open to the stars, lit by bright torches rippling with flames and lanterns strung about. Acrobats balanced on ropes high over their heads, and fire-breathers spewed flames up into the night sky. The music was familiar to her; the orchestra played songs without the lyrics, but they were songs she knew from home. Farvor dragged her over as soon as the music started and made her dance the first tune with him. She was too disorientated to resist, and found herself dancing elbow to elbow with the nobility of Rochidain. When it ended, they sat down in the chairs around the periphery of the deck to catch their breath, watching the other dancers and taking in the sound of music, laughter and the clink of glass against glass.

"Not so bad, eh?" Farvor panted, hand resting on his stomach.

"Not quite what I was expecting," she admitted. "Are these really the songs the court dance to?" Farvor waved his hand.

"Hardly!" he exclaimed. "The Queen hosts the proper court balls and they're all stiff and conventional, but the Princess seems to prefer people enjoying themselves. She has her ear open for what the people like to dance to."

As if his words had summoned her, Hellevir saw a golden figure step onto the deck, handing her cape to an attendant as she cast her eyes over the dance floor. Hellevir found herself staring with the rest of them, her eye drawn as if to the moon among the stars.

A woman made of fire, all the brighter to you because of what you have sacrificed for her. She could almost hear him murmur the words again, as if he were beside her, watching with her. She brushed the thought aside. What did he know?

She stiffened as the Princess's gaze alighted on herself and Farvor sitting on the farther side of the deck, and her heart skipped a beat as Sullivain inclined her head in a gesture.

"I think she wants to talk to you," Farvor remarked, grinning at her. "What circles you move in."

"I won't be long," Hellevir murmured, getting up and straightening out her jacket.

Sullivain saw her approach and extricated herself from her party with a brusqueness only a Princess could muster, calling over a servant carrying glasses of wine. She picked up two, and held one out to Hellevir. Hellevir tried not to feel the eyes of everyone watching her as she accepted it.

"Goodness, you brush up well," the Princess remarked with a smile. "You look lovely." Her flattery was so sudden that it stopped Hellevir's breath for a moment.

"I . . . Thank you," she replied, rather clumsily, and before she could say anything else Sullivain had moved away to the rail overlooking the canal waters, expecting Hellevir to follow. Her hair trailed down her back, braided through with gold thread. It glinted in long strokes in the torchlight, complementing the way she moved, the fencer still despite her formal wear, all grace. The gravitas that Yvoir had so envied.

"Are you enjoying the ball?" Sullivain asked.

"It's starting to improve," Hellevir found herself saying.

"Herbalist, that was almost a compliment." Sullivain leaned against the railing, her wine glass grasped loosely in her fingers. Hellevir joined her, looking out over the night canals rippling with the lights from the pleasure boats. Their arms rested on the rail next to each other.

"What news of the investigation?" Hellevir asked. "Has anything been found?" The Princess grimaced, as if she thought the subject distasteful.

"Oh, nothing yet," she said. "I can't say I'd be surprised if it was the Hannotirs, though. They're probably still bitter that Grandmama didn't give them any of the House Molako fleet when we divvied it up among the allies after the war ended. Or they're annoyed that I refused to marry one of their sickly children. Or that I used to chase their swans with sticks when I was little. Take your pick."

"You don't seem too upset. I thought they were loyal?"

"It's the ongoing balancing act of the Crown; keep the Houses' powers on a leash, but not so tightly that they bite. If the Hannotirs really did do it, clearly Grandmama misjudged somewhere along the line."

Hellevir swallowed, glancing back at the dance floor. All those dancers, weaving between each other. If only the politics of the Houses were as predictable in their steps.

"What will happen to them?" Hellevir asked. "If you do find evidence?"

"They will be stripped of their title. Hanged for their treason." Sullivain said it dismissively, as if she hadn't known them since she was a child. She glanced at Hellevir with a smile, although Hellevir was struggling to control her dismay. Hangings, and all because Loris had been cooking swan in his memories. "And then we will need a new Knight of the Court to replace them," Sullivain was saying. She acted as if she were thinking about it. "How about Lord Redeion?"

Hellevir blinked.

"Lord Redeion? But . . . he's young. I thought court knights needed experience."

"I don't mean Calgir. I mean his uncle, Auland Redeion." Sullivain turned around, leaning her elbows on the railing behind her and crossing one heel over the other, her arm pressed against Hellevir's as she did so. The picture of resplendent ease. "It would be a rise for Auland, and a rise for his nephew. Quite a leap in status for your brother too, I should imagine."

Hellevir looked out over the waters towards the palace grounds, where the trees and lawns were lit with lanterns and groups wandered laughing to and from the dance floor.

"Why are you telling me this?" she asked carefully. She was finding it difficult to think straight, distracted by the lull of the wine, the gentle whisperings in her ear about fire and brightness and bonds.

"This is to show you I'm not all tyrannical," Sullivain laughed. "Nor is my grandmother. She made threats, I will admit it. Threats are just the way of things around here, but what you said when you first arrived in Rochidain, that you'd have brought me back without threats, so stubborn on your high horse that you'd martyr yourself for any soul that tripped and fell down the stairs, it got me thinking. While you work for me I'll help you too. And your family."

Hellevir took a sip of wine to buy herself time to respond.

"You'd use the fall of the Hannotirs . . . to reward me?" she said.

"No need to sound so shocked. I've already suggested it to Grandmama, and she was open to it. You struck a chord with her the other day, you know. She realized we've been treating you unfairly when all you've tried to do is help."

Hellevir didn't know how to react. She was getting thoroughly fed up with this sensation that she was lost in a world she didn't understand. She had found herself in a web, her clumsy movements attracting all the wrong attention, and now here she was, responsible for Houses rising on the tides of another's blood.

"I don't want to be the cause of hangings," she found herself saying. She heard the edge, a note of desperation, in her own voice. Sullivain clearly did too, glancing at Hellevir with sharp eyes that cut through her, saw more than Hellevir had wanted to be seen. She was reminded of the charcoal drawing Sullivain had made, her own eyes wide and candid, so easily readable, and wished for the first time that she had been trained in court life, taught to act the part, to hide how she really felt.

"I forget, sometimes," Sullivain said quietly, "that you aren't from Rochidain. How different it must be in your village."

"It had its own problems," Hellevir remarked, remembering a dark bundle left on her doorstep. She felt Sullivain's hand brush hers, a simple gesture, perhaps an attempt at consolation. It sent a bright gleam of heat up her veins, a glint to it like the gold Sullivain threaded through her hair. She drew in a breath, wishing the man with black eyes had kept his observations to himself.

"I envy you, you know," Sullivain said quietly. Hellevir looked at her, met her copper eyes.

"Envy me?"

"The way you see things. You don't see the threads."

"Threads?"

The Princess gestured out towards the dancers, as if she could observe marionette strings holding them all up, sliding limbs this way and that. She seemed so completely comfortable, entirely at ease in her own skin, her own bearing. That ease, Hellevir realized, was what captivated people so. There was something almost artful about the way she controlled herself.

"The threads between each one of them," Sullivain said. "Some made of silk, others of iron. You don't see how they link each one of my court, each one of my guests. Some are fastened around belt purses, others like nooses around throats." She took Hellevir's hand, extended it so they were both looking along her arm. Caught off-guard, Hellevir let Sullivain make her point at a young man standing on the other side of the boat. "His thread is tied around his writing wrist, a paper trail leading all the way to the old man drinking whisky as if he thinks the world will end tomorrow." Sullivain let her arm drift over to a small group being served drinks, and settle on a whiskered nobleman. "The old man pays for his schooling, in return for favors from the boy's papa. The boy doesn't even know about the thread, has no idea how his scholarly endeavors are paid for, believes Papa has it all in hand. Which he does, of course."

Hellevir flinched, and Sullivain felt it.

"And that old buffoon there." Another shift of her arm, like a compass needle pointing to immorality. "Her daughter developed an unladylike gambling habit, so she paid off her debts to that distastefully dressed man over there with her husband's inheritance. Her former husband believes she lost it in a bad investment. He never forgave her for it, left her and married another woman. He still loves his daughter, though."

"Why are you telling me this?" Hellevir asked again. It took her a beat longer than usual to form the words. She could feel too many eyes watching her, but Sullivain didn't seem to care. The Princess was standing so close, pressed near to look along her arm, and when she sighed, as if she were perplexed, Hellevir felt the sigh, Sullivain's ribs against hers. Hellevir swallowed. Sullivain smelled of rosewater and wine.

"It changes things, doesn't it," the Princess murmured in her ear, her gaze lingering over the dance floor, "seeing the threads? The gold doesn't shine as brightly, the music isn't as pleasant. But it doesn't matter. It's a fair price to pay." Hellevir heard the smile in her words. "Even I don't see as many as Grandmama does. But when I am queen, I will be the one holding on to all these threads, not her, and I will be able to feel every vibration of every little sin. And I will know just which ones to tug to make each person dance." The music trilled and the dancers swirled, as if the world conspired in that moment to make Sullivain's point. Her face was close to Hellevir's as they watched the dancers, her breath brushing along Hellevir's cheek.

"So are you telling me I'm another dancer on your strings?" Hellevir said. "That you can tug me any way you want?" She had meant it to sound defiant, dismissive, but it just sounded young. Even so, Sullivain withdrew a little, her expression frustratingly unreadable.

"I'm telling you this so that you know if the Hannotirs fall, it will be because they have been found guilty," she said quietly. "All these threads are anchored in truths. If the House falls, it won't be on your conscience."

Hellevir blinked, surprised by her candor. All this talk of threats, bribes, sins . . . and Sullivain had just been trying to be kind, in her own way, to show Hellevir that it wouldn't be her fault, whatever happened to the Hannotirs. It was so painfully practical. The Princess's eyes were such an odd copper color. This close, Hellevir could see they were flecked with greens, golds.

"You talk about sins," Hellevir replied. "I thought forgiveness was a Pillar of your faith."

Sullivain smiled, a sideways smile that reminded Hellevir of the way Death grinned when he found her amusing.

"Onaistus can forgive all he wants," she replied. "But I am not a god. It's not for me to forgive sins." The Princess *hmm*ed as if in thought, her grip tightening around Hellevir's hand. Before she could react, Sullivain was leading her in a slow one-handed dance, twirling her in a lazy circle. "You know, I have been wondering something," she mused. "I suppose now is the time to ask." She let their arms grow taut, then pulled Hellevir back in smoothly so that their hips brushed. They weren't moving in time to the music, but to Sullivain's own inexplicable rhythm. The orchestra seemed to grow distant, the dancers on the deck of some other boat. "This exchange you make, blood for souls."

Hellevir didn't like the direction in which this was going. Something in the timbre of the Princess's voice put her on edge. She was acutely aware of the brush of Sullivain's touch as they moved, distracting her, tensing her whole body like a violin string.

"What about it?" she asked carefully.

"So . . . how do you know?"

"How do I know what?"

Sullivain shrugged, raising her arm and leading Hellevir behind and around her and back to face her.

"What the exchange should be? Do you just feel it, or . . ." She pulled Hellevir in, palm to palm. The scent of rosewater was intoxicating. "Does someone tell you?"

"It is Death," Hellevir made herself say. "It has inherent rules."

"Yes, yes," Sullivain said, impatient. "Blood for souls. But who *takes* the blood? Who *gives* you the souls?"

"You assume it's a person? Death has a mind of its own."

Sullivain's fingers slowly laced with Hellevir's. Hellevir swallowed.

"I assume," the Princess said, "because I remember. I didn't before, but I do now. I remember you. I remember you talking to someone. You asked their name, and they wouldn't tell you. You shook hands with the darkness."

Hellevir said nothing. She wanted to pull away, hating how Sullivain's closeness made her tremble like a moth caught under a glass. She found she did want to tell Sullivain, and tell her everything, but it felt wrong. A breach of trust. She almost felt as if Death's dark eyes were on her, then and there, regarding her through Sullivain's, watching to see which side she would pick.

"I want to know who you were talking to," Sullivain said.

"How can I tell you?" Hellevir replied with affected lightness. "Like you said, he wouldn't tell me his name."

"He?"

Hellevir could have bitten off her own tongue. She made herself pull her hand away from Sullivain's, a surprisingly difficult thing to do. Her skin felt cold after Sullivain's warmth.

"I can't tell you what I don't know," she said honestly. "I know nothing about him, other than that he can make the exchange. He is the . . . gatekeeper."

Sullivain's gaze became intense, and she caught Hellevir's wrist. Her grip was tight, and her golden rings bit into Hellevir's skin, although Hellevir didn't think she meant to hurt her.

"Tell me the truth," she asked, voice low. "Is he Onaistus?"

Hellevir blinked at her, at the low earnestness of her tone. And she nearly burst into nervous laughter. In that moment, the sound of the orchestra, the other dancers around them, came crashing back into full color and sound, as if Sullivain's spell had been broken and the heated pressure of her presence had been dissolved.

Onaistus. The thought had never even occurred to her.

"I doubt it," Hellevir said with a smile, trying to quell the chuckle in her voice; although, really, who was she to say he wasn't the God of the Galgoros? For some reason, it just seemed absurd.

Sullivain took a step back, her lip curling with displeasure, and Hellevir realized she was insulted. Hellevir forced herself to be more sober.

"I do not think so," she amended. Sullivain's look could have cut through the side of the boat, and Hellevir winced internally. She hastily added, "It's not my faith, and I can't say whether Onaistus exists or not, but I don't think the person I meet in Death is him." She shrugged. "Honestly, he's too bad-tempered to be the god I've heard the Peers talk about."

Sullivain sniffed and looked away, before downing the rest of her wine in one go. Hellevir realized she had embarrassed her, but far from feeling victorious, Hellevir found she felt guilty. She'd created a chink in that artful control.

"I'm sorry if that's not what you wanted to hear," she tried, but Sullivain dismissed her with a wave of her hand.

"What else can you tell me?" she asked instead, her tone hard as flint. "Anything useful at all?"

"I'm afraid not. He will not speak about himself to me." *Although he warned me away from you. Said that you were fool's gold.*

"Then perhaps you should ask him more questions," Sullivain suggested icily. "If I were the one raising the dead, I might want to know more about the person with whom I was bartering my soul."

Sullivain snared another passing wine glass, and without a backward glance left Hellevir and returned to her retinue.

Hellevir watched her for a moment, feeling the chill that came in her wake, and took a large mouthful of wine. She felt Farvor come up beside her and accepted the refill he offered with a grimace.

"What on earth was all that about?" he asked her. "That looked . . . snug."

"Death and gods," she muttered. Calgir Redeion appeared a moment later, his eyebrows raised.

"Goodness," he remarked. "The Princess dancing with someone other than foreign royalty. She either loves you or hates you to put you through that."

"The latter," Hellevir remarked, then gestured with her glass. "Is there anything stronger than this around here? I'd put this in Elsevir's water bowl."

Since the Princess had called her over so publicly, she kept catching eyes watching her and then looking away, saw people discussing her over their crystal glasses. It felt like she was back in the village again, and she wanted nothing more than to get away. She paused on the gangway, looking back at the dance, and caught sight of Farvor arm-in-arm with Calgir as they threaded through the raised hands of the other dancers. Her brother was beaming from ear to ear, gazing at his knight. Hellevir's scowl softened. She was glad he was enjoying himself, at least, but what Sullivain had said disturbed her. She wondered what threads Sullivain held that were knotted around her brother and his lover, and knew suddenly what she had meant when she said the gold shone less brightly.

The gardens were alive with the sound of laughter and running feet, the flash of bright silks and the shine of jewels at throats. Every corner she turned there was a bench or clearing full of people, some with their necks being lightly kissed by lovers, others in groups hotly debating this or guffawing about that. Hellevir just wanted somewhere quiet to sit and collect her thoughts, but there was nowhere.

She ducked behind a tall metal sculpture of a lion and caught sight of an open doorway leading into the palace. It didn't look like an area for guests, but she didn't care.

The corridor inside was blissfully quiet, the sounds of the ball distant and muted. It was lined with oil paintings depicting various battles. She found a window seat and sank into it with a sigh. She wished Elsevir were here.

She sat with her elbows resting on her knees, not caring how improper the posture was, and looked down at her left hand with its missing fingers. She kept catching stray traces of rosewater scenting her jacket.

Why could the Princess unnerve her like this? Every look, every word, every touch had lodged themselves within Hellevir and she didn't know why. She suddenly wished she could go back on deck, find the Princess, apologize for how she had reacted, but the thought of everyone watching her, of Sullivain's sharp and haughty gaze, made her shrink back in her seat.

She stiffened as she heard footsteps entering the corridor, wondering what excuse she could give if a servant were to catch her, and was surprised when Calgir appeared, his collar loosened and his hair in artful disarray. She stood up quickly, straightening out her jacket, but he waved for her to sit back down, leaning against the wall to catch his breath.

"Oh, you don't have to stand," he said. "Honestly it makes me uncomfortable when people act all formal around me."

"You must be uncomfortable a lot of the time," she remarked, and he laughed.

"I suppose I am. My father hated it too."

"Is your father . . ."

"No longer with us, I'm afraid. Died in the War over the Waves."

"I'm sorry."

"Oh, don't be." He said it with a shrug. "I don't remember much about him, I was only a small child. Besides, he may have hated the appearance of subservience but he had no fears about drumming it into people in other ways when they didn't do as he wanted. That I remember." Hellevir blinked, surprised at the easy way he'd told her that.

"He sounds . . ." She stopped herself, not wanting to insult his father.

"Hypocritical? It's true." He glanced at the seat where Hellevir had been hiding. "Forgive me if I overshare. I tend to do that when I've had a drink, or when I'm trying to cheer someone up. Not a great tactic, I know. Are you all right? That looked like quite an intense conversation you had there."

"*Intense* is one way of putting it." She liked the way he talked to her, openly and honestly. Oddly, it did cheer her up. "This is the second time you've found me hiding. You must think I'm very unsociable."

"Not at all. I understand perfectly." He smiled. "Farvor was worried, so I thought I'd see that you were all right."

"That's . . . very kind, thank you. But I'm fine."

"You're like your brother, always on the periphery."

"I'm not sure Farvor would say that. He's always liked to be at the heart of things."

"He likes to watch what's going on in the heart of things, but I think he keeps them at arm's length." Hellevir didn't know what to say to that. It felt odd to her that someone might know her brother as well as she did. But then again, there had been a period of ten years when he'd been in Rochidain, and she'd been living with Milandre. Lord Redeion probably did know him as well as she did, if not better, and the thought made her sad.

Calgir's eye had caught upon one of the paintings lining the hallway, and he leaned over to inspect it. Hellevir joined him, glancing at the plaque; *The Battle of the Prye, 385.* One of the last battles of the War over the Waves. The painting showed a maelstrom of tiny figures locked in various forms of combat, horses rearing with wide eyes, and fires blazing in the distance.

"We were on the wrong side of the war, you know," the knight remarked, still studying the artwork. She wondered if his father had died at the Prye. "House Redeion, that is. I was only small at the time."

Hellevir looked at him in surprise. "Your House sided with the original king?" she asked. He brushed some dust off the frame.

"My father was one of the leading generals," he said. "At least in the beginning. He defected when it started to look like the war wasn't going our way. Apparently, a few of our House adorned the battlements like that cook, before we swapped sides." He glanced down at her, perhaps realizing talk of bodies wouldn't help cheer her up, and smiled lightly, putting a finger to his lips. "But don't tell anyone. We're not supposed to advertise it." Hellevir made herself smile back, although his words had sent a cold finger brushing down her spine.

"Did your uncle take over the business from your father?" she asked.

"Yes, thank goodness. He likes overseeing negotiations personally and being in the thick of it all, but I haven't the head for that. With Farvor's help, perhaps one day I can be more involved, but for the moment I'm just enjoying being free, before the responsibilities hit." He smiled, hands in his pockets. "Farvor is teaching me to shoot properly."

"You couldn't before?"

"Not well, apparently. He says I was lucky to hit the side of a cow at five paces."

Hellevir laughed. "He enjoys being your squire, you know."

"I hope so," he said quietly. "Before I hired him as a squire it was . . . well, to be honest, the long winter had left me feeling grey, colorless. It happens, the grim skies and the cold have that effect on me. This time I couldn't seem to shake it. I was considering moving away from Rochidain, perhaps somewhere farther south. When Farvor came along he . . . he brought a bit of wildness from your woods, some life. He has an instant understanding when I tell him things, as if he can see me more clearly than anyone else. He . . . he brought fierceness, he brought color."

Hellevir nodded, knowing what he meant. Her brother had always lacked patience for wasted time, wasted words, which meant he could usually bore through the nonessential details to reach the truth of things. It did display itself as a kind of fierceness.

Calgir glanced at Hellevir, and when he saw how closely she was paying attention he gave a nervous laugh, as if embarrassed.

"I always thought he was a bit of a clod," Hellevir remarked, trying to ease the knight's nervousness, and added with a smile, "but I suppose you see a different side of him than I do." She paused. "I think this is where I say if you ever hurt him I'll throw you into the canal."

He looked down at her, eyebrows raised, and then burst into laughter.

"Perhaps fierceness is a family trait. But you won't have to throw me," he promised. "I'll jump in with the weights around my feet." He glanced back through the doors as a group of guests stumbled past, laughing and shouting. He turned to Hellevir and held out his arm to her.

"I don't know about you, but I could use a drink. Shall we find my squire and get roaring drunk?"

"I thought you'd never ask."

CHAPTER FIFTEEN

The Peer's voice rang like a low bell through the temple hall, the timbre seeming to complement the rain-dense clouds outside, the heavy stone of the pillars, the incense burning on the walls. Hellevir sat with Ma in one of the rows.

Hellevir had been delivering produce to the temple kitchens when Peer Laius had spotted her. She had been reluctant to set foot near the temple, but Sathir had insisted that an occasional offering of herbs and vegetables was a wise way to maintain good relations between the faiths, especially following the edict making Onaistian practice the religion of the state. Quite oblivious to her mother's reticence, Peer Laius had insisted Hellevir should come to the service he was about to give. His insistence made it difficult for her to refuse, and she also had a morbid curiosity about it.

"We are defeated by our own urges," intoned the Peer. A murmur went through the assembly. Hellevir saw heads nodding. "Our own base instincts," the Peer went on. "We are pulled down, drowned, by our own weaknesses, by our sins against the God of Light. Drunkenness, violence, greed: these are the things that prevent us from reaching the light he offers us, the light of his Promise, and yet we allow ourselves to give in to them, each and every day." More nodding heads. "I remind you now that while Onaistus may bear us towards the greener lands, towards the Promise that he made us, it is up to each and every one of us to help him as he is helping us, to resist our base urges and not give in to temptations or our own evil thoughts, or, most importantly, to false promises and false whisperings from those who would seek to watch us drown. For if we fall from his Promise, we condemn ourselves to an eternity without him, an eternity of nothingness."

He stood in front of the circular pit of sand, on a slightly raised platform. He gestured down to the pit, and picking up a long staff he slowly drew a pattern in the white sand. It was hypnotic, watching the end of the staff drift over the sand, drawing a Dometik that grew steadily more intricate. The pattern almost seemed to glow in the low light, caught by the sun behind the Peer, and Hellevir blinked, her eyes momentarily tricked into thinking it *was* glowing. "It is our duty to control our own urges," the Peer continued. "And to exert what control we have in the world in order to help each other stay on the Path of Light." The staff reached the center of the pattern, and stopped. "Control," the Peer intoned, his voice resounding through the hall. Hellevir jumped as the assembly around her repeated the word back to him. He bowed his head, and put a hand to his forehead. "Thank you. May your ways be eternal and blessed."

The assembly stood—Hellevir hurriedly got to her feet—and put their hands to their foreheads too, intoning, "And yours also."

The performance over, a general murmur of conversation filled the hall, as the assembly began to filter down the steps to the center of the room. One by one, they stepped into the pit of sand, ruining the design, closing their eyes as the Peer traced the same pattern on their forehead with his thumb. As each person received the blessing, they did seem to stand taller, their heads held higher.

"Do people really need to be told this?" Hellevir muttered to no one in particular.

"We can't all have your level of enlightenment," her ma replied stiffly behind her. They were the first words she'd said to Hellevir in weeks. "Respect that the lost may need guidance." Hellevir let herself out of the side door while her mother received her blessing, feeling like it would be somehow blasphemous, to her own beliefs as well as theirs, to accept one herself.

When Ma emerged to join her in the courtyard, Hellevir made to excuse herself to return to the Order, but she was interrupted by Peer Laius as he came out of the hall and her mother's attention was distracted. He caught sight of Ma and made his way over to her, taking her hand and folding it in his.

"I can't recall a time before I saw your face among the assembly," he said, his smile as wan as the dawn sunlight. "You bring such good to the Temple."

"That's kind of you, Peer," her ma said, inclining her head. The Peer's gaze fell on Hellevir.

"Ah, Hellevir," he said. "I'm so glad you agreed to stay. It's been a while since we last had a chance to speak. How did you find the sermon?"

Hellevir searched for the appropriate words. "It was interesting," she said.

"You should come again. I know your mother would like to see you embrace the religion of her home nation." Hellevir snorted. It was an involuntary sound, regardless of how rude it was. Before the Peer could take offense, her mother swooped in and asked if he would still be coming to the house that evening for dinner, as he usually did on Markdays.

"Of course. I would be honored," the Peer said. His eyes slid back to Hellevir, and she wished he would look elsewhere. "I hope to see you there too, Hellevir. Perhaps we can discuss the Onaistian faith in more detail, if you still have an interest in our lore. Now it has been officially adopted as the faith of the Chron it would be useful for you to have a firmer grasp of it."

Hellevir parted her lips to remark—in politer terms—that he should stop trying to convert her because he would have better luck converting the fish in the sea to a life in the sky, but her ma interrupted before she could speak.

"Hellevir will be busy with her work at the Order," she said. "She won't be able to make dinner."

"Oh, but she should," Peer Laius insisted, his tone taking on that chiding sweetness that set Hellevir's teeth on edge. "I know you and your mother have been at odds recently, but forgiveness is a staple of the Temple." Hellevir tried not to find this uproariously funny, as she and her ma avoided looking at each other. The Peer seemed to realize—finally—that he'd misjudged. "But perhaps another time," he said.

"Another time," Hellevir said through her teeth, but the Peer had already been snared and was being led away by another member of the assembly. Her mother became busy talking with another Peer. Without a word, Hellevir slipped away. She was late to meet Sullivain.

*

Hellevir climbed the steps to the aviary with trepidation. The service had left her on edge, as if she'd just washed in someone else's bathwater, but the faith was in every corner of the city; it was her ma's religion, and Sullivain's too, so why did she have such difficulty acclimatizing herself to it? As time went on she sympathized more and more with her father, distrusting the new ways but unable to convincingly explain why.

She was aware she had dismissed the Princess out of hand at the ball. Sullivain had only asked a really very sensible question. The Onaistian doctrine promised eternal life in the arms of Onaistus after Death, so why wouldn't the Princess be curious about the being that Hellevir met in the afterlife? And yet Hellevir had laughed in her face. The memory made her wince.

When she took the last step—out of breath and trying not to show it; Elsevir's weight on her shoulder wasn't helping—a guard opened the door to her and she was met with the roaring light of the setting sun, as sweet to the eye as honey to the tongue, cascading over the perches and soft feathers of a hundred doves. Their purr filled the domed circular room, echoing lightly, and she saw Sullivain standing by one of the large arched windows with her back to the door. The Princess didn't seem to realize Hellevir was there, but stood looking out over the red roofs of the city below, the glinting waters and, in the distance, the sea. Hellevir went to stand at her side, watching the ant-like people below, the miniature boats. She listened to the murmuring of the birds; they didn't have much to say besides which gardens had put out nice seeds, and how the seagulls were such bullies.

The Princess held a dove the color of sea foam in her arms and was stroking its head. She didn't turn to look at Hellevir. Her expression was closed, her gaze distant, as if she were thinking about things Hellevir couldn't fathom.

"You can leave the tea and go," she said.

"Sullivain . . ." Hellevir began. The Princess glanced at her, expression hard. In the sunlight, her eyes were molten, and for a moment Hellevir had no idea what to say. Something fluttered within her.

"Well?"

"I . . . I feel I should apologize. I was rude, at the ball. You only asked me a question."

Sullivain's lips pursed, and she looked back over her city. "An inappropriate one, judging by your response. I'm not used to being laughed at, herbalist. I should have had you dismissed." Her tone was sharp, staccato. Hellevir considered for a moment how to explain herself without betraying Death. He had never forbidden her from speaking about him with anyone in life, but it felt like doing so would somehow break an understanding they shared.

"Onaistian is very foreign to me," Hellevir said at last. "I was raised in the old ways, worshipping the old spirits. The being I meet with . . . he feels more like their ilk. Something older."

"I see. And you think my god is a new-fangled idea, rootless and peripheral?"

"No! Not at all, I . . ."

"Onaistus has been worshipped for hundreds of years, in far more kingdoms than your 'old ways.'" Sullivain was angry, her words barbed.

Hellevir bit her lip, wondering if she should just cut her losses and keep her mouth shut.

"I laughed at the ball because I honestly can't imagine eternity in his company being pleasant in any way at all," she said, a little helplessly. "Let alone a reward for a good life in devotion to the Pillars."

Sullivain was frowning, and Hellevir wondered if she was just digging herself a hole, so she was surprised when Sullivain sighed, and said, "Perhaps I am being unfair." She hesitated, as if debating whether to continue speaking. "I reacted strongly because I had hoped, I suppose, that he *was* Onaistus, that it was all true. Because if he was, then . . . I don't know. It might have been a way for me to explain myself." She seemed hesitant, the first time Hellevir had heard her unsure of herself.

"What do you mean?" she dared to ask. Sullivain stroked the dove's head distractedly as if it were a cat. For a moment it looked like she would reply honestly, give Hellevir a glimpse into whatever darkness was churning away behind those copper eyes, but then she just passed Hellevir the dove, pressing it into her hands, and reached up to coax another from the rafters.

"My grandfather liked to keep doves," she told Hellevir, as if continuing another conversation they'd been having. "I remember him training them to come home. You know we're the only House allowed to eat them? See the tags; that means they're ours. De Neïd doves." She nuzzled the bird, the tip of her nose vanishing into its soft plumage. "But who would want to eat these beauties?"

Hellevir felt suddenly on the back foot, like she'd missed something important.

"Sullivain . . ."

"Herbalist." The Princess stopped her with a look. Hellevir opened her mouth to speak, saw the light tremble on Sullivain's hand as she stroked the dove's head with one finger. Something clicked in Hellevir, remembering what Death had said about the torture inflicted on Loris the cook; not caused by the Queen, he had said, but by Sullivain. Hellevir had pushed the thought to the very back of her mind, wanting in blinkered denial to pretend she hadn't understood his meaning. She remembered a throwaway remark Sullivain had made, which had lodged itself in Hellevir's head because, for all its apparent flippancy, it had been said with a sourness making acid of its tone, *It's not like I'm on the way to the Promise anyway.*

I'm an idiot, Hellevir thought. *She wanted to talk to her god because she's afraid she's fallen from the Path of the Promise.*

Hellevir felt a twist of guilt in her stomach for being so dismissive. Sullivain had her back to her, and Hellevir raised a hand almost without thinking. Her fingers hovered over the Princess's shoulder. The words poised themselves on her tongue, almost as close to utterance as her fingertips to the embroidery of the Princess's jacket, brushing the raised threads.

You can tell me, she almost said. *Whatever it is. You can confide in me.*

"They're lovely birds," she said instead, a little helplessly, and let her hand fall to her side. Sullivain set the bird on its roost, turning back to her.

"This one came with me from the Galgoros, a gift. She's immaculate, isn't she? Not a blemish on her." She spoke quickly, filling the silence with words, seemingly any words. She gestured to the raven on Hellevir's shoulder. "How do you keep your bird so well-tamed?" she asked. Elsevir bristled.

"He needs no taming," Hellevir said quietly. "He's wild."

"But how do you make him stay?"

"I don't. He chooses to." Hellevir scratched his ruff of feathers, and he leaned into her. She glanced up to see Sullivain watching her closely.

"Is he one of the beasts you brought back?" she asked.

Hellevir blinked, surprised at her shrewdness. "Yes."

Sullivain put out a hand, stroking Elsevir's chest. Hellevir was surprised that he let her. Her wrist came close to Hellevir's face, and she caught the scent of rosewater again.

"So the bird and I have something in common," the Princess mused. "We each have a slice of your soul?"

"Yes, you do."

The Princess's gaze was distant as she studied the bird, running her hand gently over his feathers.

"Are all the creatures with a share in your soul so drawn to you?" The sunlight streaming through the arches of the tower brought out the blues and greens of Elsevir's wings. The question caught Hellevir off-guard.

"I don't know," she admitted. "You tell me." Hellevir noticed how much Sullivain looked like her grandmother, from the high cheekbones to the firm set of her jaw. Again, she felt that urge to invite her to talk, to ask her about the shadows behind her eyes. It occurred to Hellevir that she was the only one in the world, separate as she was from the court—unable to see the threads, one foot in the afterlife—who might be able to listen without prejudice, without Sullivain feeling like she was risking herself by being open. But it felt like asking for her confession. The Princess would just give her that hard glare, perhaps remark that her affairs were no business of a country herbalist, and dismiss her. Hellevir didn't want to be dismissed. A curl of the Princess's hair spiraled perfectly over one ear, and Hellevir had the urge to brush it back. She barely had the presence of mind to stop herself.

What's got into me? she wondered.

"How odd," the Princess said, and dropped her hand from Elsevir's chest. "Well, I can't dally all day." As she turned away to the door, Hellevir felt the sudden void left behind like a cold draft. Everything about her was so *vibrant*, it made it hard to see anything else while she stood there, like the sun blotting out the rest of the world. Hellevir swallowed, collected herself, and followed.

"Can you bring a larger dose of the tea next time?" the Princess asked over her shoulder as they descended the winding stone

staircase. "I get through it too quickly." The light spilled in from
the thin window slits at intervals, lighting her hair in gold-white
shafts.

"Yes. Does it help?"

"Marginally."

"I can make it stronger?"

"Please. But not too strong. It won't do for the future queen to
fall asleep in court." They reached the bottom of the stairwell, but
before they went their separate ways Sullivain reached out suddenly
and plucked a loose feather caught in Hellevir's hair, pale as snow.

"Don't tell anyone about what I said, will you?" Sullivain asked
quietly. "It wouldn't do for people to hear and think me ridiculous."

"Of course not," Hellevir replied. "Why would I?" Sullivain
just smiled at that, letting the feather drift to the ground, and
walked away down the corridor.

The question might have seemed foolish to Hellevir when it was
first asked, but the more she thought about it, the further it
burrowed into her thoughts. Onaistus, God of Light, giver of the
Promise. There were no religious images of their One God, but
from the way the Peers talked she had envisaged a deity of gold
and blinding white, something exuding goodness and peace. The
very opposite of the man with the black eyes.

Is he Onaistus?

Hellevir didn't know who or what he was. Part of her had
assumed he was simply a spirit, like the willow tree and the creature in the sea cave, the being who oversaw the passage of souls
from life to death. But in honesty, she had no idea. Perhaps her
mother had been correct, perhaps she had no right to make bargains
with such an unknowable being.

Onaistus. It was a bizarre thought. And yet as the days slid by,
it grazed at her ribs like an arrow lodged in her side, incessant and
oddly painful. She had to know, because . . . because what if?

What if he was? Then she could tell her mother, and perhaps
when Ma realized that her daughter communed not with dark
things, but with the God of Light himself, she might welcome her
back home, might regret casting her out. Then she could help
Sullivain, argue for her with the god, show her that her soul was
safe and whatever crimes she had committed could be wiped clean.

It was a wishful thought, childish, a fantasy that she let loose through her mind in the moments before she fell asleep, unable to resist the sweetness of it. She took out the old book the Peer had given her about the faith and read it cover to cover, but it held nothing useful.

The priestesses had said Hellevir could use the Order library whenever she chose. It was a maze of grey rooms and corridors above and below ground, lined with books and scrolls on everything from agriculture to architecture, history to collections of sagas. Hellevir combed the rows of books, but the Onaistian faith had been an oral tradition until relatively recently, and there wasn't much she could find committed to paper. Anyone who had been caught trying to write anything down had been criminalized until particular recorded versions became official.

One evening, after a day spent helping Sathir in the infirmary, Hellevir sat in one of the tucked-away rooms where the windows were high and let in dusty light. The cold was beginning to rime the edges of the glass, and she was wrapped up in her heavy coat against the chill of the cold vaults. A splay of books on the history of the Galgoros, where the faith had originated, was arranged before her. Elsevir sat on the back of her chair, preening her long hair.

Her findings were sparse. She had learned a lot about the Galgoros, though; it had been under a dictatorship until not that long ago, before an internal struggle had led to the formation of a consulate, made up of ten representatives from among the people who rotated yearly.

It was frustrating. There were mentions of temples, of people doing things in the name of their god, but no actual mention of what happened *in* the temples. It was like trying to grip sand; the tighter she clasped her fist, the faster it streamed between her fingers.

It was late by the time she sat back with a sigh, rubbing her eyes, no further forward than she had been hours before. She wondered if she was being stupid, spending so much time on learning about a faith with no written history. She would be better off asking one of the Peers, but the thought of approaching a temple on her own made her recoil. She heard footsteps coming up the corridor and glanced up to see Edrin, the priestess who had first admitted her to the Order. A lantern was tied to her belt as she did her evening rounds.

"I thought I saw lamplight," she commented, stroking Elsevir's head. "You're up late, Hellevir."

"I've just been reading, but I'm done for now, I think." She stood, collecting the books in a pile to put back on the shelves. Edrin turned one of the books around and read the cover.

"*Culture and Craft in the Eastern Archipelagos,*" she read. "You are researching the Galgoros?"

"I'm trying to find out more about the Onaistian faith," Hellevir admitted, stifling a yawn. "But there's nothing. I'm wondering if it's a fool's errand." Edrin hummed and gestured for Hellevir to put the books down and follow her. She took her to a narrow passage lined with thin leather-bound notebooks.

"What are these?" Hellevir asked, picking one off the shelf. It didn't have a title, only a name and date.

"Journals," the priestess said. "Written by members of the Order, or sometimes by visitors. Some of our priestesses travelled to bring us news from outside, and their writings are kept here." She scanned the shelves, and picked out three notebooks in a row. "These belong to Priestess Ollevin. A century ago she travelled through the East, and wrote about what she found there, including the Galgoros, and drew a lot of pictures too." She held the notebooks in her hands for a moment, looking down at them with an unreadable expression, and then offered them to Hellevir.

Hellevir leafed through one of them, and found that it was full of sketches. The pages fell open on a picture of a busy marketplace, behind which loomed a large building, with a twelve-pointed star on its door.

"Thank you," Hellevir said. "Can I take these to my room?"

"I don't see why not. You should take her assistant's journal too. This is his." Edrin pulled out another book, tattered and squashed with no particular thought between two heavy volumes, and added it to the pile.

Hellevir sat up reading all night. The priestess's journals were beautifully written, and Hellevir found time slipping past in her observations and anecdotes. Ollevin had travelled everywhere with her assistant, Alcifer; the length and breadth of the Chron, through the southern kingdoms, and up and down the Eastern Archipelago. The sketches she drew were simple but captured what she was looking at with easy perfection. Hellevir found herself eye-to-eye with people long dead: workers carrying hay bales on their backs up country roads, fishermen standing on long boats as they repaired nets, wearing odd clothes and sun-shielding hats, soldiers in foreign armor watching peddlers in the market through slitted helmets.

Ollevin had spent a year in the Galgoros, which ruled most of the isles, and had stayed at one of the temples as a guest. But that's where there was a gap. The last written entry was dated early in 291, and although the priestess had kept meticulous notes until then at least once every week, the next entry wasn't until the spring of the next year.

I am forbidden to write about the Onaistian faith, the next entry read. *If I did, I would be treated as an enemy. Their laws say nothing about sketches, but somehow I doubt they would make such a pedantic distinction. It would be enough for them to know that I have committed anything to paper.*

I have entrusted Alcifer with the sketches of the things I have been told about—and dare I say, things that I have seen myself—but I cannot keep them here. He will look after them until we are both back in the Chron at the Order, perhaps until we are both too old for it to matter anymore, and in the meantime may they act as warning to the Priestesses of the Nightingale, that the Galgoros is no place for those like us. We must get out before they know.

Curious, Hellevir picked up Alcifer's notebook. It was a plain thing, but when she opened it a sheaf of drawings spilled out onto her desk. Many of them were in sharp charcoal, a little too rough to be Ollevin's, but Hellevir recognized some of the priestess's among them. A lot of them showed Dometiks, laid out like lists, and notes beside them in another hand, written so harshly that they had indented the paper. But most of the pictures were scenes of people.

There were drawings of the temple Ollevin had stayed in, of the main hall which looked remarkably like the Rochidain temple where Hellevir's ma worked. There was an altar laden with bounty, symbols of eels and ornaments showing flames, a pit with one of the Dometiks of the faith drawn into the sand. Even though she'd only been using ink and charcoal, the priestess had managed to portray the gloom, the stream of light coming in through the decorated windows.

The next image showed a Peer mid-sermon, his arms raised and silhouetted against the light behind him. The crowd of worshippers watched him with reverence, and the sign in the pit was in stark silhouette. Hellevir realized with a start that she recognized this Dometik; it was the same symbol Peer Laius had drawn in the sand during the service, the symbol for Control.

One seemed to follow the other. Hellevir knelt on the floor, bringing the lamp beside her, and placed the pictures side by side, beginning with the one she had found in Ollevin's diary of the temple overlooking the marketplace. The sketches weren't all in order, but as she sorted them, they began to tell a story. When they were all laid out she knelt back, and read them grimly.

The temple and the Peer. The worshippers hanging on his every word.

Another picture, seemingly unrelated, was like something out of a fairy tale. Women talking to trees with figures leaning from the trunks, their hair made of leaves and catkins. Men holding discussions with creatures half-emerged from the sea, their skin encrusted with barnacles. Smoky figures sitting cross-legged in fireplaces, their eyes glowing. Creatures made of wind and stone, their eyes of leaves and feathers. Beautiful images, drawn with a tenderness, as if the priestess had been drawing kin.

And next came fire.

Men and women tied to pyres, the flames engulfing the wood as the Peer pointed an accusing finger at them, the Dometiks carved into the wooden pole they were bound to, into the earth around them. Their mouths were wide O's. A woman forced into a cage, the fire beneath it fed with burning coals. And much, much more; everywhere their Signs, everywhere their fire.

Hellevir had to look away, pressing her hand to her stomach. She reached for Elsevir and held him close, surprised to discover that she was shaking. What had she stumbled upon? It wasn't what she'd been looking for, certainly. She'd hoped to find stories about their One God, hidden secrets about the origins of the faith, but not . . . this. Not this.

"Why would they do these things?" she whispered to the raven. Elsevir just clicked his beak. He didn't know.

Hellevir made herself look back. There was one more picture she hadn't seen, she realized. Half of it was hidden, and she drew it out from underneath the other pictures. With a start, she recognized it.

Peer Laius's book was still in her bag. She leafed through until she came to the page with the wood carving of the kneeling man, surrounded by black things with claws and teeth. Depictions of dark things of the world made of lies, intent upon pulling men and women from goodness, from the Promise. It was the same wood carving as from Alcifer's journal.

The Galgoros is no place for those like us.

"Is this why Ma was so afraid?" Hellevir whispered. "Not because of what I could do, but because of what they might do to me?"

Elsevir perched on her knee, his beady eyes clever.

"I think perhaps it is both," he said.

"But such things happened over a hundred years ago," Hellevir protested. "In a kingdom hundreds of miles away. Nothing like that could happen here."

Elsevir's feathers ruffled.

"I think you know they could," was all he said. Hellevir looked at him. It wasn't that long ago the raven had been left dead on Milandre's doorstep, his neck wrung and adorned with hemlock, a message and a threat. Hellevir looked down at the pictures again, feeling cold.

"It's the same kind of fear, isn't it?" she whispered. She flicked through the book to the description of the Pillars, each Sign above the corresponding point of the star. She compared the list to the Dometiks carved onto the wood, branded onto skin, but they were so complicated she couldn't tell if they matched. Some were different symbols altogether from the Signs of the Twelve Pillars which guided devotees along the Path of Light.

"What does all this mean?" she asked the bird.

"It was long ago," he said. "Perhaps their ways have changed for good." He tugged affectionately at Hellevir's hair with his beak, and she buried her face in his feathers.

She'd been hunting for the truth of Onaistus. She'd found a truth, of a sort, but not the one she'd wanted. If the man with dark eyes was Onaistus . . . she'd made a bargain with a deity in whose name unspeakable things had been done.

*

The autumn had set in quickly, and was colder than Hellevir had hoped. Frosts bit into the fruit and vegetable crops in the priest-esses's gardens, causing even the herbs she had grown in the conservatories to shrivel and die. The Order received more guests than normal, people who had nowhere else to go once the streets became too cold to sleep on at night.

Hellevir was kept busy in the infirmary with Sathir, tending the sick and bringing blankets and hot food to anyone who was shivering. She kept her pockets full of apples for children who looked like they were about to burst into tears. The movement kept her from getting cold, at least, and from thinking too much about the daggers which hung over her head. Her life felt so very knotted, like a fisherman's net twisting in and out of itself, her thoughts heavy with assassination attempts, with the House insignia of swans, with the two pearls wrapped up in the riddle in her pocket, awaiting the moment she would need them to bring someone back. And now too the looming terror of Peers, lurking in the dark to trap her in a burning cage. But when she moved, when she crushed herbs in her pestle, when she boiled decoctions and applied salves, those thoughts felt somehow less important, peripheral to the everyday needs of the hungry and the sick before her. With Elsevir's warm weight on her shoulder, she felt solid, useful, needed.

Eventually Sathir ordered her to go and rest; she had been on her feet for fourteen hours. But Hellevir felt too on edge to relax, so instead she went into the garden to sit at her usual spot by the weeping willow. She'd just turned the bend in the river when she saw something on the bank, halfway out of the water.

"Poor thing," Hellevir murmured, kneeling beside it. It was a cat. Scrawny and grey. He looked like he had fallen into the river, and hadn't had the energy to pull himself out before the water had become too cold. Hellevir set her jaw. She brought the little body up onto her lap, ignoring the water leeching ice into her trousers. She hesitated a moment, one hand upon the apple in her pocket, the other on the creature's head, wondering if she dared do this.

"You're going to bring him back?" Elsevir asked.

"Yes, I am," she replied, her tone firmer than she felt. She closed her eyes, and rested her hands on the small creature's head.

*

Death was not colder than the Rochidain winter, but it was a different sort of cold. Deeper, as if the blood in her veins were being siphoned from the river.

Far above her, the mirrored sky reflected her upturned face, and it no longer frightened her. She didn't feel the urge to cling to the earth with vertigo, as if she were about to lose her grip on the ground and fall up, up into whatever lay beyond the mirror. If anything lay there at all. She had grown accustomed to looking up at herself. She nearly laughed. *Accustomed.* As accustomed as she could be to anything in Death.

She stood, brushing the frost from the backs of her legs, and looked around for the cat. She caught movement across the river, its tail vanishing through an open door in the high wall surrounding the gardens, a door she'd never noticed before. Without a second thought she followed, crossing the small footbridge over the water now frozen solid, and running across the rimed grass on the other side. She slipped through the open door.

She found herself in the small circular grove where Death had first offered his bargain. The only difference this time was the statues. Grey stone figures in armor, the pommels of their swords clasped in their hands, and the point dug between their feet. The style of their armor and weapons looked old, very old, and yet despite this they looked more threatening than the Rochidain guards in their finery. It was the type of armor made for war, for taking the side of a blade, not for beauty. They were weapons for cutting through bone.

Hellevir felt his presence before she saw him. She looked towards the fountain where he sat, his cloak swept back and his elbows resting on his knees, watching her with black eyes.

He was frightening in a way not too different from the armor and swords of the statues. A practical type of frightening that dealt in blood and would not shrink from tearing her apart.

"Hello," he said.

"Hello."

"Have you come to bargain?" The air of the world trembled with his words as if they were the rumble of an approaching tidal wave.

"I . . . I suppose I have. But I didn't expect to see you for souls that weren't human."

"All souls cross through here. Human and otherwise. All concern me."

Hellevir was about to reply when she saw the cat curling about Death's legs, rubbing his grey head against his knee. The man with the black eyes reached down absently and stroked his back. It was a strange sight to see.

"A small soul, perhaps," he went on. "But a soul all the same. You may take him."

"You do not want anything in exchange?"

"A few drops of blood will do. The apple in your pocket."

Hellevir walked over, and sat down slowly by the fountain. The cat jumped up beside her and settled himself on her lap. She scratched behind his ears. Her heart thrummed with apprehension over what she was about to ask, so loudly she could half-imagine it resonating in the air around her like ripples upon a lake. She swallowed.

"Can I ask a question?"

"I will not promise to answer it," he replied.

She bit the inside of her lip, wondering whether she was about to say something unbelievably foolish. Foolish, because she might be completely wrong, or because to ask it was to risk his wrath again. She could feel it, even now, at the edges of her vision. Shuddering like a heat haze. An ever-present threat.

"Are you Onaistus?" She pushed the words out before she could give herself time to reconsider. There was a silence, and she dared to look up at the dark man. Sure enough, he had raised one eyebrow, giving her a perplexed look that suggested he thought her very stupid. But perplexed was better than enraged. The knot within her loosened a little.

Of course he wasn't Onaistus, she realized. She'd known it really, just as she'd known where to look for his treasures. Sullivain had been wrong after all.

"No, I didn't think so," she said, suddenly embarrassed. "I just . . . had to know."

"And why is that?"

"He suddenly seems to be everywhere I look." She hesitated, and then added, "I found journals, accounts of things that had been done against people like me, in Onaistus's name. Did that really happen?"

The world darkened ever so slightly; if she hadn't been paying attention, she might have missed it. The shadows in the statues' visors seemed to watch her.

"I can't disclose the affairs of the dead," the world murmured.

"So it's true?" There was no answer, only a curling melancholy that brushed cold against her skin. Hellevir pressed her lips together, but didn't push him. "Does he exist?" she asked instead. "Onaistus? Is he real?"

The man with the black eyes leaned back and stood, giving her the sudden impression of a dark cloud passing over the sun, before he began to walk slowly around the fountain, trailing his hand through the falling droplets and letting them cling to his fingertips.

"You've been talking," he remarked. The droplets trembled. "Talking about me with your Princess."

"The Princess remembered you." She paused. "I told her the bare minimum to make her stop asking questions, and then I . . . I fell down a hole of wondering. I had to know who you are. If you're not Onaistus, who are you?"

The pressure within the copse held, made her wince, and then slowly lifted. She let out a small breath.

"I am a gatekeeper," he said without looking at her, adopting the same word she had used. She wondered if he had been watching when she talked to Sullivain. "I am a guardian. And if I were more, it wouldn't be something for the living to know about." His tone became sardonic, taking on the mocking edge she'd grown to know so well. "As for Onaistus, I don't know if he exists. But I will say I . . . hope not."

"Why?" she dared to ask.

"Why?" he repeated. "Because they don't know what they are hoping for, when they preach eternal life in the arms of their god. Their god who will save them from the horror of becoming nothing."

"What do you mean?"

"You are impatient, aren't you," he remarked. "There is no real horror in nothing. They do not understand the *gift* of being nothing. That eternal life is awfully long, no matter how blessed or blissful." He paused, his lip curling. "Because they are children who see an apple upon the tree and do not think to stop and check it for worms before taking a great big mouthful."

The withdrawal in his eyes seemed deeper than before. That Death could be exhausted by eternity . . . it was a bleak thought. It was a rare moment of introspection that made her almost wish she could reach out to him. Despite the somber note of truth in what he said, she felt suddenly stronger than she had in days after reading those journals, and was glad she had come. She found it hard to pinpoint exactly why; perhaps because—despite the very real things that had been done in the Onaistian cause—Death had reminded her she did not believe in their One God. Her mother and Sullivain did believe, but it was not her burden to bear whatever that meant for them.

She said nothing, but stood with the cat balanced in the crook of one arm. With her free hand she reached into her pocket, and brought out one of the apples she kept for patients' children. She offered it to the man with the black eyes.

"For the cat," she said. "And I'll give my drops of blood."

He regarded it, surprised, and then laughed. The sound rolled around the empty grove like an echo in a cave. He took it from her, and tossed it from hand to hand. It shone red, almost glowing with vibrancy in the greyness of Death.

"Why this sudden curiosity?" he asked. She shrugged, not quite knowing how to voice the worries Sullivain had created within her with that one simple question.

"I don't think their faith, their god's Promise, has room for people like me," she said at last. "Perhaps I wanted to know whether to be afraid of Death."

"Would you have truly been afraid of nothing, if you knew that was what awaited you?"

She thought about it, the first time it had occurred to her to wonder, although it must have been in the background of her thoughts ever since she'd first talked to Peer Laius.

"No," she replied honestly. "Nothing wouldn't be so terrible." She considered. "Perhaps I'm more afraid of being nothing before I die. Because then it would be my fault."

"Then you're wiser than most Onaistian devotees," he remarked.

"I don't know about that." Hellevir shook herself, wondering if it were possible to waste Death's time, and held out her hand for him to take her blood. He regarded her outstretched palm, but didn't reach out to her.

199

"Before I take from you, I have something of yours you may have missed." He drew out her hairpin, the one she'd left behind when she'd saved Ionas. He didn't give it to her; instead he gestured for her to turn around, and she waited as he wound up her long hair. She was surprised he did not pull it too tight, as her pa had done when she was small. It felt odd to have her back to him, as if there was an icy draft from an open door behind her. She felt the brush of his cold hand on the back of her neck; from any other, it might have almost seemed a caress, a gentle touch. She didn't know what it meant from him.

She felt him slide the pin into her hair, felt the chill of it against her scalp. She turned back around to face him, and held her hand out wordlessly.

"So willing," he remarked wryly, and drew his nail across her thumb until blood dripped onto the ground. She felt no pain at all.

"You never will tell me who you are, will you?" she murmured.

He smiled and leaned forward as if about to impart a secret. He took a breath, and said, "Perhaps one day you'll guess."

She emerged from the cold into the different chill of autumn, shivering. She found herself coated in rime, and as she caught her breath she realized the sun had long since set and there was a light dusting of frost on the ground. Elsevir landed heavily on her shoulder, and pecked her irritably.

"You were gone for hours," the raven chided. "I was about to go for help."

"It didn't feel that long." She shuddered, her teeth chattering.

Something in her arms stirred, and she looked down into the bright yellow eyes of the grey cat. He yawned, showing a little pink tongue and sharp teeth.

"Me too," Hellevir murmured. "Let's get you some food."

She got up stiffly, the frost on her coat cracking and the cat docile in her arms, and headed back towards the main buildings. Elsevir nestled in close to her jaw.

"Did it go well?" he asked.

"Yes," Hellevir said, surprising herself as much as Elsevir with the good humor in her voice. "Yes, I think it did."

*

Hellevir put the journals back on their shelves. The priestesses had a right to know what had been done against people like them, people who talked to trees, listened to the waters, told stories to the fireplace. At the same time, she felt the need to be careful about exposing what she had discovered. Relations between the Order and the Peerage were guarded but amicable, and she didn't want to create tensions by unearthing atrocities from so long ago, committed by people long since dead. She thought it likely that a few of the priestesses already knew; Edrin certainly did, or she wouldn't have given the journals to Hellevir to read.

The next time she was due to go to the palace, she felt oddly tense, trepidation hot in her gut. She made mistakes throughout the day, burning some sage she was trying to dry as her thoughts snagged on what she might tell the Princess, if anything, about what the man with black eyes had said. The cat watched her fumble, curled up in Hellevir's coat at the end of her bed, purring warmly when she paused to give him scratches behind the ears.

The morning passed and no boat came for her. The light began to fade, and Hellevir was beginning to wonder whether something was amiss, when at last a priestess informed her that a boat was waiting outside the gates. She left the cat batting at the tail of an increasingly belligerent Elsevir, and went out to meet it. A light pattering of rain had begun, and she breathed in the earthy scent of wet stone, pulling up her hood and gathering her thoughts to meet the Princess.

The lights from the windows played on the surface of the canals; the soft sounds of water and the trill of distant music were synonymous to her now with the name Rochidain. The palace was quieter than she'd yet seen it, as she followed Sullivain's manservant from the docks and through to the Princess's study. The room was lit by a low-burning fire and lantern light, dim and warm, casting Sullivain's hair a deep bronze.

"Forgive the late hour," the Princess said without turning around, stacking some papers on her desk. "I was attending court today. Grandmother wouldn't hear of any interruption." She gestured vaguely for Hellevir to sit by the fire.

"Was it an important meeting?" Hellevir asked, pulling off her cloak and setting the packet of tea on the low table.

"No more than normal," Sullivain remarked. "The Temple is

making its usual demands. Nothing new." Hellevir's ears pricked up, curious. What could the Peerage want from the Crown?

"Demands?" she asked, she hoped nonchalantly. The Princess glanced at her with a smile, not fooled.

"Demands I cannot divulge, I'm afraid. Brandy?" She unstopped a decanter and poured out two glasses without waiting for an answer.

"I understand." Hellevir tried to hide the frustration in her voice.

"You seem very interested in what the Temple could want."

"I . . ." She took a breath, looking down into the amber liquid in the glass Sullivain had handed to her. "I've been reading up on Onaistian, doing some research. I found out things about them that worried me."

"What sort of things?"

Hellevir flinched, trying not to recall the figures, hastily and harshly sketched, the paper still dented with the hard press of the charcoal.

"Historically they've not looked favorably on people like me," she said vaguely.

"You're talking about the heathen burnings?"

Hellevir looked up sharply.

"You've heard about them?"

Sullivain remained standing, leaning her elbow against the mantelpiece with her drink in one hand.

"I've heard stories. Burnings, torture." She gave Hellevir a wry smile as if they were talking about the weather. "The Temple hasn't asked for leave to execute heathens, if that's what you're worried about. As pushy as the Peers are becoming."

Hellevir made herself smile back. "No," she said. "It was a long time ago."

"Your research wasn't inspired by my question at the ball, was it?" Hellevir glanced at Sullivain, met those copper eyes, unblinking and with a frankness that for a moment made her unsure what to say. Hellevir was again taken aback by her perceptiveness; it had happened so often now she wondered how she could keep being surprised.

"Yes," Hellevir replied, honestly. "It was. I wanted to know more about the faith, figure out for certain whether the person in Death is Onaistus."

"And?" There was a tension to her voice, like a cat coiled to spring.

"I found nothing in the books I read, but in the end it didn't matter. He told me himself he's not."

There was a stillness, a held breath, when even the fire declined to crackle or pop.

"I see," the Princess said. "He's not Onaistus." Her tone was unsurprised but disappointed, and something deeper than disappointed as well. "But does he know of him? Does he know if Onaistus is real?"

"He doesn't know." She was admitting dangerous things, things she doubted the man with dark eyes would want her to say. But seeing the Princess like this—lit by the firelight, her expression unreadable, which in itself betrayed how much she was disturbed, just as the Queen went still when she wanted no one to see her reaction—Hellevir only wanted to help.

"He doesn't know," the Princess murmured. Her scowl deepened. "How could he not know?" she demanded sharply. "He is a god of the afterlife."

Hellevir put down her glass, jittery with nerves.

"He's not a god. I don't know what he is."

"Don't you want to know? He lets you raise the dead, herbalist, are you not curious?"

"Of course I am," Hellevir replied. "But . . ." How could she explain it, how the world of Death constricted when she asked questions that were too pointed? How the emptiness of his eyes deepened every time she angered him, threatening her with the promise of the void?

The Princess made a visible effort to rein in her irritation.

"I suppose it does defeat the point to know," she said darkly, although from her tone Hellevir wondered whether she believed it. "Like Peer Tadeus says, proof leaves no room for faith." She took a gulp of brandy, expression glowering.

"I'm sorry," Hellevir found herself saying, wishing she could comfort her. "I . . . part of me had hoped he would know."

"And why is that?" the Princess shot over her shoulder as she helped herself to another drink.

"So that I could help you." The words slipped out, and even as they escaped her teeth Hellevir knew they were the wrong thing to say. The Princess's gaze flicked to her like a whip.

"Help me?" she repeated. Her tone was low, calm, but there was an edge to it, a dagger concealed under silk which made Hellevir wince. "Help me? What on earth makes you think I need help?"

Hellevir swallowed.

"I just . . . I know you hoped I could speak to him for you, plead your case."

"You know, do you?" The brandy was hot in Hellevir's veins and gave her courage she might not have otherwise had. She got to her feet, standing opposite the Princess before the fireplace. The heat cocooned them both, made thick the air around them and caused the rest of the world to fade away.

"You told me once that there was no Promise waiting for someone like you," Hellevir pressed. "You're afraid that you've done something to make you fall from the Path of Light."

The Princess stared at her, and for a moment Hellevir doubted herself, wondering whether she'd got everything horribly wrong. But there was something hounded in the way she looked at Hellevir, like a rabbit caught in torchlight, and for the first time she seemed less predator than prey. Hellevir had the sudden urge to reach out, take her hand, brush the fears from her forehead.

"You don't know what you're talking about," Sullivain said quietly.

"There's no shame in hoping I could have provided a way out. That I could have saved you." Hellevir hesitated, wondering if she was about to go too far. "Whatever it is you feel you've done, you can talk to me, tell me." Those were the words she'd been too afraid to say in the aviary. They fell from her, releasing a weight as they did so, and she was glad she'd spoken, regardless of how the Princess might respond.

That silence again. Heavy as a storm, silent as the calm before it. They were standing close, Hellevir realized, the scent of brandy on their breath. Hellevir felt her heart beating quickly, and her eyes flickered over to trace the line of the Princess's jaw; her neck, the curl of hair like a snail's shell over one ear. She could hear Sullivain breathing, and wondered what would happen if she leaned forward.

An intrusive thought. It was so sudden that she almost acted on it, her body half-moving even as she panicked and pulled back as if from a ledge. The Princess sighed, unaware.

"All this talk of saving," she said, perhaps in an attempt at light-heartedness. "All this talk of gods, it's exhausting." She seemed to hear the discordant note in her own voice, as she pressed her lips together and looked away. "I've been unguarded around you. To both our detriment."

Hellevir felt the rebuke like a slap, and leaned back. She clenched her jaw, feeling her cheeks flush.

"I'm sorry," she said. "I spoke out of turn."

"You say 'sorry' too much. I hear what you've said, and I appreciate it. But there are things you're better off not knowing about, herbalist. For your own good, as well as mine. And how can you save me when you don't know what I need saving from?"

Hellevir made to speak, but the Princess raised her hand. She smiled, a guarded thing that peeked from behind the persona she wore to court, so different to the woman Hellevir had come to know who simply liked to draw and spar.

"Let us not do this," the Princess continued quietly, her tone like a stagehand at a play, carefully whispering words to an actor who has forgotten her lines. "I like what we have." She gestured between the two of them, and the motion wafted with it the scent of the rosewater that Sullivain dabbed on her wrists. "At court I . . . I feel myself glancing towards the darkness for the glint of a blade. I reach for fruit and then think twice about eating it. I am not *safe*, Hellevir, but with you I feel as if I don't wear a crown, because I know you don't want me hurt. As if we're in your village by the woods, and you've just nodded your head at me to tell me everything will be all right. It's sad, isn't it, that I would enjoy someone's company just because I know they mean me no harm? But I don't need more from you than that, until the time comes when another Hannotir assassin gets too close."

Hellevir folded her arms over her chest, trying not to feel as if she were suddenly standing in a cold draft, although Sullivain's words coiled into her, made her chest tighten. She knew she'd crossed a line. It surprised her when the Princess raised a hand to her elbow, and Hellevir felt the warmth of her palm through her shirt. She was struck by how lovely the Princess was, just as she had been the first time she'd seen her in Death. Her heart skipped like a stone over water, and it made her feel all the more foolish for thinking she could aid this creature of gold and copper, a lion where she was just a crow.

"I just wanted to help," Hellevir said. She took a breath. "But I'll go."

"No," the Princess said. "Finish your brandy at least. I won't have it wasted. You make it difficult to feel angry at you, herbalist. You are too honest for you own good. I wish . . . I wish there were more like you in court. I'd feel less like I was at the mercy of a pack of wolves."

"I don't like the sound of court."

"It's a dance," her lip quirked. "One mistake and I'm out of step with the city, ridiculed and in danger of a knife in my back."

"Tangled threads," Hellevir said quietly. Sullivain laughed at that, but Hellevir felt suddenly tired and helpless, like she'd stumbled in a dance of her own, relying only on the Princess's good grace to keep her in time. She should never have been so bold, and thought tiredly that she'd be ruminating about this exchange for a long time. She finished her brandy and put it aside.

"I should go," she said, wanting suddenly to hide. "I'm . . ."

"If you say you're sorry again I'll have you clapped in irons."

Hellevir allowed herself a faint smile.

Don't ask it, she thought to herself. *Don't make this worse.*

"The Queen," she said. "Your grandmother. Did she make you do whatever it is that made you fall from the Path?"

The Princess's brightness faded. It was the only way Hellevir could think to describe her sudden absence of light. She turned away, the dismissal blatant. Hellevir took her cue and left.

CHAPTER SIXTEEN

The knock came at night. The cat was curled up on her knees and let out a cantankerous mew as she pushed him gently aside to get out of bed. She already knew, with some odd prescience, exactly what she would find on the other side of the door.

The servant from the royal palace, the one in red who always collected her from the docks. Bion. Behind him Edrin stood rubbing her eyes, tired from her nightly rounds.

"The Princess demands your presence," the servant said, holding out a letter. "I've come to fetch you."

"Can the Princess wait until morning?" Hellevir muttered, although she already knew the answer.

"No. You must come now." Hellevir took the letter and snapped the seal. The words she read stilled her heart, stopped her breath. There was only one sentence, with the Princess's curling signature beneath it. It was dated midsummer, when she had first ordered Hellevir to bring her back if she were ever to die.

Time to fulfill your promise.

"Is she . . ."

Hellevir glanced down and saw blood on the white cuff of Bion's sleeve. He tugged at it when he saw her looking, pulling his jacket down to cover it. His cheek seemed swollen with the beginnings of a black eye.

"Let me dress," she said, and closed the door. She stood there for a moment, holding the letter to her stomach as if to quell the nausea tugging at her insides. She took a breath and let it out slowly. Elsevir cocked his head to one side in question. "The

Princess is dead," Hellevir murmured. The words didn't seem real. They were spoken by a character in a book, an actor on a stage, not her. Her pulse hammered in her temples, loud as the beating of a drum, and she sank into a chair before she fell.

Elsevir ruffled his feathers and nervously preened his tail.

"Will you bring her back?"

"I have no choice," Hellevir replied. "Her threats are still real."

"Then you will need the pearls."

Hellevir pulled herself together. She stood and dressed hastily, fastening her hair up with the hairpin which she now always thought of as Death's, and pinned the Princess's brooch to her collar.

She pulled out her bedside drawer. Inside were her herbalist's notes and Sathir's lessons. At the back, folded in their riddle, were the two pearls, glinting like droplets of milk. She heard again that cave creature's cackle, dry as tinder cracking under pressure.

Elsevir alighted on her shoulder, and they both looked down at them.

"It's a shame," the raven remarked. "If only they could each save a soul. You could keep one for the next time the Princess is killed."

"That would be too easy. Together they are a single precious thing." Hellevir picked them up and put them in the pocket of her heavy coat, wrapping her fist around them.

The servant was waiting anxiously, tapping his foot, and led her back to the gate at a brisk trot. Edrin caught Hellevir's elbow as she was leaving.

"Is it serious?" she asked.

"It won't be."

"Is it . . . does someone need to be raised?" Hellevir couldn't think what to say that wouldn't betray Sullivain's secrets, so she just nodded.

"I will be back soon," she said. "Ask Sathir to feed the cat if I'm not back by morning?"

Hellevir was always tempted to wander the streets of Rochidain at this time of night, to let the silence and the echoing canals soak into her, but it was no place for a young woman—or anyone—to walk alone. She felt eyes watching her from doorways, and wished the servant had thought to bring a guard, but they made it to the carriage on the main thoroughfare without issue. Hellevir watched the silent canals slip by, rubbing her thumb over the pearls again and again until they were warm.

"Do you think someone killed her?" she asked the raven on her knee.

"What else would it be in the dead of night?" Elsevir replied, clicking his beak. "She has her own physicians if she is simply unwell."

"Another assassination, then." The fear that had been hounding her since she first came to Rochidain, and now it had happened.

When the carriage arrived, the manservant rushed her through a side door and up the servants' stairs. Hellevir could hear music and laughter from the gardens, saw lights and moving figures through the windows.

"Where are all the guards?" she asked Bion.

"At their party," he muttered as he led her down the corridors.

"The guards have a party?"

"Yes. A yearly ball, to thank them. We keep a skeleton crew working, but . . ." He didn't finish the sentence, and said nothing more as they came to a door and he opened it for them. The door turned out to be a bookcase on the other side, and Hellevir found herself in one of the royal chambers.

Sullivain was lying on a bed. At first Hellevir just thought she was wrapped in dark red sheets, but then she saw her sightless eyes, her lips half-parted. She saw the deep gash across the Princess's throat. The image seared Hellevir as if she had been branded, and she sucked in a breath of air that tasted like iron. The edge of the wound was a brutal slash, cleaner than she had ever thought flesh could be cut. It was deep, violently deep. Sullivain's hair lay in bloody ringlets on her silk pillow.

For a moment Hellevir couldn't hear sounds, beyond the sharp rasp of her own breath, the pounding of the blood in her ears. The smell became overpowering, whipping her back to the times when the cottage by the woods had reeked of offal after a successful hunt, her father's hands slick as he pulled back the hide. The thought occurred to her, rapping quietly on the back door of her thoughts, that she was going to be sick. She realized that the servant had taken her arm as she swayed.

Silly girl, she told herself. *You've seen the dead before. You've seen Sullivain in a worse state than this.*

A maidservant stood in the center of the room wringing her hands. When she saw Hellevir and the manservant she dashed forward and seized Hellevir's arm.

"Can you save her, miss, please, can you save her?"

"Enough, Lilia," the manservant said sternly. "Wait outside and make sure no one comes in." The maid bobbed a frantic curtsy and did as she was told.

Hellevir walked over to the bed, her legs unsteady as a colt's. There was so much blood. As she approached she saw that there was someone lying on the floor on the other side. For a moment she didn't know which body to examine first.

"What happened here?" she breathed.

"The mistress was asleep. Two men broke in through the window, climbed the ivy outside. One held her down, and the other . . ." He couldn't finish, averting his eyes from the cut across her throat. Hellevir went over to the open window and looked out. It was a straight drop down to the water. A small, unmarked boat knocked against the side of the wall, at the foot of a thick vine of ivy. She could see some places where it had been pulled away from the brick by the climbers' weight.

Hellevir glanced over at Sullivain's body, forcing herself to look more closely. The blood was drying to brown where it hadn't pooled.

"I heard the struggle," Bion said. "I sleep in the room next door."

"You came in and fought them both?"

"Yes, I tried to. One came for me, but I fought him and hit his head until he stopped moving. I was between the other man and the window, and he dashed through the door to get away." He glanced at the body on the bed. "I tried to stop the blood, but it just kept coming. It soaked through everything I tried to wrap around the wound."

"I'm not sure there was much you could have done. Where is the Queen?"

"She's on the trail of the one that got away." He shivered. "Her Grace will likely find him. She has a single-mindedness when it comes to the Princess."

Hellevir nodded, about to speak when a peal of laughter rose up from the gardens. She gestured angrily outside. "A party at such a time. Did no one think this would be the perfect moment for another attack?" The manservant shrugged helplessly.

"The Queen ordered us to keep it quiet and alert no one but you," he said.

Hellevir stood by the bed, looking down at the red-slicked face. It was hard to believe this was the same woman she had visited only the week before, bringing her weekly supply of tea. The same woman who had laughed at her for being so tense. Had drawn her picture in charcoal. It just felt *wrong*. Hellevir felt a resolution harden in her chest, tattered with an odd panic. The question she'd never dared ask herself directly now forced itself into her mind.

What if he won't let me raise her a second time?

She dismissed the fear. She would bring Sullivain back. There was no alternative.

"Keep watch?"

"What?" the manservant asked.

"Not you," Hellevir told him.

"Of course," Elsevir replied. "Be careful."

"It's Death, how dangerous can it be?" She picked up a velvet-upholstered chair from next to the gilt dressing table and placed it beside the bed. She took off her heavy coat and sat down. Putting one hand in her pocket over the pearls, and slipping Sullivain's fingers through her own, she took a deep breath, as if preparing to dive, and closed her eyes.

The greyness, the silence, were becoming as familiar to her as her old home by the woods used to be. She stood looking about her, but there was no sign of the Princess.

"Sullivain?" she asked. "Are you there?" No answer came, just her own shallow, muted breaths. She walked towards the corridor, and started as she saw movement out of the corner of her eye, but it was just her own reflection in a long gilt mirror. It was the first time she'd looked in an actual mirror in Death. It was unnerving, reflecting her a thousandfold as if there were another mirror right behind her. It made her feel as if she were being watched, scrutinized by something that breathed upon her shoulder, but when she glanced back there was nothing there. She shuddered and turned away, reflexively putting her hand to the back of her neck.

Hellevir walked through the corridors, letting instinct guide her. She came to a broad staircase that descended to the main hall, through the double doors that led to the ballroom. There, Death was waiting. He stood in the center of the room, looking away from her with his hands clasped behind his back.

The light of the room sank and ebbed as if he were absorbing it. The many windows of the ballroom looked out onto the dark nothing. On the walls between them were mirrors, reflecting many Hellevirs from many angles; she tried not to look at them, but her eyes had already caught on their infinitude, and left her disorientated, not entirely sure which version was the real Hellevir or where in the room she really stood.

Her footsteps rang mutely on the checkerboard floor. She ignored the hairs rising on her arms and the back of her neck.

"So the Princess has got herself killed," the world rumbled, the darkness wavering with it like drapes in a breeze, "as we knew she would, in time. And here you are, her sacrificial lamb."

Hellevir straightened, and tried to keep the indignation out of her voice.

"I wouldn't put it like that," she remarked. Her voice should have rung around the great hall, echoed back to her, but it was as if the air clapped the sound back into her throat. Her voice in comparison to his was as weak as the guttering of a candle before the roar of an open fire.

"You keep her from me, giving yourself away piece by piece, and in return she and her grandmother refrain from destroying everything you hold dear," the black figure said. He still hadn't turned around, and Hellevir wished he would, at the same time glad not to be beneath his penetrating stare. "What else should I call you but a sacrificial lamb?"

Hellevir's eyes flickered to the nothingness outside of the windows, but she couldn't look for long; it made her feel blind.

"Blackmail is a sort of bargain, I suppose," she said. "I simply deal with her as I do with you. Odd that I should prefer my bargain with Death," she added, more to herself than to the black figure in the center of the room, "but here we are."

He turned around before she had realized he was moving. A heartbeat later he was in front of her, and she sucked in a breath.

"What a compliment," he remarked, "that you would prefer to deal with me."

"A choice between the rocks or the storm," she retorted.

"Am I the storm or the rocks?"

"I haven't decided."

They regarded each other. The light from the chandeliers seemed to die as it touched his eyes, to be swallowed whole. Looking into them, she felt as if she were at risk of being swallowed too, lost in an emptiness. There was just no one there. She shuddered, and he saw, and she wished he hadn't seen.

"Do you plan to do this forever?" he asked. He reached out quickly and she winced, but he just tucked a stray lock of hair behind her ear. "Pluck her from Death whenever it finds her, like a child being pulled from the river it insists on jumping into again and again?"

"She didn't seek out Death. It finds her because of who she is as heir to the throne."

"Death finds those who don't fear it more easily than those who have learned to do so."

Hellevir scowled.

"What do you mean? Are you saying she will become careless?"

"Yes. No jump will be high enough, no horse swift enough, no current deep enough. She will play with the immortality you have given her. She has no mortal fear, and you are the reason why. Her fearlessness saturates the footprints left behind her leading into Death. She has no fear, that is, until the moment she feels the knife cut into her throat, the very real sting of mortality."

Hellevir swallowed, her jaw tight.

"I don't have a choice," she said quietly.

"If you insist." He looked disappointed. "Although I wonder what you would choose, if there were no threats." She said nothing, unwilling to admit she'd wondered the same thing herself. What would she do now, if there was no danger in refusing to bring the Princess back? "Perhaps at first you were her lamb out of fear. But now . . ." He trailed off. "Now you've seen her in the only two forms she'll ever take. Living and dead. You've seen for yourself what rot can do to her face, and after all you've given to bring her back once, and now twice, I wonder whether you could leave her here, even without your hands tied."

She swallowed, indignation hot on her tongue, but the words to refute him wouldn't come. The sight of Sullivain's slashed-open throat pulsed behind her eyes, vile and *wrong*.

Something clicked within her. An understanding she'd been unconsciously trying to subdue, hiding it behind anger, indignation at Sullivain's threats. She recalled the moment by the firelight when she'd last spoken with Sullivain, the sudden impulse to lean in, lean closer.

Oh, she thought.

He held out his hand, smiling triumphantly at her wordlessness. Numbly, she reached into her pocket where the two pearls lay in their riddle. She hesitated, just for a second, and then drew out only one—a thousand Hellevirs in the mirrored walls did the same, watching her from behind and beside and above and below—and dropped it onto his palm. She wondered if he could hear the heavy pound of the blood in her veins, but he simply picked up the pearl between thumb and forefinger and examined it. For a moment there was something there, behind those eyes, but she blinked and it, and the pearl, were gone.

"It's unfortunate that such precious things are to be wasted on the same life again and again," the man dressed in black remarked. His disapproval pressed against the glass of the windows with such pressure she half-expected them to splinter. "When so many are in need of saving, and you are so quick to help anyone who comes to you. One day you may find yourself without a means of payment, and you must not think that I will make a false trade. Then you *will* pay the full price from yourself." His words grazed like nails down the inside of her ribs.

"In our bargain you never said I couldn't bring back the same soul more than once," she said boldly. Her skin felt tight from the density of the nothing outside.

"I suppose I did not. More fool me."

"The next riddle?" she asked, her voice cracking slightly. The pressure at the windows eased, but did not leave entirely.

He held out his hand, and between his fingers was a slip of paper. She reached out to take it, but the edge of the paper slid into her finger and her blood welled and dripped freely down her hand. She hissed and put the finger to her mouth.

"You could have warned me," she muttered, taking the riddle with the other hand. For the first time since she had entered Death, that smile dwindled and died. The sardonic lines from nose to mouth faded. He pressed his lips together.

"I *have* warned you," he said, and the great hall quivered with the sound of his voice.

He reached to the side and brought back Sullivain's hand from nowhere, pressing it into Hellevir's. The Princess was frowning as she looked out of the windows, and tugged at Hellevir's grasp like a child. Something within Hellevir unknotted in relief. She'd been so afraid Death would refuse this time. She held on tightly.

"I wish it would stop raining," Sullivain complained.

"It isn't raining," Hellevir pointed out, her voice high.

"It's so dark. I want to go outside, Kory's waiting."

"I don't think you'd like it out there."

"You don't know. I may love it. Do you think he'll have my new bow?"

Hellevir wound her fingers through Sullivain's and held them against her chest. She enjoyed seeing Sullivain like this, willful and unaware of any bargains or threats, unjaded by the court, just wanting to go outside.

"Thank you," she said to the man dressed in black. Something of his usual mockery pressed crow's feet into the corner of his eyes.

"That's the first time you've thanked me," he remarked, and she was dismissed with a wave of his hand.

She awoke to the taste of sickening fear. Not her own fear, but coming from elsewhere, roiling through her like a wave in a storm and drowning her in its sudden ferocity. Blinding white and blood-red, sharp and nauseating, within her and upon her and pressing the air from her lungs, and all she could taste was her own blood, and all she could feel was a white-hot pain at her throat. But whiter, hotter, more searing, was the mouth-foaming fury.

She came to with a gasp to find that her fingers had gone white and numb in Sullivain's grip. She winced and pulled away, startled, reeling from whatever she had felt as she left Death.

A hand gripped her shoulder, pinched tight like a crab's claw.

"Did you do it?" the Queen demanded. Hellevir couldn't find her voice. She just nodded shakily.

The Queen scowled at her, and then sat on the bed beside

Sullivain, taking her hand and pressing it between her own, kissing her fingertips as she looked down at her granddaughter. Already the broad split like a second smile across her throat was beginning to seal, the muscles knitting together, the tendons re-twining. Hellevir sat back and watched as she felt the cold of awakening course through her, a faded thing after the scorching torrent she'd felt on waking. Her limbs began to tremble.

It was her, she thought. *Somehow I just felt what Sullivain was feeling. Gods. Such anger.* She'd never felt anything like it before. The very thought of it caught in the back of her throat like an unreleased scream.

Sullivain suddenly sat up and retched, vomiting blood from her lungs and stomach. Her hand clutched the Queen's so tightly Hellevir could see that her fingernails were indenting the skin, but the Queen didn't release her, only brushed the hair from her clammy forehead and waited. When she was done Sullivain sagged, exhausted, and yet somehow managed a bloody grin when she saw Hellevir sitting by her bedside. Hellevir had to admire how she took things in her stride. After feeling all that, Hellevir could not have grinned.

The Queen stood, letting Sullivain sink back into the cushions. She turned and clicked her fingers, and Hellevir looked back to see Bion push the bedroom doors open, and two guards walked in, carrying a man Hellevir guessed to be the second assassin between them. He strained at their hold, baring crooked teeth. Hellevir was taken aback by how *normal* he looked. Shouldn't assassins have one milk-eye, tattoos of their guild insignia, an air of evil? She wouldn't have given him a second glance in the street. He looked like he could have been a fisherman, some kind of worker; he was lean with muscle, and his hands, chained in front of him, looked rough, his fingernails black with dirt. Not with dirt, Hellevir realized. Black with Sullivain's blood.

"This is the man who slit your throat," the Queen said to her granddaughter. The man was staring at Sullivain, at the absence of a scar on her throat, as if he couldn't believe the evidence of his own eyes.

"What witchcraft is this?" he snarled. The Queen seemed to find this amusing.

Sullivain rose stiffly from the covers to look at the man in the guards' grip, her lip curling slightly, teeth bared. She looked braced to do harm, ready to hurl herself at him, but the Queen's touch on her arm kept her knelt on the bedsheets.

"Two of them?" the Princess demanded. Hellevir noticed for the first time that the body of the other assassin had been dragged into the center of the room. He was a larger man, heavier set.

"Yes," the Queen said. "Bion killed this one." The Queen kicked him onto his back, and his head lolled and his eyes stared up blankly at the ceiling. Hellevir saw that his forehead had been caved in, and her gorge rose. She looked away. "That one tried to escape through the cellars."

Sullivain snorted. "He should have known better. No one knows the cellars like you."

"No. No one knows the cellars like me." The Queen jerked her head to the guards holding the second man. "Take him downstairs." The guards did as they were told, ignoring the man's struggles.

There was a beat of silence, and Hellevir looked up to find herself pinned by two pairs of eyes, one copper as coins, and the other—the Queen's—the color of iron. She had to try hard not to visibly shrink.

"What . . ." she started, and then saw Sullivain's meaningful glance at the body on the floor. Hellevir got to her feet, already shaking her head. "No," she said simply. "Absolutely not. Why would I?"

The Queen arched an eyebrow.

"No?"

"This is no different from that man in the prison cells, Loris. I won't raise a man just for you to torture him." She gestured to the door. "There were two assassins. If you must interrogate someone, interrogate the one who is still alive."

"Miss Andottir," the Queen began, her tone tinged with impatience, but Sullivain cut across her.

"Two is always better for an interrogation," she exclaimed, exasperated. "You work on one, and the other will hear the screams and talk before a hand is laid on him. Don't you want to help me find out who's doing this?"

Hellevir flinched, appalled. "Of course I do," she replied through her teeth. "And I will. But not like this."

She felt the Queen's hand on her arm, perhaps intended to be a conciliatory gesture, but it felt like a prison guard seizing her before clapping her in irons.

"Miss Andottir, two men just killed my only grandchild. I am no closer to finding out who is hiring these assassins than I was months ago. The Hannotirs have been as slippery as soap; not a bad thought for the Crown can be evidenced between them. I must know who is doing this, and your qualms are becoming an irritating obstacle." Hellevir felt a sliver of fear wriggle through her at the threat in her voice. "The man downstairs may not talk," she said. "Just as the cook did not talk. I would like to double our chances of a confession. I need you to bring him back."

"You raise him, we interrogate him, find out if it's the Hannotirs once and for all," Sullivain said, and her tone was hard, harder than Hellevir had ever heard it before, as hard as her grandmother's. She'd never used that tone with her, the tone of command.

"Don't you care what it costs me?" Hellevir demanded.

"Frankly," the Queen said, "no."

Hellevir wasn't looking at her, but Sullivain. She knew full well that the Queen didn't care how many body parts Hellevir might lose if it meant the threat to her granddaughter was annihilated, but the Princess surely gave a damn, after all this. Sullivain opened her mouth, then closed it and looked away. Hellevir felt disappointment settle hard as sediment into her stomach.

"I could talk to him again," Hellevir suggested, doing her best to keep a hold on her own temper. "Like with Loris."

Sullivain snorted. "That hardly worked last time," she muttered.

"I'm not bringing him back," Hellevir said again, her heart beating loudly with her own stubbornness. "I will only save lives that are going to be lived."

There was a heavy pause. At last the Queen took a breath, as if she were about to place a bet on a dog that she had just seen lose a race.

"Fine," she agreed. "Get to it, then. Bion, fetch Sulli a washbasin, for Onaistus's sake. She smells like a dead thing."

It was unpleasant, entering Death so soon after she'd left it. Like rubbing a bruise that she'd only just made.

The room was the same. The covers had been rumpled in a different way, the chair had moved, but otherwise nothing had changed. At least, nothing she could see. There was something different about the atmosphere, though, and she tensed, looking around her. It felt . . . the only way she could think to describe it was like the theatre where Farvor had sometimes taken her, but after the show; the lights down, the props put away, the curtains drawn. The stillness was a different sort of stillness. Lighter, without the heaviness of watchfulness that usually dragged it down. Was this how Death felt when he wasn't giving her an entrance?

Sure enough, the mirrors were empty, lifeless, reflecting nothing, as if they weren't mirrors at all. The place felt truly dead.

Hellevir walked through the corridors, realizing that even the ambient grey light that seemed to come from everywhere and nowhere was dimmer than it usually was. It made her feel nervous, as if she was somewhere she wasn't supposed to be. She opened her mouth to shout for the dead man before remembering she didn't know his name. She half-wondered whether she should call for Death, just to let him know she was there, but something stopped her. It felt furtive, sneaking around the empty place, and it made her wonder what she could get away with.

She walked out through the front doors and into the gardens. The gravel was almost silent under her boots. She could see the city from here, across the still canal, and it looked oddly like a set made of wood, an empty thing with no lights or sound, no infinity of tiny movements. She looked up out of curiosity. No mirrored sky, just the blackness without stars. Nothing.

"Back again so soon?"

She jumped violently, betraying her nerves. The man with the black eyes was watching her, amused, but there was something colder about him now, which warned her he was not pleased. The blackness of his cloak seemed somehow blacker than usual, as if its outlines were cut out from the fabric of the world.

"I . . . I was sent by the Princess," was all she could think to say.

"Quite her little lapdog, aren't you? Or perhaps I should say little lamb."

She clenched her jaw, but ignored the jab. "I've come for the man who killed her. I want to know who sent him."

"Odd. I didn't think you'd have the time to find the next precious thing. But then again, time doesn't quite work here, so perhaps it's been longer than I thought."

She said nothing. The world darkened, infinitesimally, but enough for her to notice. He watched her closely, and she tried not to feel intimidated by him. She wished suddenly and abstractly that she were taller, or he shorter.

"I see. You simply want to talk with him again. Such bravado, for a lamb," the world remarked. They regarded each other, the old arguments and threats strung between them like gossamer, trembling at their touch. Eventually he growled, a guttural sound, and waved away the unsaid things as if they were tangles of flies that irritated him. "Do as you will, I do not have the patience. If you can get him to talk to you, he is all yours."

She followed his gesture and saw a figure standing on the great bridge crossing the royal canal, looking into the water. A low whistle drifted towards them, odd in the still air. She approached him, and when he didn't seem to notice her, she tapped him on the shoulder. He stopped whistling and glanced around in surprise.

He was an older man, his head close-shaven in the manner of the city guard. He had a rough look to him, and a scar crooked his stubbled chin. Looking at him, she didn't think he was a professional killer, just a soldier from the countryside who had been paid to do the job.

"What do you want?" he demanded in a thick rural accent. She bit her lip, wondering where to begin. "I'm waiting for my missus. If she sees me talking to you she'll get all het up."

Missus, she thought unhappily. This man had left a wife behind. What he'd said wasn't a lot to work with. She wondered how she could possibly guide the conversation somewhere useful. She wondered why he was stuck in this memory in particular, standing on a bridge waiting for his missus, and who he thought she was. Perhaps some passer-by with whom he'd talked.

"Don't worry, I'll be gone by the time she arrives," she said.

"Are you going to arrest me?" he asked, without looking at her. A guard, then.

"Should I?"

"I done nothing wrong."

"Then why do you think I'd arrest you?"

His eyes glazed a bit as he looked over the canal, and he didn't reply, as if he hadn't heard her. She repeated her question, and he glanced at her as if seeing her for the first time.

"What do you want?" he said. She blinked. "I'm waiting for my missus. If . . ."

". . . She sees you talking to me she'll get all het up," Hellevir muttered. "Right." She tried again, taking him through the conversation.

"I done nothing wrong."

"You know that's not true," she tried, keeping her responses vague, the meaning clear even if she didn't know the exact wording that the guard in his memories had used. He turned to her, his rough face chipped with anger.

"And why must I? It's not my fight. I've a life here, a missus, I'm not like to throw it all away in another man's battle." He turned away, back to the canal. "Good day, sir."

"They want to conscript you?" Hellevir guessed. "In the War over the Waves?"

"It's not my bloody war," he spat. "What do I care who wears the crown?"

Hellevir hummed to herself. This wasn't really getting her anywhere. She needed to direct him to a useful memory, perhaps using a trigger, and he would switch, the same way Loris had when she mentioned Rochidain.

"Did you fight for the Bergerads?" she asked. That glazed look, confused, half-seeing her. Then the slow turn away. She sighed. She'd lost him.

"What do you want?" he grumbled. "I'm waiting for my missus. If she sees me talking to you she'll get all het up." She tried again, led him through the memory. When she reached the end, she asked him about the Queen instead. Something flickered, and she wondered if she'd caught him, but he just looked away, back to the canal.

"What do you want?"

She tried to turn him this way and that, like guiding a stream with stones and mud, but always he became caught, flooded, and returned to his source, standing on the bridge and waiting for his missus. It felt like she was steering his memories for hours, uselessly.

When he'd turned away from her for the hundredth time, she

put her hands on her hips, her patience growing taut. She glanced back to the head of the bridge, where the man with black eyes stood watching, smiling at her performance. She wondered what would happen if she had to go back into life, face Sullivain and the Queen, with no new information. She would be made to raise him. A waste of her soul.

Before she could reconsider how wise it was, she turned back to the man on the bridge and took his arms, pulling him around to face her, forcing his attention away from that eternal canal.

"Enough of this," she said firmly. "I know you killed the Princess!" He blinked, and for the first time seemed to look at her, properly look at her.

"What? I . . . ?" he started, but she didn't give him time to think.

"And they killed you too. You are dead."

Behind her, around her, the world darkened. The canal waters rippled as if the earth had quaked. She ignored it.

"What . . . I'm . . . ?"

"Who hired you to kill the Princess?" she demanded. "They have your friend too. He's alive and will probably confess everything, so you may as well tell me."

"Is this some trick?" he asked, glancing around him and behind. "I won't be part of no trick."

"No trick! Just say a name."

"I'm . . . I'm . . . that's . . ." He rubbed his forehead with a frown—the area where the blow had struck him—blinking repeatedly as if to clear his mind. She caught his face in her hands, his stubble prickly under her palms, and made him look at her.

"You are dead," she said slowly. "But you killed the Princess too. You did what you were paid to do. Now I need to know who hired you both, and it doesn't matter if you tell me because they can't do anything to you here. You're already dead."

"I . . . You're talking nonsense, girl." He tried to move away, but she didn't let him.

"I'm not. Look around you. This *feels* like Death."

"I . . ." He looked up, around, but found no words to deny the truth of it.

"The name."

"They can't . . . this is it? It *does* feel like it, the cold . . . How did I . . ."

"Your wife won't come to harm, I promise. I won't let them punish her, if that's what you're worried about."

"The missus? She's been dead for years. Can they reach her here too?" Hellevir softened her grip on him.

"No, they can't," she said. "And they can't get you either."

He shook his head, shook her off, pressing the bridge of his nose as if he had a headache.

"I can't," he said. "If they found out . . ."

"They can't do anything to you, not anymore. Any promises you made to them ended when you died."

"This isn't happening," he muttered. "It's . . ."

"Please, tell me."

"It's . . . Gods, I need to think."

"Tell me!"

He shook his head again, closing his eyes. He turned away, and for a moment she thought she'd lost him again, but he put his hands to his head. He looked back at her.

"Did he do this?" he demanded. "After everything we did for him? Did he do me in?"

"Who?"

"Did he turn on us?"

"Who are you talking about?"

"Don't ask me bloody who. Auland, that bastard . . . did he do me in? Was he the one who killed me?"

Hellevir felt her stomach drop. "Auland?" she repeated. "Auland Redeion? He's the one who paid you?"

"Yes, the bastard. Me and my mate, we owed him a favor from the war, and he called it in. We fought together; he saved my life, and Mattis's." He rubbed his forehead again. "Did he turn on us? Gods, I knew him a cold man but . . ."

Hellevir didn't know what to say. She was reeling. She started as he gripped her wrists.

"Take me back," he demanded, his eyes clear and angry, tinged with something like madness. "I don't want to die, not yet, lass, I'm not ready. I got to . . . I got things to *do*!"

"I can't, I . . ."

"You must be able to! Don't lie to me! I don't want to *be* here!" He shook her violently, and her head pounded from it.

"You're hurting me!" she gasped, trying to pull away, but he was three times heavier and his arms were twice the size of hers.

"I'll hurt you more, lass, gods help me, if you don't get me out of here," he growled at her.

"That's quite enough of that," the world around them remarked, and a hand gripped the soldier by the back of the neck and pulled him away like a dog. The soldier stumbled and fell, and Hellevir braced herself for his attack, but he just pulled himself up the bridge barrier, and his eyes caught again on the canal. His shoulders sagged and he returned to standing, waiting for his missus and whistling.

The man with the black eyes turned to her, and she realized she was gripping the back of his dark cloak like a child. She dropped it quickly, embarrassed that she had needed to be saved.

"Thank you," she said curtly. The man's lip curled at the edge, as if he'd enjoyed the show.

"Twice you've thanked me in one night," he remarked. "I shall have to start keeping a tally." ⸱

"I didn't think he'd react that way."

"To being told his life was finished? How did you think he would react?"

"I don't know," she admitted. She swallowed, trying to quell her shaking nerves. "I should go back," she said. "They'll want to know what I found out."

That House Redeion is behind the attempts on Sullivain's life. It wasn't the Hannotirs. I was wrong. Her mind whirled with everything that meant.

Auland was Calgir's uncle. It would ruin the House, result in them all being hanged. Would they hang Calgir? And what would happen to her brother? He was the knight's squire, they'd assume he was an accomplice to the whole thing. She didn't doubt for a second that he was ignorant of it all, and Calgir probably was too, but it wouldn't matter; the Crown would hold the whole House accountable. She recalled the bruises on Loris's skin, the unnatural bend to his arm. The Queen would show no mercy. Sullivain would show no mercy. She had no reason to.

She suddenly felt both enclosed on all sides and lost in a vastness like the sea. She had no idea what to do, and panic gnawed at her. Her brother might be hanged. Even though she knew she could bring him back, if it came to it, such a logical thought had no place in the face of that visceral fear: her brother might die. And what if she couldn't bring him back? What if he was the one life she couldn't save?

The darkness drew around her as she thought, until she finally realized that the man with the black eyes was regarding her, entertained by watching her realize the position she was in. He offered her no help, and she did not ask for it.

"I should go," she said again.

"Then go," he replied.

She opened her eyes groggily, her body protesting against sitting still for so long, and then at the flush of cold through her skin that set her teeth chattering. Her soul had barely caught up with her when a shadow loomed over her.

"Well?" Sullivain demanded. Her hair was clean, now, if still damp, and she had dressed in fresh clothes, but there were still brown specks of dried blood on her skin. The Queen was leaning against the wall behind her, arms folded, and Hellevir had a sudden and horrific anxiety that she already knew everything, and would simply humor any lies Hellevir told while the jaws of some sharp-toothed trap slowly closed around her.

"Can I at least have some water first?" Hellevir muttered, hoping it didn't sound like a delaying tactic. She *was* horribly thirsty.

"You were ages!" the Princess snapped as Bion poured her a glass of water. "What took so long?"

"Time works differently there," Hellevir said and took a gulp.

"So? What did you find out?"

Hellevir put down the glass, not looking at her, not looking at the Queen, who remained silent.

"He didn't know," she lied quietly.

"He didn't know?" Sullivain exclaimed. "How could he not know?"

"He took orders and payment from a stranger, he didn't know him. He was dressed in a dark coat." She wasn't used to lying. It felt like something foreign on her tongue, and she wanted to spit it out. "His friend, the one you caught. I think he's called Mattis."

"So you've learned nothing, then? It was a waste of time?"

Hellevir swallowed, knowing the motion was a giveaway but suddenly very aware of how dry her mouth was.

"Yes."

"And you refuse to bring him back?"

"I do." She looked up at Sullivain. "Our deal is for me to keep you alive, not to raise anyone at your beck and call. And to keep you alive, I can't waste myself on every man you want to torture." She glanced at the Queen. "Despite your threats. If you make me raise this man, there will not be enough for Sullivain next time she dies. I can feel it." At that moment she wasn't certain whether it was a lie. She felt exhausted.

Sullivain whirled away with an annoyed growl, and began stalking up and down her bedchamber. Hellevir was glad she was seated, the quivering in her limbs hidden. The Queen reached out a hand to stop Sullivain's pacing, an almost lazy gesture that halted her granddaughter at once.

The Queen came to stand in front of Hellevir. There was something ruthless about her, a ruthlessness Hellevir didn't think Sullivain was yet capable of, but even so Hellevir met her eyes and held them. If she could stare down the god of Death, or whatever he was, she could stare down one woman. But it was a much, much harder gaze to hold, and she willed her features to settle into tiredness, resignation, the real emotions she felt. Fear curled like a live thing within her, desperate to get out, to claw its way up her throat and become evident in her eyes, but she squeezed it brutally until it settled whimpering within her. Panic gripped her, so that her lungs ached to breathe quickly, but she forced the air in through her nose and out just as slowly. At last the Queen nodded, and turned to Bion.

"Put the body on the pikes," she commanded. "Let the world know Sulli survived an attempt on her life."

Bion flinched.

"The pikes, mistress? Like Loris?"

"Did I stutter?"

"Mistress, you want people to know there was an assassination attempt?"

"Why not?" Sullivain interrupted, whirling around, her tone flippant. "It'll make me look invulnerable to the people. Because I lived." She glanced at Hellevir. "And I am invulnerable, aren't I, herbalist?"

Hellevir made herself nod.

"Yes," she muttered. "As long as I am here."

Hellevir left the palace feeling like a different person. Two visits to Death had left her hollow, a ghost. Exhaustion dogged her every movement, and the truth she had learned traipsed after her with every step.

She began to hurry in the direction of House Redeion. Her ears still rang with the shouts of the second assassin as he was dragged to the cells by the guards. She had no idea how long a man like that could keep quiet, whether he had any motive to remain loyal to Auland Redeion, and the uncertainty drove her faster. She had to warn them.

She was halfway there when common sense stopped her.

I can't, she realized. *It's too much of a risk. If there's even the slightest chance the Queen didn't believe me, and sent someone to watch me, I'd be betraying House Redeion by going to them at this time of night as surely as if I'd told her the truth.*

She glanced around, though she knew she'd never see one of the Queen's network if they didn't want to be seen. She felt watched, hounded. She could write a letter, send it by Elsevir, but he was hardly inconspicuous. A letter could easily fall into the wrong hands.

Auland Redeion was hosting a dinner tomorrow night. Then she would talk to her brother, to Calgir, tell them what she had discovered. She had no choice but to wait, as painful as it was.

She made herself walk back to the Order, her mind churning over the new riddle in her pocket. Whenever she passed a street-lamp she took it out to read it by the light.

Fell treasure must be guarded
Under lock and key,
Or else it will break loose.

Unsolvable, until the right moment called for her. Its abstraction incensed her, all the more because she felt the weight of time on the back of her neck. She could sense something brewing, a corner turned, and knew she would need the next treasure soon. The second pearl sat in her bedside drawer, but she didn't want to have to rely on it; Death hadn't seemed aware that there were meant to be two pearls. Who knew whether he would accept the second when he discovered she'd split them? She couldn't take the risk.

When she returned to the Order, she made her way to the libraries. She found every book she could on Rochidain, its history, geography, trying to find anywhere that might hide treasure. Any small hint she seized and ran with, but each time it led to nothing. The meaning of the riddle remained stubbornly locked away.

As she studied, the weight of the night growing heavier, she found she was shivering, but it was not from the chill of the library corridors. When she closed her eyes she saw her behind her eyelids; Sullivain, eyes sightless, her hair clotted with blood. When her mind wandered, the thought had a magnetic pull, drawing her to it unawares like a fish on a hook.

It was a pain she'd not felt before, nor believed she could feel. She'd recognized the truth the moment Death asked her what she would choose to do if there were no threats, whether she would still raise Sullivain. The answer was resoundingly simple: yes. Yes, she would always raise Sullivain.

As she gave herself over to research, buried among the books and maps, it was as much to give herself a place of peace, a haven, while her thoughts tangled and retangled themselves in her head, reminding her of the stench of wolfsbane, of how deeply a throat could be cut, whispering of what might have happened if she'd succumbed to the instinct that night by the fireside, to lean in closer and touch her lips to Sullivain's.

And yet, the next day, when she was due to take her insomnia medicine to the palace, she sent Elsevir instead with the small parcel. She felt cowardly, but she feared for her secrets in the face of Sullivain's shrewdness, and in the face of . . . whatever had happened when Hellevir had woken. She had felt what Sullivain had felt, her pain and rage, and Hellevir didn't know what had caused it, or how to avoid it happening again. It occurred to her that if it did happen again, it might be a two-way street; what if Sullivain could feel what was pulsing through Hellevir, just as Hellevir had felt the tidal wave of Sullivain's emotions? What if she felt that Hellevir knew the truth about the Redeions? And what if—a side-glanced what-if, one she couldn't look at truly because she barely understood herself what was beating in time with the thrum of blood through her veins—Sullivain felt the truth Hellevir had learned about herself?

She felt frightened of herself, wondering if there was a boundary she wouldn't cross to bring back the Princess, and what limits she would put on the cost to her soul. She wondered if she should stamp out this feeling like an ember, reminded herself of how willing Sullivain had been for Hellevir to expend her soul to save her own life, how idly threats had dripped from her lips, even if now Hellevir knew they had been fed to her by the Queen . . . but even so it felt like a treasure not unlike those she found for Death, a precious thing. She couldn't quite bring herself to crush it, although she had a presentiment that she would wish she had.

When Elsevir returned with a note in his beak, tidily sealed and stamped with the galleon, Hellevir held it in her hands, looking down at the neat cursive lettering that spelled her name.

She cracked it open, read it quickly.

This is the second time you've saved my life, Sullivain had written. *I wanted to tell you this in person, but letters delivered by raven have some romance to them. I have something for you, as a thanks. He's in the Wall Stables, an ex-racehorse called Dune. Four legs and everything. I don't have the time to ride him, so he's yours. If you want to use him to travel to your little village, I won't tell Grandmama. No longer than a short stay, though; I still need you here as my guardian against demise.*

There was a postscript, an afterthought, written hastily.

Do come next Markday, she said. *I miss how we used to talk.*

Hellevir folded the letter and put it in her journal. A horse of her own. It was a peace offering, an apology, as much as Sullivain could ever apologize, for the way she had behaved when Hellevir had brought her back. It meant she could go home at last, see Milandre, if only for a little while; the goal she had been driving herself towards for all the months she'd been in Rochidain. She let out a laugh, humorless and solitary-sounding in the small library reading room.

Yet now that she could go, she found she didn't want to. She would have loved to see Milandre again, her workshop, the garden, but it seemed suddenly less important now. Instead, she found she wanted to go to the palace, to make sure Sullivain was all right after the ordeal of her death. It tugged at her in the same way as the afterlife drew her, beckoning her back into the half-light of Death.

She returned to her research, the bit held even tighter between her teeth. Her memory of Sullivain's terror on waking only made her more desperate to find the next precious thing.

CHAPTER SEVENTEEN

Hellevir was ready two hours before Farvor was due to take her to the Redeion dinner. She wore the dress her mother had bought her; sewing the torn hem had distracted her for a while. Every passing hour had felt like a band around her chest slowly winching tighter, until she wondered whether the air was being slowly siphoned from the room. At last there was a knock at the door and a priestess told her a boat was waiting, but as the task before her loomed heavy and dark she wished suddenly she didn't have to leave at all.

Farvor was waiting in one of the knight's boats. It had a nightingale painted in black on the stern, and was steered by one of the household servants. Her brother looked resplendent in a cloak the color of a peacock's breast.

"Another gift?" she remarked in an attempt at normality as he helped her down into the vessel. He gathered it up in one arm and let it fall in shining ripples.

"Splendid, isn't it?" he said. "But no, I bought this myself. I saved for it for half a year."

"Half a year's savings, and you spend it on a cloak?"

"It's a splendid cloak."

"It's *half a year's* savings."

"And they're my savings to spend entirely as I wish."

"I suppose I can't argue with that," she muttered. She glanced at the boatman as they settled into the plush seats, and wished Farvor had brought himself here. The need to talk to him was a weight on her chest, but she breathed past it and told herself to be patient.

"Are you all right?" her brother asked.

"Fine," she said, trailing her hand in the water. "How are Ma and Pa?"

"Getting on. Pa is doing well at the shop. Being a partner keeps him busy; I don't think he's home much." He paused. "He misses you," he added. "So do I. I feel like I haven't seen you for a while."

Hellevir put her arm through his and gave it a squeeze.

"I'm sorry," she said. "I've been busy."

"You're getting covered in river water," he remarked. "You're going to smell terrible for the entire evening." She pushed him away and flicked the droplets from her fingers at him.

The dinner was a small affair, by Redeion standards. About fifty people were present, a collection of knights and their squires. Lady Ava Hannotir was present with Yvoir.

Auland Redeion sat at the head of the table. He was a regal-looking man, his hair an iron grey and his eyes sharp as thorns as he regarded the guests and listened to them talk. Hellevir watched him as subtly as she could. On the previous occasions when she'd been in the same room as the knight, she had dismissed him, considering him a little old and a little set apart from the reality of the city in his ivy-clung canal home, but as she listened to him she realized she had been too quick to label him. He was an alert man, with his ear to the ground and his eye on the room. Although he spoke rarely, when he did so it was to contribute something insightful. He delicately sipped his wine, and throughout the whole meal he only consumed one glass while his guests' were refilled time and again.

The conversation was light and consisted entirely of posturing; Hellevir found herself growing twitchy, watching pleasantries and trite gossip being exchanged over a torturously long set of five courses which she couldn't even taste, anxiety boiling in her belly.

Calgir laughed and drank and talked, oblivious to Hellevir's glances his way. She somehow had to get him alone after the meal. She felt like she was walking along a cliff edge and was just waiting for the moment when she would throw herself over; it wouldn't be pleasant when she did, but at least the painful wait, the trepidation of knowing it was to come, would end. Hellevir realized she was knotting her napkin on her lap and made herself smooth it out.

At last the dinner ended with sherry and cheeses. Hellevir found she'd gulped her sherry in one mouthful and hoped no one noticed as the servant came forward to fill the glass again, but her brother did, of course.

"Are you all right?" he asked her. "You've been on edge all evening."

"Fine," she said. "Pass the grapes, would you?"

After the meal, the guests stood to go into an adjoining room that looked out onto the garden, where they'd take coffee. Hellevir couldn't bear to wait any longer. She lingered behind with Calgir as he let his uncle and the other guests precede him, and before he could follow she caught his elbow. He raised his eyebrow, surprised, but hung back with her without comment. Farvor noticed and stayed too.

"Everything all right?" Calgir asked her when the door had closed.

"I would like to have a word, if we can talk somewhere?" Hellevir asked. "It's nothing serious," she added with a glance at the servants coming in to clear away the food. "I just wanted to talk to you about your next hunt." Calgir was perceptive enough to realize she was wary of someone overhearing and gestured her out into the corridor. He led them into a small sitting room lined with books, where a fire was already laid and burning low in one corner. There were two large chairs by the fireplace, and a small side table with two books, a pipe and a tobacco pouch.

"What's this about?" Farvor asked irritably. "Something's been wrong with you since I picked you up from the Order."

Hellevir motioned for Calgir to close the door, and, mystified, he obliged, before expectantly turning back to her. Now that she had their attention she suddenly found she didn't know where to start.

"I heard a rumor," she began slowly. Calgir motioned for her to sit down in one of the chairs by the fire. Hellevir caught sight of one of Farvor's waistcoats resting over the arm. This must be where they both retired to of an evening. Hellevir felt like she was standing inside a private place.

"What sort of rumor?" Calgir asked, sitting down opposite her on a footstool, and she was relieved that he hadn't immediately written her off as a gossip. Then again she shouldn't have been worried; he'd always been a gentle man, taking her as seriously as he took her brother.

"There was an attack on the Princess," she said. "You may have heard. Two men broke into her bedroom."

Calgir nodded, grimacing. "Yes, I saw the body of one of them out on the palace wall," he muttered. "The second in a year. Go on."

"I was summoned to help the Princess as her herbalist," Hellevir said, bending the truth to avoid telling Calgir more than he needed to know. "She trusts me. I was there after the attack, when one of the men who was hired to kill her was being questioned."

Calgir's expression became grim. "Hellevir, what have you heard?" he asked her quietly. She swallowed, and forced the words out.

"He named House Redeion as his employer," she said, and it felt like a weight was dropped from her mouth as she said it. "Specifically, he named Auland, your uncle."

The knight's blood leached from his face. He sat back, staring at her.

"What?" he demanded.

"He said they had fought alongside Auland in the War over the Waves, that they owed him a debt. Auland called it in. The killers climbed through the window from a boat on the canal, slit her . . . tried to slit her throat."

Calgir shook his head, running his hands through his hair. Farvor stood straighter, unfolded his arms.

"That's . . . that can't be true," her brother insisted.

"I'm afraid it is."

"But that's madness," he protested. "I'm not the greatest admirer of Auland Redeion but he wouldn't stoop to . . ."

He trailed off. He wasn't looking at Hellevir, but at Calgir, who was still sitting with his head in his hands.

"Calgir?" Farvor said quietly. The knight looked up, but instead of surprise or fear his expression was one of resignation. Realization speared Hellevir.

"You already knew," she guessed. "Didn't you?"

Calgir didn't reply at once. He just looked at the floor. Farvor went over to him as if to comfort him, and then hesitated, standing awkwardly at his elbow. After a moment he knelt beside him.

"Calgir?" he pressed. "Is this true?"

Calgir's jaw worked as he tried to find a way to speak.

"He told me," he said slowly, "what he planned to do." He took a breath, released it sharply. When he spoke again his words came out shakily, as if they were reluctant to emerge from behind his teeth into the cold open air. "He told me that he was going to force the cook to put poison in her food. Then when that didn't work, he said he'd hire someone to do it more directly."

He hesitated, not looking at Farvor. "We . . . we knew one of them had been captured. Auland managed to ensure the cook's silence." Hellevir flinched, remembering the twisted body of Loris, strangled when no one was watching. "But the man he hired to get into the chambers, he can't get to him. He's too heavily guarded. We think he'll stay silent for a while, Auland's ensured it, but we can't expect him to hold out forever. Auland has arranged us passage out of the city, before the Crown finds out who's behind it all."

Farvor stared up at Calgir, aghast, dark eyes wide.

"Passage out?" he whispered. "You were going to leave me?"

Calgir shook his head, miserable. He gripped Farvor's hands but he pulled away.

"The Queen's methods are brutal," Calgir said. "It's only a matter of time before she learns the truth from the man she captured. We *had* to make plans to leave. If we left you they would have known you had no knowledge about any of it."

"What nonsense are you talking? You should have told me. I could have helped, though I don't know how. Why not tell the Crown it was all Auland?" Farvor demanded. "There's no love lost between you and that old fool."

"He's my uncle, Farvor," Calgir said tiredly. Hellevir sensed a weight in his words, as if they were the culmination of many nights' weary soul-searching. "I couldn't just give him up."

"But he's a malicious old man! You owe him nothing! You would have picked him over me?"

Calgir flinched.

"No, love, please don't think that!" he said. He stood, taking Farvor by the shoulder, and her brother didn't shake him off. "I was picking you over me, your safety over what would have made me happy. I wanted to tell you. I *ached* to. But what would that have done? Lightened my soul but burdened yours, and to what end? Just to put you in danger? I didn't want to make you leave this city, your home, subject you to a life of running, because of my fool uncle's stupid plans. I couldn't have asked that of you."

"You didn't even give me the choice, Calgir!"

"Did you have any part in it?" Hellevir interrupted quietly.

Calgir glanced up at her sharply, lips parted, but whatever vehemence he meant to inject into his tone seemed to be expelled as he let out a sharp breath of air.

"No. No, I tried to talk sense to him in the beginning, but . . ."

"But what?"

"Hellevir, the Queen killed most of my family in the war," he said darkly. "My father, my brother and sister. My mother died not long after from grief; she refused to eat." His tone became grim, hard. She'd never heard him sound like this. "Why should I stand in the way of an arrow pointed right at the Queen's heart?"

"Calgir," Farvor murmured, voice edged with surprise. "You don't mean that."

"Why shouldn't I?"

There was a beat of silence.

"Sullivain wasn't alive when the war happened," Hellevir commented.

"No, but she's her grandmother's image. A dynasty in the making." Calgir went to stand by the fireside. He leaned against the mantelpiece and put a hand to his mouth, eyes wide with worry.

"Hellevir, how did you find this out?" he asked her.

"I was there when one of them was being interrogated," she said. "Before he died."

"Was anyone else there?"

Hellevir shook her head.

"He died before he could tell anyone else. He confessed only to me." She noticed Farvor's head rise sharply, and knew he had an inkling of what had happened. She gave a helpless shrug. "I'm not sure what I expected you to do with this information. I just had to warn you. I didn't know you were already aware, that you had plans to get out of Rochidain."

"What will we do?" Farvor asked. His tone was unhappy, but firm. Calgir looked up at him.

"We? I don't want you involved in this, you don't have to . . ."

Farvor shushed him. "Of course it's 'we.'" This wasn't your fault. We just have to decide what we're going to do now."

"We're leaving the day after tomorrow," Calgir said quietly. "We have chartered a boat to take us overseas. We have some contacts in the Galgoros who will give us haven. I can only pray to Onaistus that the man Auland hired keeps quiet until we can get away."

"Why not sooner?" Hellevir asked. "Why not leave tonight?"

"The harbor schedule is booked weeks in advance. If we try to leave sooner it will raise questions, especially after the body was piked so publicly. The day after tomorrow is the earliest a ship of our fleet is scheduled to undock. Until then, we must act as if nothing is amiss."

"Is flight our only choice?" Farvor asked. "Had Auland no contingencies?"

"Flight was his contingency. I think he assumed the attack would be successful, and he'd be free to target the Queen while she was without an heir. He always assumed success; it was what made him such a brilliant politician at court."

"And such a piss-poor conspirator," Farvor remarked angrily.

The crackling fire filled the silence, gave music to the thoughts that lingered like smoke between them; thoughts of imprisonment, of interrogations, of hangings. Calgir covered his face with his hands. To Hellevir's surprise, his shoulders shook once with a single, helpless chuckle. "You know, it was just like him," he said, his voice muffled in his palms. "To attend the same dinner where he intended to have her poisoned. I told him it was reckless, inviting misfortune, but he didn't listen. Always the man for over-seeing things firsthand, never leaving it to someone else."

Farvor looked like he was about to speak when a knock came at the door. The three of them straightened up. Calgir visibly braced himself, and called for the visitor to come in. A servant put her head around the door.

"Lady Hannotir and her squire are leaving for the evening, my lord," she said. Calgir nodded and stood up.

"I'll be there in a moment."

He glanced at Hellevir after the servant had gone. He took her hand.

"Thank you for trying to warn us," he said. "And for being careful." He hesitated. "Do you plan to tell anyone else about this?" he asked, without looking at her.

Hellevir sighed. "I can't," she said. "I won't put my brother in danger because of his association with you. And . . ." She paused, seeing the shadows that had bled under Calgir's eyes, how haunted he suddenly seemed. "I don't think you asked for any of this. I don't think you really believe the Princess should be punished for her grandmother's crimes. I think it's just what Auland has told you to think."

A common affliction among the elite of Rochidain, she thought bitterly, remembering the threats the Queen had made Sullivain use against her. *The battle-worn generation has the younger dancing to their tune as if there's still a war.*

Calgir flinched.

"Hellevir, you don't know what I think."

"No." She sighed. "I'm not sure what I can do, but if there's anything, tell me."

Calgir left the two of them there. She and Farvor stood in silence for a moment.

"So you bring people back for the Princess, now?" her brother asked. She could hear the disapproval in his voice.

"No," she said. "I just went into Death to talk to him. I . . ." She hesitated. "I was there to bring the Princess back." Farvor blinked, unfolding his arms and putting his hands on the back of the chair.

"She died? The assassins actually killed her?" Hellevir nodded grimly, and he let out a long whistle. "So you may have averted civil war," he remarked. "A second one."

Hellevir wrapped her arms around herself. "I can't believe Calgir knew," she murmured. "I thought he was innocent."

Farvor gave her a sharp glance.

"He *is* innocent," he said. "He wanted no part of this."

"That's not how the Crown will see it." She rubbed her eyes, suddenly very tired. "I wish I could advise him," she said. "But honestly, in his shoes I don't know what I'd do." She looked up at her brother. "You're really going with him?" she asked.

"I have to," Farvor muttered, looking at the door rather than her. "I wish he'd told me, I hate that he didn't. But I have to. You don't have much choice when you're both bound and one of you decides to jump."

It felt like a storm was brewing, and blowing straight towards Hellevir. She could feel the pressure of it building, tightening the air around her until it made her teeth ache. It didn't vanish, as she'd hoped it would, after telling Calgir; perversely, it only seemed to grow heavier with every step as she made her way back to the Order.

She realized that she'd stopped walking halfway across a bridge. She turned and leaned heavily on the railing overlooking the canal, welcoming the cold bite of metal against her palms. The waters swept past her, winter-smelling and unsympathetic. She swiveled on her heel, winding her way through the streets until she reached the doors of her pa's house. She pulled the bell and waited. A few moments later she heard footsteps and the Temple servant opened it, scowling into the growing dusk.

"Yes?" she demanded, as if Hellevir hadn't once lived here.

"I've come to see my pa," Hellevir said. The servant looked like she wanted to refuse her entry, but after a moment she sniffed and stepped aside. Hellevir stepped through into the courtyard, where the babbling fountain cooled the air. The pomegranate tree at its edge still glimmered with fruit, despite the chill wind.

Her pa was sitting in the front room with a drink, looking over his business accounts, and glanced up with a mixture of surprise and concern.

"Hellevir, what are you doing here?" he asked, returning her hug one-armed. "I thought Farvor was meeting you at House Redeion?"

"He did. Is Ma here?"

"No, at the temple."

"Can we talk?"

He frowned, perhaps noticing the heavy smears of dark under her eyes, the solemn set to her jaw. He moved some papers away from the other chair for her to sit.

"What is it, my girl?" he pressed. Hellevir pulled off her coat, and took a breath. Then she told him everything. The threats the Crown had made, every instance when she had raised Sullivain. She told him about what she had learned in Death, and about Auland Redeion. When she was finished, her father looked like he had aged years in a few minutes. He didn't reply at once, but instead stood to stir the fire in the hearth. Hellevir caught sight of white-hot eyes, blinking at her from between the gleaming wood, hair made of steam.

Her pa didn't ask her if she was certain. He didn't berate her for putting her family so at risk of royal threats. He didn't demand to know why she had enmeshed herself within the web of Rochidain politics so completely, tangled by wrist, ankle and throat.

After a few minutes of thought, he turned back to her and put his heavy hand on her hair.

"I'm so sorry," he murmured. "What a sorry excuse for a father you have."

Hellevir shook her head, appalled. "Why would you say that?"

"Because it's my job to protect you," he said sadly. "A part of me knew, really, why the Crown had called you here, and yet I let you keep working for them. I was just proud, I suppose, and so happy to have all my family in the same city again. Even if not under the same roof. I didn't let myself think about the cost." He brushed the empty knuckles of her left hand.

"Pa, I . . . I chose this."

"I know. You are grown and you will always make your own decisions. But it actually grieved me, you know, when you arrived. You looked so young, barely older than when I'd last seen you. I remember wanting so very much to send you home again, back to the forest. It's where you really belong. And now I hear about the danger you've been flung into, the threats, the torture, and now Farvor is at risk and I . . ." He stopped and sat down heavily. He pressed his lips together and swallowed thickly. "I should have protected you from this, all of this. I should have sent you home the moment you got here."

Hellevir knelt down in front of her father, putting her hand on his knee just like when she was a little girl and he would tell her stories by the firelight.

"I brought this on myself," she said, "the moment that I first raised Sullivain. Milandre tried to warn me, and I didn't listen."

He took a breath, released it slowly. He appeared to think, studying her.

"My girl, we have to get you out of Rochidain," he said. "The Crown will guess how the Redeions discovered the truth." He said it gently, but still it went through her like a snake striking from the darkness. She wondered bleakly how she could have been so stupid, how everyone seemed to be a step ahead of her. Of course she would have to leave Rochidain, once it was discovered that the Redeions were behind it all. And Hellevir had been on her merry way back to the Order, as if she could return to her life there. And if she was in danger, so were her parents. They would have to flee as well.

Hellevir couldn't look at Pa. Her eyes were affixed to a chip in a floor tile, filled with dust and ash. He took her hands.

"I will talk to Farvor," he said. "We'll see if we can get passage on the same ship."

"You've built so much here," she said softly. "I've ruined it all."

He put his palm to her cheek.

"No. No, you didn't do this. You just tried to warn us all. This was Auland Redeion's doing, the idiot of a man."

"Ma will hate this. She found a home here."

"Ma won't find it very homely when she's thrown in a prison cell with her entire family, let me tell you."

"But they won't imprison me. They need me, in case Sullivain ever dies again." Hellevir felt tears begin to well, and tried to swallow them down, even as the treacherous things slid down her cheeks. "I'm the only one who's safe," she muttered. "I'm the only one they won't hurt. They can't afford to. I call them cruel, but if they really were they would have locked me in a tower like a witch from the stories, bound up tight to raise their dead until I didn't have a tooth or bone left to me."

Her father winced, his old features tightening. He stood and poured her a drink of brandy from the sideboard, and she noticed that he made it as large as he usually made for himself.

"It will be all right," he told her as he handed it over, but she knew he was lying. They sat in silence, watching the firelight. The brandy burned a hot trail down Hellevir's throat. She welcomed the gentle fuzz it brought. She jumped, almost spilling it, when her father slammed his hand against the arm of his chair.

"I just don't understand why," he growled, glowering into the flames. "Why did he have to risk it all? A mansion, servants, wealth, safety. What more could he possibly want?"

Hellevir looked into her drink, remembering Calgir once explaining what a civil war would mean for the Houses. Upheaval, chaos, and, most importantly, opportunities.

"What all Houses want," she said. "The Crown."

CHAPTER EIGHTEEN

The waiting became unbearable. Hellevir stayed up late that night, grinding up herbs and making tinctures into the early hours, too anxious to sleep, her mind flickering over all the worst scenarios. What would happen if the Queen found out Auland Redeion was the perpetrator before they left? What would the punishment be for him, for Calgir Redeion, for her brother? Hanging, Sullivain had said. And then their bodies would be displayed on the pikes. Loris's body had been removed, but she could remember how small it had looked, pierced through like a fly on a thorn high above her head.

In the morning she received word from Farvor that their family had been granted passage on the Redeion ship. It was leaving at dusk the next day.

Hellevir quietly began to prepare, cleaning her clothes and packing a bag before stowing it under her bed. She checked the storerooms and made sure she'd left the dried herb stocks high, the shelves full of tinctures, salts and poultices. She weeded the conservatories, nipping dead leaves between her fingernails and rubbing garlic on the brick intersections to keep the pests away. All the while she did these things she tried to memorize the smell of the greenhouses, the way the sunlight shone through the dripping leaves of the willow tree, the comforting rise and fall of the priestesses' voices as they sang their evening chorus. She didn't let herself think about what it would feel like to leave, and not be able to return. She just made sure she had a bank of memories stored away, ready for those dark nights on a boat, drifting on waters she'd never crossed before, ready to draw out of her pocket and keep her warm like a hot stone. If Edrin and Sathir noticed her preoccupation, her quietness, they said nothing.

She continued her search in the library, anxious that the final riddle was somewhere near Rochidain and she was almost out of time to find it.

In the depths of the night, when the Order was still and bats flickered like dreams between the rafters, Hellevir sat with a pile of books, leafing through a volume on local flora and fauna. Elsevir was perched on the back of her chair, and hopped over onto the table by her flickering lantern.

"Tomorrow is Markday," he commented.

Hellevir flipped to the next page of her book. "Hmm."

"Also the last day you will have in Rochidain for the foreseeable future. You leave tomorrow night."

"Hmm."

"Are you going to go and see her?"

Hellevir kept her head bent over the page as if she were able to see any of the words past the image of Sullivain.

"I can't," she muttered, flicking the page. Her chest felt tight just saying it. He waited. She sighed. "There're a million reasons. I can't risk her finding out the truth from me. I felt her heart when I raised her, I have no idea if she felt mine. I can't risk it, no matter how much I might want to see her."

She stared down at the pages, unseeing.

"I'm betraying her, Elsevir," she said quietly. "I'm turning my back on her, abandoning her. Even if she can't feel what I feel, she'll read the guilt on my face clear as day."

A priestess found her slumped over the book, snoring softly, her hair in witchy ringlets about her face. Hellevir awoke to her gentle tapping on her shoulder, and a letter being slid under her hand. Hellevir mumbled a sleepy thanks, glancing outside to see that dawn had dragged itself over Rochidain. The last dawn she would see in this city. Tonight, they were leaving.

The letter was from Milandre. The first paragraph was a scolding for not sending more letters, the second paragraph contained the affairs of the village. Hellevir felt a pang as she read, missing the

cottage and the crotchety old healer. She would have given anything
for Milandre's brusque advice.

*You promised me another package of seaside treasures; where's
my dried seaweed? And the yellow-flag iris seeds you never sent?
The irises may still be seeding in the fens, although it's a bit late
in the season. I expect a few pods within the fortnight. Have you
got any mustard plants out there? Send me some of the leaves to
make a good old-fashioned poultice for my joints.*

Write to me more often. Boredom is the bane of old age.

Hellevir folded up the letter. It struck her fully then, the truth
she hadn't brought herself to comprehend, that she was leaving
not just Rochidain but the country. It was unlikely she'd ever see
the old woman again. She pictured the healer in her cottage, by
herself, kneading dough or winding twine around a charm, waiting
for a letter from her, and felt a twinge go through her that was
so painful she folded over the letter, pressing it to her stomach.
She hated Auland Redeion then, a hate so sudden and vicious that
she wondered if she *should* hand him over to the Crown. All of
them were suffering for one man's greed.

But no, she couldn't. The Queen wouldn't be lenient to the
Redeions, to anybody who had known the truth and said nothing.
Hopelessness weighed her down, threatened to bury her in the
stone floor of the library. She raised the letter to her nose. It smelled
of woodsmoke and herbs, of Milandre's old workshop.

Her resolve hardened. She would write back, explain everything
that had happened, and she would get her old mentor yellow irises.
She had one more day; she could do it. One last good thing she
could do in this damned city.

"Do you know what fens she's talking about?" she asked Elsevir.
"I've never seen yellow irises here."

The raven paused his preening and cocked his head to the side.

"If she means the yellow fields, they're to the north," he
remarked. "I haven't been close so I don't know what plant it is.
I assumed it was gorse."

Hellevir thought about it. Something tickled the back of her
mind about the yellow irises, the yellow fields.

She stood, putting aside her books and the letter. She found the
map room and paused in front of the display of Rochidain and
the surrounding lands which she must have passed a hundred

times. Near the top right of the map, not far from the road she'd first taken into the city all those months ago, was a smudge of yellow, with the neat calligraphic label: *The Golden Moors*. It was dotted with blue, little lakes labeled as *Loch This* or *Loch That*.

She felt her body still.

No, she thought. *It can't be that easy.*

She took the riddle out of her pocket, and read it to herself, her heart beating staccato in her chest.

"*Fell treasure*," she muttered. "Fell is something evil, deadly; a fell beast. But can't it also mean *moor?*"

Elsevir wiped his beak on his claws.

"These riddles are for you," he said. "If that's what you think it means, then follow it."

"It's a stretch. Golden Moors to fell treasure."

"They all are. But they're meant to make sense only to you."

She stared at the map a little despairingly, and then glanced outside at the rising sun.

"We're going tonight," she said. "I can't leave the city, not now. What if I don't get back by dusk?"

"It might be your last chance," Elsevir pointed out. "Don't you have a horse now, anyway?"

The stables were set into a long stretch of the wall surrounding Rochidain. Sullivain had said the horse which she'd gifted Hellevir was named Dune, and when Hellevir first laid eyes on him, she understood why: he was the color of sand on a hot day, his mane and tail long and dark.

She passed into the cool interior of the stables, breathing in the scent of hay and animal. The ostler appeared with saddlebags and riding gear, all made from fine red leather, all prepared for her. A rummage in the saddlebags revealed brushes, a hoof-pick, a few other bits and pieces, and riding gloves, sewn with fewer fingers on the left hand. She looked at them for a moment and then pulled them on, a perfect fit over her bare knuckles, and felt carved out by guilt. Sullivain had taken such care to have these made, even having a stamp pressed into the leather, a raven.

I'm a coward, Hellevir thought again, looking down at the pack with a wretched feeling. But the thought of seeing Sullivain again . . . it strummed two notes in her, one high and keening, tinged with panic, that the Princess would see through her. And the other was low, sonorous, a harmony made up of their conversations, and the memory of Sullivain's breath on her cheek as they'd danced by torchlight to the Princess's inexplicable rhythm.

Dune whinnied as she saddled him up. He was a little big for her, but didn't seem likely to buck or spook. When she was up the ostler helped make sure her saddlebags were secure, and patted Dune's flank fondly.

"Such a beauty," he said. "I was surprised the Princess let him go."

"He's quite a gift."

He nodded in agreement.

"The Princess doesn't give horses away lightly, and when she does it's to get rid of the ugly ones. Not stallions like this."

Hellevir stroked Dune's neck.

"There's no such thing as an ugly horse," she said with a smile.

"Tell that to the last person she gave one to," he remarked. "Lady Hannotir's squire." Hellevir frowned down at him. "Never seen a girl sneer so much at a gift, ugly as it may have been. Piebalds are just out of season; they're not bad horses. I had one back home, and there was no better workhorse in the world, nor a gentler creature."

"Why did she gift a horse to Yvoir?" she asked.

He just shrugged. "How should I know?" He glanced behind him as someone called his name. "You all right up there, then? Know your way?"

"I think so. Thank you."

He tapped his cap and she nudged Dune forward, settling into the horse's gait. She had fond memories of racing up and down the field edges on her pa's old mare, although back then she hadn't been quite so high off the ground. Elsevir flapped a little until he got his balance, and as they made their way out of the gates Hellevir thought they must look an odd sight: a commoner on such a fine horse with a black raven perched on her shoulder.

She pushed Dune faster than she would ordinarily have found comfortable, aware of the hours slipping by and the hinterlands of Rochidain broadening as the city faded from view. The thought of her family and the Redeions waiting at the harbor, night falling and making their lingering on the dock ever more noticeable to the eyes of the night watchmen, made her urge the horse faster. Unlike her, Dune had no qualms about their speed, clearly thrilled to be out of the stables and allowed to run free.

Elsevir circled overhead as Hellevir shot down the road, bent low over Dune's neck. She lost herself to the rush of the wind, the whip of her cloak flapping like wings behind her, her eyes watering and her mind blessedly empty as she focused on staying in the saddle, letting the beat of Dune's hooves pound her dread into the dust. Eventually she let him slow, her heart thrumming and her legs buzzing with the force of the road. Dune shook his head, nostrils flaring in the sea air.

As they went the road became muddier, and tall grasses started to prick the path. Hellevir reached the top of a hill and looked down into a basin of sorts, the land muddied and swamp-like, and it was from here that she saw the first yellow irises. The golden flowers bobbed and bent gently in the breeze, bright as stars amid the rolling reeds. The road diverged, returning up the side of the small valley, but Hellevir saw a narrow path leading out into the mire. It was boarded with wood leading deeper into the fen, perhaps for people to fish in the pools and lakes she could see glinting in the sunlight among the gold and green.

Hellevir dismounted and led Dune down the path, careful where she put her feet, but there didn't seem to be any rot. Nevertheless, when it started to get marshier she left him tied to a post.

"Don't let anyone steal you away, all right?" she told him. "I need you to get back in time." He shook his head, and said he would stay put.

She was surprised there were so many flowers still fresh, though they were very late in their bloom and most were browning at their edges. The majority had turned to seed. Hellevir pocketed a few that had split to send to Milandre. She followed the boardwalk between the tall walls of grasses and reeds, the waving irises, the heavy air smelling of silt and water, until at last she came to a small lake. The planks extended over the water, and there was a little fishing boat moored alongside. Hellevir stopped at the edge.

"*Under loch and quay,*" Hellevir muttered to Elsevir. "Though I'd call it more of a jetty than a quay."

"Do we take the boat out?" the raven asked.

"I suppose so. Although I don't see any oars."

She let herself down gingerly into the boat, nervous of the way it rocked. She pushed away from the pier, letting the boat drift over the waters along the edge of the bank, trying not to imagine scenarios where she was trapped without a means to get back to shore while the sunlight faded.

It was actually quite pleasant, being on the boat, listening to the seabirds and the rush of the wind in the grasses, surrounded by a high circular wall of green and gold. Elsevir perched on the prow.

Fell treasure must be guarded
Under lock and key.

"*Or else it will break loose,*" Hellevir finished quietly, looking back towards the jetty. "Perhaps I should have started looking under the quay itself." The boat knocked against something, making Elsevir flutter his wings to keep his balance, and she clambered carefully to the front. They'd hit a submerged object. Hellevir peered over the edge of the boat, but couldn't see anything properly.

"What is it?" Elsevir asked.

"I can't tell," Hellevir said. "It's under the water; I can't make it out." She pulled up her sleeve. "I'll see if I can feel what it is."

"Just don't tip the boat."

Hellevir reached in, her hand vanishing into the murky water. Cold wrapped around her searching fingers, leaching up her sleeve. She stretched as far as she could, feeling down along the slimy wooden boards of the boat.

Something gripped her wrist. Something hard and bony, something icy and slick with weed.

Hellevir screamed, yanking back with such force that the boat rolled dangerously. A ripple went over the water, a rumbling from somewhere deep in the mire. The irises on the edge of the loch shuddered.

Something began to rise from the water, splitting the surface like ruptured skin. A creature's curving back, riveted with steel but ridged like a spine; then came its shoulders, and finally its head rose from the lake, water showering from the grooves of its bones.

Hellevir could only stare as the creature cast slowly about, its skull—a horse's skull—roving the lake with blank eyes. The steel clasping its neck to its body groaned torturously. One limb rose from the water, made from bone and wood, and rested on the bank, long claws gouging into the earth. Hellevir's heart stopped as the creature's head swayed around, and she found herself the subject of its empty gaze. The water was still dripping from its jaw, the holes of its eyes, the bridge of its nose. Hellevir was vaguely aware of Elsevir cowering in the stern of the boat.

The horse creature said nothing, it only watched her. It breathed laboriously as if it were exhausted, sending plumes of mist from the gaps in its skull, along its warped spine. It shifted and Hellevir realized the creature's whole body was wrapped in chains, pinning its other limb at a twisted angle around its torso, which vanished into the muddied waters, dripping weed with the rest of its body. It smelled of silt and disturbed earth.

It waited. Hellevir thought she should probably speak first, but her voice had run away and hidden somewhere far at the back of her chest. The creature moved closer, impatient, and the metal screeched so loudly it made Hellevir's ears ring.

"I'm sorry to wake you!" she gasped. "Please!" For some reason that seemed like the right thing to say as the beast loomed over her, likely to tip the boat with one plunge of its arm and send her into the black waters, where she imagined unspeakable things curling in the silt.

"I'm sorry to wake you," she said again. "I've . . . I'm looking for a treasure. A precious thing. I was told to look here." It felt suddenly insolent to demand treasures from this thing. The caverns of its eyes were old with pain. The chains churned the water. "I need it to bring back souls from Death," she went on, although the more she justified her claim the less she felt she had a right to it. "If I have a precious thing it won't cost me when I bring people back."

The creature rolled its head, the metal sound horrific and low, scratching against Hellevir's bones. She thought it would capsize the boat then and there as it reared high, but instead it lowered its free arm into the water, tugged at something deep below, and slowly drew up the end of the chain. It dropped the great padlock, dripping and netted with weed, into the hull of the boat, sinking it a few inches deeper into the water. The padlock was huge and heavy, unmarked, the keyhole yawning like the mouth of a leech. Hellevir shuddered.

"I don't have the key," she said quietly, looking up at the horse's skull leaning down expectantly towards her. "I'm sorry." A quiver went through the creature from its head down its ratcheted spine. "But I'll try!" she exclaimed. "I'll try." She crawled over to the heavy lock, rubbing off the mud and pulling away the weed. She cast about her hopelessly.

"Elsevir, can you bring me the hoof-pick from Dune's saddle-bags?" she asked, her voice uneven. The raven launched himself into the air without a word. Hellevir drew out her pocketknife and felt inside the lock with the tip. She'd never picked a lock before, but she knew the theory. When Elsevir returned, dropping the long pick into her lap, Hellevir fed the knife into the padlock's arch, tensioning the internal lever, and with the pick she began to push up the teeth. She could feel the creature's blank stare, waiting as she pushed up the levers one by one. At last she had them all and she felt it click. Her heart skipped, grateful that it had been so easy, and she made to pull the lock open. It wouldn't come.

She tried to pull out the pocketknife and found it was stuck tight. She tugged at the pick and it was solid within the lock. The whole thing seemed to be fused as one, and wouldn't give even slightly as she pulled it this way and that. The padlock wouldn't open.

She looked up at the creature, mortified that she had failed.

"I'm sorry," she said. "It won't let me open it."

The creature shook its head with a screech, pulling away so sharply that the padlock was jerked back overboard into the water, taking her knife and hoof-pick with it. The creature began to wrench at the chains around its body, neck straining. It pulled and pulled, its free hand gouging deep scars in the bank, tearing irises and reeds from their beds as it tried to heave itself free from the mire. The noises it made, the deep screeching of metal and bones like a hull scraping along the side of stone, made Hellevir's teeth ring, and she clapped her hands to her ears as the boat rocked in the thrashing waters.

At last it ceased, its energy spent, and it sank slowly, its body sliding back into the water until only its head rested within the boat. It was so heavy that it slowly dipped the bow, and the water began to pour inside. Elsevir clambered onto Hellevir's shoulder away from the growing pool.

"I'm sorry," she said to the creature. "Please, stop! You're sinking us." The creature showed no sign of hearing, its skull motionless and the weight of its head bearing them down. Hellevir hesitated, and then inched closer, aware that her own weight was making them sink faster, and tentatively put her hand on the creature's nose. It huffed, exhausted, the water misting from its nostrils.

"I'm sorry," Hellevir whispered again, the bone slick under her touch. "Go back to sleep. I'm sorry I woke you. It's all right." The creature rolled its head, chin dipping into the water in the boat. "Go back to sleep. It's all going to be all right." With a weary heave it pulled itself up, and the boat bobbed back with a jolt. The creature turned its skull away and dipped back into the water, sinking back beneath the surface. The whole lake shuddered, and went still.

Hellevir sat, out of breath and dripping. She stirred as she realized the boat was drifting again, uncaught. The final ripples of the creature's movement had pushed them back towards the jetty.

"What now?" Elsevir asked, ruffling his feathers and shaking off the water.

"I suppose we didn't get this one," Hellevir murmured. "It just . . . it seemed wrong to ask it for things. It seemed so unhappy."

"What happens when you next need to bring someone back?"

"I . . . I suppose I'll cross that bridge when I come to it. I could enter Death and ask for a different riddle."

The boat clicked against the side of the quay, and Hellevir clambered out, her legs stiff from the cold and her cloak heavy with water. Elsevir nestled against her neck for warmth, although Hellevir was shivering too. She made her way back down the jetty, rubbing her arms.

A movement caught her eye where the boardwalk entered the high grasses. There was a long shoot of green pushing up out of the earth beside the jetty, where the bank met the lake. It rose up and up until it was hip-height. As she watched a flower bloomed, unfurling and spilling open with a triple-petaled yawn, golden and bright, before it faded and grew thin, withering and dropping. In its place grew a green pod, which swelled and swelled, turning brown, until at last it split open, revealing rows of small round seeds.

After a moment's hesitation, Hellevir plucked the seedpod and held it flat in her hand.

"The treasure?" Elsevir asked. "You found it after all?"

"Perhaps I wasn't meant to free the creature," Hellevir said, looking down at it. "'*Fell treasure must be guarded Under lock and key, Or else it will break loose.*' Perhaps it wasn't meant to be loose."

"Poor creature," the raven muttered.

"Why should it be forced to stay here?"

"Perhaps it would do harm if it broke free."

"Then better for it to sleep?"

"Perhaps." Hellevir shuddered, and slipped the seedpod into her pocket. She wrapped the riddle around it.

"Let's go back. It's getting late."

The ride back was uneventful and blissfully swift, but very cold. Hellevir was sodden and the autumn breeze cut through her like a knife. By the time she reached the city she was aching from head to foot, coughing and shivering. The encounter on the Golden Moors had depressed her.

She was relieved that she still had some time. Long enough to stop at the Order to change and gather her things. She stopped by the Wall Stables, making herself rub Dune down and check his hooves were clean, before she kissed his nose goodbye. He'd been hers for only a little while, but she would miss him. She hobbled back to the Order of the Nightingale, wrapping her cloak tightly around herself as if she could thaw the ice in her bones and very aware that she must smell of swamp. Elsevir tugged worriedly at her hair as she coughed into her hand.

Edrin opened the gates for her, eyebrows raised as she took in Hellevir's disheveled appearance.

"Are you all right?" she asked, ushering her inside. Hellevir made to reply and just coughed instead, her chest making a rattling sound. She didn't protest as Edrin hurried her back to her room. "Where on earth have you been?"

"The Golden Moors," Hellevir managed.

"On your own? It's not a good idea to go there by yourself. People can fall into the marshes and then they get sucked down into the mire. The Queen lured people into it during the War over the Waves, you know. What were you doing out there?"

"Lovely," Hellevir muttered as they went up the stairs. "I went to gather iris seeds. There were boardwalks down, though, so I was all right."

"Boardwalks? They must be new. I didn't see them there the last time we went for sweetgrass." She shook her head as she opened the door to Hellevir's room. Hellevir sat down heavily as she convulsed with a coughing fit, sending Elsevir fluttering into the air to land on Edrin's shoulder. The grey cat slipped through the door and hopped up beside her, leaning close to her hip and purring.

"What do you know about the moors?" Hellevir asked breathlessly.

"Just the folktales." Edrin tutted over the boot-prints she'd left on the floor. "Great battles, grand sacrifices, the usual. It wasn't always a mire. It used to be fields."

"What happened to it?"

"The founder of the city fought one of her final battles of the Nightingale War there, before the earth sank into swampland."

Hellevir nodded, trying to think through the fog in her brain. The Nightingale War, the name kept coming up.

"Get out of those wet clothes and into bed," Edrin said. "I'll get Sathir to bring you something."

"M'fine," Hellevir muttered, although she had to admit she was feeling a little dizzy. "And I can't." She heaved herself from the bed and knelt down, pulling out her bag from under the bed. She'd prepared it that morning. She felt Edrin's hand go stiff on her shoulder.

"So you *are* leaving," the priestess said. "Me and Sathir wondered."

Hellevir pulled out some dry clothes and looked guiltily back at Edrin.

"I'm sorry, Edrin. I couldn't say anything before, in case . . ."

"In case the Princess found out," Edrin finished for her. Hellevir shrugged a little helplessly. "Won't you tell me why?"

"No. The less you know the better."

"You're leaving now?"

"I have to."

Edrin nodded unhappily, looking like she was trying not to cry. She shook herself and smiled.

"Wait just a little," she said. "I have something for you." Before Hellevir could say anything she'd whisked away.

Hellevir changed out of her damp clothes, bundling up the wet cloth. The temple bells began to chime, ringing out across the city, and Hellevir spared a worried glance outside for the fading light. She was pulling on her heavy coat when Edrin reappeared, carrying a small string-tied parcel in her arms. She pressed it into Hellevir's hands.

"Just something of us to take with you."

"Edrin . . ."

"They're only small, won't weigh you down. I know you have to run, so open them later."

"Thank you." They looked at each other for a moment, before Hellevir flung an arm around her and hugged her tightly. "You gave me a home when I had none," she said into the rosemary-smelling fabric of the priestess's scarf. "Thank you. Tell Sathir I'm sorry that I couldn't say goodbye."

Edrin hugged her back tightly. "She'll be grumpy and take it out on me, hope you know that."

"Sathir's always grumpy."

Hellevir stooped and picked up her bags, hauling them over one shoulder. Before she left she paused at the door, looking around the little room that had been her home. It looked empty without her pestle and mortar, her alembic and rows of jars. The smell of dried herbs hung in the air, and she hoped it would linger a little.

She left the room and closed the door with a click.

Hellevir found a carriage to take her to the docks. The first stars were beginning to peer through the night sky, and she felt her stomach twist, wondering if she was already too late. The carriage clattered loudly down the narrow streets, moving far too slowly. Hellevir leaned out, memorizing the brightly colored houses, the long canals like sweeps of paint, the light glinting on the cobblestones as the lanterns were lit by boys with flames on long tapers.

The bundle Edrin had brought her sat on her lap, and by the light of the passing streetlamps through the carriage windows she untied the string and pulled aside the paper. Inside were two books. The first was an empty notebook, with Edrin's neat looping writing: *I noticed your journal is getting full. Hope this comes in handy.*

The second was a small leather-bound book with green edges. It fell open at a page bookmarked by a long twine of leaves, dried and neatly braided. Leaves from the willow tree, she realized. Edrin had included a note: *A little something of our willow to keep you company.*

Hellevir held the leaves to her nose as the carriage trundled farther from the Order, and took a breath of the fresh green scent, wondering why she was always being moved on from her home. The leaves had been marking the title page, *Folk Tales of Rochidain*, where a neat woodcut print showed the willow drooping down into the river. Hellevir flipped through the book, and realized it was a collection of fairy tales, each one centered on the willow. The story of the lovers from different Houses who used to meet beneath the boughs, to the dismay of their families, and chose to die tragically in each other's arms rather than be separated. The story of the wicked banker who thought to hide his wealth in the tree's roots, depriving his family of the food from their mouths, until the willow swallowed the bag of gold whole and dragged it down into the depths of the earth.

The very first story was of course about the founding of the city and the planting of the willow tree on the river bank. The chapter was entitled "The Antlered King."

That name again, the Antlered King. She'd heard it more often in Rochidain than she ever had in her village by the woods. The Antlered King who had been consumed with malice, had burned the land and eaten his enemies' hearts. The name resonated in her, like a copper bell.

The Nightingale Queen was the founder of Rochidain, the chapter began. *Her enemy was a darkness from the west, bringing war and laying waste to the lands from the mountains all the way to the sea. The darkness was an army from the snows, an army dressed in black led by a king with an antlered crown, a king with a black cloak and a black heart astride a black horse. Nothing is known about the army, nor why they started their march, and even less is known about their ruler. He has been scrubbed clean from history, a blight and malice upon memory.*

The war lasted ten years, and the land was scorched from the fires. It seemed all the black army wanted was to pillage and slaughter, raze the realm to the ground and see the sky turn red.

They ruled the whole kingdom with steel under a cloud of smoke, until the country forgot the touch of sunlight.

After many long years, the Nightingale Queen emerged from the fires, and began to raise an army of her own. Battles raged all along the coasts, and thousands of men and ships were cast against the rocks. Fields were torn and shredded by boots and horses' hooves, but at last it looked like the Queen would win. The final battle was long and bloody, fought upon the Golden Moors, and in the fray the Queen's brother was slain. At last, the black army was finally routed, and sent fleeing to their ships. The Nightingale Queen deployed her fleet in pursuit, and a second battle was fought amid the roiling waves, until the dark fleet was dashed against the rocks and the Antlered King was cast into the seas. And so, by land and by sea the dark army was conquered.

The Antlered King was dragged onto the beach, and executed for his crimes. They say his body was burned and ground to dust, and his head was taken and buried in secret, a thing of evil and violence that would poison the ground wherever it rested.

The Nightingale Queen brought her brother to the banks of a river, and where she buried him a weeping willow grew. Here the Queen put aside war, forming alliances with the last of the enemy soldiers, and vowed to keep the land peaceful as long as her line reigned.

There was a woodcut of the Nightingale Queen, resplendent in armor, her long hair braided and her expression sharp. She actually looked a lot like Sullivain. On the next page was the illustrator's rendition of the Antlered King, facing the Queen across the battlefield.

The carriage passed into a less well-lit street, and in the gloom Hellevir could just make out a spread of darkness like an ink-stain, seeping at the edges. The sound under the horse's hooves changed from that of cobbles to brick, and Hellevir glanced outside. They were nearing the harbor. When she looked down again at the page now lit by the harbor lights, she saw that the king was depicted as ugly and crooked, shrouded in rotten armor with a cruel-looking sword at his hip, notched from use, his nose hooked and his hair long and unkempt. His shield had the head of a stag etched onto it, its face brutish and its tines sharp. As Hellevir looked down at it, tracing the antlers with her fingertip, she noticed that her mire-fevered limbs were burning with energy. It was there, the logical next step. There for the seizing.

Elsevir pulled gently on a lock of her hair.

"An antlered king with a black cloak and a black heart," Hellevir said to the raven, stroking his ruff of feathers. "Does that sound familiar to you?"

"He sounds like the man you've described to me. The man with the black eyes."

"Yes," Hellevir said grimly. "He sounds like Death."

The carriage stopped at the top of the pier, and the driver helped her down. She paid him, peering into the growing sea-mist to see if her family was waiting for her. The air smelled greasy with brine, and when she licked her lips she could taste it. There were distant sounds emerging from the gloom: the clang of a harbor bell, the loud conversations of fishermen, the endless glug and thunk of boats bobbing by the wharves.

Footsteps approached, and she tensed, but she recognized the broad frame of her father as he jogged up to meet her. As he entered the light, she saw that he was pale, his expression grim. Before she could speak he had wrapped her in his arms.

"Oh, thank the gods," he gasped, gripping her tightly. "I thought they'd got you too."

Those were the worst words he could have spoken. Her heart plummeted into her feet.

"What do you mean?" she demanded, pulling herself from his embrace. "Got who? What's happened?"

"Farvor and Calgir," he said. "They didn't leave in time. They've been arrested for treason."

CHAPTER NINETEEN

Farvor loved the smell of the city. It was so different to the smell of the country, which was all pine and wheat. Here in Rochidain, he could smell the sea, the old musty stone of the buildings, the sweetness of the tended gardens. He walked upon the wall of the canal, his arms held out wide for balance. He put back his head and took in a great big breath before releasing it in a slow plume that ignited the cold, sunlit air, and closed his eyes. In the distance he could hear music from a garden party in one of the other Houses further up the canal. Birdsong trilled all around him in the Redeion gardens.

"You have no idea how tempting it is to push you in," came Calgir's voice. Farvor smiled.

"If I go in, you're coming with me," he said. He opened his eyes and glanced down to see the knight standing at the edge of the wall, looking down into the bright waters. His blond hair gleamed in the sunlight. "Come up here," Farvor said, holding out his hand. Calgir smiled—a sad smile—and shook his head.

"You need to help me finish packing," he said gently. "We need to be ready to leave tonight."

Farvor made an unimpressed sound in the back of his throat.

"Packing can wait a few more minutes. Got goodbyes to say. Have you said yours?"

Calgir's smile faded as he avoided Farvor's gaze, looking over the canal and the drifting swans. Instead of replying he reached up and took Farvor's hand, letting himself be pulled up next to his squire. Farvor rested his other hand on his hip and let Calgir's

258

sit on his shoulder, swaying them gently to the music in the distance.

"We're going to fall in," Calgir remarked, but he didn't make them get down.

"Then we'll just climb out, and we'll be all wet so we have to go inside and undress and then we'll have no clothes on." He glanced down at the water, contemplative. "You know what, that sounds all right to me."

Calgir laughed, looking down at him, and brushed a wayward black lock from Farvor's eyes. "And when we both catch the chills we'll be too ill to look after each other, and too ill to catch the boat." His lips pressed thin with very real anxiety at the prospect.

Farvor reached up and smoothed out the furrows in Calgir's brow with his thumbs, and then took his hand and gently spun him around, his feet moving cleverly on the wall to keep his balance. Calgir wobbled, for a moment looking worried that he really would fall in, but Farvor kept him upright, hand to hip.

"I won't let you fall," Farvor assured him.

"You'd have every right to," Calgir muttered. Farvor pulled away a little so he could look at him.

"And why's that?"

Calgir sighed, not meeting his eyes.

"This . . . situation. I wish I'd done more to stop Auland when I had the chance."

"Do you really?" Farvor challenged. "You gave me the impression you were happy to see the Crown suffer."

"I . . . Part of me did. My family suffered during the war because of them, Farvor. But I was only a child; I don't remember much of it. My father . . . well, I've you told you about him. All I really remember is how hard the rings on his fingers felt when he knocked me down. Uncle . . . he was the same, long after the war ended. Until I was a teenager. It was only when we both realized I was his height that he stopped."

Farvor took Calgir's hand, sliding his fingers through his, and gave it a gentle squeeze. "I'm sorry," he said. Calgir shrugged.

"Ancient history now. Or at least I thought it was. But as time passed I just kept feeling this surge of hate. I don't like feeling hatred, Farvor, it's too much like a disease." Farvor brushed his hair, let him speak. He wished with every ounce of his being that

Calgir had told him all this sooner. "I kept thinking about turning Auland over, I kept looking at Auland and thinking *Isn't it time for you to face your own messes? You wanted the crown so badly you would risk your wealth and kin, and we all have to pay the price.*" His voice devolved into a growl, low and angry, as he looked out over the grounds of the home he was being forced to leave. "The arrogant, callous *idiot.*"

He sighed, covering his face with his hand as he always did when he was ashamed of what he was feeling.

"Every time I heard that the Princess was alive, I felt relieved," Calgir said. "We weren't about to be hurled into another war. And I felt ashamed of my relief. Because that's the way of Rochidain, isn't it, an eye for an eye? I should want revenge. That big word they use in all the stories. I *should* want it, but all I want is to fly my falcons, sail the lagoon. All I want is to sit by the fire with you. I don't want war, I don't want to be constantly afraid that the machinations of my uncle will get us all killed. I just . . . I want *peace.*"

He expelled the last word from his chest, and they both watched it dissipate on the chill air.

"I *do* wish I'd found a way to convince Auland to stand down," Calgir muttered. "But he kept saying the Crown was our birthright, that our ancestors wore it long before any other House. When he said that it felt like the weight of all the Redeions who died in the War over the Waves were pressing down on me, telling me I should let Rochidain be Rochidain, my uncle be my uncle. That I was a coward for wanting something else."

Farvor sighed.

"This place," he remarked. "It's pretty but, gods, it has a lot to answer for. Calgir, you're not a coward for enjoying a good life while you have it." Frustration marred his tone.

"I should have stopped Auland. I should have turned him in while there was time."

"You know what would have happened to him then. You're not pitiless. He put you in an impossible situation."

"But our lives are ruined because of him. If I'd given him up, you wouldn't be caught in this mess with me. You wouldn't be having to flee the city . . ."

Farvor stopped him with a kiss. Calgir felt wonderfully warm in the chill autumn air, and Farvor held him close, letting the heat seep into him and through him.

"Let's get one thing straight," Farvor murmured. "It hurt when you told me you were planning to leave without me, without telling me anything. I don't think I've ever been hurt like that. But it made me realize that I would follow you to any country, over any sea. I would traipse after you until the moment you told me to go away. Even then I might stick around."

"If we're confessing, then know that I will never tell you to go away." Calgir sighed unhappily. "Although I wish I could have kept you safe, even if it was safe a thousand miles from me. It's the only reason I didn't tell you the truth from the start."

Farvor put his head on Calgir's shoulder as they stood there, gently swaying to the distant music, and let his eyelids drift shut as Calgir's hand played lightly in his hair.

"What did I ever do to deserve you?" he heard Calgir whisper. In his arms, Farvor could almost forget about the sword hanging above their heads, ready to swing down with the breath of one man's confession deep within the palace prisons.

He heard them before he saw them. The snap of a twig under a boot, the gentle drawing of a blade. His eyes opened and he stared into the tree-shaded gloom of the gardens beyond the sunlight's reach. Calgir felt his body tense and glanced up, just as the soldiers stepped into view, the sunlight gleaming from their swords and the gold of their armor.

"What are you . . . ?" Calgir demanded angrily, but before he could utter another word he'd been dragged from the wall by his wrist and flung onto the ground. Farvor cried out and tried to go to him, but another soldier seized his shoulder and slammed him down. He tried to get to his feet, pulling his dagger from his belt, but the blade was knocked from his hand and he was given a quick kick to the temple which sent him reeling against the stone, his vision going dark at the edges. Blearily, heart hammering, he turned over, and watched as Calgir was struck on the head with the pommel of a sword and went sprawling. Farvor made a sound and tried to crawl closer, but a soldier put his boot between his shoulder blades and pressed him down until he could hardly breathe.

"By order of House De Neïd," one of the soldiers intoned,

although Farvor couldn't tell which one, "I hereby arrest you, Calgir Redeion, for conspiracy to murder the Princess."

"No, I . . . !" Calgir started, but one of the soldiers kicked him in the gut. Farvor gasped, reaching out, but the boot pressed down harder on his back.

"You will be tried at dawn and any witnesses called to your defense. If you are found guilty, you will be hanged by the neck until dead." Farvor watched, bright spots in his eyes, as Calgir was heaved to his feet and handcuffed, and one of the soldiers gripped him by the back of the head. He was bleeding from a cut on his hairline, a long trail of red.

"What about this one?" the soldier standing over Farvor asked.

"He's the squire," the other said. "Bring him with us."

"Don't hurt him!" Calgir shouted. "He has nothing to do with any of this!" He was silenced by a blow to the head that nearly knocked him down again, and Farvor tried to heave himself upright. He had to get up, he had to get to Calgir, that was all that ran through his head. The boot pushed, and he thought he felt something crack. It didn't matter; he had to get up. He was vaguely aware that Calgir was shouting, angrier than Farvor had ever heard him before, and this upset him in a deep way that felt like claws burying into his chest, but the world was turning steadily darker and he couldn't seem to keep his head upright.

The guards appeared too quickly for any of them to react. One seized Hellevir before she could think to run, pulling her arms behind her with such force that she heard her shoulders click and pop. Elsevir erupted into the air with a shriek, flapping his wings at her assailant and attacking with his claws, but he was swatted aside.

"Elsevir!" she shouted, before a hand was clamped over her mouth. She struggled and kicked, but strong hands gripped her and lifted her bodily, throwing her onto the hard floor of a prison carriage. She stood quickly and pressed against the barred window, watching as figures churned in the mist, listening to the shouts and the scrape of boots, her heart in her mouth. The carriage jolted forward, knocking her head against the metal bars, and she fell back with a cry. She struggled to her feet and beat her fist against the driver's window.

"Let me out!" she shouted. "What are you doing?" She heard a voice mutter something on the other side, then a second voice let out a loud guffaw.

She knew the route well enough to know exactly where they were taking her. As the carriage was drawn through the gates, up the long avenue over the waters, and turned around the courtyard at the front of the palace doors, Hellevir clenched her hands to keep them from trembling and tried to breathe evenly. The carriage door was unlocked and a surly-looking guard jerked his head to indicate she should get out.

Hellevir tried not to be frightened. She'd need to be as strong as she could, as clear-headed. She held her head high, as high as her ma did, and forced her steps not to falter. It was Bion who met her at the doors, took her by the elbow and guided her firmly through the palace corridors.

"What's happening?" she demanded through her teeth.

"You can ask the Queen yourself," he said shortly. He led her through to a broad portico, a rectangular pool lined with columns and long seats lit by torchlight. The leaves hadn't been brushed from the paths or collected from the water, and it gave the garden an abandoned feel, despite the flickering brazier lit at one end, its light shining on Sullivain's golden head. She was wearing a wine-red waistcoat and knee-high boots that shone as if they were wet. She was reclining in a seat and watching the fountains trickle water into the pool. Beside her was the Queen. The sovereign wore light armor and the coils of her hair were slightly loosened as if she'd been riding at speed. In the torchlight the lines of her face looked deeper as she sipped from a glass of wine. It made her look harder, like she was carved from stone, rather than older.

She glanced up, and the way she looked at Hellevir made her want to flee. She looked at Hellevir as though she were a sword she had purchased that had shattered with the first blow. Hellevir had been found wanting, and there was no fixing a shattered blade without melting the whole thing to be recast.

Hellevir listened to her own bootsteps ringing in the still air, and told herself that she would not be afraid.

Sullivain heard her approach and turned around, resting her elbow on the back of her seat.

"Hello, herbalist," she remarked. "Come and pull up a chair."

"What are you doing?" Hellevir demanded. "Why have you arrested my family? We've done nothing wrong." She'd hoped her voice would be firm, unwavering, but it sounded too high.

Sullivain brushed some dust from her boot.

"Nothing wrong, eh?" she remarked. There was a bowl of dried dates on the table at her elbow, and she speared one with her pocketknife. "Did your kin not know that it was House Redeion who sent the assassins, and fail to come forward?"

Hellevir swallowed. The fear was making it hard to think straight. She swept it aside, and prepared the lie on her tongue.

"I . . ."

"In fact, weren't you the one to tell them all?" Sullivain demanded, slamming the knife into the table with startling violence, embedding it in the wood by an inch. She got to her feet in a fluid movement, but the Queen put a hand on her granddaughter's shoulder, stilling her.

"I have no patience for more of your lies," the Queen said to Hellevir. "We've given you a life here, Miss Andottir, and you have thrown it in our face."

"You gave me threats," Hellevir found herself retorting. A pair of soldiers appeared at the edge of the pool, and the Queen put down her glass.

"I have no more patience, and now no more time. Sulli, ask what you have to, then lock her up." She flicked her hand to the two soldiers and strode towards the house, her cloak snapping at her calves as they followed behind her.

Hellevir watched after her, heart beating hard, and then flinched as Sullivain pried the knife from the table.

"We know you did get a name," Sullivain said.

"The other assassin confessed?" Hellevir guessed.

"No, actually," the Princess replied. "He's a tough one. We're still trying to crack him." Hellevir shuddered, trying not to think about whatever part Sullivain was playing in that interrogation.

"Then how?"

"We know you found a name because someone overheard you blabbing everything to Calgir Redeion and your brother."

Hellevir's stomach felt like it was full of lead. She didn't know what to do.

"It was Yvoir, wasn't it," she said.

Sullivain inclined her head. "Yes. Hannotir's squire." Hellevir parted her lips to speak but Sullivain waved her hand for silence, and Hellevir stopped before realizing she didn't have to obey her. "Grandmama interrogated Auland earlier, and he confessed everything before we touched a hair on his head. Gave it all up remarkably quickly. I suppose he thought a confession would get him leniency. It was an interesting conversation all around, really. I learned all sorts about his plans, his spies."

Her words gleamed coldly, and she shook her head with a smile, as if she could hardly believe what he had admitted. "The intelligence that man had about the other Houses, it almost puts our network to shame." She barked a laugh, an abrupt sound. "Do you know how he got our cook, Loris, to put wolfsbane in my food? Loris was a Hannotir spy after all, planted by Ava Hannotir at the palace to keep an eye on us as I grew up. Auland discovered him and threatened to turn him over to Grandmama, tell her everything, unless he did as Auland told him to. Turns out Loris's loyalty to Hannotir secrets was greater than his loyalty to me." She pressed her lips together. "And not just Loris. The spies he knew about in my own household . . . Like bats in the attic, rats in the walls." She sounded bitter, but unsurprised. Hellevir shivered, but before she could respond Sullivain took a step closer suddenly, menacing in her closeness.

"But his treason, however repugnant, was almost to be expected. I can't pretend I'm surprised by it. It's the way of Rochidain, and how it has always been, how it will always be. But you," she spat. "I thought . . . I thought we had an understanding. You had my favor and you lost it. You have lied to me."

"And what reason have you given me to trust you?" Hellevir demanded hotly. "Or your grandmother? I wanted to, truly, but what reason have you given me to think that if I'd come to you with this, you wouldn't have punished us all anyway? After all your threats, after what you did to Loris, I had no reason to think I could rely on your good grace, that me and mine would be safe. That's why I was running."

There was a beat of silence, filled only by the light trickle of the fountain. Sullivain tilted her head to the side, like a curious hound.

"And why should I not punish you all?" she asked, tone low

and dangerous. "Have you all thrown in the cells beneath the palace? You know what happens down there. Your mother, father, brother, why should I not have them all thrown into the darkness?"

Hellevir felt as if she were on a knife edge, teetering over some unspeakable future.

"Because they didn't know anything until the moment I told them," she said. "And then only acted to keep their loved ones safe." She hesitated. "Safe from you."

Sullivain stepped back. Hellevir's fear flickered through her veins.

"What will you do to the Redeions?" she made herself ask. Sullivain's copper eyes narrowed.

"Auland will be hanged," Sullivain said slowly, enunciating the words. "As will all those of his kin who knew and failed to come forward. The rest who claim Redeion heritage will be sent to the mines."

Hellevir felt her legs begin to tremble. She had to fight hard to stay upright.

"No!" she exclaimed, the word dropping from her like a glob of molten iron. "You would destroy an entire House for the actions of one man?"

"Do you think it will be the first House ever to be annihilated? There were more than nineteen Houses before the war, herbalist." She perhaps intended it to sound mocking, but it just sounded bitter. Hellevir stared at her, stricken.

"Sullivain . . ."

"You would do better to argue with the turning tide." Sullivain picked up the Queen's half-empty glass, swirling the red wine by the lantern-light. There was a faint line of lipstick on the rim. Sullivain took a sip. "It's Grandmama's order, and her orders are law, Hellevir."

Hellevir tried to marshal her thoughts, wondering how everything could have gone so wrong so quickly.

"But Calgir Redeion," she insisted. "He's my brother's partner. I can't be the reason that he dies. *Please.*"

Sullivain sighed angrily, flicking her hair over one shoulder.

"I cannot give you Calgir. He's the Redeion heir, and he has known the truth for months. None of the Houses can be allowed to think we would show mercy for such treachery. Don't you see that we have no choice?" The last words were a growl, impatient, frustrated. The Princess turned around, picking up her pocketknife again and cleaning it on a napkin as she considered the pool and the back of the palace. Hellevir took a step forward, putting her hand on Sullivain's shoulder. Sullivain didn't move other than to turn her head.

"I have brought you back twice," Hellevir said. "And I have asked nothing for myself. This I ask. This I *beg*. Please give me Calgir. He might have known but he had no part in it. My brother doesn't deserve to lose the man he loves." She took Sullivain's hand—thinking to beseech her on behalf of the whole Redeion household—but it was a mistake.

Emotions not her own, sour and sickly, unguarded and unbridled, flooded through her as if she were a broken dam. She had felt this sensation before, when Sullivain had emerged back into life a second time. Then, she had felt Sullivain's fury, her terror. Now, it was a different sort of dread. Hellevir breathed out sharply.

"You feel guilty," she said before she could think not to. "You don't want him to die."

Sullivain was watching her. She pulled her hand away and the sensation was gone, jerked back like a dog on a leash. Hellevir was left feeling cold and shaken.

So, the flood of emotions came when they touched. Hellevir backed away, unwilling to let it happen again, even by accident.

"I do not feel guilty," the Princess said stiffly. She seemed agitated, as if she'd had a taste of Hellevir's heart as well, and didn't like it. The lie hung in the air like a dead crow strung up over a farmer's field, swinging slowly from a cord. Sullivain heard its discordant creak and grimaced. "We can't show mercy, Hellevir. We can't seem weak. We once let the Redeions live, live and thrive, after they took the wrong side in the War over the Waves, and look how long Auland let his wounds fester. There can be no heir left."

Hellevir's thoughts battled with each other. She felt the sudden urge to heave herself into the water of the pool, submerge herself and drown out that awful ring of finality in Sullivain's voice.

"Calgir has to appear to die," Hellevir said, her voice sounding distant as if someone else were speaking. "But you could still let me have him."

There was a beat of silence, heavy and churning.

"You would raise him?" Sullivain asked.

"No one would need to know. To the public eye, he would have been hanged." She couldn't believe she was bartering this way. Bartering Calgir's life away, using his death as a tool. But she could bring him back.

"And then what?" Sullivain scoffed. "Release him into the wild? He's a Redeion, he can hardly fade into the crowd."

"Then they go away somewhere, both him and my brother. Let them have passage overseas where no one knows them. Just let them get away like they intended to. I know you don't want to do this." Her voice cracked a little.

Sullivain's jaw worked as she thought. She tapped her finger against her elbow, watching the fountain's water.

"You should have told me the truth," she said at last.

"Will you give him to me?" Hellevir asked again.

The silence was dreadful.

"I remember Calgir's mother," Sullivain said quietly. "I was born after the war but I remember her, how she wasted away. Every time I saw her, she was thinner, greyer. The grief wasn't kind." She shook her head, as if frustrated with herself for what she was about to say. "I will give him to you. But he cannot stay in Rochidain. He cannot stay in the Chron. Because if he does, he will *not* be safe from Grandmama."

"You won't tell her?"

"I . . ." She gritted her teeth. "No. I suppose I can't."

"Thank you." The band of dread around Hellevir's throat eased slightly, allowed her enough room to swallow. "What about us?" she asked quietly. "What are you going to do with me and my family?"

"Grandmama wanted to throw you yourself into the darkest cell we had, let you rot there until we needed you." She said it flippantly. "Have your family carted off to a pit somewhere. But I told her it affected your gifts if you were miserable and cut off from the sky. I told her that it wouldn't pay to have my resurrectionist despise us more than she already did. Your family will be sent home, and you're to be placed under house arrest at the palace, until we can decide what to do with you."

"Why did you tell her that?" Hellevir had to ask. "You know it's not true."

"Do you think I want you to be miserable?" Sullivain demanded angrily. "Do you think I haven't felt. . ." She stopped, glancing briefly at Hellevir's hand by her side as if it still brushed her own. Hellevir took a step forward, tension making her limbs shiver.

"And why," she demanded, "do you care how miserable I am?"

"I . . ." Sullivain pressed her lips together. For a moment she was in perfect silhouette against the sconce behind her, half-turned as she was towards Hellevir. Hellevir thought she might be about to say something truthful, but Sullivain just clicked her fingers to get the attention of a guard standing on the other side of the pool. He strode over, the red shades of his leather cuirass the only color in the gloom.

"When the Redeions have been hanged," she said to Hellevir, "and Auland's body has been affixed to the battlements, then maybe you can see your family. Until then, you're in my custody." She turned to the guard. "Lock her in one of the guest rooms," she ordered. "Make sure she can't leave." The guard inclined his head and took Hellevir in a tight grip at her elbow, but she shrugged him off.

"You don't have to do everything your grandmother tells you to," she said quietly.

Sullivain said nothing, watching her with lips pressed thin as the guards took Hellevir by the arm and pushed her back towards the palace.

CHAPTER TWENTY

The guest room was well-kept and rich, far richer than Hellevir was used to, but she barely took in the gold brocade, the uphol-stered chairs. It was still a prison cell, with finer trappings. She sat with her head in her hands, and tried not to think.

She only looked up when she heard a flutter at the window. Elsevir had landed on the window ledge, and she went over to let him in.

"There you are," the raven exclaimed. "I've been looking for you everywhere." Elsevir put his head to the side, avoiding looking at Hellevir. "I saw House Redeion being ransacked, soldiers throwing their things into the courtyard." He sounded distraught. She gathered him to her chest and sank to the floor, relieved that he was okay.

"I've made a mistake, Elsevir," Hellevir murmured, fighting back the tears but unable to stop them completely. "I didn't realize what a dangerous game I was playing." She told Elsevir what had happened, wiping her face with the back of her sleeve.

"It's my fault, I should have told the Princess outright," she concluded quietly.

"The Queen would have had the House destroyed anyway," Elsevir replied, nuzzling at Hellevir's hand. "You've heard your father's stories of the war, what the De Neïds did. There's nothing you could have done."

"But it's not the end," Hellevir made herself say. "I have a chance to bring him back."

"Do you think the Princess will do as she promised?" the raven asked.

"I have no choice but to trust her." She took a breath, forced herself to release it slowly. She could hear her pulse pounding in her head. "I knew Sullivain could be harsh. I didn't know she could be brutal. I don't know anymore how much of it is the Queen's influence, and what's just her."

But Hellevir had felt it, when she touched her. She had felt Sullivain's guilt, churning within her like vertigo, her fear that she was making a dreadful mistake. More than that, she'd felt regret, cloying and thick. It had been suffocating.

The days passed in a blur. Hellevir tried a few times to leave her room, but the guards stopped her. Food was brought to her twice a day. The fire was lit for her in the evening. When night fell she lay down on the enormous bed but could barely sleep.

Death was watching her. She felt it, waiting gleefully for the approaching moment when she would bring him another of the treasures. She gripped the iris seeds in her pocket, the second pearl she'd never used, and thought about what she had read in the book of tales that Edrin had given her. Her bags had been left in the room with her, the book among them, and she read the whole thing from cover to cover, straining her eyes by candlelight as she studied the woodcut of the king dressed in black with tines growing from his helmet.

Day dawned. She sat on her bed, knees tucked up to her chin, and watched the sunlight filtering around the heavy curtains like an eclipse. She got up and pushed them back, letting the brightness flood the room. Her eyelids drifted shut, red-tinged, and she wished she could throw open the windows, let in some fresh air, the sound of birdsong, but the locks were tight.

Hellevir was taken in a carriage into the city. Bion sat opposite, his knee bobbing with nervous energy. She could see it out of the corner of her eye, jittering, and she wished he would stop.

As they travelled down the main thoroughfare, the crowds grew thicker and louder. Vendors shouted out, their wares clinking from the portable stalls they wore on their backs, glinting with jewelry and trinkets. The shops they passed were heaving with customers.

"Why do I have to go?" Hellevir breathed. Bion glanced at her, seemingly surprised that she had spoken.

"We discovered the killer because of you," he explained. "That's earned you a seat."

"I didn't mean to."

"It doesn't matter whether you meant to. The result is the same." He looked out of the window at the passing crowds. Hellevir squeezed her eyes tightly closed, and didn't listen.

The crowds tightened and then spilled out into the town square, where the flagstones were blinding white and the houses around them bright as tulips. The autumn sunlight shone fiercely down on the heads of hundreds of onlookers, their voices loud and abrasive in the small chamber of the carriage. Bion took out a pair of irons, and Hellevir let him fasten them around her wrists.

"Why would I run now?" she asked. He shrugged, slipping the key in his pocket.

"The Queen gave you freedom before, and look what you did with it," he remarked.

He got out and helped her down to where a line of guards was waiting, holding the crowd back to allow Hellevir to pass through and up a flight of stairs onto a temporary viewing platform. Hellevir scanned the square, seeing that there were other platforms dotted around, all crowded with the elite of Rochidain. Her heart froze as she saw the heavy silhouette of the gallows at the head of the square, made of timber so dark it looked burned. She saw windows flung open with people hanging out to watch, children climbing the fountain to get a better view.

"Sit," Bion said, and pushed her down into an empty chair.

"I don't want to see this," she murmured, but he didn't hear her. She heard bootsteps beside her and sensed Bion stand up straight and move away. The chair beside her creaked as someone sat on it. Feeling numb, she turned to look at the aquiline profile of the Queen. The monarch surveyed the crowd, one ankle resting lazily upon her knee.

"You know," she mused, as if to no one in particular, "the city hasn't seen a good execution in years. The odd murderer, of course, but not a family of traitors. Not since the last of the Bergerads were brought to justice."

Hellevir said nothing, feeling like she wore a muzzle as well as irons.

"There were several Bergerads who fled at the very start of the war, wanted nothing to do with it. They hid in the fens, or the mountains, or abroad. Not one of them had spilled De Neïd blood, nor conspired to. But still I hunted them down, herded them back to Rochidain like wayward cattle."

She turned at last to Hellevir, eyes iron-dark and twice as hard.

"I fought for the Crown for four years, and I have held it for twenty-five. How do you think I have done that?"

Hellevir didn't reply.

"Terror," the Queen murmured. "Terror of a thousand different breeds." She gestured, the vambrace on her arm glinting in the sunlight. "The people are petrified of another war. Many remember the last too well to want another. The Peers are terrified of losing control when they are just beginning to claw it away from the heathens. Heathens like you." She smiled, a cruel hook at the corner of her lips. "And the Houses, we know what scares them. Their secrets coming to light, their indiscretions, their sins. By their secrets I have kept them bridled."

Laughter erupted from a group standing near the platform. Guffaws and shouts. Hellevir flinched.

"I always worried my grip would slip. When all sin equally, what does it matter who knows? But after today, not one of them will dare to oppose me again. Today is an opportunity for me to remind them why the De Neïds won the war, and why they should still be terrified of us."

Hellevir found she was quivering. The irons were clammy around her wrists, and she gripped her hands together tightly.

"You've given me the means to keep them under control a little longer," the Queen mused. "And for that I owe you my gratitude."

There was a surge in the crowd, a cheer went up, and they both raised their heads to watch Sullivain ascend to the royal platform. She was resplendent in white and gold, a crown glinting in her wheatsheaf hair. She looked beautiful in the daylight, like a shard of the sun.

A feeling surged through Hellevir. Unexpected and powerful. It swept down to find her in the well the Queen's words had dug for her, scooped her up and brought her to the light.

There is hope, she thought. *Sullivain has made me a promise. Calgir Redeion will live, despite you and your terror.*

273

"And how do you keep Sullivain terrified?" Hellevir asked, watching the Princess as she smiled and waved to the crowd.

She felt the Queen turn to her, the full attention of her regard like the burning torch of Death's heavy gaze.

"Sulli is the only one in the city who doesn't need to be afraid," the monarch said softly.

Hellevir turned and faced her, met her gaze, and said nothing. A heavy beat passed.

The Queen stood and left the platform, flanked by guards. A minute later and the crowd cheered again as she ascended to stand beside her granddaughter. Above her the De Neïd standards drifted in the still air, red as blood.

Drums sounded. All eyes turned to the gallows, where five figures were being led up the steps, wrists and ankles shackled. In their center was Auland Redeion, looking far less noble than Hellevir was used to, dressed as he was in a simple shift, his beard unkempt. And beside him was Calgir. His blond hair was ruffled, his usual careless curls close and limp to his head with days of being unwashed. Hellevir's heart twisted.

It'll be all right, she thought, as if he could hear her. *I promise. It'll be all right. I'll bring you back and you'll be free.*

A Peer stood on the edge of the platform. He wore finer robes than Hellevir had seen Peer Laius wear. The head of the Temple, Tadeus, she remembered. He had an old-fashioned scroll in one hand, and once the crowd's murmuring had died down, he unravelled it and began to speak in a booming voice that echoed around the square. A speech about treason, about the fate that awaits traitors, cast into the non-being, destined to become nothing, as befits all those who fall from Onaistus's Path of Light. Hellevir couldn't really hear it; the blood was too loud in her ears. She was suddenly parched, her throat grating as she tried to swallow. She was breathing heavily. She couldn't tear her eyes away from Calgir, his head held high even now.

Auland Redeion stepped forward when the speech ended, stumbling in the chains around his ankles before the Peer could stop him. He looked out over the crowd, face contorted with anger.

"We are descendants of the Nightingale!" he hollered. "Onaistus be my witness, the Crown is ours by blood!" No others on the platform from House Redeion joined him, or looked at him. A couple grimaced, sickened.

A man in a black mask was standing behind the Peer, and he heaved Auland back so violently he almost fell. Auland struggled as a noose was forced over his head, his shouting muffled, but guards had ascended the platform and held him tight. Calgir stood tall and unflinching as a rope was tightened around his neck as well. When Auland knocked into him, Calgir shook him off, as if he couldn't bear his touch.

At a nod from Peer Tadeus, the man in the black mask placed his hand on the timber lever at the end of the row of House Redeion. An expectant hush fell over the crowd.

"No!" Hellevir heard a voice she knew ring out through the silence. "No, Calgir!" She stood abruptly, eyes darting over the crowd to find her brother. She saw Farvor pushing forward, elbowing his way through the throng. She surged towards the stairs, but Bion roughly caught her wrist and yanked her back, making the irons bite into her flesh. Guards slid through the crowd like sharks catching the scent of blood, and Farvor was seized.

"You can't do this!" her brother shouted as he was dragged away. "You bloodthirsty bitches, you can't do this!"

Hellevir didn't look at the Queen as she barked orders for the execution to go on. She didn't turn back to watch her brother being heaved away, his sobs loud in her ears. She didn't watch Calgir. She only watched Sullivain, because Sullivain was watching her. She was all Hellevir could see.

The Queen's hand appeared on her granddaughter's shoulder, gripping the fabric of her cloak like an eagle's talons. Sullivain flinched. Then she looked away from Hellevir, down at the ground, her eyes wide and glassy.

"No," Hellevir breathed. The lever was pulled and somehow, over the distance and over the myriad noises a throng of thousands will make, she heard the sound of ropes snap taut.

They carted her back to the palace and left her in the bedroom again. All the while Bion ignored her demands to see the Queen, to see the Princess, to see her brother. He only stayed with her long enough to remove the irons, and then he closed the door in her face. She stood still as the lock clicked.

She had imagined it, she told herself. Sullivain wouldn't go back on her promise. She must have imagined it. Any moment now, a guard would come to take her to some small underground room, somewhere no one else would go, and Calgir's body would be on a slab or a bed or even the floor. And then she'd kneel beside him, take his hand, and barter for his soul. Then they'd collect Farvor from whatever cell he had been thrown into, and they'd be shipped off somewhere, somewhere warm, where they could smoke pipes together and read books and . . .

She realized she was crying, her whole body shaking. That sound, that snap, she kept hearing it. She knelt by the fireplace, unable to move, until Elsevir came tapping at the window.

Hellevir woke groggily to Elsevir snapping at someone's hand on her arm. She stroked him quiet and sat up, pushing her hair out of her face to find Bion looming over her. She had been asleep a while; the fire had burned low. She got to her feet, knowing exactly where she was being taken, and Elsevir settled on her shoulder with a glowering eye.

Bion brought her down the long, high corridors of the palace, back to Sullivain's rooms by the training grounds. It was a cold day and raining hard, but the Princess had the bay doors wide, the lace curtains drifting in the breeze.

Hellevir usually enjoyed being in Sullivain's study. But right then, she had no eyes for the books, or the beautiful paintings, or the statues and the ornamented hearth. Even for the drawings on the tables, Sullivain's own sketches of swords, of the gardens. Sullivain watched the rain without turning as Hellevir was let in. Her hair was loose and flowed in gentle waves over her shoulders.

"You may go, Bion," said a voice that was not Sullivain's. Hellevir turned to see the Queen standing by the bookcase.

"What is this?" she demanded as Bion bowed out of the room. The Queen turned to look at her granddaughter.

"Sulli?" she asked. The Princess didn't move, watching the rain with her arms folded. The Queen sighed. There was a large wooden box on the floor by her feet. The rainwater on the windowpanes was reflected on its rough surface; it looked like bloated veins. The Queen leaned over, pulled back its latch, and opened it. There was a smell of something burned, charcoal and embers, something greasy.

"You wanted to raise Calgir," she said. "Here he is."

Hellevir looked into the box. It was filled with grey softness, interspersed with black, crooked-looking things. It reminded her of a snowy terrain in the hills, dark spikes of rock and trees amid the white.

The rain filled the silence. Hellevir stared into the box, part of her mind refusing to acknowledge what was in there, that this was all real and not some horrific dream.

"Why did you do this?" she murmured. Her voice trembled.

"Because after everything, you still seem to think I'd let a threat like the Redeion heir escape the city," the Queen remarked.

"I wasn't asking you," Hellevir said bluntly. She looked at Sullivain's back. "Why did you do this? You made me a promise. Why did you tell her when you knew what she would do?"

Sullivain said nothing. Her shoulders were stiff, her posture rigid. She didn't turn around.

Hellevir clenched her teeth together until her jaw ached.

"Will you at least let me try?" she asked the Queen.

"Please," she replied, eyebrows arched. "I'm curious to see if you can raise the dead without a body."

Hellevir felt ill. Elsevir squirmed, uneasy on her shoulder. Hellevir knelt before the box, her nostrils filled with the cloying smell of bones, burned and ground. She reached her hand inside, and her fingertips brushed the greasy softness of ash. They were still warm. In her pocket she grasped the seeds.

Don't think about it, she told herself. *Don't think about what you're touching.*

Gods. Poor Calgir. What had she done?

She closed her eyes, and let herself sink into Death.

The cold rushed to meet her like an old hound. The silence stopped her ears, and all she could hear was her own beating heart. For a moment she just sat there, her hands on her lap, staring at the grey floor.

It felt like all the world weighed down on her shoulders, but somehow she stood up anyway, and went over to the garden door, looking out into the blackness beyond. No mirrored sky greeted her this time, not even a path; just blackness, above and below, as if the room were drifting in the empty night sky.

"Are you there?" she asked the black.

"I'm always here," the world whispered back, the words on the air itself that pressed against her skin. She turned around and found the man with the black eyes seated by the fire. His elbows rested on the arms of the chair, his fingers steepled.

"Do you know why I'm here?" she asked him.

"You're here for the boy," he said, watching her with those dark eyes.

"He was a man. They hanged him for a treason he didn't commit."

"He was a boy still. Not in years, perhaps."

"Then what am I? A girl still?"

"No. You are no longer a girl. You haven't been since you were ten years old and you learned that there is more than the pale mortal world."

Hellevir looked away, fighting back tears. She wanted to ask the question, but she was terrified she already knew the answer. She clenched her jaw, and told herself she would not cry here, not in Death. She would not let Death see her cry.

"Can I take him home?" she made herself say. "I have your precious thing." She took the seeds out of the pocket and held them out. The man with the black cloak stood up and was before her by the doors in the next breath. He looked down at the seedpod, his eyes bright with their life and his hunger for it. These moments were the only time she saw anything besides darkness within them. A human being pulled forward to peer through the eyeholes of his mask. She realized—suddenly, abstractly—that she recognized what the darkness was by the absence of it as his eyes filled with the light of the seeds. The horse creature on the moors had the same eyes, black with pain. Eons of pain.

Her body shuddered as he took her hand, his skin cold as iron, and gently closed her fingers around the seeds again, hiding them from sight.

"Not this time," he said. "But you already knew that."

"Why?" she demanded. She would not cry. She would not.

"Your boy has no body, not anymore. Some things cannot be raised."

"Your rules change every time I come here," she hissed, her anger surging. "Now you tell me I cannot bring everyone back. You never told me there were limits to who I could bring back."

His expression darkened. The world darkened.

"There are no limits," he said quietly. The air around him shivered with his words. "But the price would be too high, even for you."

"I brought you your precious thing. I will give you my blood. Just tell me the cost!"

"The ones you take back, they have wounds, nothing more. Wounds, illnesses, they are fixable, easy things, that the body could right itself given the time and the force of life. The treasures you find, the few drops of blood you give, can fix these things. They cannot recreate bodies from nothing. Not without the price of another body."

"Another body?"

"Yes."

Hellevir looked away, into the gloom. Her fist tightened around the seedpod, and she felt the shell crack a little.

"My body," she murmured.

"Yes."

"I would have to die."

"Yes. To recreate a form from such complete destruction."

"I . . ." She didn't know what to say, what to think. She reached into her collar and brought out the lion pendant Pa had hung about her neck when she was a girl. The pendant she'd worn against her heart, its warmth reminding her that she was not alone. His dark eyes went to it as if drawn there. "What about this? You once said it could raise legions, that it was soaked in blood. Surely I can trade this for him?"

The darkness churned, and she had the sudden impression that he wanted to accept her offer, but would not. She stepped forward, thinking to beseech him, but he shook his head, moving away as if to touch it would burn him.

"It carries too much blood for one body," he said. "It would not be a fair trade."

"I don't care if it's an unfair trade." She hesitated. The next words sat on her tongue, heavy and leaden, begging to be allowed to fall from her lips. The words she'd read in the carriage by the light of streetlamps. The words that had been slumbering in her chest these last awful days.

Antlered King.

She swallowed them back, thick in her throat. She didn't want to anger him, she wanted him to bring Calgir back. The idea of naming him, flinging the words at him just to goad him to a response, felt deeply wrong.

"Please," she said instead. "Take it."

"No. You might not care, but I do."

"Please . . ."

"No. I will not make false exchanges." The words rang with finality. Hellevir put her head in her hands. The air roiled around her like disturbed silt, as if it could sense her distress.

"Can I at least talk to him?" she asked quietly.

"As you wish."

She glanced back and saw the figure of Calgir standing by the doors, looking out into the black. She drew her breath in sharply.

"Calgir?"

He turned around, his expression bright and cheerful. "I wondered where you'd got to," he said. "Avoiding the party again?"

"You know what I'm like," Hellevir murmured. "Always on the periphery." He laughed, and it was an odd sound in this place, deadened as if it had been caught in a glass vial.

"Well, come on, let's get back. I know Farvor was looking for you."

She caught his wrist, stopping him from stepping into the blackness. He looked back at her, surprised. Her throat felt tight.

"I . . . Farvor loves you," she said. "You know that, don't you?" It felt trite to her ears, something from a story. Trite dying words. He smiled, and it was the brightest thing in this place.

"I am aware," he said drily. "Come on." He made to move away, but she held him.

"Is there anything you want me to say to him?" she asked.

"To whom? Farvor?"

"Yes."

"Why? He's waiting out there for us."

"I know, but . . . humor me. Please?"

"You can tell him to please stop cracking his knuckles, it makes my toes curl. And to learn to polish his shoes as well as he does mine. He is my squire, after all."

"And to stop smoking out of the bedroom window?"

"No, I made him stop that. It was making the curtains stink."

They smiled at each other. Calgir patted her hand on his wrist. His eyes glazed over and shifted to the darkness outside, and he tugged again, pausing as he noticed her grip on his arm.

"I wondered where you'd got to," he said. "Avoiding the party again?"

"I . . . yes. Calgir, I'm so sorry."

"Oh, don't worry, I sometimes slip away too. Sometimes you have to."

"I'll join you in a minute," she said. "Farvor said to tell you he loves you." It all felt so clumsy. When it mattered, at times like this, shouldn't the words come easily? She made herself loosen her grip, and her arm dropped to her side.

"Oh, I know it," he replied with a blue-eyed wink, and trotted down the steps. She could see him for a long while as he walked, but when she blinked he was gone, and the emptiness had swallowed him whole. Hellevir watched the shadows, feeling hollow as a cave. She felt the man in black come up beside her and felt his breath in her hair.

"So your life wasn't worth his?" he asked tauntingly.

"I can save other lives after his," Hellevir said.

"So you weighed the scales, and your life was worth more?"

She turned to him with a bitter scowl.

"Stop goading me," she said sharply. Her voice cracked as she said it. "I *must* live, if others are supposed to."

"Can it be you're as afraid of dying as the rest of them?"

"Of course I'm afraid of dying."

"Of the nothing of death, or the pain?"

"I . . . I don't know." She closed her eyes, feeling nauseous. Her thoughts wouldn't sit still, wouldn't make sense to her. "What does it matter to you?"

"A great deal. If it's a consolation to you, I would not have let you make such a trade anyway."

She opened her eyes and turned on him. "What?"

He shrugged, his hands in the pockets of his coat, his black eyes resting somewhere in the gloom. It was a nonchalant gesture, improper for talking of life and death.

"I need you alive to keep finding the treasures I set you to hunt. No one else can do it."

Hellevir put a hand to her stomach. She suddenly wanted to get away, from Death, from the Princess, from Rochidain. From everything. Nothingness suddenly didn't seem so awful.

"Then this was just a trick to see what I would do?" she asked quietly.

"I suppose it was."

"And? Did I do what you expected?" she hissed.

"No, actually. I thought you were a martyr, ready and willing to give each and every part of yourself away for anyone in need of saving. I did expect you to give yourself in place of the knight. It turns out you have more depth to you."

Hellevir didn't know what to say to that. A hundred reasons churned away in her head, ready to be presented as an excuse, a clever philosophy to counter his cynicism, but they turned to ash upon her tongue. She had no good excuse, no clever logic, other than her own fear and the weight of lives she would save against Calgir's. A black-and-white equation, devoid of any moral component. The easiest decision in the world to make.

"I'm tired," she said quietly instead. "I want to go home."

He took her hand, and bent over it, as if they had just finished a dance at a ball. She was too taken aback to withdraw, but he had enjoyed all of this, she knew. It had entertained him. She felt sick.

"Why can I feel her?" she asked. "Sullivain? When I touch her, I can feel her heart."

When he looked up, still bent over her hand, it was with an amused satisfaction. "You already know."

She swallowed.

"Is it because I've brought her back twice now? Our souls are twice bound?" Like two pieces of string that had been twisted together, once, and then once more. It seemed as if her fear leached into the world around her, seemed to taint it red. The thought of their souls forever bound terrified her.

"Yes," he said simply. "But I do not think that your twisting souls can be held accountable for how afraid you are that she will die. For how you miss the sight of her, even now. For how the seed of your obsession has taken such firm root. I did try to warn you."

She shuddered. She wished he would let go of her hand.

"I want to go home," she whispered again. Although right then she couldn't have said where home was.

"Then go," the world rumbled, and she awoke.

The soldiers dragged Farvor somewhere dark, somewhere he couldn't see Calgir, although he shouted out his name. Every time he did, a fist came from the darkness and battered him, until he spat blood and his chest felt like his bones had turned to shattered glass. The floor was cold and wet but he didn't care, it was a balm against his hot skin. He thought day might have come, but one eye wouldn't open and the window of his cell was high and deeply recessed, so he couldn't see the sky.

"Please," he gasped when food was brought to him. "Where is Calgir? Please tell me what's happening." He knew what was happening, knew it but didn't think it.

Hours, days, who knew how long later, he heard the door creak open, and a moment later Hellevir was by his side, her hair smelling of the incense the Order burned and her hands gentle as she checked over him.

"Farvor, I'm here," she murmured. "It's all right, we're leaving." She drew away. "You broke his ribs!" he heard her snap over her shoulder. "Why?"

"He resisted," came a male voice from a figure on the other side of the bars.

"Of course he resisted!" she said. "What sort of man wouldn't?" She turned to address the guard. "You're going to help me carry him back to the city."

"I don't . . ."

"It wasn't a request. Check with the Princess if you want. Go and prepare a carriage." The guard must have obeyed; the red-and-gold shape vanished.

"It's all right," Farvor heard her murmur, putting something cool and wet against his eye. "It'll all be fine." His hand drifted up of its own accord and gripped her elbow.

"Did they do it?" he demanded. He heard her swallow, saw the outline of her head turn away. He gripped her tighter, shook her arm with the strength he had left. "Tell me!"

"Farvor, let me just get you home . . ."

"Please, Hellevir, tell me. Please just tell me."

She was silent. His chest felt like there were iron bands around it, but he didn't let her go.

"He . . . yes, they did it."

Farvor closed his eye, his head rolling to the side as if she'd struck him. He'd known it, though. What else could possibly have happened? He knew his grip was too tight, because she winced with the pain, and he made himself uncurl his fingers. He coughed, and tasted blood again. He caught her hand as she tried to turn his cheek.

"You bring him back," he spat, staring at her through his good eye. "Right now. You bring him back." His other hand was gripped around her cloak, scrunching it up like a child holding his mother's skirt.

He saw Hellevir look up and away, silent. Her hands were tight around his, cold and clammy. He could tell she was desperately trying not to cry by the way she was holding her breath. What right had she to cry?

"I tried," she said as if she was speaking around a lump in her throat. "I did. But they . . ."

"What?" The word fell like a rock. He heard it echo back to him from the stone wall of the cell.

"There was nothing left to bring back. They burned the body so I couldn't save him."

He felt like he was going to be sick. And he was, right before the shadows at the corners of his vision engulfed him whole.

CHAPTER TWENTY-ONE

They let Hellevir go home. Two weeks, the Queen said, to tend to your brother's wounds. Take it as a gesture of good faith.

Farvor was bedridden. She made compresses and ointments for his bruises and wrapped him tightly so nothing would move too much. The compress for the swelling was Milandre's recipe, soaked in a bowl of dried witch-hazel leaves, among other things, and she made a poultice of comfrey, nettles and butter, with a few drops of yarrow and elderflower-infused oil. He accepted her attention as if she were a hired nurse, his gaze distant and his expression blank.

"Has he said anything?" her pa asked as she prepared Farvor some dinner in the kitchen. He had barely eaten, scraps here and there that she'd practically force-fed him. Hellevir shook her head.

"Nothing," she said. "It's like I'm not there. Like *he's* not there."

"It'll pass," Pa said, worrying the tablecloth in his big hands. "It'll pass. He's a strong lad, a hunter, he'll be all right." Hellevir didn't reply. She picked up the tray and made to go back up the stairs, but her father called to her. "Are you still going to be her herbalist? After all of this?"

Hellevir looked down at the tray, the willow-bark tea and the small vial of poppy extract for the pain.

"I have no choice, Pa," she said. "Two weeks and then I'll be trapped at the palace again. Besides, the Queen could still make our lives worse. And if Sullivain did die it would mean war." They were rote-learned words now, tasting stale.

"Not Farvor's," Pa remarked, his tone dark. "She couldn't make Farvor's life worse." She heard him sigh. "I'm sorry, my girl. It could always be worse. I shouldn't tempt fate so." She glanced back at him, seeing his eyes were downcast. She laid the tray aside and put her arms around him, breathing in his smell of leather. He patted her arms around his neck. "I'm just angry," he said grimly. "So damn angry I could set the whole palace on fire and walk away without a backward glance. The thought of you serving that girl after what her grandmother did . . . it makes me swallow bile. I wonder how you can stand it."

The first thing on her tongue was an excuse for Sullivain. *If she was free of her grandmother, she might be different*, she wanted to say. But the excuses dissolved, because it was just her own stubborn hope that gave them substance.

Her pa shook his head. She knew he felt as powerless as she did, and she knew he hated it.

Hellevir took the tray upstairs, feeling like there was a hole in her chest that was cold from the wind blowing through it. Wretchedness was a feeling she was growing used to.

Farvor was sitting up in bed, looking out of the window at the life of the city below. They'd positioned the bed so he would have a good view of the street.

"Cook has given me free rein of the kitchen," Hellevir said. "But I'm a herbalist, not a chef." Farvor didn't reply. He was watching something out on the thoroughfare; she paused by his bedside to see what it was.

There was a procession passing by, for one of the Onaistian festivals. They both watched as the grey-robed Peers walked in columns down the streets, swinging incense burners that breathed white along the path, spilling smoke down between the railings into the canal waters. Between them they carried long effigies made of stretched black fabric that they held over their heads, weaving them back and forth. She could smell the incense: sandalwood. It was pleasant. Some of the Peers carried instruments, and they played a lively tune, the sound bouncing cheerfully between the houses. Some of them had bright green ribbons trailing behind them, fastened to their buttons and wrists like river weed.

Along the edge of the flowing worshippers stood still forms, glinting sharp as stones. Guards with pikes stabbing into the sky, the galleon symbol stark on their armor. There were more guards everywhere, now, ever since the hangings. They watched the people like wolves, waiting for the weakest to stumble.

"They're walking along those golden discs," Farvor said quietly. "The ones we saw embedded in the paths." Hellevir glanced at him, surprised. It was the first full sentence he'd said in days.

"Those effigies are eels?" she asked, watching the black things being wound between each other in intricate zigzags down the road.

"I suppose so."

They watched as the procession continued, the Peers vanishing down the street with a long trail of followers behind them. Somewhere down among them was their ma. Hellevir had only recently learned where Ma had been all through this; she had just hidden at the temple. Never mind that her daughter had been arrested at the palace, or that her son's lover had been executed. Hellevir shook herself awake, her mind wandering in unwanted places.

"You should eat some soup," Hellevir said. "Though it might be a bit cold now. I made it from leftovers." She put the tray on his lap, careful to avoid the lingering bruise on his thigh.

Farvor looked down at the soup, the spoon loose in his fingers. Hellevir plumped the pillow to put behind his head.

"Is it all right?" she asked when he didn't look like he was going to eat it. She wished he would just eat *something*. She saw the muscles in his jaw work.

"Is this it, now?" he said quietly. "We eat leftovers?"

Hellevir sat on the end of his bed. "What do you mean?" she asked gently.

"This . . . this is normal," he murmured. "It's normal. It shouldn't be, though. How can they not feel it? How am *I* supposed to not feel it? Everyone should be wearing black. All the rivers should be stained black. There shouldn't be parades. No incense or songs. But there *are* parades, and markets. Soup." He let the spoon drop from his fingers onto the tray with a clatter. "Leftovers."

Hellevir swallowed, not knowing what to say. The soup grew cold between them.

Edrin came to see Hellevir at the house, and brought her news. They kept finding members of House Redeion, those who had escaped Rochidain by other means, those who had known of the plot. The Queen herself left Rochidain to hunt them down, and one by one they could be seen swaying from their ropes by the pale dawn in the city square. Such things had not happened since the War over the Waves, and Rochidain sat upon the edge of the sea in a frozen shock, a frozen fear. The Gallows Month, some started to call it.

Soldiers marched through the streets, sending townsfolk scurrying to their homes. Arrests were made in the street: anyone voicing dissent, anyone daring to ask why the entirety of House Redeion must pay for one man's felonies. The taverns still played music, but few people danced, and conversation was hushed, spoken low over barely-touched pints. The marketplace seemed muted, the usual roar of sound quelled beneath eyes watching from the gloom of helms.

A thump woke Hellevir, startling her. She went over to the window, and saw a sparrow lying on the sill. It must have thought the glass was the sky. It wasn't moving. She opened the window and took the tiny creature into her hands.

"Elsevir," she called to the raven, who sat perched upon her chair. "Will you bring me one of the violas from the Order, from by the willow?" He cocked his head to the side, but did as he was asked without question. He returned not long after and dropped a single flower, purple and yellow, on the coverlet. At Hellevir's gesture, he pecked her finger sharply, drawing a bead of blood.

Death brought a blissful silence. The noise of the thoroughfare, the old women talking outside her window, were all banished, leaving the comforting sounds of her own body; her steady breath, the brush of her hair against her shoulders. She stayed there for a few minutes, sitting cross-legged with her eyes closed, enjoying the completeness of the quiet.

"Did you come here to sleep?" the air around her asked. She kept her eyes closed.

"Is it another thing forbidden in our bargain?" she replied. He paused. She felt his dark eyes on her.

"No," he admitted.

"Then I'll sit for a little bit."

A pause. She waited.

"As you wish," the world murmured.

She sat there for a while, enjoying the stillness, the silence. She knew he observed her; his presence was so total throughout the world that she would have felt him watching her wherever she was. Right then she didn't care. It was almost comforting, something familiar that she knew held no threat. How odd that something she had once found so terrifying could now bring her respite.

At some point she heard a flutter of wings and felt a small body alight upon her shoulder. She sighed and opened her eyes, withdrawing back into life. The noise from the thoroughfare hit her almost as heavily as the cold.

The viola in her lap was gone, and the coverlet was stained with the drop of blood from her finger. The sparrow on her shoulder chirruped and flickered to her hand, and onto the top of her head, and back to her shoulder. She stood up and went over to the window.

"Even the small ones will cost you," Elsevir remarked as they watched it flutter away.

"I know," Hellevir replied quietly.

Hellevir got dressed and went to check on her brother, but found to her alarm that he wasn't in his bed. Frantic, she ran downstairs, calling out for him, only to find him sitting outside by the fountain, wrapped up in his black hunting coat.

"There you are," she said, letting out a breath as she sat beside him. "I was worried."

"You shouldn't have worried," he said quietly. They sat in silence, listening to the robins squabbling among the heavy fruits of the pomegranate tree. The silence became heavier, weighed down by all the unpleasant things they didn't want to talk about, until Farvor at last let out a breath.

"I wish you'd stop," she heard him mutter, and she glanced over at him. He met her gaze tiredly. He'd had trouble meeting her eyes for days, and now it felt odd.

"Stop?" she asked.

"I don't think there's anyone in the world who embraces guilt like you do. I can almost see it emanating from you. It's exhausting."

"I'm sorry," she said meekly.

He made an annoyed sound, tired, and she almost apologized again. He rubbed his eyes.

"I know you blame yourself for what happened," he said. "But it wasn't your fault. It was Auland Redeion's." The name sounded toxic the way Farvor said it, like he wanted to spit it from his lips.

Hellevir swallowed. She hadn't told him about the possibility of trading one body for another. Death wouldn't have let her give herself away anyway, so there was no point in mentioning it, surely?

She couldn't bring herself to say the words. Instead, ashamed of her own spinelessness, she said, "At the dinner party I should have waited until the guests had left to talk to you both. Then Yvoir wouldn't have overheard us."

"You weren't to know she was listening."

"No. But I should have been more careful."

"Auland should have been more careful. Not you. He got his whole family killed. I don't know what he thought would happen."

"He got himself killed, too," she said softly.

"Small mercies. He always was a nasty old man. You know he used to beat Calgir? When he was a boy?" Farvor put back his head and let out a breath, watching it curl in the cold morning air. "What am I supposed to do now, Hellevir?" he asked quietly. "I can't stay here forever."

"Heal first, worry about the future later," she said. "You're still broken."

He smiled at that, as if she'd said something amusing. It wasn't a full smile, just the facsimile of one, without humor.

"Yes," he remarked. "Still broken."

"I just meant your ribs. Your eye. Everything else will take longer."

He said nothing for a moment, his hands in the pockets of his heavy coat and his head still tilted back to look up at the white sky.

"I feel . . . nothing. Just empty. Like I can't convince myself anything happened. Is that normal?"

She put a hand on his knee.

"You're in shock," she said. "You're still numb. It'll pass."

"And then what? It'll just hurt? When the nothing is gone there'll just be pain?"

"Maybe for a while. But it'll get better."

He moved his leg away from her hand.

"You've never had to grieve for anything," he said. He didn't say it with venom, or with an intent to hurt her. It was just a statement. "You've brought back anyone you'd have missed. What do you know about death?"

He closed his eyes as if he were suddenly dizzy. She opened her mouth but no words came to her. She wanted to say that she missed Calgir too, the way he tried to make her feel at ease, his comfortable laugh, but she knew it was nothing compared to what Farvor felt.

Someone pulled the bell at the gate. Her body moved to open it while her mind stayed seated beside her brother, struggling for something to say. And so when she opened the door, saw who was standing there, it took her a moment to catch up with herself.

"No," she breathed. "No. I won't go."

Bion grimly held out the letter. It was stamped with the wax seal of the golden ship.

"I'm afraid you must," he replied.

Sullivain wasn't dead. Not yet. But there was certainly no hope that she would live for long.

Her spine was broken, Hellevir didn't know in how many places, and her arms and legs lay unnaturally limp upon the covers. There was a gash on her head and, where the physicians had lifted her shirt to apply leeches, bruising spread across her abdomen like a sick flower. Milandre had always thought leeches were a quack's tool. *Leech for this, leech for that, they'll use a leech for anything they know they can't fix,* she'd said. *Leech to bleed you when you're already bleeding.*

The Princess was spitting up bloody foam. From the way she was wheezing Hellevir guessed one of her lungs had collapsed. She'd seen it once in one of Sathir's patients; the priestess had lodged a pipe into his chest to let the trapped air out, but nothing like that would help Sullivain. She was broken in too many places.

"This was an accident?" she murmured.

"He was too wild, too big for her," Bion said quietly as they watched the physicians work. "We thought she had him, though. He seemed to have calmed. They got up a good sprint, I've never seen such a fast horse. But just as she was relaxing in the saddle, he bucked, and when she still didn't come off, he rolled." He shuddered. "Every time he bucked, she laughed. Like a fey thing."

No jump will be high enough, no horse swift enough, no current deep enough, Hellevir thought. She nearly turned around to leave the room right then. So what if Sullivain died? After everything she had done, the hangings, the desecration of Calgir's body, why should Hellevir save her? She should leave now, for Farvor if for nothing else. Let the creature be held accountable for her careless nature.

Her anger boiled hot in her chest, acidic after the days of watching bodies swaying in the morning air, of seeing her brother wane to a shadow of himself, covered in the yellowing bruises Sullivain's guards had inflicted on him.

But she didn't leave. She told herself later it was because of the risk to her family, because of her fear of what the Queen would do if her granddaughter died; and that was part of it. But she never admitted to herself that it was also because the sight of the Princess, blood-soaked and limp, caught her. Arrested her and made her chest feel so tight that it hurt. Sullivain looked . . . fragile.

At the sound of voices, Sullivain's eyes flickered open and her gaze roved across the ceiling before settling on Hellevir by her feet. She coughed, bubbling blood.

"Hello, herbalist," she replied, and grinned. It was a gruesome sight, all red. "Come to save me again?"

Hellevir felt something within her sag, helpless before the whistling hollowness that the sight of the dying Princess opened within her. She observed the feeling with detachment, as if it were a part of her she could remove and hold in her hand, a part she wished she could fling far, far away from her. She came forward, her movements wooden as a puppet on someone else's strings, and stopped by the end of the bed.

"Hello, Sullivain," she said, voice hoarse.

One of the physicians, a small man with a white beard, glared at Hellevir sharply.

"With all due respect, the Princess does not need a *herbalist*." The sneer was inherent to the word in his vocabulary. "Regardless of the supposed help you may have been in the past."

"Shut up, Fortlight," Sullivain muttered. "Get out." The physician stared at her, wide-eyed.

"But my lady . . ."

Sullivain huffed in pain, cutting him off.

"Take the black things too. Can't feel them but . . ." She coughed, blood misting the white bandage across her chest. "Onaistus, they're ugly."

"But . . ."

"You heard her," Bion said from behind Hellevir. "Out." The physicians fluttered and removed the leeches, and reluctantly left the Princess's bedside, casting baleful glances at Hellevir as they went. When they were gone, Hellevir came and sat in the chair they'd left by the bedside, removing the basin of blood from the coverlets. As she did so her hand brushed Sullivain's bruised arm.

The sensation shot through her like an arrow. A rotten braid of fear and pain, intertwined with each other and knotted with other things that the touch was too fleeting for Hellevir to feel properly. Fear of true death. Agony over mistakes. Something deeper, inherent to her nature, that Hellevir could taste but not quite identify. But mostly it was just pain.

She flinched, unable to keep herself from pulling away, and saw that Sullivain was watching her. She knew, Hellevir realized; she felt it too. She was just better at hiding it. The Princess turned her head away.

"Can feel it getting closer," she muttered, her eyes glazing. "Can't have those old coots here when you bring me back."

"What makes you think I will?" Hellevir demanded. "After what you did?"

That grin again. Humorless, tinged with something almost mad. As if she wasn't in agony, body and soul.

"Don't be stupid," was all she said, wheezing. "If you fail to bring me back do you think Grandmama will let you live? Do you think she ever planned to let you live if you failed? Your naivete, it's baffling." Red dribbled from the corner of her mouth. Bion came forward and wiped it away as it started to slide down her jaw. "The edict making Onaistian the state religion has even given her an excuse, should she need it. You are an agent of deceit, who has led devotees away from the Promise of the God of Light."

The words sank into Hellevir's mind. Her thoughts flickered to the images she had found in Priestess Ollevin's journals, pictures of fire. *It can't happen here*, she'd thought. And yet she couldn't find it within herself to be surprised. She'd known her family was in the shadow of the gallows, ever since House Redeion had been destroyed.

"You would have me executed as a heathen?" she asked quietly. She felt ill.

"You *are* a little heathen," Sullivain said with a gurgling laugh. Hellevir wondered if she was becoming delirious. "What good devotee of the God of Light talks with Death?" She said it so mockingly that the words didn't sound like hers. Hellevir wondered how much of her grandmother she was parroting.

"Do you think your people would accept that? Too many of them worship the old ways."

"But many more of them are converts to Onaistian," the Princess gasped. "The old ways can't withstand the tide. You are a dying race, herbalist, and soon your kind will all be gone, you the first of them in Rochidain."

Hellevir shivered. Only the first. Those in the Order would not be safe, not forever. No one who talked to beings others couldn't see would be safe. And if there was one there would be more. The first execution would be the breaking of the dam. She had to avoid setting the precedent.

"Is there nothing you won't use to stay alive?" Hellevir asked, but it didn't matter. Sullivain's eyes stopped seeing her, sealed over with pain. Hellevir automatically took her hand, ignoring the surge of agony that coursed through her, the terror. Sullivain coughed and wheezed, tears slipping from the corners of her eyes, and finally she died. Hellevir felt it happen, dying with her, felt it when the surge went silent.

The room suddenly felt very quiet, and very empty.

Bion looked over at her, expression grim.

"You will save her," he said simply. It wasn't a plea, or a request. It was a simple statement of how things would be.

Hellevir didn't answer at once. She just looked at the body, and drew her hand away. She knew what it was, that element of Sullivain's nature that was so profound. One thing that had been threaded through the fear, through the pain. A shame resigned to itself, old and hard. A shame for what, Hellevir didn't know. But the resignation, that frightened her. It was as settled within Sullivain as the heart in her chest. Resignation that this was the way it had to be.

Why do you do these things? she asked the body. *Who told you that you had to?* But she knew already. This was the Queen's doing, her training, just as the threats had been hers as well, using Sullivain's voice to utter them. The Princess's eyes stared up at the ceiling, and when Hellevir brushed her cheek again, there was nothing.

"Yes," Hellevir replied. "As stupid a death as it was, I'll bring her back." She tore her gaze from the body to him. "And you?" she demanded. "You're all right with all this? You'd watch innocents hanged?"

"Yes," he said simply. "Of course I would, for her."

"And how has she bought you? Or are you just terrified like the rest of us?"

"Neither. When her mother died and her father . . . well, she had no one besides her grandmother, and me. I helped to raise her. She's the only child I'll ever have or would ever want."

Bion said nothing more. He just pulled up a chair by the bed and folded his long legs, watching her with his arms crossed. The look he gave her was made of steel, unmoving, unflinching, his loyalty facing her with the bare brutalism of a wind-beaten rock. He wouldn't let her leave, Hellevir realized, not until Sullivain was raised. Hellevir took a deep breath and released it slowly—shakily—and turned back to the body on the bed. She found herself asking Farvor for forgiveness.

She put one hand in her pocket, grasping the seeds, and slid the fingers of the other through Sullivain's. Her skin had already grown cold to the touch.

The room had no doors, not anymore. The windows were gone too, the walls blank as if they'd never existed. Only the balcony doors remained, the lace curtains suspended in the moment of a gust of wind, floating like flung handkerchiefs.

Hellevir stepped out onto the balcony, except it was no longer a balcony. White steps led down, flanked by a delicate balustrade, curling in a gentle, broad spiral. When she looked over the balustrade she couldn't see the bottom, and when she looked up, the mirrored sky showed the eternal descent, vanishing into the black hole of its depth like a curling snail shell. She swallowed and swayed, gripping the balustrade until the dizziness had passed. Having little choice, she began to descend.

She circled down and down, taking each step with patience, knowing eventually it would end. The steps wound clockwise, and her vision began to spin from the monotonous descent. When she looked into the darkness it seemed as if it twisted and swirled, used to the motion from her eyes trailing down the stairs.

When it stopped it came as a surprise. She found—rather to her tired irritation—that the stairs had led her back to a balcony, and as she looked through the doors leading onto it she realized it was the same balcony as the one she'd left. The stairs kept going, inviting her to continue the downward spiral. She did, following the winding path, until she came to the balcony again. She didn't take the next set of stairs. Instead she pulled a chair from inside the room and sat on it facing into the darkness, her arms folded.

"Are you enjoying watching me wander like a rat in your maze?" she asked the empty air. In this place her words sounded too hushed, as if she'd tried to stopper them before they could pour from her lips. She heard a chair being picked up and placed out on the balcony next to hers, and the man with the black eyes sat down beside her, the hem of his coat hanging over the arm and brushing against the marble floor. He crossed his ankle over his knee and leaned back with a sigh.

"I don't enjoy it," he replied, or the air replied. The sound didn't come from beside her but all around her. "That's the wrong word."

"Then why?" she asked, but he didn't reply, whether because he had no answer or because he didn't want her to know it. Instead, he stood, restless, and looked out over the blackness. She got to her feet and went to stand beside him. They observed the darkness as if they stood on a promenade watching the night ocean.

There was a glass by her elbow, she noticed, another by his, filled with dark wine. He picked his up and took a thoughtful sip, but there was something about the way the wine slid around the glass which made her think it was not wine. It was too thick. She picked hers up and smelled it, and put it back down again. He watched her actions out of the corner of his eye and smiled at them.

"Rochidain will not be safe for you for much longer," he remarked without looking at her. It always struck her oddly, seeing him in profile; it felt similar to when she'd entered Death before he had been expecting her, the stage not ready and the theatre dark, an unwariness that had made her feel like she was witnessing something she shouldn't. She traced with her gaze the sharp black of his hair against the white of his skin, the cut of his jaw.

He looked at her then, black eyes giving her their full attention, and she had to fight not to glance sharply away.

"Why now more than before?" she asked.

"The new faith has little room for other deities besides its God of Light," he said, his mocking tone directed somewhere other than her, for once. "And your activities haven't gone unnoticed by its followers."

"Who?" she asked, with some dread.

"There are suspicions, here and there. Flickers in the dark where I assume you want to go unseen."

"You *have* been keeping an eye on me."

He turned to her fully. It felt like an eclipse, the illumination of a dark intensity.

"I would rather you did not die too early and ruin our trading relationship. There have been very few over the years who can come and go so easily between life and Death." Before Hellevir could ask about this, he went on, "You are young. Very young. The last burnings the Onaistians committed were a hundred years ago, long before your mother's mother, but I remember when their victims came through here and they stumbled into non-being with the relief of the tortured. The things that they endured at the hands of the supposed devout . . ." He leaned forward. "The history of the Onaistian faith, it is *soaked* with blood."

Hellevir felt her knuckles tightening on the balustrade.

"I don't need reminding," she said. "But that was long ago."

"The zealotry tastes the same."

The silence of Death pressed against her ears, made her breathing seem loud. The brush of her shirtsleeves echoed. There was an ache within her, although it was too new a feeling for her to be able to explain. A feeling as if something were about to be lost, grief of a sort. He sipped his wine that was not wine, looking into the blackness as if he could see things out there.

She shook her head.

"I can't leave Rochidain," she insisted. "Sullivain will hurt my family if I am . . ."

"The Princess has cheated me long enough. If she dies again, it is well past her time."

"With respect," she said curtly, "it's not you she's threatening. And it's not your city that will be torn apart by civil war. I don't have a choice." She growled it through gritted teeth.

The world around her let out a slow breath. She could tell he wasn't pleased with her, and she told herself she couldn't care less.

"One day there may be more of your soul within her than you have left within yourself," he remarked, and the air brushed against her cheek as if he were standing close in front of her. "Already you are more bound together than I think you care to be. You do have a choice, and one day you'll wish you'd made it. Death, war, it will happen with or without you."

"You really want me out of Rochidain, don't you?" she said. She looked up at him, met his empty eyes, made herself hold them. "The things I've found have been linked, telling the same story. They're all to do with the Nightingale War and the founding of the city. But the story began somewhere else. There's somewhere else you need me to be."

Your story, she dared to think, still not knowing if it was true. *Antlered King*. She saw a flicker, deep in the darkness, something that heard her. The man far behind the mask peering through the holes cut out for eyes.

"Observant girl," the world remarked, although she hadn't seen his lips move and, thinking on it, she wasn't sure if she'd heard the words at all.

Hellevir reached into her pocket and drew out the iris seeds. The flicker became a flame, caught upon the treasure.

"Will you give me Sullivain?" Hellevir asked. He blinked and drew himself away.

"You should get yourself out of this, Hellevir," he said. She realized with a sliver of surprise that it was the first time he had said her name. It sounded odd to hear him say it, as if here she was not Hellevir but simply the One Who Bargained With Death. "Your deal with Sullivain has trapped you, and you'll reap no benefit from it."

"I will reap the benefit of not seeing my family swinging from the gallows," she replied. She looked down, realizing that the seedpod was no longer on her palm. The man with black eyes was holding it as if up to the light, his jaw tight as his eyes wandered over it. A blink later and it was a slip of paper, which he held out to her. The next riddle. She took it and put it away.

He held out his hand to her, and obligingly she put her palm across his, trying not to flinch at the metallic cold of his touch. It didn't hurt as he drew his nail across her thumb, letting three drops fall, one by one, onto the white marble of the balcony floor.

"Your Princess will bring you ruin," he said. He didn't say it as if the idea brought him any particular pain. "But I should know better than to try to steer the living from their destruction. You're not just drawn to it, you actively seek it out. If it's ruin you want, you will find it. But I have warned you many times now, and you will do as you are wont." Before she could reply he looked over her shoulder, and she turned to find Sullivain leaning against the balustrade, her flaxen hair loose about her head.

"Do you think I could jump it?" the Princess asked, looking down at the darkness. She was leaning so far over the balustrade that her feet left the floor, and she balanced on her stomach. Hellevir glanced down.

"Probably," she said. "But I don't know what happens if you die in Death. I'm not sure even I could bring you back."

Sullivain laughed, and it was a pure sound. Not the triumphant laugh as she'd died for a third time, confident enough in her threats that she would wake up again. The sickly fear, the pain, the burden of mistakes, it was all gone. Hellevir liked seeing her this way. It made her wonder if—had the circumstances been different, if they had met some other way and Sullivain had never died at all, had she never had a taste of what it meant to cheat death, had her grandmother not been the way she was—she and Sullivain could have been real friends. Real . . . something.

"You are so strange," the Princess remarked. "Fetch me something to toss, would you? I'd like to see how far down it goes."

"Come inside, and we'll find something," Hellevir said, holding out her hand.

"A shoe, I want to toss a shoe."

"I'm sure we can find a shoe." Sullivain took her hand without hesitation, swinging their arms between them as she led Hellevir back inside. In Death, their touch did not relay emotions as it now seemed to do in life. Hellevir glanced over her shoulder to see the man with the black cloak leaning against the balustrade, watching her go with an inscrutable gaze as his glass of wine that was not wine hung limply from his white fingers.

Hellevir groggily opened her eyes, feeling like she'd been away for a long time. She braced herself against the cold, and when it had passed she looked up to find the Queen leaning over her.

"Well?" the Queen demanded, her voice hard, but before Hellevir could reply movement from the bed caught their attention. Sullivain's body was moving, but she wasn't yet awake. Her chest expanded as the lungs reinflated, her ribs clicked as they straightened. Her body twisted and lurched, dragging across the sheets as her spine unbent back into place once, twice, three times, and she awoke with a gasp, sitting up sharply and retching bloody foam from her throat. She wiped her mouth with the back of her hand, hair slick to her forehead with sweat, and grinned at Hellevir, her teeth still red, unfazed and lucid. Before Hellevir could react Sullivain seized the back of her head and pulled her down to kiss her once, hard, on the lips.

Bone-shuddering relief, joy and fierce exultation that was not her own overwhelmed Hellevir and she felt suddenly blind.

"I knew you wouldn't let me down!" Sullivain crowed as she released Hellevir. Her own thoughts came flooding back like water rushing to fill a void. "I knew it! And you did, you came through!"

"Sullivain!" the Queen rebuked.

"Oh, hello, Grandmama! Look, I'm back!"

Hellevir shakily wiped the blood from her mouth and chin, as Sullivain pushed up onto her knees and stretched this way and that with her arms high in the air, seeming to enjoy the feel of her own muscles and the pop of her joints.

The Queen half-reached for her, and then stood with her arms folded, watching her. If Hellevir hadn't been sitting so close, she might have missed the slight tremble to her frame, the way she kept blinking.

"Onaistus, that feels good!" Sullivain exclaimed, oblivious. "Can't tell you what a drag it was to just *lie* there, I'll never complain about doing circuits again!"

"Sulli, stop jumping around like that," the Queen said sharply. "You should rest."

"I don't want to rest," the Princess said with a wave of her hand. "I feel fantastic, more than fantastic. Bion, get me a bath ready and fetch fresh riding gear, we can saddle that beast yet." Hellevir felt something wither inside of her at that. Her lip curled, and she got wobbling to her feet, sharp-edged words pushing up against her teeth, but before she could unleash them the Queen's voice cut across her.

"You won't be saddling anything today, Sullivain. Sit down."

Sullivain plopped back down onto the bed, still stretching her arms. "But, Grandmama, I *almost* had him! We got up a good speed, you should have seen him fly . . ."

The sound of the slap was loud, like the crack of ice. Light refracted in a blink from the heavy rings on the Queen's fingers as they caught the sun pouring in through the window. Hellevir stared in shock as Sullivain raised a hand to her cheek, where the skin was already reddening. The giddy light in her eyes faded, became mottled, as she looked up at her grandmother. Her other hand clenched into a fist on the coverlet.

"You just died, Sullivain. Again." The Queen was leaning over her, her shadow over Sullivain thick as she blotted out the sunlight. "Do you think on top of everything I make my worry I must add my granddaughter's stupid and willful death to the list?" Her voice quivered with anger, and beneath it Sullivain visibly bent.

"Grandmama, I . . ."

"Do you think I need you tempting fate further on the back of wayward beasts? Have you no sense?"

Sullivain was silent, curled up on the bed.

"I'm sorry, Grandmama," she said quietly.

The air was charged between the Queen and her granddaughter, so pressured Hellevir felt it in her ears. Sullivain was staring down at the covers, frail in her bloodied clothes, wisps of Death still strung about her like cobwebs, made small beneath the heavy regard of the Queen.

The matriarch seemed to recede, her hackles lowering, and she leaned over Sullivain, putting a hand on her arm and drawing her into a rough embrace.

"You will not leave the palace until an appropriate amount of time for recovery has passed," she said into her dusty hair. "We can't let anyone suspect what Miss Andottir is. And if you must ride, you can ride one of your forty broken horses."

Sullivain drew away.

"But we were so near . . ."

"Do not argue with me. Besides, you won't be saddling him, I've had the brute killed."

Sullivain withdrew sharply, looking like she'd been slapped again.

"You did what?" Her eyes were wide, the whites stark against her dirty cheeks.

"He was a danger."

"But he was mine!" Sullivain exclaimed, voice shrill. "I chose him from the herd, brought him . . ."

"Enough, Sullivain," the Queen said tiredly. "I don't have the patience. This has been a waste of my day, and your resurrectionist's abilities." Her face closed, the high arches of her cheekbones pronounced as if carved from stone. "I'm disappointed. I didn't expect such folly from you."

Without a further word she turned and left the room, leaving Sullivain crouched there in her grimy riding gear, torn where her bones had ripped through. The sounds of the bustling building were muted, in another world, as the Princess shuffled to sit on the edge of the bed.

"I'll get your bath ready," Bion said, and left as well.

Hellevir glanced at the door, wondering if she should go too, but Sullivain looked suddenly very alone, a small figure in the middle of such a vast golden room. The air still smelled of her blood. Hellevir half-turned towards the door, then hesitated.

She betrayed me, she thought. *She doesn't deserve anything from me.* Even as she thought it she found herself walking around the bed and sitting beside her. She put a hand on Sullivain's shoulder.

Sullivain looked up at her, as if surprised to find her still there. Her eyes were glassy, her jaw tight against tears. She smelled of the stables.

"They were going to kill him anyway," she muttered. "Unsaddleable, they said. I wanted to show them anything could be saddled. He was such a lovely color, like burnt rowan." She looked down at her hands, at the dirt ingrained into the creases of her palms. "How could she?" The question fell from Sullivain, her voice collapsing at its edges like wet sand. "He was mine." She shook herself. "Doesn't matter in the end, does it?" She sniffed, and turned away, perhaps so Hellevir wouldn't see her face. Hellevir's hand slipped from her shoulder and brushed her wrist, quite by accident.

It happened again. Hellevir felt a surge of anger, sickly and roiling, not her own, a flood from outside that gripped at her gut and twisted. Sullivain stood abruptly, yanking her hand away before Hellevir could pull the strands of emotion apart.

"Stop doing that," the Princess snapped.

"I don't do it deliberately," Hellevir remarked. "Do you . . . what do you feel?"

"I feel things I don't want to. Make it stop."

"I'm sorry, do our knotted souls cause you discomfort?" Hellevir found herself retorting, getting to her feet. "Perhaps you should have thought of that before dying three times."

"Is that why it keeps happening? Because you brought me back?"

"Yes."

Sullivain half-turned away, her hands over her arms as if she were suddenly cold.

"So that's how you really see me, then," she muttered. She gave a half-laugh, bitter. "I'd hoped it wasn't true, that I was imagining it all."

"And how do I see you?" Hellevir found she was clenching her fists tightly by her sides and made herself uncurl her fingers. Sullivain looked at her, expression for once unguarded. She just looked like a hurt woman.

"You hate me," she said simply. "You hate me for what I've done."

"Of course I do," Hellevir said bitterly. "You broke your promise. Calgir is dead and my brother lies at home broken in body and spirit because of you. My family lives under a shadow of fear."

"But you also . . . you don't hate me. You wish you could hate me more."

The silence that followed was heavy. Hellevir could hear her own breath, loud and far too fast.

"I don't know what's wrong with me," Hellevir said quietly, "because I really, really should hate you, completely and utterly, after what you did."

The way Sullivain was looking at her felt dangerous. Her copper eyes gleamed in the dull light like coins at the bottom of a well. Hellevir hated how that curl of hair fell over her ear, a perfect spiral. She hated how the bones of her hands pushed against the flesh to reach up and brush it back. She hated how Sullivain was looking at her, and yet wished suddenly that she would look at her no other way.

"Hellevir," Sullivain murmured. "I wish I hadn't done it. I wish I hadn't told her. I didn't think she would. . . destroy him like that."

"What else did you think she'd do?" Hellevir demanded through clenched teeth. "But it doesn't matter what you wish. You did it. It's done."

Sullivain did something surprising then. Her face crumpled, and she leaned forward, and the only place for her to lean was on Hellevir's shoulder. Hellevir's breath caught as she found suddenly that the Princess's forehead was on her collarbone, the rosewater scent of her hair brushing against her cheek. She automatically gripped Sullivain's arms, mindful of the thin fabric keeping their skin from touching. Her muscles tensed, braced to push her away, but she did not.

"There's no disobeying her," came Sullivain's voice, and Hellevir found herself imagining the warmth of her breath upon her shirt front. "I cannot disobey her. I thought I could, for you, but I can't."

"Yes, you can," Hellevir murmured into her hair, her eye tracing the way the light caught it. "She's not a god. She's just another woman like you and me."

"No, she's not. She's not. She's my mother and my father and my grandmother, but more than that she's my queen. Everything I have, everything I am, I owe to her."

Hellevir risked it. She pulled away and reached up her hand to Sullivain's chin, tilting up her head. The moment their skin brushed, she felt the flood, the simmering anger like a cauldron, and yes, the regret. She really did wish she hadn't broken her promise, but more than that, she felt she'd had no choice. Hellevir let her hand fall, and found herself looking up into Sullivain's eyes.

"You do have a choice," she said. "There is always a choice."

Sullivain studied her, eyelashes spiked with unshed tears.

"Why *don't* you hate me?" she asked. "I've given you every reason to."

"Because you may act in your grandmother's image, but I know you're not her."

"And how do you know that?"

Hellevir wasn't really certain. Perhaps it was just a stubborn, stupid hope. Perhaps it was because she'd sunk so much of her soul into Sullivain, that the thought of it being wasted on someone just as twisted and brutal as the Queen might have driven her mad. Instead, she just said, "I've gone into Death three times for you. I know you better than you think."

Hellevir didn't know what might have happened next. If she might have turned away, reminding herself of the harm this beautiful creature had caused. Or if she might have held Sullivain's face and kissed her. If she might have made a terrible mistake.

A knock interrupted them, and they both froze, caught for a moment as if they'd forgotten that the rest of the world existed.

The door opened before Sullivain called for them to enter, and Hellevir's heart shrivelled in her chest. Peer Laius, of all people, put his head around the door. His expression was one carefully tended, nipped and goaded to be one of sad resignation in the face of tragedy. The expression froze when he saw the two of them by the bed.

"Forgive me," he said stiffly. "I . . . I was led to believe you were bedridden, my lady . . ." The expression coagulated into one of confusion, and Hellevir glanced at the blood on the bedsheets.

"Why bother knocking if you don't wait for an answer?" the Princess barked. "What are you doing here?"

"I was informed by one of the physicians that you were . . . in a worse way than you clearly are. He implied I might be required for last rites. Tadeus is unwell so I thought . . ."

"You thought wrong, Peer. I am quite well, if in need of recuperation. Please wait outside until I call for you."

"As you wish, my lady. My apologies." He made to duck out of the room, but not before he cast Hellevir a curious glance through narrowed eyes. His hand on the door had one of the Signs of the Pillars drawn in ink on the back, and Hellevir wished she knew which one it represented.

The silence that followed was stricken. They glanced at each other, both wondering what the Peer would make of what he had seen.

"He'll have been told you were at death's door," Hellevir said. "He'll want to know how you've healed."

"I'll tell him the physicians were misinformed," Sullivain muttered. "Meddlesome idiots. When he comes back in I'll play up the bruises."

"Will it be enough?"

"It'll have to be. But you should go. I don't want him to see . . . whatever it is that we share." Whether she meant the empathy or something else, Hellevir didn't know.

They regarded each other for a moment. Hellevir had the urge to put her arms around Sullivain, tell her it would be all right. Instead she shook herself, bowed her head, and left, trailing a long train of things left unsaid.

In the corridor, Hellevir felt for the new riddle in her pocket. Opening it, she read,

A wise mouth imparts sound advice:
When blind and breathless,
Do not try to sing.

CHAPTER TWENTY-TWO

Hellevir didn't go home. She couldn't face Farvor, not after bringing Sullivain back again, so she took advantage of her sudden lack of a guard, and instead went to the Order. She sank down on the grass by the river, among the late-blooming violas. She drew her knees up and hugged them, wishing she was back home. She missed Milandre. The old herbalist would know what to do.

Everywhere she looked she was trapped. Trapped between life and death, trapped between two religions, trapped between hate and . . . not hate. The irony was, she wanted to do exactly what Death had told her to do: leave Rochidain, get out of harm's way. She just couldn't.

Why did Sullivain have such a grip upon her, even now, after everything? Was it just the binding of their souls that drew Hellevir to her? But after everything she had done, seeing her so broken, taking her hand and feeling the sheer torment she was enduring, all Hellevir felt was fear. She was afraid of losing her, afraid that her Princess was trapped as well. Even now, she couldn't push aside how much she just wanted to *be* with her.

Am I twisted, somehow? Hellevir thought. *No one should feel these things for a person like that. A person who would betray me, who would watch my friend hang, who would cause my brother such pain.* She put her head on her knees. Overwhelming hopelessness gnawed itself a hollow home within her.

"Hellevir, are you all right?" a voice asked, and she glanced up to see Edrin walking towards her, a basket full of blankets for the infirmary hanging from one arm. Hellevir realized she'd been crying, and dashed the tears from her cheeks, impatient with herself. What good would crying do?

"Fine," she said. Edrin came over and sat down beside her, spreading her robes like a soft pool around her.

"Did you have to bring someone else back?" she asked gently. Hellevir looked at her, surprised. Edrin shrugged. "You get this hang-dog look about you," she said. "Like you haven't slept." Hellevir snorted, twisting a blade of grass around her finger. "Was it someone from the palace?"

"The Princess," Hellevir muttered, tired of secrets. "She fell off her damned horse." Edrin put a hand to her mouth.

"Is she all right?"

"She's fine. Right back in the saddle," she commented bitterly. Hellevir tugged at the grass and began peeling it strand by strand. Edrin took her hand, stopping her.

"Hellevir," she said. "What's wrong?"

Hellevir didn't answer at once. She kept remembering Sullivain's last words: that she would have her burned as a heathen, and she the first of many. She didn't know whether she should say anything, and worsen Edrin's fears.

"Edrin, do you . . . are you worried about the edict they've passed?" she asked quietly.

"The one about the Onaistian faith?" Edrin hummed, pursing her lips. She was looking towards the willow, and Hellevir found herself doing the same. "Yes," Edrin said quietly. "If I'm being honest. I am worried. They've done no violence to us, but it feels . . . there is something inhospitable. Like this is their land, now."

"They used to burn people like us," Hellevir said. "People who talked to things, heard things. In the Galgoros."

"I . . . I know." Edrin shook her head, and her headscarf came a little loose at her ear, showing dark hair underneath. Hellevir tugged it straight for her. "But that was before. You've heard their sermons; they preach kindness, acceptance. Twelve Pillars teaching them how to be good."

"I worry whether anyone who needs a set of rules to be good can know how to be good."

"Everyone has their own way of defining what it means to be good. Perhaps a set of rules is a way to create common ground."

Edrin took her hand. "You've had too much happen to you recently, with your brother and House Redeion. You're expecting the worst."

Hellevir sighed, and sank back onto the grass, looking up into the sky.

"Can you blame me?" she muttered.

The grass whispered as Edrin lay down beside her. They watched the clouds drift overhead.

"That one looks like a cat," Edrin said, pointing up at a cloud. She was trying to distract Hellevir, and Hellevir was grateful for it.

"How's that a cat?" she asked.

Edrin shifted over so Hellevir could look down her arm, and began tracing the outline.

"See? Ears, back, tail. Cat."

"That one's a tortoise."

"Where?"

"The cat's standing on him. The cloud's moving—it looks like he's putting his head back in his shell."

"Looks more like a bear who's bitten something he doesn't like, so he's wrinkling his nose."

"Now that I don't see."

"No imagination."

They lay there for a moment, eyes watering a little from the brightness of the sky.

"Should I be worried, Hellevir?" the priestess asked quietly.

Hellevir didn't answer at once. She didn't want to frighten her.

"Just be careful," she replied at last. "More careful than I have been, anyway."

Edrin looked like she was about to reply. But then they both heard quick footsteps coming towards them, and propped themselves up to see who it was. It was Sathir, her apron stained with what looked like river water.

"I'm so glad you're here," the priestess said to Hellevir. Her tone was grim. "I need you to come quickly."

"It doesn't rain but it pours," she said to Elsevir as she looked at the tiny body on Sathir's table. The child's mother stood nearby, her fists working and creasing in her skirt with such anguish that the fabric was starting to rip. She was making awful sounds.

"Can you help?" Sathir asked Hellevir grimly.

Hellevir approached the table, looking down at the little girl. She was only five or so years old. Her skin was pale, almost translucent. Her hair may have been blond but it was hard to tell because it was soaking wet and covered in silt.

"What happened?" she whispered.

"She fell into the canal, her skirts dragged her under."

"She drowned."

"Yes. Her mother, she works at House Greerson." Hellevir looked up.

"The noble boy's House? Ionas?"

"Yes. She heard what had happened," Sathir said. "Or at least the rumors of what happened."

"She's desperate. She would have believed anything."

"Can you blame her?"

Hellevir shook her head.

"Will you bring her back?" Sathir asked. The mother looked up and fixed Hellevir with bloodshot eyes.

"Can you do it?" she said, her voice rough. "Please, please say you can. Say you'll try. Whatever you want, I'll give it to you."

Hellevir stared down at the child. The body was so small, there was a part of her mind that couldn't wrap itself around how small it was. The single pearl sat in her pocket. It had been burning a hole in there since she'd brought Sullivain back a second time using the first. The fear sat within her, curling like a live thing.

A third time, it had happened. A third time, Sullivain had died. And what about the fourth, the fifth? Sullivain would always be in danger, and, regardless of the bulwarks the Queen built around her, one stray arrow would always find its way inside.

It was only sensible, only prudent, to preserve the treasures for the inevitable moment Sullivain was attacked again. Only sensible.

"I can't," she heard herself say, as if another person had said it. Sathir stared at her, frowning.

"Hellevir?"

"I'm sorry." She turned abruptly to go, the sobbing of the child's mother loud in her ears and soul. Her fists were tight at her side, unclenching only to reach for the door handle. She stilled, unable to twist it. She felt herself wilt, suddenly despairing.

What had this city done to her? This wasn't her. Hadn't she

told Milandre that she would save anyone who needed it, bring back anyone it was in her power to bring back? Save those whose lives had been cut off too soon? When had that become so muddied, so blurred by the politics of the Crown, by Sullivain's sideways smile? This wasn't her.

It was in that moment that she saw herself, as if side by side with the version of her that had come to Rochidain, only a few months before. The version of her who was wide-eyed at the city around her, bracing herself for unknown terrors, ignorant of the mire of threats and intrigue hidden behind every wall, a mire which, if it had form, would stain the canals a color dark as rust. That Hellevir wouldn't have thought twice about raising a little girl who needed her. She found another reason to hate Sullivain, then; she hated her for what she'd made Hellevir become.

She couldn't do it. Imagining walking away, closing the door behind her, made her feel wretched.

"Damn it," she muttered, and turned back. She pulled a chair over to the table, the legs grating harshly on the stone floor. She took the little girl's stiff hand, and asked, "What was her name?"

"Ismund. Her name's Ismund."

Death awaited, cold and still.

It was a relief that the body was gone when she stood up. A relief not to hear the anguished sobs of the child's mother. She left the room and descended the stairs. She found herself outside quite quickly.

"Ismund?" she called. "Are you there?"

She thought she saw the flicker of a dress vanish out of the gates, out towards the canal. Hellevir followed, sweeping aside her cloak to keep herself from tripping. The mirrored sky reflected her like an ant.

"Ismund!"

Outside, the paths were empty, the canal water unmoving. She followed a vanishing heel as it ducked through an archway, and wondered to herself why the dead always ran away. The path wound through the buildings, the walls high and dark on either side, and spat her out onto the edge of another canal. She stopped, stunned despite herself. There wasn't just one canal, cutting across her path. There were hundreds. They lay in neat rows one beside the other, separated by small paths with railings, connected by arching bridges. It looked like Rochidain with the buildings stripped away, and only line upon line of water vanishing into the gloom of Death with their grey reflections in the sky.

It felt horribly exposed. But out there, dashing over the bridges and running along the water's edge, were the forms of a little girl and her reflection. Hellevir braced herself and followed.

The canals were endless. There were none of the sounds she expected of them, no gentle drip and hush of water, no gurgling as it was drawn into pipes. None of the swish and clunk as the boatmen dropped their poles into the water and pushed their vessels along.

She came upon her quickly. Ismund had stopped at the edge of one of the canals where there was no railing, looking down into the featureless water. Before Hellevir could do anything but let out a shout, the little girl had dropped over the edge. The water parted around her like mud, leaving behind the path of her fall open to the air, and as Hellevir rushed over the bridge towards her it snapped shut like a mouth, and all she could see was the pale crown of the child's head under the surface, shining and undistinguishable as a pearl under murky water.

Hellevir dropped her cloak and dived in after her. The water felt bizarre, both wet and solid as she pushed through it, splashing droplets that froze mid-air and creating eddies that spun and stiffened but kept on pushing against her. She gripped the girl under the arm and heaved her upwards, catching hold of the ladder on the wall of the canal and pulling her up one rung at a time. She landed them both on the pathway, gasping from the effort, and turned the little girl over. She looked as dead and bloated as when Hellevir had first laid eyes on her, her eyes flat.

"It doesn't rain but it pours," the voice said, and she looked up to find the man with the black eyes leaning against the railing, looking at her with his arms folded. "Twice you have come here for a soul in one day."

"Couldn't you have helped me bring her out?" she demanded.

He tilted his head to the side like a curious crow.

"Bring out whom?" he asked.

"The . . ." She opened her arms to gesture to the girl's body, but it was gone. She cast about for it, stricken, and her eyes caught again upon the canal. Under the water, her pale hair gleaming, floated the little girl. "Why?" she asked, breathless. "Why is she doing that? Going back into the river?"

"I imagine it scared her," the man in black remarked. "Her soul keeps taking her back to it to learn why. Children's souls do that; they go back again and again to what frightened them most to try and understand it. Older souls have learned that understanding isn't always conquering."

Hellevir stood, straightening out her skirts. They weren't wet at all. A hand appeared holding her cloak and she started, surprised, before taking it from him and wrapping it around her shoulders.

"I've come to take her home," she said quietly.

"I see. And did you find the next treasure already?"

Hellevir swallowed, her hand clammy around the second pearl in her pocket. She'd seen his anger before, and it frightened her more than anything else in the world. And yet here she was, tempting it, like stabbing at a wasps' nest with a stick.

"No," she said. "I haven't, not yet. But I do have this." She made herself take the pearl from her pocket and held it out in her palm. It shone blood-red in the dim light of Death.

The world was still but somehow it stilled further, as if it were closing and pressing and clamping around her, as he looked down upon it in her hand. It suddenly became difficult to breathe, and she found the thought of needing to breathe in Death absurd, ironic, even as her lungs struggled to draw in air. The man with the black eyes had not moved, but the shadows of his face had grown darker, his sockets hooded.

"Stop," she demanded through her teeth.

"Why should I?" he asked, his voice low and thrumming through the world around them.

"Because you never said I couldn't split them. It was not forbidden in our bargain." She saw his lip rise, the black shadows deep around his teeth. He came closer and took her jaw in his hand, and she thought then and there that he'd give one sharp tug and she'd be thrown back into the nightmare, the void. She gripped his wrist reflexively, but he was as immovable as stone. "You said nothing," she snarled, unable to get the words out properly while he had her jaw. "You never said I couldn't. You can't make new rules at your whim."

"You clearly already knew it would anger me. And yet you risked it all the same."

She felt her eyes narrow, her resolve harden.

"Your anger is worth less to me than bringing back the little girl," she said hotly. "I can endure your anger." He drew his head back at that, his hooded eyes regarding, thinking. The hand dropped from her jaw and she gasped, but didn't let herself rub where he'd gripped her. Her heart was beating at three times its normal speed, and not just with fear. An anger of her own was building in her, and she returned his gaze with an equal resentment. She was so sick of being terrorized. Terrorized by the Queen, the Princess, the Peers of old, and Death, ever-watching, ever with that smile. She was sick of it. Beneath her feet the cobbles of the path cracked with the weight of his displeasure, and yet for a moment he seemed surprised, as if he hadn't expected it.

Slowly, the world became less dim. The pressure in her ears, pressing the blood into a dull roar, became fainter. They regarded each other amid the endless sea of canals, and far, far above their heads, their reflections did the same.

"I *am* going to make a new rule," he said, and the canal waters rippled. "That is the last time you will split the treasures I ask you to find." He held out his hand. Wordlessly, she reached out and opened her fist, letting the pearl drop into his palm.

"Can you say it has any less worth than the first pearl?" she asked fiercely.

"No," he replied, holding it up as if to the light. "They are both cheapened equally."

Hellevir kept her hand held out, and he slid his nail across her palm, letting the blood flow freely. She hissed, surprised by how much it hurt, but she did not protest at the pain.

She felt a tug on her skirt, and looked around. The little girl stood there, her eyes wide and blue, her dress too big for her. Hellevir bent and picked her up, putting her on her hip. Ismund pulled the pin from Hellevir's hair and began to play with it until she took it away and slid it into her pocket.

"Do you want to go home?" she asked. Ismund just nodded. Hellevir turned and looked back at where the man with black eyes had been standing, but he was gone.

*

She was growing used to waking. She bore the storm of her body returning to itself, and found for the first time that she wished she had a stiff drink to hand. She slumped, and might have fallen off her chair if Sathir hadn't righted her.

"Did you . . ." the priestess began, but she jumped as the body on the table shuddered and sat up, spewing up river water. Ismund hacked and coughed, and for a moment the three of them just watched her. Then her mother let out a sob that Hellevir would remember for a long time and dashed towards the child, gathering her up and pressing her hands to her cheeks, patting her arms and legs as if to make sure she was real, stroking her blond hair. The girl just coughed.

Hellevir sagged, suddenly exhausted, and Sathir felt the weight against her hip.

"Are you all right?" she asked, taking Hellevir's shoulder. Hellevir nodded, waving her away.

"Fine," she muttered. "Just took more out of me, I think." *As punishment*, she thought tiredly. They both looked up as the girl's mother approached. She reached forward and took Hellevir's hands, kissing them.

"Thank you," she said, her eyes bright from crying. "Thank you."

Hellevir just nodded, having no idea what to say. "I . . . you're welcome. But please don't tell anybody. It will be a rumor and then more people will come knocking. I can't bring back everyone." She paused. "But I'm glad I brought back Ismund. She's such a quiet thing."

The woman stroked her daughter's hair. "She's mute. That's why no one heard her call for help."

In her dreams Death watched her, but when she searched for him, he was gone. She walked the canals, and that was all she did, looking for the crown of Ismund's head shining like a pearl under the water. Except it wasn't Ismund, but Sullivain, her hair gleaming in the gloom. Hellevir didn't know if it was real, or if this was her own mind bringing her back to what frightened her most.

The dream shifted, took on a strangeness she'd never felt before. If she'd been lucid she would have likened the odd light of the dream to the half-gloom of Death. She sat helping the Princess to polish her saddle with beeswax.

"Pass the cloth, would you?" she asked, and Hellevir obligingly handed it over. "We should go racing, sometime. A country girl like you, bet you could give me a good run. I won't break next time."

Hellevir smiled.

"I'm used to riding ravens," she said. "I don't know which is faster."

"Will you teach me? I've always wanted to ride a raven."

"If Elsevir will let you on his back, I'm sure I can."

"Grandmama used to ride a ship called the *Oystercatcher*, named after the Antlered King's." She held up the saddle to the dream-light. "There, good enough, do you think?" She whistled, but Hellevir woke up before she could see what beast the Princess had summoned to ride.

CHAPTER TWENTY-THREE

Hellevir busied herself all the next day at her pa's house, trying not to think about the dream, about Sullivain in general. She made a poultice in the kitchen for her brother and brewed him some more tea. He received her care without a word, but she caught him watching her a few times, his expression guarded and his lips pressed together.

"What is it?" she asked, but he just shook his head.

That evening she sat downstairs helping the Temple servant clean the silver. Weira seemed to begrudge her help, taking it as a personal insult that Hellevir would do housework, but she needed distraction. When the knock came at the gate, every nerve in Hellevir's body trilled like a plucked string. She could only think that it was some further evil news, that more of House Redeion had been found and condemned to hanging, but it was Peer Laius whom the servant led in. He smiled at her, tapping his forehead and pushing back the hood of his coat.

"Miss Andottir," he said pleasantly. "How nice to see you."

"Peer. I'm surprised the guards let you through."

"Oh, there's no harm in a Peer coming to visit members of his congregation." That wet smile, eyes drooping and sad like an unhappy dog. "Besides, it's my duty to come and aid in times of calamity." The Peer gestured to the house as he spoke, as if blessing it, and Hellevir noticed again the Dometik inked on the back of his hand. He saw her eyes following it.

"The Sign for Kindness," he explained. "In general we draw a Sign on our skin when there is a particular Pillar we wish to strengthen ourselves within."

"Have you failed to be kind, Peer?" She couldn't help herself asking the barbed question.

"Rather I wish to find further kindness within myself. With everything that has occurred this year, so much upheaval, I have been endeavoring to have an open heart and mind, to consider the plight of those affected. Your brother especially could probably do with a kind ear after all he has been through."

The Peer's tone was vaguely accusatory. She was saved from having to answer by her mother appearing at the door.

"Peer!" she said. "How good to see you. Hellevir, ask Cook to send up some refreshments?" She didn't send Weira, Hellevir noticed, and couldn't pretend she minded the dismissal. She did as she was told, ducking into the kitchen to let Cook know to prepare some tea, then in a bid to keep herself busy she put on her coat and went into the courtyard to collect herbs for drying. The outside smelled fragrantly of mint and sage, the sweet rot of the late pomegranate fruits as they began to wither on the boughs, unpicked and uneaten. Hellevir sat by the edge of the fountain, plucked one that still looked edible and pried it open, thinking what a shame it was to let it go to waste. It was past its prime, but each seed burst in her mouth with sweetness; she took a moment to enjoy how they popped. She picked a couple more for the table, thinking to save one for Elsevir.

She could hear her ma and the Peer talking, their voices low, and with the lilt of Galgarian. She felt something in her sour, as it had done the moment she'd learned her ma had fled to the Temple when the rest of them had gone to the boat on that awful night. The Temple before all else.

She glanced up as she heard the door, and saw Farvor emerge. In the cold light of day he looked haggard, but his lip twitched in the semblance of a smile as he saw her and came to sit next to her on the fountain wall.

"I would have gone for a walk while the Peer was here," Farvor remarked. "But . . ." He gestured to the gate; they could see the guards' boots underneath. The bough of the pomegranate tree brushed his shoulder, and Hellevir briefly spied pollen-stained fingers resting lightly on his coat, as if consoling him, and eyes round and bright as pomegranate seeds winked at her from the foliage.

Farvor took out his tobacco pouch and opened it on the wall between them. Dark green leaves, speckled with yellow, dried and fragrant, which he pinched between his fingers and pushed into a pipe. Hellevir recognized it as the one from Calgir's study. He lit the leaves, breathing in to air them, and exhaled a long cloud of smoke, leaning his head back so his jugular rolled when he swallowed. He held the pipe out to Hellevir, and she took a breath.

"That's an odd taste," she said, handing it back.

"Harpseed tobacco," he replied without looking down. "Calgir's favorite, he likes the plum flavor. He gets it imported from the Archipelago somewhere. I should have got the name of his trader; this is the last pouch left." He took another puff and let it out slowly, filling the air with sweet smoke.

Hellevir took another lungful, trying to taste all the flavors. It was too sweet for her, but the smell was familiar. It reminded her of Calgir's study.

"Are you all right?" she asked quietly. She wanted him to say yes, half-hoped that he would lie. He didn't reply at once, watching the house martins criss-cross overhead. He flicked his hair out of his eye.

"No," he said. "I'm not all right, Hellevir. I can't imagine what all right feels like anymore." Hellevir could sense her brother wanted to say more, so she kept quiet as they passed the pipe between them. It went out a couple of times, and Farvor puffed it back into life. "I sometimes think it can't have happened," he said, watching the smoke drift. "When I've just woken up. For a tiny, tiny moment, I wonder if it was all real. I emerge from sleep and it feels like I'm still trapped in a nightmare, and it's right then that I feel most hopeful; that it wasn't real at all, that it was all a horrible dream, and I just have to wake up. Then I do wake up, properly, and it is real, and I wonder how I'm supposed to *stay* awake."

She took his hand, resting on the cold bench between them.

"I saw him," she said quietly. "When I tried to bring him back." Farvor looked down at her, green eyes like sea glass. She made herself go on. "Death let me speak to him."

"What did he say?" he asked. His voice was only half-there, a thing she could have missed if she weren't listening for it.

"He didn't know what had happened," she said. "I think he

thought we were all at a ball. He was eager to get back to you. He said you were waiting for him."

"Waiting for him?"

"Somewhere outside. I . . . I told him you loved him. He just smiled and said he knew."

Farvor gave a half-laugh. His eyes were glassy.

"Bastard couldn't even say he loved me too," he said, but gently, without force. "And I did. I did love him."

"He knew."

"He knew. At least he knew."

His smile faded, and when he looked down again his eye rested on the galleon brooch pinned to the lapel of her coat. He reached out, unpinning it, and held it in his palm. He traced the sails with the tip of his finger. "I feel like they've robbed me, Hellevir," he murmured. "That Princess, the Queen, up in their palace. Not just robbed me of him, but of myself. I'm not sure what I felt like before this, and I just have this sense that I've been altered, suddenly and irreparably, in a way I hadn't prepared for. Like I've lost part of who I was, a part I didn't realize could be lost. And all because of them."

Hellevir swallowed, not knowing what to say. The words rose in her—unwelcome, inconsiderate—to defend Sullivain, explain that she had only done what she thought was necessary, that she had regretted her decisions, that it was the Queen alone he should be angry with, but it didn't matter. He knew all that already. There was no excuse.

"Hellevir . . ." He hesitated.

"What is it?"

"I have to ask you something. Will you tell me the truth?" She nodded, not trusting herself to speak. Dread coiled after his words like dust in their wake. "Yesterday, when that servant came to the door. The royal servant. What did he want?"

Hellevir swallowed.

"Hellevir?" His tone was harder.

"She fell from her horse," Hellevir said quietly. "She needed my help." There was a pulse of silence.

"She died, didn't she," he whispered.

"Yes."

"And you brought her back."

320

"I had no choice. They gave me no choice." Gods, those words. How many times had she said them? Farvor made a harsh sound in his throat. His fingers closed over her pin. The pipe had gone out, but he didn't relight it.

"And if you'd had a choice," he remarked, "would you have done it anyway?"

She wished he wouldn't ask her. She didn't like the answer, either.

"I don't know."

"You don't know." He laughed, a horrible sound. "You don't know."

"Farvor, I . . . it's complicated."

"No, it's not, Hellevir. That woman had Calgir killed. How many times has she died now? How many times have you brought her back to life?"

"Three," Hellevir whispered. She wished she could vanish into the cobblestones at their feet. She couldn't meet her brother's eyes.

I deserve this, she thought.

"Three," Farvor repeated. "You've brought her back to life three times, and you couldn't give me back Calgir once?" She closed her eyes. He was standing in front of her now, shaking with anger, with pain. "What is she to you?" he demanded, voice cracking. He took her shoulders. "How could you? After everything she's done? What is she to you?"

Hellevir opened her eyes. Tears ran down her cheeks. Farvor looked like a different person, one she'd never seen before. She'd known the serious boy in the woods, the carefree squire dancing by the canals, but she'd never known this man, gaunt with anger, his voice like iron filings.

He stared at her, a long moment. Reading her.

"Do you love her?" he asked her suddenly. "Is that why?"

"No!" she said. "No." She didn't know how she felt. She didn't know if she was lying. Her own heart felt so prodded for answers that it was bruised.

"Is that why she gets to live and Calgir doesn't?"

"It's not that simple!" Hellevir exclaimed, desperately. "Please, Farvor, she wanted me to bring him back, it's the Queen who . . ." It felt like talking to a steel wall. She didn't think he could hear her.

"No." He backed away, shaking his head. "Is she worth so much more to you than me?"

"Of course not, Farvor . . ."

"No, I can't. I can't do this." He turned away, unlocking the gate. The soldiers on the other side turned and glared, ready to push him back.

"I need to get out of here," Farvor demanded. "The market, a tavern, anywhere, I don't care. Just take me somewhere else."

"Farvor, wait! What are you doing?"

"Leave me be, Hellevir!" He turned back to the soldiers. "Will you take me?" They exchanged a look, and one of them shrugged.

"Hold the fort, will you?" one said to the other. "I could do with a pint."

"Farvor, stop!" She tried to follow him, to reach out and grip the back of his coat, but she was halted in her tracks by the flick of a word across the courtyard behind her.

"Hellevir!" She startled, glancing back, away from the gate closing on her brother's heels, and saw her mother standing at the open door. Behind her, in the hallway beyond, she could see the Peer. His expression was stony. Hellevir felt the blood drain from her cheeks.

"I'd best be off, Piper," the Peer said, sliding through the doorway past her ma. Without looking at Hellevir he crossed the courtyard in three long strides, as if eager to get away. She felt her mouth open and close, desperately trying to find words to explain away the conversation he had just overheard, but couldn't find a single convincing lie before the gates had closed. She stared at the green-painted wood.

"How much did he hear?" she whispered to her mother.

"Enough."

"I . . ."

Hellevir braced herself for a demand to know what was going on, for her mother's endless judgment, but to her surprise she took her hand. Her ma traced the sensitive scars of her knuckles, her jaw tight.

"You've raised her three times?" she muttered. "Her and how many others?"

"Ma, I . . ."

"All this darkness," she interrupted. "I wonder how much of it could have been avoided if you'd refused to deal with Death."

Hellevir wanted to pull her hand away, to push her way through the gates and go running after Farvor.

"It is who I am," she said impatiently. "I cannot change it." Her mother looked up at her, green eyes unhappy, and put her hand to Hellevir's cheek. The gesture surprised her.

"I know that," she said. "And I've come to terms with it. Which is why I'm telling you to leave. Not just this house, but Rochidain. We have to get you out of this city."

Hellevir nearly laughed. After all of Death's warnings, it was ironic that her mother would agree with him. But she couldn't deny the truth of it, the fear that coiled around her as she pictured the Peer standing in their hallway, deciding what to do with her. She could almost taste it, a new danger on the air. She had to leave.

"The city is not a place for someone like you," her mother said.

"You actually seem sad about that."

Her ma pressed her lips together.

"The Peer has been good to our family, but even he cannot ignore what he just overheard. I cannot protect you anymore." There was an earnestness to her voice, a very real fear.

"Protect me . . . ?"

"He's had doubts for some time. Suspicions. Inexplicable things happen around you, Hellevir, and rumors follow you like a shadow. It's why I sent you to the Order, to keep him as far away from you as I could. I managed to assuage his concerns, until now."

There are suspicions, here and there, the man with black eyes had said. *Flickers in the dark where I assume you want to go unseen.*

Hellevir opened her mouth, then closed it again. She didn't know what to say. Her ma had sent her to live at the Order to protect her? All this time and the thought had never occurred to her.

"Why didn't you say anything?" she demanded. "I thought . . . I thought you just wanted me gone."

"I didn't want to scare you, Hellevir."

"Scare me? Ma, what do you think they'll do to me?"

"I don't know. I don't know what would happen, but I don't want them to decide what their policy will be using you as an example. Please, get somewhere safe, away from here."

Hellevir put her hands to her face, wondering at the knot she found herself wrapped within.

"Ma, there are guards at the gate," she said, voice muffled. "And the Queen's threats are still real. I can't just leave."

"There's one guard at the gate," her ma countered. "Who I will deal with. As for the Queen, she won't let you be hurt; she needs you too much. She might even help you."

Hellevir had to laugh.

"I doubt it," she remarked. She hesitated. "The Queen would just lock me in one of the palace rooms, but . . . but Sullivain might see it differently. I should talk to her."

Her ma turned without another word and went back inside. Hellevir wasn't sure what to do, until she heard an almighty crash, and her ma came running out again and pulled open the gate where the remaining soldier stood.

"Come quick!" she ordered. "There's been an accident." The soldier hurried in after her, and the gate was left unguarded. It was that easy. Hellevir didn't dawdle, but hurried out, her footsteps brisk. Her heart was thumping as she hurried along the canals. She had no idea what she thought she would say to Sullivain, but the urgency to leave felt like a physical pull within her. She had never seen her ma so frightened before.

As she neared the main thoroughfare leading to the palace, her hand strayed up to the galleon at her lapel, preparing to show it for admittance.

She stopped in the middle of the street. The brooch wasn't there. She hunted about in her pockets, turning them inside out.

"Where . . ." She froze. Of course, Farvor had unpinned it, had still been holding it when he ran off. The thought made her uneasy, something nagging at the back of her mind. Perhaps he hadn't realized he was still holding it, because why would he take it deliberately?

Realization sank into her stomach, heavy as lead. She broke into a run.

The guard led Farvor through the palace. He walked as if in a dream, the edges of his vision blurred, his limbs not quite attached to his body. He couldn't have said whether his feet were even touching the floor. His ribs, still healing, protested at so much movement, and the ache fed the roiling fever within him, stoking it. His body hummed, his bones throbbing with Calgir's name and the need to cause pain.

Farvor had always found that city folk couldn't hold their liquor. It hadn't been difficult to get the guard drunk. After four pints of Overdawn it had been easy enough to give him the slip, and Farvor had made his way to the palace, where he'd flashed the royal insignia for admittance.

The guard knocked on a door, and on hearing a voice let herself in. There was a short discussion inside, the voices muffled, and the door was held open for Farvor to enter. The study beyond reminded him of Calgir's. A room he had not entered for weeks, closed now to mere squires, the memories locked away and untouchable as the House was claimed by the Crown.

A servant in red passed him as he went inside. He frowned at Farvor, looking him up and down, and glanced back into the room.

"Are you certain?" he asked the person inside. "Your grandmother would not allow this."

"Just leave, Bion," came *her* voice.

"As you wish."

The door closed behind Farvor. He was alone with her. He hadn't thought it would be so easy. A fire crackled to the side, illuminating books and sketches. There was one of Hellevir laid out on a table, done in charcoal. So candid a picture. The Princess sat at her desk, watching him with those snake eyes of hers.

"I had to talk to you," he said. He studied Sullivain, the way she held herself. He studied her expression for shadows, for the shadow of what she had done to Calgir, for the shadow of shame. For the shadow that Hellevir seemed to be so drawn to.

"What about?" She turned her back to him and folded a letter into an envelope.

"Please face me."

She sighed and looked at him, seeming reluctant.

"What do you want?" she asked tiredly. He remained standing, his fist so tight around the dagger in his pocket that his nails bit into the flesh of his palms around the hilt.

"I want Calgir back," he said. She stood, her hand on the back of the chair. She was tall, strongly built. He wondered if she knew he had a knife.

"But that's not why you're here," she remarked.

"Do you think you're untouchable?" he found himself saying.

He hadn't planned anything, but these were the first words that fought their way out of him. "That you're entitled to your life?"

"Hardly." She sniffed. "After dying three times, no, I don't think I'm untouchable." He didn't believe her. She turned away from him, deliberately showing her back again. "You've come here to tell me about the pain I've caused you," she said, stacking her letters together. "The moral bankruptcy of my soul. You've come here to tell me how ashamed I should be. You've come to tell me my many sins." She half-looked at him over her shoulder. "Something you and your sister have never grasped is that it doesn't matter what I've done, what Grandmama has done. As long as we retain the Crown, as long as we have deterred further treason, it will have been worthwhile. Would you rather that the city had sunk into the mire of civil war, and Auland Redeion had emerged from it victorious with the crown upon his head? Would you prefer the city he would have built? You know better than most what that man was capable of."

Farvor felt her words trying to worm into him, but there was only so far that they could burrow. Once, he might have heard her, but he was a different creature now. She'd stripped him of anything resembling his old reasonable self. He had been eaten from within by anger and pain, and now he was a hollow shell, home only to what had consumed him.

"The things you will say," he murmured, "to excuse your crimes." His grip tightened on the dagger. "The lot of you. Every last one of you. Auland, the Houses, the Queen, you. You're all alike. All rotted, all fetid."

Sullivain was quiet. Still, she wouldn't look at him.

"Yes," she whispered. "But even rotten things like me can desire to live." She looked at him, her head high. The touch of her gaze left him feeling unclean, her presence polluting the very air he breathed. Everything about her was offensive to him, offensive to the memory of Calgir. And it had polluted his sister too, his sister who until she had come to Rochidain had only wanted to save people. His sister who would martyr herself for any soul that crossed her path, his sister who had never tried oranges before, now caught in a web so tightly she could barely move, her eyes growing hunted by the shadowed dangers around her. The candid picture on the table watched him. She looked afraid. She hadn't always looked afraid.

All of this was because of Princess Sullivain. All of it.

"You're wrong," he said.

"What am I wrong about?"

"I didn't come here to tell you anything."

He felt her study him. His body sang with tension, with an unreleased need.

"Don't do this," Sullivain said quietly. "It won't help."

The dagger was out in the open, and he drove it forward. She blocked him. The very end of it slid into her and she grimaced in pain, but didn't let go. They stood there, locked, an immovable object and an unstoppable force. He saw fire in her eyes, felt the tremble of wrath in her grip. He wanted to pierce that anger, let it pour out and show its true hideous face for all the world to see, for Hellevir to see.

"Farvor," she said through her teeth. "Please, don't. Hellevir wouldn't want this."

"Like you give a damn what Hellevir wants," he retorted, and pushed with everything he had. She twisted lithely out of his way, knocking him back so harshly that he lost his balance, his heel catching on the edge of the carpet. He felt a sickening thud go through him as his head hit the floor, and his vision went momentarily dark. Nausea rolled through him but he fought it, opening his eyes to find Sullivain crouched over him.

He used the moment, seized upon it as he wished he'd been able to when Calgir was taken from him. He still gripped the blade, and she wasn't prepared when he drove it into her thigh. She cried out, and he pushed her backwards before she had a moment to collect herself. He heaved himself to his feet, ready to fight, but she wasn't moving. He looked down at her, tears blurring the darkness that pooled underneath her head where it had struck the edge of the hearth. His blood was burning, roaring in his ears to mute the sound of the door behind him, the heavy shout. He stood as if paralyzed, even as the sword was thrust through his back and into his heart.

No *no no*. Dread coiled within Hellevir as she sprinted up the street. *Please no*. She didn't know why she was praying, as if one of the old gods would answer her.

Farvor, what are you doing?

But she knew full well what he was doing. She would have done the same in his place. The only thing that was left to him to do.

The palace gates loomed before her, closed at this hour besides a single swinging door guarded by one soldier. She stood to attention as Hellevir hurtled towards her, a hand to the hilt of her sword. Hellevir recognized her as Kélé, one of Sullivain's guards.

"Stop right there!" Kélé exclaimed.

"I have to see the Princess," Hellevir gasped, sweat dripping down her temples.

"Herbalist? What are you . . ."

"Did a young man come through here with a royal brooch?"

"Yes, not five minutes ago. He asked to see the Princess. Not sure why she said he could come in at such a late hour."

No no no.

"Please, I have to see her. Something's wrong, please let me through."

Bells sounded, somewhere deep in the palace. Loud, picked up again and again as more chimes joined the first throughout the grounds. The guard started, turning abruptly, and Hellevir used her distraction to push past her, pelting up the stairs towards the main doors. The soldiers usually stationed there had already rushed inside to see what had caused the alarm.

No no no.

Shouts were flung past her, stomping feet, and she was submerged amid the general madness of soldiers and servants running in different directions. Hellevir ran towards the Princess's study, dread pounding with her every footstep. She heard shouting from farther up the hallway. Maids and servants were clustered around the door, their gasps and cries filling the corridor. Hellevir elbowed her way past, shoving her way through into the room.

No. Farvor, what have you done?

Sullivain lay on the ground. She was bleeding, her bright hair matted and dark. The Queen knelt beside her, hands blood-slick and shaking as she lifted her up against her chest. Hellevir froze, dread coiling through her, but the Princess shuddered and coughed. Her eyes fluttered open for a moment, and then closed, but she was breathing. Alive, gods, she was alive. Farvor had failed.

"Why would you let him in?" the Queen hissed to her limp

body. "Why would you let him in, stupid girl!" Hellevir surged forward, only to see the prone form of her brother on the floor.

"Farvor!" Hellevir dropped down beside him with a sob. She took his head in her lap, held her palms over the wound soaking the white of his shirt. He didn't react to her touch, didn't respond at all as she called his name. The wound was right over his heart.

Breathe, she willed him. *Please breathe.* He wasn't moving. His eyes weren't fully open, but gazed sightlessly over her shoulder.

No no no.

"What did you do?" she cried at the Queen.

"Get a physician!" the monarch was shouting, ignoring her. "And for Onaistus's sake clear the room." Kélé barked orders and started herding people away, but Hellevir had no mind for them. Her brother wasn't moving.

No no no. This can't be happening.

She closed her eyes, reaching for the frost-rimed curtain of Death to draw it back, but a hand snatched her by the arm and dragged her away before she could pass over, shoving her violently backwards onto the floor. It hurt in a way she hadn't experienced before, as if she'd been thrown into deep water and dragged up again too quickly for her body to handle.

"Don't you dare!" the Queen snapped at her.

"Why are you stopping me?" she demanded, lunging again for her brother. "He's my brother!" But the older woman wouldn't let her close.

"Do you think I care? Do you think I'll let you raise him after he just tried to kill her? I barely made it in here before he attacked her a second time."

Hellevir couldn't breathe. Farvor's blood was soaking through the fine rug. She began to put a hand to her face, stopped when she saw it was red. The Queen knelt down beside Sullivain again, and Hellevir crawled over to her, reaching out for the Princess's hand.

An indistinct miasma of pain and hatred, churning like boiling water. Bubbling rage, indistinct but lancing hot. Before she could feel anything more, the Queen shoved her aside roughly, severing their connection.

"Kélé!" she shouted. The soldier turned around, arms wide to keep the staff from pushing in. "Throw her in the cells." The Queen cast Hellevir a look, dark as blood. The glare pierced through her and Hellevir had a sudden prescience that she knew exactly what the older woman was going to say. "Take the body to the furnaces."

"What?" Horror slid under her skin. "No! You can't . . ."

"Yes, I can. Take her!" Kélé seized Hellevir, hauled her bodily away from Farvor.

"Please! Don't!" The soldier grimly ignored her as she kicked and bit and clawed, dragging her out of the room. She screamed, frenzied as she tried to break free, but it was no use against the metal of the soldier's armor, the strength of her grip.

"I'm sorry, herbalist," Kélé muttered as she hauled her like a sack of flour down the stairs to the prisons. "Orders are orders."

She opened a cell and threw Hellevir in. She hit the ground hard, but was up and on her feet, ignoring the pain.

"Please, Kélé!" she exclaimed. "I have to get through! Sullivain would let me through."

"Your brother just tried to kill her," Kélé remarked over her shoulder as she left her there. Hellevir put her hands over her face. She wanted to vanish, to dash her head against the wall, become victim to the dark.

She stood there for a long time, resting her fevered forehead on the bars.

"Miss Andottir?" The words reached her through the maelstrom in her mind, found her huddled within it. She raised her head to face three men. They wore the grey robes of the Peerage, the twelve-pointed star glinting on their chests by the torchlight. The third man, she saw, was Peer Laius. He watched her with those moist eyes, his expression unreadable, and didn't look away when she faced him.

"What do you want?" she whispered.

"We're here to take you to the temple prisons. You're under arrest for crimes against the Path of Light."

The floor was cold under her cheek. The thought that haunted her, that ran circles in her mind until she felt bruised by it, was *This is how Farvor felt when Calgir died.*

It was dark. She couldn't tell if her eyes were open or closed, but as she stared the darkness took on form. The cot, the locked door, a figure with tines that seemed to grow from its head watching her from the murk, but when she blinked it was gone.

Farvor was dead. She'd lost him. He'd been right, she'd had no idea what real grief felt like. It pinned her to the floor of the room where the Peers had brought her, marching her furtively from the palace. It weighed her down and smothered her until she could hardly breathe, hardly bear to exist. It roared in a synchronous monotone with the blood in her ears, held as obstinate and leaden a place within her as her bones.

She lay there for a long time, trapped. She couldn't have moved if she wanted to.

Dawn slowly lightened the tiny stone cell.

Burned by now, she thought. *Turned to ash. Ground to dust. And Death won't even let me save him.*

Sullivain. My Sullivain. Please let her be all right.

Footsteps, voices, which stopped outside the cell door. She didn't move.

"Hellevir?"

It was Peer Laius. She didn't turn to face him. She heard the rustle of fabric as he came close to the bars. She could smell the incense of the temple about him.

"I had no choice, Hellevir," she heard him say. Those words, the mantra she had spoken to herself so many times. "You gave me no choice."

"Can we proceed, Peer Laius?" another voice asked. Peer Laius sighed.

"Yes," he said, his tone pained. "Open the cell."

There was a jingle of keys, and a creak as her cell door opened. She was gripped and forced upright. She didn't resist as she was taken out, her hands tied in front of her with rope by a guard who wore the twelve-pointed star on his armor. They led her through the white corridors of the temple, their footsteps echoing as they walked.

Hellevir looked back at Peer Laius.

"Does my mother know you're doing this?" she asked him quietly.

"Piper shall be made aware," he replied. "We will hand you back to her when the punishment has been meted out."

Punishment. It threatened to spark fear in her gut, but she raised her head high, and an odd calm smothered the fear, irrational and unexpected. Perhaps it had all been too much, and this was the only way she could cope. She faced the heavy double doors in front of her with resignation, acceptance.

"This isn't even official, is it?" she asked. "You're doing this without the Crown's authority. They think I'm still in the palace prisons."

"We need no higher authority," the Peer replied.

Before her was an empty room, windowless except for a single skylight letting in a pillar of watery dawn air. It shone upon a sandpit in the middle of the room, not unlike the one in the temple congregation hall by the altar. A group of Peers, some she half-recognized from her mother's house, others who were strangers, lined the small chamber, all dressed in somber grey. They looked down at her like statues as she was made to take off her shoes and stand within the pit. She felt the sand between her toes. Two guards stood by the door, their faces hidden beneath visors.

She could hear her own breath. High and wavering.

"Is this really necessary?" she heard one of them whisper behind her. "The new edict does not outlaw other practices."

"*Any heathen practice shall be tolerated, except when it appears to risk the eternal souls of those on the Path of Light, and then it shall be deemed a threat to the faith*," another patiently quoted the scripture. "*And the punishment for such heathenism shall be decided by the Council.*"

It can't happen here, she'd said. *It can't happen here.*

Hellevir clenched her jaw.

"Don't I get a formal trial?" she demanded. Her voice rang around the small chamber. "Or are you all the judge, jury and executioner?"

"Miss Hellevir Andottir," the leading Peer said. She recognized him as the Peer from the square when Calgir had been hanged, Peer Tadeus. He was tall, greying, with a nose like a beak. "You are being tried for three counts of endangering the eternal soul of Princess Sullivain De Neïd, first of her name, heir to the Crown, and one suspected count of endangering the soul of Ionas Greerson, of House Greerson."

"And your proof?"

"I have seen it with my own eyes," Peer Laius said from beside her. "By all accounts, the Princess was crushed by her horse, her body damaged irreparably. Miss Andottir was alone with her for hours, and when she left the Princess was unharmed."

"I am a good healer," Hellevir said. "This is not proof."

"A further witness, Miss Lilia Greyson, the Princess's maidservant, confirmed that she had seen the Princess appear to die on at least one occasion, her heart unbeating, only to be alive and well again after a visit from Miss Andottir." The Peer paused. "Further, I heard her speak about her offenses with her brother, admit to them openly."

"If you talked to her maidservant, you know that the Queen threatened me into doing it, I suppose."

"The why is irrelevant. The instance must be punished. How do you respond to these accusations?"

Hellevir raised her head, as high as her mother had taught her.

"I brought Sullivain back to life," she said. "Under her threat, to keep my family safe, to avoid civil war. But I would have raised her anyway, as I raised Ionas, and as I would raise anyone who came before me needing to be saved. I will not be browbeaten into regretting it." Anger flushed through her, and she raised her bound hands before her, clenching her fists until the ropes creaked. "And all of this, because I do not believe in your god. Do you think I don't know about the history of your faith? About the burning of people like me in the Galgoros? Your Twelve Pillars preach kindness, forgiveness, tolerance, and yet you burn anyone who threatens your ways. Death has told me of the victims tortured by your followers, thankful for the release of death. How do you answer for this hypocrisy?"

Silence rang through the small chamber. For a moment she thought they had no answer. The scent of incense was sickly in the close air, devoid of freshness. Her head swam, but she stood taller. It created a perverted stubbornness within her, the fact that, after everything, the Peers had still been waiting to catch her, arrest her, punish her, kick her while she was down. It fed into a seething anger which made her want to goad them to do their worst. She almost laughed at the irony; the only time she had ever felt such wrath was when she'd raised Sullivain, and felt her fury through their touch like a blistering heat.

"All in favor of a guilty verdict," intoned the leader, voice dispassionate. "Raise your hands." One by one the Peers lifted their hands, the chamber rustling with their movements. The leader looked once around. "Miss Hellevir Andottir, by unanimous vote of the leading members of the Peerage, I pronounce you guilty of heathenism, and of disrupting the sacred passage of eternal souls along the Path of Light. May Onaistus forgive you. I hereby proclaim your punishment to be twenty lashes."

The guards seized her from behind. She did not shrug them off as they removed her jacket, but maintained the gaze of Peer Laius. It was only when they tore the fabric of her shirt, exposing her back to the cold, that she felt a sound slip through her lips, and saw him look away. She held her bound hands close to her chest, holding up the remains of her shirt, as they made her kneel in the pit.

One of the guards stood behind her. She heard the creak of leather, the crackle of the tails against his leg. She braced herself, clenched her fists against her shoulders, felt the press of the expectant silence around her as he raised the whip. Her back tensed for the first blow.

I hope you're watching, she thought to Death. *I should have listened to you.*

Her blood was pounding in her ears. She felt her body rock gently with the force of it. It was so loud she barely heard the footsteps in the corridor beyond the doors, the clamor as they were thrown wide open. She only saw the Peers glance away, looking up like vultures interrupted in their meal.

"Stop this at once!"

The voice rang through the hall like a tolling bell. Hellevir breathed, almost sobbed. It was Sullivain.

In the next moment the Princess was beside her, enveloping Hellevir in her clean scent of rosewater, wrapping her jacket around her shoulders.

"What is the meaning of this?" the Princess demanded. Anger bled from her. Her voice was rough, damaged at the edges. The Peer Tadeus scowled down at her, but when Sullivain stood tall he seemed to become diminished, taking a step backwards. Palace guards, Bion with them, lined the corridors outside.

"My lady, this heathen has committed acts against the Path of Light. She put your eternal soul in danger . . ."

"On *my* command, Tadeus. Are you punishing those who obey my commands, now?"

"My lady, this crime cannot go unpunished. The precedent would undermine the Temple's authority." He paused. "And your own. If there is no justice here today, word will spread that the Crown flouts the edicts of the Temple."

The threat was transparent. Sullivain looked down at Hellevir, and then spared a glance around the chamber.

"Out," she barked. "The lot of you. I wish to speak with Peer Tadeus alone."

The congregation hesitated. Then at a nod from the Peer, they began to filter out of the chamber, their shoes shuffling on the cold stone. Bion collected Hellevir, picking up her boots in one hand, and guided her out of the chamber. The doors shut behind them, leaving only Sullivain and the Peer within.

Bion undid Hellevir's bonds and lowered her onto a seat outside the temple. The tree in the center of the courtyard rustled in the breeze, lit by the twofold light from the torches and the strengthening dawn. Hellevir's mind felt tangled, knotted like kite strings caught in a branch, and so it took her some time to notice the dusky figure standing in front of her. She looked up at the Queen, silhouetted against the clouds soaked lavender and gold by the rising sun.

They regarded each other.

"Did you do it?" Hellevir breathed. "Burn him like you said you would?"

The Queen didn't reply. Her lip twitched, as if a pile of words were building up on her tongue but she didn't think it worth the energy to spit them out. It struck Hellevir as odd, and it took a moment for her addled thoughts to line up and tell her why. The Queen's expression was no longer stone-carved, unreadable. The De Neïd mask had slipped.

"What do you want from me?" Hellevir growled. "What more could you possibly want? Why are you even here?"

"I'm here," the Queen remarked, "because my idiot of a granddaughter insisted on running into the night with a fresh stab wound to help her herbalist. I am here because it seems like the moment I take my eyes off her, she meets with some calamity."

Calamity. What a word to describe her brother's attack, fueled by grief and pain. Exhaustion flooded over Hellevir, and she felt the blood thrum behind her eyes.

"What did you think would happen?" Hellevir demanded. "That the city would just take it all in stride, the hangings, the bodies pinned to your palace like trophies? Did you think there would be none like Farvor?"

"Don't lecture me, child."

Hellevir struggled to her feet, ignoring the shuddering in her limbs. The Queen stood a foot taller than her, but Hellevir wasn't intimidated, not anymore. Her bare back brushed against the fabric of Sullivain's coat, evidence of her ordeal.

"Tell me this, Your Grace," she said, her tone brazen. "Would you have fought so hard for the Crown if you'd known the target that would be forever painted on your back? On Sullivain's?"

The Queen glowered down at her, and Hellevir assumed she would not answer, perhaps simply turn on her heel and leave, but instead she spoke with a discomfiting steadiness.

"Sullivain was not born until after the war," she said. "But my daughter was old enough to lift a sword. We both fought for queendom knowing exactly what it entailed, and we fought with equal ferocity. It is the same ferocity I see in Sullivain, and I know she will do whatever it takes to keep the Crown, because I have taught her how. We are a family accustomed to the dangers of power."

"And if Sullivain doesn't want to fight? If she wants safety?"

The Queen didn't reply at once. She just studied Hellevir.

"There is no such thing as safety," she said slowly. "Not for us, or for you. Not in Rochidain, and not even in your little village by the woods where we found you. There is no such thing in this life. I would have failed Sullivain if I'd only taught her how to live in peace."

Hellevir parted her lips, about to argue that the Queen's view of the world was warped, but found that she couldn't. She remembered how long and cold the winters had been when she was a child, how worried her father became that they wouldn't have enough to eat. She remembered her mother dying in childbirth, her sister not drawing a breath. She remembered the villagers driving her from her home for being something they didn't understand. She thought about the ire of Death, and the shuddering void where he had thrown her.

The sound of the doors opening caught their attention, and they both glanced over to watch the Princess emerge from the temple's chamber. Peer Tadeus appeared behind her, and they spoke briefly.

The Queen folded her arms, watching the exchange, and Hellevir felt her presence beside her as tall and heavy as a raincloud.

"You won't let her die, will you?" the Queen asked her.

Hellevir didn't answer at first.

"I don't think I can," she murmured, honestly.

"I'm glad. She's caught you in a tighter bond than any terrors I could threaten."

"It is a kind of terror," Hellevir replied. "I'm terrified she will die, and I won't be able to bring her back."

The Queen looked down at her.

"That is my terror too," she said softly. For a moment, just a moment, fleeting as the glance of sunlight off glass, they shared an understanding.

Sullivain started walking towards them, and the Queen turned to wait by the water's edge, the hem of her cloak brushing the cobblestones.

"Come on, herbalist," Sullivain murmured, taking Hellevir's arm. "Let's get you home." Hellevir could feel the warmth of her through the fabric of her sleeve. She felt suddenly weak, although no lash had landed across her back. She noticed that Sullivain's hands were bandaged, almost like a boxer's, as the Princess lightly brushed the hair from her forehead.

"You came for me," Hellevir whispered.

"Of course I did," Sullivain muttered back gruffly. "What do you take me for?"

"What did you promise the Peer? In exchange for me?"

"Oh, the usual. I've given him a legion in the city militia for Temple cadets. Nothing horrific." She said it glibly, but Hellevir sensed it had been a higher price than she liked. Before she could ask about it, Sullivain sagged, and suddenly Hellevir was the one supporting her. Her features were taut with pain.

"Your wound," she said. "Your head. You shouldn't be walking after that."

"Had to get my herbalist out of trouble, didn't I? Even though your brother tried to kill me." Hellevir flinched. Nervous energy was coursing through her, giving her strength, but it would wear off. Then she was afraid of how completely she would crumble.

"I would have, too," Hellevir replied. "You killed his lover. For a crime he didn't commit."

The Princess winced, but said nothing. She didn't try to defend herself.

They didn't speak as the guards led them out of the temple gates, towards a group of boats gathered by the pier. Sullivain paused them by the waters.

"There's a boat to take you home," she said.

"Sullivain . . ." There was a lot to say between them. It hung in the air, uneven and ridged.

"I am sorry," Sullivain said, her voice scratching over the words. "About your brother. I didn't mean for that to happen."

"Is . . . is he . . ."

"I've sent his remains to your home. You'll find him when you get back."

Remains. She felt the word go through her, become a part of her. *His ashes.* She closed her eyes.

"Hellevir, I . . ."

"I should go. My parents will want to know what happened." She could feel the Princess beside her, radiating heat. It would have been so easy just to sink back, brush against her, fall into her, give up.

"As you wish," the Princess said.

CHAPTER TWENTY-FOUR

Hellevir felt as if her mind were detached from her body. All through the boat-ride home, the walk to her gate, she watched herself as if she were a figure on a stage. When she pulled the bell she barely heard it.

It was her mother who opened the gate. Her eyes were red from crying, her hair wild about her. Before Hellevir could speak she seized her hand and dragged her inside. There was a muted silence about the house, deathly quiet. Her pa was standing by the door, aged and grey.

"You will bring him back," her ma was commanding. "You will bring him back." Hellevir felt dizziness overwhelm her. There was a smell, something charred . . .

"Ma, I can't . . ."

Her ma didn't listen. She just shoved Hellevir ahead of her into the dining room. For a moment Hellevir wasn't certain what she was looking at. The dining table was laid with white, covering a heavy form underneath it. She found herself looking suddenly into her mother's eyes. Green like sea glass, green as Farvor's. Her mother took the front of her shirt, crushed it in her fist. Hellevir watched it as if she were standing on the other side of the room, as if it were happening to someone else.

"You bring him back," her ma demanded. "Right now, you hear? Bring him back!" She pushed Hellevir away, her lip quivering and tears sliding down her cheeks. Hellevir looked at the body on the table, because that was what it was. Not ashes, not ground bones, but a body.

Hope budded within her, and she drew in a breath. She reached over and lifted the sheet. She made a sound so foreign to herself that at first she thought it was her mother. Her brother had been burned, his lovely dark hair singed, but . . . he was whole. Whole enough.

"Ma, I . . ." She couldn't even begin thinking about it. She didn't let herself think. She just turned and ran out of the door, out into the courtyard. The pomegranates were bright in the sunlight, far past their ripest, turning to rot and beginning to litter the ground around the roots of the tree, but still with a dewy sheen to them like glass. A hand dripping pollen plucked one and held it out to her, the ripe seeds of its eyes intent. She whispered thanks and ran with it back inside. Her ma looked up at her from under wayward black hair, eyes red and stare unwavering.

"You really want me to do this?" Hellevir breathed.

"Now," was all her mother said.

Without another word, Hellevir sat down heavily by her brother's side, her heart thumping and her skin cold with the sweat of anxiety. She took his hand again and closed her eyes.

The silence of Death felt physical. As if it could knock her over.

She got to her feet. At first she thought the walls were blurred, until she realized she was crying, and she dashed the tears aside. They wouldn't stop flowing, as if they had nothing to do with her. The grey walls regarded her, the black nothing pressed against the glass of the windows, as if the room were a box floating in the void.

"Come out," she whispered. She turned, and saw one of the walls of the room had gone. The edge of the floor met the blackness and fell away. She looked back again and saw the window behind her had gone too. So had the wall to the left, and as she looked, the wall to the right. She stood on a platform suspended in the endless darkness.

"Come out!" she demanded. "I have endured too much today for your games!"

"This has never been a game," the air murmured, and she whirled around. The man with black eyes stood there, his coat pooling on the floor around his feet. It pooled and kept pooling, until its edges spilled across the floor and into the darkness. Her eyes hurt from watching it.

She walked towards him, and held out the pomegranate. It shone, radiant like a gemstone held up to the light. Facing each other in the darkness, the two of them were lit only by its glow. Dew dripped from it onto the ground, burning like embers.

"Please," she said. "I want to take him home."

He tilted his head to the side and watched her tears with the same uninterest as the falling rain. It was the fruit he had eyes for, but he did not reach for it. She held it out higher.

"It's still full of life. Full of it. Please, take it."

"You haven't found the next precious thing, have you?" Now, even now, his tone was mocking. As if she were a child come to him to fix the broken toy she had played with too boisterously.

"No," she whispered. She reached into her collar and drew out her father's pendant. It had the same light as the pomegranate, but deeper, richer, a baritone. "It's worth legions of blood, you said," she murmured. "Please, take it."

"And I will say to you what I said when you wished to raise the Redeion boy; it is not a fair trade. Legions, yes, and I am not willing to give you legions. It is worth more than one boy."

"He's not just one boy!" The air darkened, impossibly, suffocatingly. It pressed against her skin, pulled tighter at her hair, trapped the air within her lungs. The man with black eyes took a step closer, and she hated how this world obeyed him, how this world made her feel like a dog in his cage. She hated it with such venom that she could almost feel it seethe along her skin, pushing back against the gloom, and for a moment—fleeting, so fleeting—he frowned as if he were concerned. But then the moment was gone, and he was close in front of her.

"One boy among thousands," he said, and the world sang low with the word, "no, millions, that have walked through here, many younger and many who have died more tragic deaths than your brother. To me, yes, he is just one boy, and I will not make exceptions to the rules of Death, even for you."

She closed her eyes, drawing herself together. Then she slowly sank to her knees and gripped the edge of his cloak in her fist. It seeped around her fingers like smoke. All other iterations of herself that had and would enter Death flinched at the gesture and looked away, humiliated, but—right then, right there—she didn't care. It didn't matter. He looked down at her kneeling before him, his expression closed and inscrutable.

"Bring him back," she whispered, looking up at him. "I'm begging you."

"My dear," he said, putting a hand under her chin. "You make such demands, for someone who has nothing to bargain with."

"I do, though," she said. "Whatever the cost, take it."

He tilted his head again, regarding her. The silence of the world rang in her ears.

"Then I suppose we do this the old way." He put his palm to her cheek, and brushed her forehead with his thumb, tracing the line of her brow. His ice-cold touch left a trail of numbness on her skin. He paused under her left eye. "But the cost will be high," he said. "The body has been badly injured."

"It's not his time yet," she whispered. "I want to take him home."

"Not his time," he repeated, scorn in his voice. "What do you know of when someone's time is over? Perhaps he chose this as his time. He knew what was waiting for him when he confronted your Princess."

Hellevir had no answer. Instead she just held out the pomegranate, its rich scent filling the air with the unpleasant sweetness of overripe fruit. He plucked it from her fingers, and held it to his nose.

"Hellevir?" came a voice, and she jerked around. Farvor stood with his hands in the pockets of his waistcoat, the old one in Redeion blues. He shook his head with a smile. The light was back in his eyes, careless, with none of the horrible heaviness of the last weeks.

"What are you doing in here?" he asked. "Must I always drag you into the dance by the scruff of your neck?" He held out his hand to help her to her feet, and she took it, numbly. Before he could protest she wrapped her arms around him, hugging him tightly, and he laughed.

"Did you miss me?" he asked. "Come on, Calgir's waiting outside and he said he'd swipe us a bottle."

Hellevir just held him tighter.

"I thought I'd lost you," she whispered.

"Whatever do you mean? Like I'd ever abandon you at a party. Well, maybe I would, but I've only done it once. Twice."

She made herself draw away. She wanted to say she was sorry, that she couldn't do without him. That she wished she could have made it better for him after it all happened. That she wished her pride had never made her bring back Sullivain in the first place. She wanted to say a lot of things, but she didn't, aware they would spill from her lips like broken glass and only cut her to shreds, and Farvor would just be confused and would forget everything anyway. His death was too important a thing to sully with her own regrets.

"Will you come with me?" she asked instead, taking his hand, but he was already looking off into the darkness, as if someone had called his name. Her heart felt like it was being constricted so tightly it couldn't possibly still be beating, but she didn't let go of his hand. She looked back at the man with black eyes, who watched everything as if it fascinated and—even then—amused him. She felt her lips press together in anger, but she said nothing. Instead she just held out her palm.

"You cannot save everyone," he warned her, but he seemed to enjoy knowing that she wouldn't listen to him.

"Take your payment," was all she said. She didn't let herself flinch as he moved with that suddenness and stood by her outstretched arm. He drew his nail across her palm and it dripped black, vanishing into the shadowed earth at their feet. He watched the blood intently, with delight, it seemed.

"Why do you enjoy this so much?" she asked him. The salt paths of her tears cracked on her throat as she spoke. Farvor pulled at her hand, but she did not let go.

The man in black smiled, as if at something secret.

"Well, I have to savor it," he replied softly. She was surprised how genuine his tone was. "After all, it's the only bite of life I get."

Hellevir awoke to noise. Far too much noise. Sobbing and raised voices, her ma and pa fighting. She bore the wave of frost, shivering and feeling like she would never be warm again.

Her hand still held Farvor's. She felt him shudder and grip automatically, and allowed herself to sag. He was back. Nothing else mattered. She could just sleep, she wasn't needed for anything else. The noise halted at last and she wondered if they would just let her be.

"Farvor! Onaistus, you're alive, you're alive!" She felt Farvor's hand being pulled away. She curled in on herself, hoping they'd forget about her.

A hand took her arm, pulling her around in the chair. She kept her eyes closed.

"Hellevir, my girl," she heard her father ask. "Are you all right?"

She made herself nod, but didn't open her eyes. "Is Farvor . . . ?" she started.

"He's dazed, your ma's taken him upstairs. Gods, Hellevir, if you hadn't been here . . ." She heard him pause, felt him take her cheek in a rough hand, lift her chin towards the light of the lamp. She pulled her head away. "Hellevir, open your eyes," he demanded in a low voice.

"Pa, I . . ."

"Open your eyes."

She swallowed, and did as she was told. One of her eyelids, the left one, felt odd, drooping too much. She felt his dismay in the silence.

"Please, Pa, I . . . I just want to go to bed. Please."

He stared at her mutely, at the absence of her. He collected himself, and nodded.

"As you wish, my girl. Let's get you to bed." He pulled her up and half-carried her to her room. Her limbs felt leaden, as if her blood were sluggish. He lowered her onto the bed, and began taking off her boots. She wanted to protest, but the air in her lungs felt too heavy, and she just let him. When he pushed gently on her shoulder she sagged back and he drew the covers over her. She was asleep before he'd even left the room.

She dreamed of Sullivain. They sat upon the edge of a river, their shoes beside them and their trouser-legs rolled up, dangling their feet in the clear waters.

She awoke in the dead of night. Something sat in the corner of the room, something with tines growing from its head, but when she focused fully there was nothing there. She sat up groggily. The moonlight shone so brightly through the window that she could almost hear the chime of it.

There was a chest by the bedside, and she opened the second drawer from the top. There was a mirror inside. Her hand bumped the edge painfully as she reached for it. The wooden floorboards were cold under her feet as she went over to the window. After a steadying breath she raised the mirror to the light.

The empty socket stared back, black in her pale face. She wanted to look away, but she made herself study it, grow accustomed to it. It turned her stomach, but she waited until the feeling passed, until it was no longer her face with the black socket, but simply her face. Darkness loomed to her left where it hadn't been before, but she told herself she would get used to it. She would have to.

A raven and an eyepatch. At least she'd be easy to spot in a crowd.

CHAPTER TWENTY-FIVE

The next day dawned as if nothing had happened. The birds sang, the sun shone, oblivious to everything that had transpired. Hellevir awoke exhausted, aching as if she had the flu, but she made herself sit up in bed and run a comb through her hair, every action taking far more energy than it should have done. Elsevir had arrived in the night; when he heard what had happened and saw Hellevir's eye, he rubbed his head against her cheek. Hellevir loved him for his quiet acceptance, for not scolding her.

Farvor came in to see her. He sat by her bed, holding her hand. She brushed his fingers, his arms, ran her hand through his hair, reassuring herself that he was there. That he was whole. She rested her head on his shoulder.

"I thought I'd lost you for good," she murmured.

"You did, for a while," he said. He swallowed. "I assume I failed? To kill her?"

Hellevir winced, closing her eyes.

"Yes."

"Did you . . ."

"No. I didn't have to raise her."

"My clothes . . . Hellevir, they were charred, did she try to have me burned? Like Calgir was?"

"It was the Queen." She recalled the bandages around Sullivain's hands. How scorched the body had been, as if it had been laid upon a fire. She lifted her head. "I think Sullivain saved you from being burned."

Farvor flinched.

"That doesn't make this all right, Hellevir," he said quietly. He reached over and brushed her temple near her drooping eye. "None of this is all right." She braced herself, asked the question she didn't want to know the answer to.

"Should . . . should I not have brought you back?"

He squeezed her hand.

"Ask me another time," he said. "I . . . I can't think right now, Hellevir," he said. "My head's all clouded. I can't think straight. I need time."

A letter came later that day. She knew it was from Sullivain by the wax seal. It gleamed as she broke it. It requested her presence at a dinner the next evening, a party of fifty.

There was a note inside, in Sullivain's curling calligraphy.

Please come, she wrote. *Grandmama is out of the city, and I would like the chance to talk to you without her looming over our shoulders.*

Hellevir didn't linger. The house felt too small for everything that had happened, and the glances from her parents and brother lay too heavily on her.

"Where are you going?" her pa asked as she swung her coat around her shoulders. She wore a black scarf across her eye to hide it until she could find a proper eyepatch. Elsevir plucked at it nervously from her shoulder.

"Back to the Order," she said. "I can't stay here anymore."

She stopped as her father took her arms and surprised her by hugging her tightly, unsettling the raven. Her pa never initiated embraces; she was always the one to throw her arms around his neck.

"Thank you," he said into the top of her head, kissing her hair. She sagged into him, burying her head in his chest.

They both paused as the bell at the gate rang. Weira appeared from the kitchen and went out to open it, and let in Peer Laius. Hellevir looked away, wishing it had been anyone else. She began to tremble in her father's arms, her body recalling the tension as she braced for the lash, and he felt it.

"Hellevir?" he asked, but before she could explain the Peer had approached, inclining his head in greeting. Hellevir noticed that he had drawn the Dometik for Kindness on the back of his other hand, too.

"Peer Laius," Hellevir said stiffly.

"Miss Andottir, I . . . what happened to your eye, if I may ask?"

"Infection," she said. He noticed her coat.

"Are you leaving?" he asked.

"I am."

"Will you permit me to accompany you? I would like us to talk." Hellevir felt her father bristle beside her, and she put a hand on his arm.

"Don't worry," she said. She gestured to the Signs on his hands. "Kindness, see? It would be very unkind to have me flogged as a heathen."

The Peer maintained his composure well. Pa hesitated, not knowing what to make of that, but nodded.

"Fine," he said. "If there's a problem, send Elsevir for me."

"I will."

She followed the Peer out of the courtyard and through the gate as he held it open for her. There was still a soldier on the other side who made as if to stop her, but she cut him off with a single black look.

"Stop me and I'll tell the Princess how your drunken negligence allowed my brother to get away," she remarked. He hesitated, and then stepped aside to let her through.

It was cold, her breath pluming in front of her. The paths along the canal were too narrow to walk side by side, so they went in silence until they came to a bridge, where the Peer stopped her. It took him a moment; she did not see him on her left side until he caught her elbow.

She faced him, bracing herself. In the morning light he looked gaunt, his skin as grey as his uniform, as if he hadn't slept at all. The grooves of his face were deep.

"I wanted to . . . discuss with you what happened yesterday," he said.

"I haven't told my mother, if that's what you're worried about," she replied. She heard the ice riming her words. Peer Laius seemed to relax slightly.

"That is good of you. Thank you."

"I didn't do it for you. The house has been too burdened with tragedy, and I don't want to add to it. Besides, my mother needs something to believe in." She looked out over the canal, watching the sparkling waters. Already she was noticing that she was turning her head more to make allowances for the darkness in her vision. "Why are we talking, Peer?"

"I've come to urge you to leave the city."

Hellevir had to laugh. She couldn't help it. So many people telling her to leave. She realized he was picking at the skin on his fingers, a nervous tic, and when he saw her looking he put his hands behind his back.

"I say this out of respect to your mother, and the Crown. The presence of heathenism such as yours, which threatens the doctrines of our faith, can only cause them harm by association. You have seen how the Peerage feels, how it has already brought the faith of the Princess into question."

"Yes, I believe I caught the gist of how the Peerage feels." Hellevir looked away, trying not to let her patience wear thin. She was so exhausted. "But I don't fear the Temple half as much as I fear the Crown, and their threats."

"You're not thinking, girl," he said, and she felt her gall rise at his tone. She'd never taken well to being called *girl*. "The Temple is growing in authority daily. If you stay, the reputation of your whole family will be in jeopardy. Your brother may find no work, your father may be fired as partner at the shop. Your mother, the Temple is her life. Without it, she will become as unhappy as she was when she first came to Rochidain."

"What would you have me do?" Hellevir demanded, her anger coloring the blind spot of her vision red. "Deny the Crown?"

He didn't reply at once. The bustle of the thoroughfare a few streets away, the drip of the canal water, filled the air between them. Hellevir wanted to be far away, out of this conversation. She wanted to get back to the Order and crawl into a bed. She wanted the whole week to be wiped clean and restarted. She kept seeing Farvor lying on the ground, felt the still weight of his heavy head on her knee, and she wished she could drown the memory, slice it whole from her mind and cast it aside.

The Peer leaned close to her, shark eyes hard.

"Find a way to leave," he told her. "For everyone's sakes."

He turned and left without another word. Hellevir found she

was shaking, anger bleaching her knuckles white on the railing. She watched him for only a second longer, fighting for words to shout after him. Fatigue clouded her mind and the socket of her missing eye ached, and she could find nothing to say. Instead, she turned with a growl and strode quickly back to the Order, knocking into people passing on her left.

She was sick of threats. She was sick of lies. She was sick of being cornered into action or inaction, into life and death. She was sick of being treated like a heathen, a witch. She was sick of being terrorized.

She felt so tattered, like a sail that had been ripped by too many winds. Her emotions assaulted her. She imagined leaving the city and . . . it hurt her. She remembered Sullivain's light touch on her forehead, the warmth of the Princess's touch as she'd helped her up from the sandpit. She didn't want to go, she realized, not if it meant leaving Sullivain behind.

But when she reached the gates of the Order, looking up at the symbol of the nightingale, she knew she had no choice. If she stayed at the Order, it would only bring attention to them, make the Temple see them as the same kind of heathens as she was; not just healer women, but women who heard voices and spoke to beings that other people could not, women who sang to willow trees, women who housed those who would risk the eternal souls of the Onaistians. Without her, they might weather the storm, and go unnoticed. It hurt her to admit these things to herself, but she looked the truth in the face with the same stubbornness with which she'd raised the mirror to look into her empty eye.

Perhaps it was time to act like the heathen that everyone called her. She began to realize, standing there and looking up at the gates of a place she had thought of as a home, that the only way she would escape a city like Rochidain was to use the weapons it had tried to break her with. Lies, threats. Terror. The thought brought her no joy at all.

She resolved on what to do. Her anger was no longer a tempest, but low burning embers within her chest.

There was a man on the thoroughfare market who sold body parts made of wood, resin and glass. The Order used his services now and then for patients who came for help. Hands with rolling digits hung from the top of the stall, legs were arranged in neat rows from simple peg-legs to jointed hips, knees and ankles. Hellevir felt Edrin balk a little as they neared the stall, their arms looped as Hellevir adjusted to her lack of depth perception. The fake arms, legs, hands, even noses and ears, all looked convincingly like body parts, chopped up and waiting to be sold.

The seller was a thin man, tall and spindly like a sapling. He had a lathe and woodworking tools behind the stall, where he worked with clever hands on new pieces. It was obvious what she was after before she'd even spoken. The black sash across her face was ill-fitting, too bulky, and he took one look at it and brought out a cloth sack, laying the eyepatches out one by one.

Hellevir picked up a bright red one decorated with white embroidery and beads.

"What do you think, Edrin?" she asked, half-serious. "I'd have to buy a dress to match."

"That's three ades, miss," the seller said.

"Then I think plain black will do."

"Just one ade, these. This one may fit. May I?"

She nodded. She took off the sash and he hesitated, seeing the empty socket, but he sized the patch without a word.

"I may have something else for you," he said when he'd adjusted the strap, and went behind his stall to bring out a large velvet box. He opened it, and inside were rows upon rows of eyes. Hellevir felt Edrin shudder beside her, but it was exactly what she'd hoped for. The seller began picking them up one by one and comparing them to her good eye, looking for a matching shade of green, but she stopped him.

"Not green," she said. "I don't want it to match." She pointed to another lying in the silk insets. He raised an eyebrow.

"Are you sure you wouldn't prefer a nice matching color, miss?" the seller asked. "They're well-made, imported from Ennea. No one will know."

"I want people to know," she replied. "That one, please."

"Very well, miss. Would you like me to fit it for you?"

"Please."

"Look up, miss." She did as she was told, as he washed the eye in a cleansing solution and rinsed it, before he gently eased it into her socket. It was an odd sensation and made her good eye water, but it didn't hurt. She blinked away tears, feeling the new and solid coldness under her eyelid.

"Well, how do I look?" she asked Edrin. The priestess smiled weakly then turned away, holding her hands over her upper arms as if a stiff breeze had brushed past her.

Hellevir caught a carriage at dusk. She wore violet, a waistcoat with a high-collared coat that her brother had bought for her when he'd first taken her to the Merchant Quarter market, delicately decorated with silver embroidery. She'd never been brave enough to wear it, complaining it made her look like a duelist. Now, with the eyepatch, she thought it suited her. Edrin put up her hair in her pin, and in Hellevir's opinion it was just as good a job as her mother used to do, piled up with delicate curls falling behind her ears.

"Are you sure about this?" the priestess asked quietly as she pinned the royal insignia on to Hellevir's lapel, bright against the clever embroidery. Bion had returned it to her, cleaned and polished. She'd tried not to think why it had needed to be cleaned. "You can stay here. We'll protect you, regardless of what that nasty Peer says." Hellevir took her hands, pressing them between hers.

"Thank you," she said. "But I have to go. I can't live under the Crown's thumb forever. It will be better for my family if I leave. I've only brought them pain."

"It sounds to me like you've kept half of them alive."

"It's been a curse. Everything I've touched with good intentions has ended up causing harm." Hellevir shook her head. "No. Better for me to leave."

"You will be missed. And you'll always be welcome back here. I hope you know that."

"This place has been my haven. I will come back when I can."

Edrin pressed her forehead to Hellevir's, and Hellevir closed her eyes.

"You'd best be going," the priestess said, brushing a wayward hair from Hellevir's shoulder. "Don't want to keep the Crown waiting."

The carriage ride took longer than usual. Hellevir couldn't figure out why there were so many people in the streets until she realized it was the night before the Light Festival, a celebration that was in fact unrelated to the God of Light. It was an older celebration, an early winter holiday before the frosts set in. Hellevir wondered how long it would be allowed to happen as the authority of the Temple grew. The thoroughfare stalls were being adorned with lanterns and paper decorations in preparation for the festivities the next day. Huge braziers and bright bunting were being pulled out of cellars and dusted off. Tomorrow there would be food and drink sold on the thoroughfare, imported especially from over the sea and farther down the coast. There would be dancing and singing competitions and theatre, mulled cider and mead, stalls selling furs and warm boots. At least the city would be seeing her off in style, Hellevir thought.

The carriage at last left the bustle of the festive preparations behind, and passed over the broad bridge leading to the palace. The courtyard was already filled with carriages, but it wasn't long before they stopped in front of the broad entrance, and the driver handed Hellevir down onto the marble stairs. Her boot-heels clicked as she ascended through the double doors. A servant bowed and took her gloves and cloak.

The hall was filled with people she didn't know, or at least not well. Faces she'd seen in passing over the months, whom she'd been introduced to once, but whose names she had forgotten. She scanned the crowd for Sullivain, but could not see her. No doubt she wanted to make an entrance.

Lady Hannotir was present, however, and beside her was Yvoir. The squire took one look at Hellevir and ducked her head, but Hellevir didn't approach her. What was done was done; the girl had probably thought it was her duty to report what she had heard pass between Hellevir and Calgir. She'd had no reason not to. All the same, Hellevir couldn't find it in herself to greet her.

"Miss Andottir," came a voice, and she turned to find herself face to face with Ionas Greerson. It took her a moment to recognize him—the last time she'd seen him, he'd been covered in blood—but he still had the complexion of a bronze statue, his hair a golden red. There was something calm about him, about the way he held himself, the way his eye flickered to her eyepatch and discreetly away.

She inclined her head, struggling to remember what story he had been told about the night he'd been stabbed through the heart.

"Lord Greerson," she said. "It's nice to see you."

"And you." He took a step closer, and Hellevir caught the sudden smell of sandalwood about him, a fashionable perfume. "I've been meaning to talk to you, actually, but never found myself in the Order at the same time as you. I'd like to talk now, if we can." There was something insistent about the way he spoke, not so much because he was used to getting his own way—although she had no doubt that he was—but because of the nature of what he wanted to discuss.

Hellevir glanced towards the dining room, but it looked like everyone was still talking and milling around without taking their seats. She itched to find Sullivain, but it would have to wait until the dinner was over anyway. She had to admit, she was curious.

"Of course," she said. He nodded and extended his arm to her. Feeling a little self-conscious, Hellevir took it lightly, and let him escort her from the front hall. He led her out into the garden, and paused beside the edge of the canal, the wall adorned with hanging plants that trailed down into the water.

"I never thanked you," he said. "For what you did for me that night."

"Sathir did a good job of looking after you," Hellevir replied vaguely. He shook his head.

"No, none of that," he chided. "I know what happened."

Hellevir took in a breath and released it slowly, her breath misting in the wintry air, looking out over the canal at the bright lights of the city. She tried not to let his bluntness put her on the back foot.

"There's no such thing as a secret in Rochidain," she muttered.

"Certainly not among the upper echelons," he replied with a white-toothed smile. "Besides," he added, "Sathir told me."

Hellevir clicked her tongue and folded her arms. She felt cold.

"I trusted her," she remarked sadly.

"And you still should. I wanted to know some details about what had happened, and when she couldn't answer my questions, I made her tell me the truth."

"Poor Sathir."

"I also know how the De Neïds threatened you," he said. "How they forced you to raise the Princess not once, but three times."

Hellevir cleared her throat. She wanted to go back inside. "Have you taken me aside just to make me face how poorly I keep my secrets hidden?" she asked.

"No. I'm not confronting you. I'm trying to say that we're on the same side here."

Hellevir went still.

"Same side?" she repeated. He took another step closer, and she wished he hadn't. The scent he was wearing was sickly this close, and she normally liked sandalwood.

"The Greersons never supported the Bergerads," he said, his voice low so no one stood a chance of hearing. "They had no more idea how to rule than an actor *pretending* at kingship on a stage."

"You wouldn't have been born by the time the War over the Waves ended," Hellevir said sharply. Annoyance flickered across his eyes.

"My House thought the de Neïds could do a better job. We helped the Queen take control. But this is not what we envisaged: these hangings, the destruction of an entire House. We did not fight for a bloodthirsty bitch and her whelp." Hellevir flinched. Farvor had used the same phrase at the hanging.

"Don't call her that." Hellevir said it automatically, then wished she hadn't.

"What, *bitch*?" He shook his head, bewildered. "What else would you call a woman who hangs an entire family to punish the acts of one man?"

"What are you saying to me?" she asked, alarmed.

"I'm saying," he said, "that it's time for another change. Myself and a few others, we're trying to come up with a plan. We want to remove Sullivain as heir, remove the whole de Neïd household, replace it with a democratic assembly. It's worked in other countries—just look at the Galgoros."

Hellevir resisted the urge to roll her eyes. It seemed too flippant a gesture for the shock that his words had rung through her. It was the last thing she had ever expected him to say.

"A democratic . . ." She laughed. "Sathir shouldn't have let you read so many books."

He breathed sharply through his nose, impatient and not a little discomfited by her reaction. This was clearly not how he had imagined the conversation going, although Hellevir had no idea what he had expected. For her to proclaim the wisdom of his plans, perhaps express relief through her tears that someone had at last—*at last*—seen the error of monarchical rule and the true way forward for the realm.

"Each House would have a representative," he pressed. "It would be fair. No single House would have the glut of power. The palace would be razed to the ground, a council put in its place."

"And you wanted *me* to be a part of this plan?"

"Yes," he muttered, a little sulkily. "You were part of the second attempt on the Princess's life, everyone knows it, and still she let you go. She trusts you, and we can use that."

Hellevir was already shaking her head, untangling herself from the net of conspiracy he had flung around them. Her boots crunched on the gravel as she stepped away.

"You think I was part of the plan to have her killed?"

"Weren't you?"

"I didn't *know* what Auland had planned," she exclaimed. "I warned Calgir when I discovered the truth so he would have time to react. I was never part of the attempt, I was just trying to protect my brother from harm. Your sources failed to mention that." She took his arms in her hands, suddenly desperate for him to listen to her. He looked like he wasn't happy about their proximity, but she just held on and resisted the urge to shake him.

"I will pretend that I haven't heard you," she said. "Out of courtesy to Sathir, because I know she cares about you. But you *must* be more careful than this, than confronting people so openly, and *in the royal palace?* Are you mad? You *must* put these thoughts out of your head, at the very least until the last few months have become just another awful memory, and the Crown has stopped looking for conspiracy. The last time I was overheard it led to an entire House being slaughtered, my brother being beaten within an inch of death and the body of the love of his life being desecrated. And the person who overheard me is in that room." She pointed back down the path, towards the lights. "I won't be responsible for that again. It took me too long to understand how real threats can be in Rochidain."

She was relieved that he looked at least a little shocked, and she hoped some of her words had got through to him. Her heart was pounding. She turned away before he could speak, and began walking back towards the lights of the dining room, hoping no one had noticed they were missing.

The guests were starting to filter into the dining room as Hellevir arrived. She was relieved Ionas was at least sensible enough to wait a little before reappearing himself. Hellevir found her seat—surprisingly near the front of the room, not in her usual place with the squires but among the lords and their aides—and let the servant push her chair in for her as the other guests mingled and wandered to their places.

She glanced up as the person to her right took their chair, and her heart sank as she realized it was Ionas.

"Lord Greerson," she remarked.

"Miss Andottir," he said brightly. "It seems you're stuck with me this evening."

"Delightful," she replied. She nodded as a servant offered her the red wine, but Ionas refused, putting a hand over his glass.

"Oddly enough, a sword through the heart after a drunken duel can make wine taste less than appealing," he remarked when she raised an eyebrow.

The doors opened again and Sullivain strode in, accompanied by a couple of courtiers. She wore periwinkle blue, her hair gathered in ornate braids about her head, and a choker that clung to her skin, glinting like armor.

"Please sit," she said as everyone got to their feet out of respect. "I'm late, I do apologize, I had an urgent errand to take care of." She reached the head of the table and raised a glass in a quick toast, before sitting down. Her eye caught briefly on Hellevir and she hesitated, as if she hadn't been expecting to see her there. The courtiers sat on either side of her. Hellevir noticed Bion quietly taking his place among the standing servants.

The dinner continued, taking far too long as usual. Hellevir could feel Ionas watching her out of the corner of his eye, assessing her, and she wondered if Sullivain had deliberately seated them together, or whether it was coincidence. She wanted to look up to see what the Princess was doing, but unfortunately she was to her left and Hellevir couldn't watch her without turning her whole head and making it obvious.

"You've become quite used to this, haven't you?" Ionas asked her at one point when she'd been served the fish.

"Used to what?" she asked.

"All this. You came from a home at the edge of a nameless wood. Your father was a hunter, a no one from the middle of nowhere. Your mother a foreigner." He gestured to the grand room, the chandeliers sparkling above their heads, the golden insignia on her chest. "Now you dine with queens."

"My father isn't a no one," she remarked.

"Oh?"

"No. He's my father."

"I didn't mean to offend you. I'm just trying to say I'm impressed by where you've managed to find yourself."

"Believe me, I'd rather be in our cottage by the woods than in Rochidain."

He raised an eyebrow.

"It seems you've kept your country manners, at least," he remarked.

Hellevir ignored the barb. She settled for just eating her fish, and he turned to talk to the lady on his other side.

The meal finally ended, and the guests drifted through to the ballroom where drinks were being served and an orchestra was tuning up. Hellevir hung back, and managed to catch Bion before he followed them through.

"Can you tell Sullivain I want to talk to her?" she asked him. He nodded and bowed, vanishing into the crowd. He reappeared surprisingly quickly, before she'd had a chance to feel like she was hovering too much, or before Ionas could find her again.

"The Princess will see you now," he said. Hellevir braced herself and followed him away from the bustle, and towards the more private area of the residence. The sounds of the party became distant, their footfalls soft on the carpeted floor. They reached Sullivain's study, and he knocked and held the door open for her.

It was warm inside, the hearth lit and the lamps flickering. Hellevir's eyes flickered to the ground where Farvor had lain, but the rug was new, the bloodstains gone. Sullivain was standing by the fire, pouring herself a glass of red wine. It glinted in the firelight.

"Hello, herbalist," she said as Bion let himself out. "Wine?"

"Yes, thank you."

The Princess held out the glass—she still wore gloves, Hellevir saw, that were a little too tight—and sat down, inclining her head for Hellevir to sit opposite.

"Did you bring him back?" Sullivain asked without looking at her.

"I did." The Princess's manner seemed to relax, if only slightly.

"Well," she said, taking a sip. "That's something at least." She gestured towards the eyepatch. "And your eye, that was the price?"

"Yes."

"It suits you. The eyepatch."

"Thank you." Hellevir paused. "What happened? Your grandmother was going to burn him to ashes. I thought I'd lost him."

Sullivain hesitated. "I had to stop her." It was one of the rare instances Hellevir had seen her consider her words. She looked pensive, as if remembering something unpleasant. "I've never fought with her like that before. We stood by the open furnace; his body was already in the flames, she'd put it in herself. She tried to stop me, told me I was being a little fool, but . . . I pushed her aside, and I got the body out. Then . . . then we argued. We both said things I don't think either of us can forget. But I wore her down, told her I wasn't one of her subjects and I wouldn't blindly follow her orders. Not anymore."

There was a pulse of silence.

"But why?" Hellevir asked. "Farvor tried to kill you."

Sullivain's lip quirked, a sideways smile.

"In case you hadn't noticed, my people do that a lot. It's the main sport of Rochidain."

"And you've had them executed for it."

"I didn't want you to suffer, all right?" she growled. "Not because of me. Not again."

Hellevir put her glass aside and reached for Sullivain's hand. The Princess didn't stop her as she pulled the glove from her fingers, revealing the gauze underneath.

"You pulled him out of the fire with your bare hands," Hellevir murmured.

Sullivain slid her hand away, as if embarrassed.

"Grandmama's gone. Ostensibly to find the last of the Redeions

359

who got away," she muttered. "But I expect it's to cool down, get away from me, or else she'd be tempted to throw *me* on the pikes. I thought this gave us a good chance to talk. I'm renewing my offer for you to come and stay at the palace. I think it would be best if you were closer. And . . ." She paused. "And I would like you to be closer."

Hellevir didn't reply at once. Instead, she raised her hand to the golden brooch on her lapel. Slowly, she unclasped it and put it on the table between them with a click. It shone, bright and polished as the day it had first been given to her. Sullivain looked down at it, expression unreadable.

"And what are you trying to say with such a gesture?" she asked, her tone hard.

"I will not be your herbalist anymore," Hellevir replied.

"What?" A word on a single breath, disbelieving.

"I will not be your resurrector either. I'm going to leave Rochidain, and I don't intend to return. You're going to let me go, and you're not going to harm my family in any way."

Sullivain said nothing, running her finger distractedly around the rim of her glass.

"Is that so?" she asked. "And why would I suddenly let you go?"

Hellevir leaned forward, feeling the heat of the fire against her cheek. It was all or nothing. She couldn't let herself be gentle.

"Your grandmother has threatened me and my family with imprisonment, hangings, if I fail to bring you back to life. But her threats pale in comparison to what I promise I can make happen to you."

The words, written in her journal, prepared, memorized, came to her with the bitter and unpleasant taste of copper.

Sullivain scowled.

"What are you talking about?" she demanded. Hellevir braced herself, ignoring the heaviness lodged in her chest.

"I walk and talk with Death," she said. "He and I have a bargain which he needs me safe and well to fulfil. If I ask him to, he will catch you when you next die, and throw you into the darkness. Not the nothing that Onaistians seem to fear so completely. He'll throw you into another place, a worse place. A shuddering darkness made of his wrath, a tortured blackness. I have witnessed it myself; I call it *the void*, empty as it is of light, of hope, of sanity. You will suffer an eternity of despair and pain, and all I have to do is ask for it. If he knows you threaten me, he will wait for you, and there is no escape from him. He wants you, Sullivain. He's angry that you've escaped him so many times."

Hellevir could feel her own heart beating, forceful and hard against her ribs. It felt wrong, saying these things, but she didn't let herself stop, didn't let herself waver. The Princess held her eye and didn't speak at first.

"Why now?" Sullivain whispered at last. "Why would you say this now?"

Hellevir reached behind her head and undid the clasp at the back of the eyepatch, removing it completely. She was rewarded by the sight of the blood draining from Sullivain's skin as she saw the eye underneath, black from corner to corner, gleaming like spilled ink in the shadow of her face.

"Because I am one with Death," Hellevir said. She brought her hand up to the corner of her eye. "He sees what I see. The last sacrifice has brought me too far over into Death, and I am his agent among the living, now." She leaned back in her chair. "In many ways I have you to thank for it." She swallowed. "My brother came here to kill you, because of what you did to Calgir, and he died. After raising you so recently, the sacrifice to bring him back was not small."

The silence was physical. Sullivain watched Hellevir, and Hellevir did not break her gaze. She willed Sullivain to believe the lie. She wished she could enjoy seeing the Princess shaken, but it just made her feel cruel.

"It will happen again," Sullivain murmured without looking away. "I will be killed."

"In which case you can send for me," Hellevir replied. "And you can rely on my good will and good faith to come. But I will not be trapped by you."

"And if you don't come when I call?"

"Then you're mortal like the rest of us."

A shudder went through Sullivain. Hellevir knew why she feared dying so much. Sullivain did not believe that there was a Promise waiting for her, a blissful eternity, not after the things she'd done. Sullivain had long since fallen from the Path of Light. Hellevir knew this, and felt cold exploiting it. She watched the war behind Sullivain's eyes, between the faith she clung to and the knowledge of the afterlife she knew Hellevir possessed.

The Princess—the Queen in all but name—looked down at the brooch on the table.

"Grandmother began all of this with her threats," she remarked. "Got us off to a bad start, when we might have been friends, you and I." Hellevir remembered thinking much the same thing when she had last saved Sullivain's life, when the Princess had wanted to throw shoes into the abyss of Death.

Sullivain looked up again. Her expression was difficult to read. Anger at herself for playing the game badly enough to lose. Irritation, and—what Hellevir had been hoping to see, and what she hated to see—fear.

Hellevir put down the glass of wine.

"I am leaving the city tomorrow," she said. "If you cause harm to my family, I will know. The only thing that stands in my way is the Queen, and I need you to explain this to her as well. Convince her to let me go."

"We have an . . . understanding, after what happened," Sullivain murmured. "I don't believe she would hunt you down if I told her not to. Not now." She leaned over and picked up the brooch, turning it over in her hands.

"You know," she said. "I could really have done with an ally in this den of wolves. I almost dared to believe that we *were* allies, just for a while there, when you were coming to visit me. But it was stupid of me, I suppose."

"Perhaps in another life," was all Hellevir said. She stood, turning to go. The Princess got to her feet, her eyes wide, as if she were about to call Hellevir back. But then she just swallowed, and held out the brooch again.

"You will need this if you do return to the city in good faith. Unless that was a lie?"

Hellevir reached across for it, brushing the Princess's bandaged palm. Sullivain flinched, and their fingertips grazed together.

Mistakes, so many mistakes. Unavoidable, ingrained into that resigned shame that formed the bedrock of the Princess's heart. How bitterly she wished Hellevir wouldn't go, that she'd had the courage to fight her grandmother sooner, had forced her to let the

Redeion boy live. Hellevir withdrew her hand, the brooch warmed by Sullivain's touch.

"Does that happen for everyone you've brought back?" the Princess asked.

"No," Hellevir said quietly. "Just you."

"You don't want to leave. Not really. There's something you aren't telling me."

"If you felt that much from me, you know I don't have a choice." Hellevir put the brooch in her pocket. "And it wasn't a lie," she said. "But it wasn't a promise, either."

"I would have let you go, you know," Sullivain murmured. "After all this. You didn't have to resort to threats."

"And I never needed threats to convince me to keep you alive," Hellevir countered. "Yet you still made them."

They watched each other, each encased in her own world of crackling flames and regrets, the music of the ball distant. Hellevir's heart ached. Sullivain looked so beautiful by the firelight, her hair filled with its glow like the red of a fox's tail. The Princess reached up and brushed Hellevir's cheek, the silk of her gloved hand soft.

"Sullivain, I . . ."

"Please don't go," she said quietly. "I need you here. I have no one else."

"Sullivain . . ."

The Princess kissed her. It went through Hellevir, through to her marrow, down the ridge of her spine, into her very roots, even as Sullivain's emotions ravaged her own. Her loneliness, her shame, her fear, they engulfed her, even as the tender peal of her longing for Hellevir rang into the core of her. She felt the Princess's fingers twining in her hair, heard the soft ring of her hairpin as it tumbled to the floor.

Hellevir never wanted the kiss to end. She wanted to drown in Sullivain, give in to her touch, to the smell of her hair, to the feel of her warm skin. But she couldn't let the Princess see her lies. It took a strength she didn't know she had to pull away, withdraw from Sullivain, and something vital within her tore in two as she did so.

Sullivain's copper eyes, like a lion's, gazing into her own. Her scent, rosewater, lingering around them.

"Please don't go," Sullivain murmured again. Her fingertip traced Hellevir's cheek, trailing her aching desire for Hellevir to stay.

"I'm sorry," Hellevir whispered. Her voice shook. "Goodbye, Sullivain."

She felt wooden as she turned away. Cold, as if she had plunged into Death, as she opened the door and let herself out into the corridor. Fragmented, as if there were more things that needed to be said. As if the wine she'd left half-drunk on the table should really have been finished.

The door closed behind her. Through it she heard the crash of a glass being thrown against the wall.

When she got back to the Order, Elsevir was waiting for her.

"Did it work?" the raven asked. Hellevir took off her eyepatch and looked down at it in her hand.

"I think it did," she replied quietly.

"And she won't come after us?"

"No," she said. "I don't think so." She closed her hand over the eyepatch, and put it in her bedside drawer before pulling off her cloak with a sigh. Her bags already sat packed on the floor in panniers, and her travelling clothes were laid out on the chair for the following day. She ran her fingers through her hair to free it from knots. It was loose without the pin to hold it.

"We'll stop by Pa's house in the morning," she said, "and then we'll leave."

"Are you ready to?"

Hellevir had no reply to that. No, she wasn't ready. The sight of Sullivain, her face so close to hers, the lingering feather-touch on her lips, had almost been her undoing. She wanted to be pleased that she had been strong, that she had resisted, but she felt only unhappy.

She went to sit at the window overlooking the canal. It wasn't too late in the night; boats still drifted here and there on the waters, carrying the low murmur of voices and the hollow slide and clunk of the poles being lifted and dropped to push the boats along. It was cold, frost lining the stone walls and beginning to creep at the edges of the waterways. She rested her chin on her hands as she sat by the windowsill. The smell of the water and the wet stone, the woodsmoke from a nearby fire.

The ivy whispering gossip it had heard through its years, through the cracks in the stone and the wooden windowsills.

She felt too alert to sleep, the tension still fizzing in her veins after the confrontation. Melancholy stole over her, intertwined with her fears. Fears of what lay in store for her outside Rochidain. But despite that—and it took her a moment to recognize this—she was relieved. She could leave, finally, and be at no one's beck and call.

Yes, she thought, *perhaps I am ready*.

There was still the matter of the treasures, of course. It occurred to her to stop looking for them, to turn her back on her dealings with Death as coldly as she'd turned her back on Sullivain, but even now she still felt the same as she did in the village, when she'd first laid eyes on Sullivain's body. That *tug*. That *pull*, to draw aside the curtain and slip into the half-light. Perhaps it was because so much of her soul had been lost there; if anything the tug was only stronger, her curiosity about that place and the dark man only more profound, now that she had an inkling of who he was. She wasn't certain she could end her bargain with Death any more than she could stop the beating of her own heart. Even now.

She got to her feet with a sigh, perplexed at herself, brushing the head of the sleeping Elsevir and opening the wardrobe to take out her nightclothes.

There it was again. That feeling, one she hadn't felt in the living world in months. Something not quite right, as if there had been an imperceptible change in the room. She paused, her hand half-raised to the linen, and then turned to the chair by the window.

The man dressed in black smiled at her. The candlelight glinted in his eyes.

"I hear you're taking my name in vain," he remarked. "My agent among the living, are you?"

She picked up the other chair, turning it to face him—the harsh click of her boot-heels on the wooden floor gave her an obstinate sort of confidence—and sat down slowly.

"It got me out of the city, didn't it?" she returned. "I'm free to find your treasures. Besides, could you call it an outright lie?"

"Yes. But you still carry her brooch. If she calls, will you come running back?"

"I don't know," she said truthfully. "Perhaps."

He leaned forward to rest his elbows on his knees, and it seemed as if the room flexed with the movement. The candlelight seemed to bow around him.

"After everything she has done to you," he said slowly, "you would still want to keep her alive? I know her. She has entered Death; the imprint of her soul has been left on its walls. I know what is within her, and what she has done . . ." He shook his head, but not with sadness. With excitement, as if he couldn't wait to see what would happen next. "It's nothing compared to what she is capable of doing. Rarely have I had the chance to sample a soul before it has become drenched in blood. The promise of war drifts behind her like a second shadow."

Hellevir wished she had a response, but she didn't. She just kept remembering the Sullivain who had met her in Death, the one with bright eyes who like a child had taken her hand and swung it between them. The Sullivain who had watched her by firelight, begged her to stay. There had been no malice in those eyes, no hardness. Just Sullivain.

"There's more to her than that," Hellevir replied quietly. "She doesn't . . . she doesn't enjoy what she's done. What she does. I believe her grandmother has told her she has to be this way, to survive. She has faced her grandmother, now, and I take hope from that."

Death leaned back, unimpressed by her answer. There were no sounds, not in this dream-state, other than the drip of wax onto the floor, overspilling the candlestick. Hellevir did not move to stop it.

"Does it matter whether she enjoys it or not?" the man with black eyes asked. "You lay so much blame for her character upon her grandmother, but she fully has the means to bring this city to ruin on her own."

Hellevir felt a shudder go through her.

"It might come to nothing," she said.

"I have seen many wars," the man with black eyes said. "Many uprisings. They flit over the years like a stone skipped across the water, intermittent arcs of peace inevitably plunged into chaos. I know the signs when I see them."

Hellevir raised her head high.

"Why do you even care?" she asked boldly.

He shrugged, and the candlelight dimmed. "I don't," he said.

"War, no war. It doesn't matter to me. Souls pass through and I watch. I suppose I find wars interesting to observe."

"Then why warn me, if war is inevitable? If what will happen next is so *interesting* to you?"

He smiled that smile.

"I'm not warning you in order to change the outcome. You misunderstand. I'm just preparing you for what I know will come next." He leaned closer. "But can it be you are as curious as I am to see what will happen? Can it be that you find it all interesting too?"

"I don't want war."

"It's certainly not peace you hunger for. You forget, you've walked in Death and I know your soul as well." His hand drifted up to his chest, where she knew the lock of her hair was still curled in his pocket, her signature agreeing to their bargain. "I know what you desire, and it's not just your Princess, and it's certainly not peace. Why do you think you first tried to raise the dead? Because you cared so much, or because you wanted to know if you could? To test your mettle? You don't fear becoming nothing in death, but being nothing in life, and times of peace are not conducive to greatness."

They regarded each other across the emptiness of half-life and half-death, she with her head high, and he with his cold grin. Her heart felt tight in her chest. No one had ever talked to her like this, and she didn't know what to say.

"I do not want war," she repeated, and it was the truth. Even so, she remembered once thinking how dull it would be to be without all this. To be ordinary. But that was before her brother had died. Before she had nearly been flogged. Nevertheless, his words rang within her, indisputable.

"Do you feel it, yet?" he asked quietly. She didn't want to ask him what he meant, to give him the satisfaction, but she did anyway.

"Feel what?"

He raised an eyebrow, unimpressed by her deliberate obtuseness.

"That you are missing pieces from yourself," he said patiently.

She paused, as if she were thinking about it, and brought a small pouch out of her pocket. Still thinking, she slid the black eye from its socket, and gave it a wipe with a silk handkerchief from inside.

"Not really," she lied.

"That's not what I meant by missing pieces," he chided. "And you know it." He leaned closer, and suddenly her chair was a lot nearer to his than it had been. He plucked the eye from her fingers before she could stop him, turning it over in the candlelight. For an absurd moment, she thought he would crack it in his fist. "I meant the missing pieces of your soul," he said as he examined it. "Do you feel the wind whistling through the gaps?"

Hellevir watched him turning the eye over, her jaw set. In the bright light of the candle, not in the greyness of Death, there was some color to his hair after all. A dark umber. A strand of it was folded over his ear, and it seemed an absurdly human thing. He sensed her gaze and met it with his own, and she felt the whole weight of Death behind his eyes.

"Who are you?" she asked.

He leaned closer with a mocking smile. "You tell me," the world said.

She awoke with a jolt, the wind cold against her skin from the open window. She still sat with her arms resting on the ledge, and she had a crick in her neck. The ivy chuckled.

Hellevir kept her goodbyes brief. Edrin hugged her tightly.

"I wish you weren't going," she said. They both looked down as the grey cat curled around her legs, saying in his own way that he wished she would stay too. It was quite a thing for him to admit, and she knelt down to pick him up in her arms.

"You should look after Grey," she said to Edrin. "He never did tell me his name. Perhaps he'll deign to tell you." The priestess smiled as the cat rubbed his head against her chin.

It was more difficult at her father's house. Her mother kept her eyes downcast as Hellevir said she had to go, and simply pursed her lips with a nod.

"It's for the best," was all she said. Hellevir sighed, impatient with her mother's coldness, and embraced her. Her mother stiffened, surprised, and then gripped her tightly.

"Don't trust Laius," Hellevir whispered in her ear.

"I know," her ma murmured. She sounded sad.

They parted, and her ma pushed her hair out of her face. She didn't say another word, but went down into the kitchen.

"Where will you go?" Pa asked Hellevir, his arms folded and his dark eyes unhappy.

"Back home," she replied. "See Milandre, at least for a little bit. And then I was just . . . going to wander. I want to travel. I have Sullivain's horse. I can earn my way as a herbalist."

"That's a dangerous thing, travelling on your own. And a young woman like you."

Hellevir shrugged.

"I'll have a raven that can peck and a horse that can kick," she said. "I think I'll be all right." As if to concur, Elsevir preened a lock of her hair.

Her father shook his head, muttering to himself.

"Will you write to us, at least? Let us know you're safe?"

"Yes, Pa."

"And if you need help, at any time, no matter where you are, tell me and I'll come for you." She wrapped her arms around his neck, unperching Elsevir, and squeezed him tightly. Pa huffed, sighing the sigh that meant he knew he wouldn't argue her out of her plans.

Farvor sat outside in the courtyard, waiting for her in their usual spot by the fountain. It was a bright day, making him appear wan. The burns and bruises were all healed after his resurrection, but there was still an absence in his expression when he looked up at her.

"So," he said. "You're leaving."

"I have to."

He nodded, understanding. For the first time she wondered if she were betraying him further, by leaving him alone in Rochidain. Abandoning him after everything that had happened. She sat down beside him.

"You could come with me." The words were out of her mouth before she had a chance to think about them. It hadn't even occurred to her before that moment.

He took a breath, released it slowly.

"Ask me again next time you come back," he said. "Right now, I don't have it in me to go beyond those gates, let alone out there." He nodded his head towards the canal.

His eyes were vivid in the morning sunlight. He reached up a hand and brushed the eyepatch with his fingertips.

"I think I want to hate you," he said, with no malice in his words. "For failing to save him. For saving her. For saving me. But I can't. Not when I see what you gave up to do it. It almost makes me want to hate you more, that you've taken the option away from me."

"I'd give up more, Farvor," she replied quietly.

His lips became a thin line. She ached to be able to do something, say something, but in the depths of her heart where the truth resided, she knew she couldn't. Some kinds of damage couldn't be fixed.

She put her arm around him. Something of the fissure in her chest, opened by everything that had happened between them, became less jagged as he leaned his tousled head on her shoulder and she felt the reassuring weight.

She brought Dune from the stables at the city wall, and made the return journey to Milandre's cottage, leaving the city with relief like that of emerging from the heat of a blacksmith's forge into the cool of the day. Looking back from a rise over Rochidain, glinting with its canals and red-tiled roofs, its brightly colored walls, the high turrets of the distant palace, she felt the same as when she'd said goodbye to Milandre, answering the summons of the Crown, watching their cottage vanish from sight. She didn't want to leave; Sullivain had been right about that. But she knew it was time, felt it in her bones.

The journey only took her six days; she didn't stop in taverns on the way, but slept curled up beneath trees under the stars. She didn't dream, of Sullivain or of anything else, and she was relieved. She would wake up with cobwebs laced in her hair, and her eyelashes spiked with ice.

It began to sleet towards the afternoon of the sixth day, and she pulled up the hood of her old waxed coat, enjoying the sound of the tapping rain by her ears, the softness of Elsevir's feathers as he crouched against her neck. The wind held winter's bite.

When the village came into sight, she paused briefly on the rise, looking out over the chimney smoke rising into the grey sky, smelling the wet pine from the forests. It was like returning from a dream.

*

Hellevir sat sipping nettle tea by Milandre's hearth. She'd gathered the nettles fresh that morning, and with some honey it was soothing and warmed the chills she'd picked up from the winter rain. A pot of elderflower cordial sat infusing on the stove, which Milandre would sell when the winter maladies started up. Some of the flowers hung by their stems from the eaves, dried for teas. Elsevir sat on his old perch, enjoying a large bowl of seeds.

"Are you drying off a bit?" the old woman asked, bustling into the workshop with a basket full of radishes from the garden. The rain never bothered her, and she wiped her hair flat with the drizzle that had gathered on the strands. "You've turned into a city girl; a little rain never would have hurt you before."

"It's all that finery and good food. Made me soft. The silks and delicious wines and sumptuous roast dinners and . . ."

"Yes, yes. We have wine here too. Far nicer than that imported city vinegar. Not just good for the body but good for the soul." She tapped her heel against a barrel under the workbench. Hellevir had to turn her head to see properly, her blind spot covering the left half of the room. She knew Milandre noticed.

"Plum wine?" she asked. Milandre didn't answer at once, until Hellevir glanced up at her.

"Yes, the trees bore a lot of fruit last year." The old woman sat down in the chair opposite, giving the fire a nudge with the poker. She said nothing, and Hellevir wished she would, just to get it over with. Hellevir could tell it was all there, bubbling under the surface. Milandre never could keep her thoughts to herself.

"Aren't you going to tell me I'm a little fool?" Hellevir asked quietly.

Milandre raised an eyebrow.

"Why would I do that?"

Hellevir just snorted.

"After everything I told you?" she exclaimed, laughing a little without humor. "If it weren't for me, House Redeion would still be standing. Farvor would still have Calgir. He wouldn't have died." The words came easily to her, spoken so many times to herself in the darkness as she tried to fall asleep. The pain they caused her was already old and worn, like a well-travelled path through a wood.

"Do you want me to rebuke you?" Milandre asked. "Tell you

that you acted rashly? You did, you know it. But if you're looking for someone to blame you, don't look to me. Auland Redeion was the fool, and you were just trying to make the best of an impossible situation."

Hellevir raised her head to look at Milandre. She wished she could believe her. The blame felt like a solid part of her now, a replacement for her missing eye. A bedrock of shame, she realized, much like what she'd felt in Sullivain.

"My concern now is for you, my girl," Milandre went on. "I never cared for Rochidain, or for the way your ma treated you there." She humphed angrily, shaking her head, and gestured to the workshop, the warmth and the good smell of herbs. "You know you can stay here, there'll always be a place. For as long as you need to gather yourself together, after everything."

"Thank you." Hellevir went quiet, thinking, and Milandre let her. "I should feel that way, shouldn't I?" she asked, looking into the fire. "Like I need to recuperate, after everything that happened? I should feel devastated."

"You don't?"

"No, I . . . I don't. I feel strong. Like I'm standing tall after months of being crouched, my back crooked."

"You're not allowed to complain of back problems. Wait until you're my age, then you'll know back problems."

Hellevir smiled.

"That's not what I meant."

"I know. I'll wager it's because you're no longer under the control of that girl. That Sullivain." She shifted angrily in her chair. "I should never have let you bring the little creature back. She's been nothing but a bane."

The softest kiss. *Please don't go.* Hellevir brushed the memories aside like wiping gossamer from her eyes.

"You couldn't have stopped me. I wanted to do it. I felt like I needed to."

"Well. We both should have known better."

"Yes," Hellevir conceded. "We should." They sat in silence for a moment, listening to the crackling fire that kept trying to catch one of the wayward feathers that had fallen on the hearth. Milandre pushed it with her foot, and the flames snatched it greedily, the fire seaming its way down the barbs.

Hellevir undid the clasp of the eyepatch, letting it fall onto her lap, and rubbed the skin around her empty socket. Milandre reached over and took her chin, turning her face towards her to study the black glass eye. She pursed her lips, brushing her thumb over Hellevir's cheek underneath, and shook her head.

"No more, my girl," she said quietly. "This is enough, now, eh? Let Farvor be the last one."

Hellevir took her hand and held it on her lap with a sigh.

"There are more of his riddles to find," she said. "And there will always be people I can save on the way."

Milandre squeezed her hand.

"I know I can't convince you to do anything you don't feel it right to do, but you are precious too, my girl," Milandre muttered, her gaze lingering on the gap where Hellevir's fingers used to be. "It's why he demands parts of you when you have no treasure. And if you're not careful there'll be nothing left of you."

"In life, I have missing pieces," Hellevir said. "In Death, I'm whole." She waggled her remaining fingers. "I have all five of them there."

"Well, if I ever die," Milandre said, leaning back in her chair and giving Elsevir's neck a scratch where he perched on its arm, "don't even think about bringing me back. I won't be responsible for another tatter in your soul."

"If? You plan to live forever?"

"I plan to, and I will," was the nonchalant reply. "Think I'll go quietly? Death will find me armed with an iron poker and a rolling pin."

That night Hellevir dreamed she and Sullivain were skipping rocks over a still lake. Sullivain was much better at it than she was.

The road stretched before them, crowded with wagons and horses, busy with farmers and travellers coming to and from the village. Some of them she recognized from her childhood, people she'd known for years but who walked past her without a glance. Hellevir felt like she was in a world apart from them, watching them all from behind a glass wall. It was just her, Elsevir and the horse, and everything else except for the long, long road was peripheral, imaginary. The breeze brushed her hair, smelling of snow.

A *wise mouth imparts sound advice:*
When blind and breathless,
Do not try to sing.

The riddle meant nothing, but she had faith she'd find the path, or the path would find her.

"Where are we going?" Elsevir asked, puffing up his great black ruff.

Hellevir surveyed the road, curving over hill after hill like loops of honey until it vanished into the distance, misty with the winter air.

"Anywhere. Everywhere." She folded the riddle and put it away, taking up the reins and stroking Dune's wheat-colored neck. "Wherever Death sends us next."

ACKNOWLEDGMENTS

I wrote this book (and book 2) during the pandemic in 2020 and 2021. I was definitely one of the lucky ones, fortunate enough to have my own space and to be able to work from home, but even so the experience left a mark, as it did on everyone. There was a long stretch of time when staying home and doing nothing became very claustrophobic and I felt like a very useless human being; it is with the benefit of hindsight that I realize this bled a lot into the book. In Hellevir there was a character who was trapped on every side, but by her abilities was anything but useless. Into her went my anxieties and through her I explored my desire to be able to do something, no matter the cost; like two of my friends, a nurse and a doctor, who sacrificed their safety to help others. This book is in part dedicated to them.

Thank you first and foremost to the Ki Agency. Anne Perry's cheerfulness and quite frankly intimidating competence were the perfect balm for debut anxieties. I've been dreaming of becoming published for as long as I can remember, and I owe it to Anne for making the dream become reality. Meg Davis then took over, and I couldn't have hoped for a fiercer champion in my corner. Thank you both, I owe you many drinks.

Thanks are owed to my inimitable UK and US editors, Natasha Bardon, Elizabeth Vaziri, Vicky Leech, Julia Elliott, Rachel Winterbottom, Chloe Gough, and everyone at HarperVoyager who believed in and supported the book: Ellie Game, Anna Bowles, Linda Joyce. I'd also like to thank Vedika Khanna for help on early drafts.

My wonderful friend and excellent beta-reader, (Dr.) Megan Shipton, made the time to read my work despite being in the thralls of a PhD and then on the other side of the world. Not many people have a go-to poison expert who won't just tell you what plants kill most effectively, but who can also explain on a chemical level why they work the way they do. Did you know that hemlock contains the alkaloid coniine, which is a powerful muscle relaxant, causing death by respiratory paralysis, and has a similar chemical structure to nicotine?

My partner, James, introduced me to the programming term *rubber duck debugging*; you have a rubber duck on your desk and explain problems to it, and in the process of articulating it you hit on the solution. James sat through a lot of plot exposition and "Does this sound right?" monologuing, providing suggestions and chocolate. So thank you, favorite, for being my rubber duck (better than; rubber ducks don't supply tea).

I owe thanks to those who made up an environment conducive to writing while trying to ignore the world on fire; work colleagues, friends who have stayed with me, and James's mother, Anna Miller, who welcomed me into the family with open arms.

And of course, I owe most to my mother, Suzanne. She fostered my love of books and writing from the moment she recognized it, reading drafts upon drafts of my writing—even the teenage works— and encouraged me unfailingly to keep going during the inevitable "What if I'm just a terrible writer?" phase of agent rejections. I'd have given up on writing a long time ago without your love and guidance. You're the wisest woman I know; thank you for everything.

A small disclaimer: the herbalism dotted throughout the book is a mixture of olde medieval practices and modern foraging. The remedies used here should not be construed as a replacement for modern medicine.

I used a number of foraging websites as sources, and the following were fun books I enjoyed having to hand:

Dauncey and Larsson, *Plants that Kill* (Quarto Publishing, 2018)

Dauncey and Howes, *Plants that Cure* (Quarto Publishing, 2020)

Wright, *The River Cottage Mushroom Handbook* (Bloomsbury, 2007)

Culpeper's Complete Herbal and English Physician (Manchester, UK 1826)

ABOUT THE AUTHOR

By day, **Marianne Gordon** works as an editor at an academic publisher, and by night, she loves to write fiction. When she's not reading or writing, she enjoys cooking, quilting or sewing, and riding around the countryside on her motorbike. *The Gilded Crown* is her debut novel.